She Creeps

She Creeps

ALEX HAIRSTON

KENSINGTON PUBLISHING CORP.
http://www.kensingtonbooks.com

DAFINA BOOKS are published by

Kensington Publishing Corp.
850 Third Avenue
New York, NY 10022

All Kensington titles, imprints and distributed lines are available at special quantity discounts for bulk purchases for sales promotion, premiums, fund-raising, educational or institutional use.

Special book excerpts or customized printings can also be created to fit specific needs. For details, write or phone the office of the Kensington Special Sales Manager: Kensington Publishing Corp., 850 Third Avenue, New York, NY 10022. Attn. Special Sales Department. Phone: 1-800-221-2647.

Dafina Books and the Dafina logo Reg. U.S. Pat. & TM Off.

ISBN-13: 978-0-7582-1882-7
ISBN-10: 0-7582-1882-6

First Kensington Trade Paperback Printing: June 2007
10 9 8 7 6 5 4 3 2 1

Printed in the United States of America

For
Grandma Chrissie
and
Kayla

ACKNOWLEDGMENTS

To my readers: I'm back and ready to take my career to the next level. Having my third novel published is an incredible blessing. There aren't any words to truly express how this makes me feel. I was happy with one novel and now I'm working on my fourth . . . God is so good! I'm sure somebody knows what I'm talking about. Wow!!! My readers mean the world to me. Thanks so much for purchasing my first two novels *Love Don't Come Easy* and *If Only You Knew*. I appreciate the love you've shown by posting my name and titles on myspace.com, message boards, and everywhere else on the Internet. Hopefully after reading this book, my new readers will love me just as much or even more than my wonderful returning readers . . . thanks for being so patient and for your continued support. Checkout my website www.alexhairston.com and please e-mail your comments to me at alexhairston@yahoo.com. I'd love to hear from you.

I'd like to thank Kim (my beautiful wife and #1 sample reader) for loving and inspiring me the way you do. . . . I'm still in love with you. I can't thank you enough for our wonderful kids, Terence, Terell and Alexis (my lil' basketball star) →PAW POWER GFS YOU KNOW!!!

Special thanks to my parents, Alex Sr. and Marie, Grandma (Betty), my siblings, Darryl, Chaz, Nokie and Erica (my #2 sample reader). Thanks to Cindy, Phillip, Decquetta and Quaisha.☺ I can't forget two of my favorite people in the world, Athena and Kiera.

I'd like to thank my agent/publicist Felicia Polk for all of her advice and hard work . . . we're almost there.

To my new editor, Selena James, you're off to a great start. I look forward to a bright and productive future working with you. Extra special thanks to everyone at Kensington Publishing Corp. for believing in me and making this happen.

LUV4 Book clubs: R.A.W. Sistaz, APOOO, Brown Suga Sistas with Books, Minds in Motion, Ebony Eyes, Sisters of Literary Excellence, DIVA, PSSST, Nubian Sistas and so many more.

I'm excited about the release of *She Creeps*. This is a unique and extra-ordinary story that I've been dying to write for a long time. I started writing this story in the third person, but Naomi's voice was so strong and passionate that I knew her story had to be told in the first person. Writing from the female perspective is always funny, challenging and at times uncomfortable.☺ Regardless of what perspective I write from, I'll try to keep things fresh and interesting. Thank you so much for supporting my dream. Enjoy!!!

Lots of Love,

Alex

Part I

FAMILY TIES

1

Naomi

I wanted to die the day they found Momma's body. It was midsummer, hot and muggy. I was eight years old and my sister, Serena, was only seven years old. We couldn't really understand what was going on. Momma was only missing for a day, and then the next thing I knew, most of our neighbors were standing around outside of our house trying to find out what had happened to that pretty white woman who was married to the big, mean, black policeman. They were talking about my daddy. He was one of the most hated men in Eden, North Carolina. That never bothered him none, but it sure did bother me.

The night before they found Momma's body, I was awakened by the sounds of adult laughter. Somebody was having a good ole time. I could hear Momma tiptoeing around and giggling like she'd had a few drinks. It was late, but my daddy was still at work. He was dedicated to his job and to taking good care of his family. Momma knew she was wrong because she had another man in our house. Brothas in Eden admired her beauty and fondness for black men. Most white men and a lot of black women despised her for that reason. I think that's why Daddy didn't allow her to work. He figured that keeping Momma at home was the best and safest place for her to be.

I couldn't figure out who was in our house that night, but I knew it wasn't my daddy. His first rule was that no man was to be in his house around his wife and daughters, especially if he wasn't at home.

Back then, Serena and I shared a bedroom. Disney was the theme of our room, all about innocence and imagery. Our bookshelves were lined with colorful children's books. We couldn't get enough of stories like *Snow White, Cinderella,* and *Sleeping Beauty.* We played and slept in a bright and cheerful environment. Mickey, Minnie, Donald, and Goofy were on everything from our bedspreads, curtains, and lamps down to our little throw rugs. Momma kept our bedroom neat and our clothes and linen smelling April fresh. One of my favorite things back then was a huge poster of the Magic Kingdom's castle along with all of the Disney characters that hung on our wall.

Serena was sound asleep, but I was wide awake listening to every little sound. That old house had the noisiest loose floorboards. They were like sensors, letting us know who was walking in what area of the house. Our bedroom door was closed, but from my bed I heard footsteps moving toward the kitchen and then out the back door. I heard the wooden screen door slam. *Wham!* It startled me, made me sit up in my bed, because it was such a disturbing sound to hear at that time of night. I assumed it was Momma's mystery man making a quick exit.

Tires screeched as a car sped off down the road. A few minutes later the phone on our kitchen wall rang twice, but no one was there to answer. Our neighbor's dog started howling. That was the third night in a row that dog made that disturbing sound. Folks 'round here said that a dog howling in the middle of the night was a sure sign of death.

The next thing I remembered was hearing my daddy's car pull into our driveway and his tires rolling over the gravel, making that familiar grinding sound. His car door slammed, his keys jingled, and then he let out his famous smoker's cough. He entered through the front door and within minutes he must have noticed that the back door was open. I could hear his footsteps move toward the back door.

I imagined him gripping the handle of his pistol as he called for Momma. His raspy southern baritone voice called out, "Barbara! Hey, Barbara, you out there?"

No answer. The sound of crickets chirping in three distinctively different tones filled the night air. I could feel the tension thicken. I slowly laid my head back down on my pillow.

Daddy asked himself, "What the hell is going on?"

Next he checked his bedroom and it was obvious that Momma was gone. Then he checked on me and Serena. She was still sound asleep. Although I was wide awake, I pretended to be asleep. I was raised to stay in a child's place, out of grown folks' business, so naturally I did as I was taught. Somebody had to respect my daddy's wishes. I could sense his frustration when he closed our bedroom door. His emotions probably shifted back and forth a million times, trying to figure out what was going on. I'm not sure what happened after that because all that pretending and the darkness of my bedroom put me right to sleep.

The next morning my daddy woke me and Serena and took us for a ride. We drove all over Eden and half of Rockingham County that morning. I guess we were supposed to be looking for Momma. What appeared to be a beautiful day soon took a turn for the worse, becoming the most horrific day of my life. When we came home later that day, the police were there and so were a lot of our friends and family. And I can't forget the nosy neighbors. People come out in droves when something bad happens.

At first no one said a word—I just saw a bunch of tears and angry faces. I sensed that something bad had happened. I started to get sick to my stomach. My white grandparents, the ones who disowned Momma, the ones who refused to claim me and Serena, the ones who I hadn't seen in God only knows how long, were there yelling obscenities at my daddy. I heard one of the officers tell Daddy that they had found Momma's body. Instantly a powerful chill came over me. I was old enough to know that when someone said *body*, they were referring to a dead person. There was no way a woman that young and beautiful could be dead. I was in a state of shock and disbelief. I wanted to know exactly what happened to her, but no one would tell me. I was a child and had already heard too much. I thought maybe Momma could have been seriously injured and needed to go to the hospital, but not dead. Then I heard the word *murdered.* At that point I knew that Momma would never come home again, and my little heart was hurt in the worst way imaginable. A feeling of pain and emptiness came over me. The woman who had given birth and loved me all of my life was gone forever. Just thinking about this makes me cry. I was eight years old then and I'm twenty-nine now. Even to this day I've never been able to find the exact words to describe how I felt at that moment. The feeling is indescribable.

All I could do was yell out, "Don't say that! I want my momma! Where is she?"

My aunts, uncles, cousins, and neighbors tried to comfort me and Serena. Family members are usually drawn closer together during a tragedy, but not my dysfunctional family. My grandparents were too busy fussing and stirring up confusion to acknowledge the fact that me and my sister were scared to death and hurting. For a moment Serena seemed almost oblivious to what was going on. She cried mostly because I was crying. Slowly she began to realize that Momma was really gone. I turned to my daddy for answers, but he couldn't tell me anything because the police were taking him away. He was a policeman, too, and it was strange seeing him get arrested. I refused to believe that my hero could have committed such a heinous crime, especially against my momma. I overheard one of my neighbors say that two little boys, Michael and Brandon, found Momma's nude body in a ditch stuffed halfway in a storm drain. She had been stabbed to death.

A few people around me including my angry white grandparents started saying that my daddy killed Momma.

My granddaddy said, "He did it. Frank killed her. I know he did. He's crazy enough to do something like that." He squinted his eyes, pointed directly at Daddy, and in a very hateful tone, said, "That's why I never wanted Barbara to marry that nigger, because I knew eventually something like this would happen."

I was the daughter of one of the most hated men in our community. Daddy was partly to blame. He never took the time to get to know the people in our community and vice versa. He always fussed about people staring at him and Momma. Daddy raised hell about simple things like kids being on his property. Seeing him with a gun, a badge, and his infamous mirrored sunglasses was a big turn-off for most people. It's hard to trust a man when you can't even see his eyes. I had seen his eyes and had known about his kind ways, but no matter what I thought, they always saw him as the bad guy. He was a black policeman. To make matters worse, my daddy was the only black policeman in Eden at that time. He was married to a white woman and now he was an accused murderer. He was one of the most hated men in Eden.

Although our neighbors hated my daddy, some of them began to defend him. Not because they believed in his innocence, but mainly because my angry white granddaddy turned Momma's murder into a racial incident. A few minutes later the media arrived, local television and newspaper reporters. This made the scene more dramatic than ever.

As his fellow white policemen took him away, Daddy cried out, "You can't do this to me. I swear, I didn't do anything! I didn't kill my wife! Let me go! I want my daughters!"

I'll never forget the look of desperation in his eyes. I'd never seen my daddy like that. For the first time, he seemed helpless. I jumped up and down and screamed, "Daddy! Daddy! Daddy!" Then I yelled at the white policeman, "Let him go! Pleeease, let my daddy go!"

A riot nearly broke out in front of our house, but somehow my daddy was able to defuse the situation a little by reassuring everyone that he'd be all right. Mostly everyone calmed down, but not me. No matter what I did or said, they still took him to jail. Daddy went peacefully and I think people respected that. Others saw it as an admission of guilt. Serena and I cried our little hearts out. I think we both wanted to curl up and die because we had no one and nowhere to run to. At that moment the world seemed so small. I was suffocating and then reality set in. All of a sudden the world went from being so small to becoming an enormous place, way too large for two little girls without parents. That's when Momma Pearl stepped in. She's our daddy's oldest sister, a real ornery, raging-bull type when she wanted to be. Other times she was a self-proclaimed prophet. This was probably the ugliest and cruelest woman who ever set foot on God's green earth. Sometimes I think Serena and I would have been better off going to a foster home instead of living with my aunt because of the way we were mistreated. But at least Serena and I were together.

Momma Pearl and her sister, Clarissa, raised us. We had a strict upbringing. Serena and I called them King Kong and Mighty Joe Young. They were two devils dressed in white garb, head-wraps and all. Aunt Clarissa never hit or ridiculed me and Serena like Momma Pearl did, but she was just as bad because she was well aware of the cruelty her sister was putting us through and did nothing to stop it.

Aunt Clarissa—or Sister Clarissa, as the church folks called her— moved in after Momma Pearl and her husband Henry separated. Uncle Henry was a good man, always had a smile and a kind word. He was a tall, handsome light-brown-skinned man. Uncle Henry was country, though, the kind of man who would wear a belt and sus- penders at the same time. That was always a funny sight. People used to call him a jackleg preacher, a real Jim Jones in the making. I never paid that much attention. He was the preachingest man I've ever known, and most of all he was really kind to me and Serena. He never actually said it, but we knew he loved us. The last I heard Uncle Henry moved up north somewhere and became a storefront preacher. When he left things really went downhill, mostly because Momma Pearl be- came ordained and took over his church, Eden Light Undenomina- tional Church of Faith. She's still alive and going strong at fifty-four, leading her cult of followers to hell. A woman like that can't teach anything except pure evil.

Serena and I lived in Momma Pearl's big, old, dirty country house in Blue Creek until I got married shortly after graduating from Morehead High School. When I moved I took Serena along with me. There was no way I was leaving my sister in that house with Momma Pearl to suffer alone. It was far from a happy home, but it was home. No home sweet home, more like home *bittersweet* home. That old house always smelled like stale bacon grease—that smell lingered and lingered forever. I could even smell it in my clothes and linen. I can still see that greasy stove with the big blue Crisco can filled with bacon grease. Momma Pearl fried chicken and fish in that same old nasty bacon grease. The thought of it still nauseates me. She claimed that she loved us and she showed it every day by whipping and calling us poor white trash or little wannabe-niggers. That was her special way of breaking us down. She was like the black version of Cinderella's evil stepmother, except we were family, her own flesh and blood. I wouldn't have treated a dog like she treated us. To this day I don't know why she hated us so much.

In a way I think my sister and I both died the day they found Momma's body. Not in a physical sense, but a major part of us went with her. There is of course a part of her that lives in us. I honestly feel her spirit inside of me, the good and the bad. She wasn't a perfect woman, but she was our momma.

From my childhood experiences, I learned humility, to expect the unexpected, to never take people for granted, and most of all, that adultery is a bad thing. Let's just say that some lessons are easier learned then others.

2

Naomi

I was born right here in Eden at Morehead Memorial Hospital. Born in May—the thirtieth, to be exact. That makes me a Gemini. My astrological sign reflects my dual personality. Most of the time I'm strong, but I do have my weak moments. I've lived in Eden all my life, but I sure don't wanna die here. So many sad memories. But no matter what, the happy memories always have a way of overshadowing the sad ones, like my memories of me and Serena dancing and playing with Momma. We used to play under this huge weeping willow in our backyard. It was the strangest-looking tree. The branches and leaves drooped down to the ground and made the perfect hiding place. At one point in the back of the tree the leaves separated like a natural archway. Of course that was where we would enter and exit. The three of us would go under the tree and sip tea from our toy tea set and eat Ritz crackers and cheese or drink milk and eat Chips Ahoy chocolate chip cookies. Right next to our weeping willow was our make-believe wishing well. Momma was so creative that she actually made us believe that it was a real wishing well. Even happy memories make my eyes water because I wanted times like that to last forever. That was one of my biggest wishes back then.

Momma sure was something special. She used to read to us. She read anything and everything from her original poetry about weeping willows and wishing wells to *Uncle Tom's Cabin, Gone With the Wind* and *Roots.* She had a subtle way of mixing our cultures together and teaching about who we were without us ever really realizing what she was doing. She'd occasionally slip a couple of white baby dolls in, here and there. Our daddy's a very dark man and because of his dominant genes, Serena and I look more black then anything. When Daddy was younger, he resembled Wesley Snipes and Momma bore a very close resemblance to Demi Moore. Sometimes it's hard for me to watch Demi Moore in movies because all I see is Momma. Other times it's therapeutic. If people didn't know Momma, then they'd never know that Serena and I were biracial unless we told them. Daddy used to tell us that we could never consider ourselves white. He said that having just one drop of black blood in our systems canceled out our whiteness and made us black in every way. He said it with so much conviction that we believed him. Statements like that confused the heck out of me and Serena. The look on Momma's face told me that she disagreed with him, but she never voiced her opinion. In a way, Daddy stole her voice, her dreams, and possibly her life.

All I know is that I have dreams and desires that can't possibly be met here in Eden because I've always dreamt of being a hairdresser, beautician, cosmetologist, hairstylist, or whatever they call them. That sounds so silly because I'm not even a hairdresser now, but I'm really good at doing hair. To top that off, I can cook my butt off too. I'd love to own a big-time soul food restaurant like Sylvia's up in Harlem or somewhere with a bunch of hungry black folks.

I wanna live in a place with busy sidewalks, bright lights, a hot nightlife, skyscrapers, a wide variety of restaurants, and fancy clothing stores. The biggest and best thing we've got going here in Eden is Wal-Mart. I've always been impressed with big cities like Los Angeles, Chicago, and New York. If I'm ever able to move away from here, then maybe my dreams will come true. Eden is a beautiful place, but its small-town atmosphere isn't enough for me anymore. It's way too slow here. I can't just sit around on my front porch day in and day out like a lot of people here do, smiling and waving at passing cars and watching life go by.

A lot has happened since we lost Momma. Daddy was sentenced to life in prison without the possibility of parole. He's been in prison for twenty-one years now. My God, it doesn't seem like it's been that long. Daddy is fifty-two years old. I often wonder if he truly belongs there or if he's just another victim of southern justice. How could they convict a man without any witnesses or concrete evidence? Only he, Momma, and God know the real answer to that. I tried my best to help him. I told everybody, including his lawyer, about the man I heard in our house the night before Momma was murdered. They discounted everything I said because I never actually saw anyone. I was an eight-year-old, and as far as the prosecution was concerned, I was dreaming. Everyone from our neighbors down to the police department seemed to have something against my daddy.

Flashbacks of my parents arguing and the day I first saw Daddy put his hands on Momma in a threatening way shed some serious doubt on his innocence. He slammed her against their bedroom wall, forcefully grabbed her by both wrists, and then slapped her in the face. If he could hit Momma, then eventually he could kill her. Sometimes that's how domestic violence progresses.

It's the strangest thing, but I used to wonder how Momma felt the day she was murdered. Did she know it was her last day? Made me wonder about her last thoughts. Did she feel afraid and did she think of me and Serena? We never got the chance to say good-bye. If Momma could have spoken to us, what would her last words have been? For a long time I had horrible nightmares of seeing hundreds of tiny maggots crawling all over her naked, pale white skin when she was in that storm drain. That was nothing but the devil trying to pollute my mind with grotesque images. The nightmares finally stopped and then Momma came to me in a realistic dream. I could see her just as plain as day, looking like herself, beautiful and healthy. She told me to stop worrying myself to death because she was doing just fine with all the other angels in heaven. I believed that and all, but I prayed to God that I'd never know the pain Momma felt the day she was murdered.

For years Serena and I visited Daddy in prison, but as time went on, the visits became fewer and farther in between. It's just that eventually we ran out of things to talk about. More then anything, it became harder and harder staring into the eyes of Momma's accused murderer. It's sad, but that's how I started to think of Daddy. Prison changed him. Maybe it was the environment or just the way he tried so hard to convince us of his innocence. He reminded me of someone who was starting to believe his own lies. The same old routine, time and time again, eventually grew old. Besides, Serena and I have families of our own.

It's morning, 5:45 A.M. The alarm clock went off about ten minutes ago and I woke up feeling kind of edgy. That feeling has little to do with my past and more to do with my present situation. My husband's back is to me. His body moves up and down with every breath he takes . . . inhale . . . exhale. He lies still, pretending to be asleep, but he's probably awake, thinking about some of the same issues that are on my mind.

I lie here thinking, *Here I go, rise and shine, up and at 'em. Another start of a new day in my predictable life.* My mind gets me going, but my body wants to continue lying here resting for a few more hours. The bad thing is if I don't get going, nothing will get done around here and that's the truth. But do I get any credit for what I do? Heck, no!

With my usual pleasant southern accent I say, "Good morning, Craig. It's time to get up. Rise and shine, sweetie."

He clears his throat and mumbles, "Uh-huh."

I gently nudge his shoulder and say, "Time to get moving."

Craig remains in the same position. "I know. I know."

"Is that all you have to say? I said good morning to you."

He mumbles, "Morning."

I put my hands up to my mouth like a bullhorn and yell, "Wake . . . up!"

That caught Craig off guard. He turns over toward me and says. "What in the hell is wrong with you? I ain't sleep. Can't nobody sleep with all this doggone noise you're making. You need to get up first, anyway. How 'bout getting breakfast going—remember breakfast?"

"How can I forget? Don't worry, I got it coming." I look up to the ceiling. "Yep, I got it coming."

A variety of breakfast foods run through my mind like a miniature slideshow. I'm in the mood for something special. I usually like to make omelets when I'm in a good mood. A night of good sex—no, *great* sex—really makes me crave omelets. Damn, I haven't had a craving for omelets in a while. Today looks more like overcooked bacon, runny scrambled eggs with burnt toast, bitter coffee, and sour orange juice.

It's a different day, but it's still the same old thing as yesterday. I haven't been happy in a long time and I'm sick of pretending. That's all I do. My pleasant tone and smile are fake. I even fake orgasms during sex to keep from dying of boredom. Sometimes I wanna scream, "Lord, help me, please!" My life is going nowhere fast. It's simply at a complete standstill. This can't be as good as it gets.

I'm a trophy. My older and sometimes wiser husband refers to me as his "beautiful, five-foot-nine-inch, statuesque memento." Craig used to think it was a big deal having a sexy, young wife, and the fact that I was a virgin when we first met really excited him. Lately it feels like he's put me on the shelf and I'm doing nothing but collecting dust, layers of dust that are really starting to wear me down. Maybe it's just me and maybe it isn't that serious. I do have a tendency to be a little oversensitive.

Before I rise I like to begin each and every day with a small prayer to ensure the safety and well-being of my family. But on the other hand, some evenings I've found myself wishing that something bad would happen to Craig and he wouldn't come home. I'd shout, "Freedom! Hallelujah! Hallelujah!" Lord, forgive me, but he does irk me. I don't hate my husband, can't hate him. I've just developed a strong dislike for him.

As I place my bare feet on our cold, hardwood floor, I stand and turn away from Craig, looking out our bedroom window at the morning sky. I've probably seen the sunrise a thousand times and each sunrise is different. God has a very distinctive and beautiful way of ushering in the new day. The trees in our backyard hold steady while their branches and leaves sway as a swift spring breeze blows through. The weatherman didn't call for rain, but I can tell that something strange is brewing.

My family consists of my husband, Craig, the control freak, and our three kids: Craig Jr. age 17, better known as C.J.; Erika age 16; Morgan age 10. Oh, and our family pet, a pretty, light-brown boxer named Chop-chop. Sometimes I hate that dog so much that I wanna kick the dog shit out of her, but I don't because she'd probably eat me alive. That damn dog howled and cried just about all night last night. I don't know how true it is, but I've heard that that's a sure sign of death. That notion is something that stuck with me from childhood.

I love my kids. Morgan is my only biological child, but I treat and love C.J. and Erika like my own.

For the most part, C.J. is a nice, quiet boy. He does have his moments when he irritates me. He means well, but sometimes I think he has a touch of attention deficit disorder or something. The child is somewhat delayed and has a tendency to be distant, in a world of his own. I can't quite put my finger on it, but I think either his daddy or his momma must have been drinking real heavy or on drugs when he was conceived. I never thought C.J. would be foolish enough to experiment with drugs, but I was wrong. Drugs are a big problem everywhere, even in a small town like Eden.

Erika is young and restless. Words like *impatient, self-centered, sassy,* and *dramatic as hell* probably describe her best. This girl is always bored if she isn't on the go or tying up our phone line for hours. She's the type of kid that has to be into something 24/7, no matter what. Erika's been boy-crazy ever since she broke up with Vernon, this little knucklehead boy from her school. He was tying her down and she felt that she was missing out on other fun things life has to offer. Next thing I knew she was dating an older man. I definitely had a problem with that, but I didn't have a problem putting her in her place right then and there. Sometimes Erika gets confused and thinks she's a woman because she's finally grown some little titties and her backside is starting to stick out a bit. Truth be told, her boobs are bigger than mine, but that still doesn't make her a woman. I almost had a fit when she told me that she thought she was ready to have sex for the first time. It's rare that a child communicates with a stepparent like that. She confides in me like a best friend and I keep all types of secrets. Craig doesn't know what's on her mind, especially the sex part. That's definitely a good thing because it'd break his heart and there's a good chance he'd kill me and her. There have been plenty of times when Craig wanted to go upside her head for being so wild. I had to play the peacemaker because I know Erika's a good kid. Sometimes it's hard, but I'm supportive of most of her decisions.

The happiest day of my life was the day I gave birth to Morgan. She was the most beautiful thing I'd ever laid eyes on. It was a thrill to finally see the pretty little face behind the muffled heartbeats that I'd heard for months. The sight of her innocent eyes, coal-black hair, and tiny hands and feet instantly made me cry. Now she's almost as big as me. Kids tease her for being a bookworm and computer geek, but that's okay because she's gonna run her own company some day. She promises to buy me and Craig a big house on a hill when she grows up and I believe she will. I've never seen a child so interested in learning about everything under the sun. Sometimes it's hard to believe that an intelligent girl like that came from me and my simple husband.

I married Craig when I was eighteen, inheriting the responsibilities of a ready-made family. Craig was twenty-five when we married. I never realized how controlling and insecure an older man could be. Mistake number one. My second mistake was letting him convince me that I didn't need to work. I worked for a short time at Belk Department Store in the Eden Mall as a sales associate and then that was it—instant housewife. Craig doesn't want me to do anything, because he thinks he's a king and his queen shouldn't have to work. We tried compromising on the work issue and he suggested that I do daycare or some other type of home-based business. What that really meant was that he didn't want me interacting with other people out in the real world, especially men. If Craig concentrated more on taking care of his home and less on his insecurities, he wouldn't have to worry about anything.

"Get up, Craig. You're just being lazy."

Craig mumbles, "I'm up. Stop nagging. So what if I'm being lazy? I got a right to be lazy. My people built this damn country for free and I don't think anybody should be bitching and complaining if I need to take a few extra minutes to get going in the morning."

As I make my way into our little master bathroom to freshen up, I put on my happy housewife act and say, "I'm sorry. Just doing my J-O-B, sweetie." I really wanted to say, *Shut the hell up and get your lame ass up and go to work.*

I don't know and I don't care about whatever Craig is yapping about. I look in the mirror and think that I'm too smart and too pretty to be at home all day, letting all this go to waste. It'd be nice to mix and mingle with some co-workers or customers like in the old days. Most sales associates are known for some harmless flirting here and there. That was good for me and my sales. Working made me look forward to coming home and now I'm just home without anything to look forward to. That's exactly what I get for trying to make my man happy. Somewhere along the way I forgot about making myself happy.

I'm a stay-at-home mom/homemaker or whatever you want to call it. My days are spent taking care of my family's needs and our house, which doesn't afford me a lot of personal time. It's my responsibility to make sure everyone gets up and out of house on time.

"Get up, Craig. Don't make me say it again."

"You're a real pain first thing in the morning, you know that?"

"I know. I know. Just get up."

"I just need a few more minutes."

"You're only making it harder to get up. Too much sleep isn't good for you. It just slows you down even more. Makes for a sluggish day."

"Who told you that, Oprah or Dr. Phil? Bet a million bucks you heard that from one of your daytime television friends. Tell me I'm wrong."

I smile, shake my head, and say, "Leave me and my daytime television friends alone. I got something for you."

I reenter the bedroom and quickly snatch the covers off of Craig, revealing his naked body curled up in a fetal position.

"Damn, girl! I think your goal in life is to get on my last nerve. Give me that blanket back or at least the sheet. I ain't playing!"

I laugh and say, "See? Told you it was chilly in here with the AC turned up like that. All we need is that nice breeze that's stirring out there. We should be enjoying that good ole North Cakalaki air."

"It ain't as good as it used to be."

"You need to get up and stop being so mean."

"I ain't mean. I'm just not a morning person. You already know that. Besides, I'm about to get laid off, anyway. Who cares if I'm late? As a matter of fact, I think they expect me to be late."

"Why, 'cause you're black?"

"Damn right!"

"That's the wrong mentality. Stop feeding into stereotypes. You're a supervisor, Craig. Forget about layoffs. You need to put forth your best effort no matter what. Shoot, you're just giving them what they want, just like the rest of 'em. You need to get your butt in there on time. It's about principle."

"Principle?" Craig sits up in bed, looks at me real crazy and asks, "What in the hell do you know about principle?"

I damn near cut him with my sharp stare. "Excuse me?"

"Don't look at me like that. I mean, when it comes to work principle. You don't have a clue, 'cause you don't work in a pie shop and you're talking about principle."

Craig laughs at me. He should be laughing at himself. He finally decides to get his narrow behind out of bed.

He gives me his usual quick little peck on the lips. "See, I'm up."

"I see."

We're talking about two completely different things. He's talking about being up out of bed and I'm talking about him being up, his erection. What a freakin' waste. Wish he really knew how to use that thing.

Things have really changed between us. Craig used to be much more outgoing and creative, but now he isn't as focused on sex or romance. We used to laugh at couples around here that kissed like he just kissed me. No passion whatsoever. Now those same people are probably laughing at us, laughing at me. I don't want anybody feeling sorry for me.

I've never been the type to seek pity from anybody. No pity party over here, no sir. Losing Momma to death and Daddy to prison kind of forced me to be strong. I had to be strong for me and Serena. God bless that girl. At least Craig stopped smoking, cut back on drinking, and most of all, he has a good job. On the other hand, Serena's husband, Darryl, is as crazy as a bedbug. I sympathize with her because there ain't nothing worse than having an unemployed drunk for a husband. They've had their share of ups and downs over the years, but somehow Serena's been able to tolerate him and their two kids. I swear Taylor and Travis are two little terrors. Craig calls them Birth Control Number One and Two. Their little bad asses are the exact reason he and I stopped considering having any more kids. Taylor is two years old and all she knows how to say is, "Shut up," "No," "Stop," "Ugh-uh," "Stink-stink," and "Doo-doo." Travis isn't any better. His first words were curse words. I'll admit, it was kind of funny hearing a one-year-old say "shit" and "bitch," but now that he's four it's just downright ignorant. Darryl and Serena are to blame for their kids acting the way they do. My grandma, Big Maw, she was my daddy's momma. She died a long time ago, but I still remember something she used to say, *Charity starts at home and spreads abroad.* Now I understand exactly what she meant.

Meeting Craig and falling in love sidetracked some of my dreams and changed the course of my life. Even if I could turn back the hands of time, I probably wouldn't. When I met Craig it was far from love at first sight. Craig wasn't my type at all. Anyone could see that we made an odd couple. I still don't understand why short men are so attracted to tall women. I thought he was a short, loudmouthed, overconfident womanizer with a fake tough-guy persona and no real sense of style. Now I'm laughing at him. He used to wear hats that matched whatever color outfit he wore. Simply put, he was country and he still is. But at the same time he was more or less my savior from the living hell my aunt, Momma Pearl, was putting me through. Over time, I guess I learned to love him and his unique qualities a little. I still don't like his pointed-toe cowboy boots, country bastard.

Craig asks, "What are you laughing at?"

"You and your mean self."

"Why me? You're the joke."

"Is that right?"

"Yeah."

I wanna joke Craig about being so countrified, but I know that's a very sensitive subject for him. I mean, I'm a southern girl and all, but I'm not *country*.

"You said you're not a morning person." I said instead. "Well, you're not a morning, noon, or night person. You're just plain ole mean all of the time."

"You're wrong 'cause nighttime is my time. Didn't you enjoy last night?"

"I was asleep and I don't enjoy your sneak-attack sex tactics almost every night, either. Slipping up behind somebody and just ramming your thing inside isn't my idea of sexy. No, I didn't enjoy last night."

"It sounded like you enjoyed it. I didn't hear you complaining none when I was doing my thing."

"That doesn't mean that I enjoyed it. I don't complain about a lot of things, but that doesn't mean I enjoy them. There's a big difference. What would you enjoy more, having a big steak forced down your throat, or if it was slowly fed to you along with your favorite side dishes and an occasional sip of wine? Do you understand my point?"

"Nah, not really. Excuse the hell out of me. I'm your husband and

I didn't know I had to ask for permission every time I wanted to get some."

"You missed the point."

"Too bad, and so did you. I don't have time for this bullshit. I gotta go to work and you have to get the kids up and get breakfast going, remember?"

"I told you already, I got it coming. You need to learn how to talk to me."

"I'm learning. Slowly but surely, I'm learning. Sorry if I'm not the little lovey-dovey type you've always dreamed of."

I don't say a word. *I love my husband. I love my husband.* That's what I keep telling myself as I make my way down the hall to wake the kids for school.

Craig and I met in church. His first wife, Debbie, had just left him and I was a young, naive girl looking for a way out of a bad situation. According to Craig, Debbie just up and left him and their kids without an explanation and never looked back. Momma Pearl was fixin' to kick me and Serena out of her house for what she called being too grown. To us, we were just growing up, having a little fun and trying to meet new people.

Momma Pearl knew Craig and liked him and his family a lot. In other words, they had money and money makes the world go 'round. Craig's family owns a little bit of real estate in this area. They sold a ton of houses in the old days. Now they mostly concentrate on their family business called the Draper Grocery Store.

Momma Pearl knew that Craig was very fond of me. She figured he needed a new wife and momma for his kids and she could get rid of me. She called that killing two birds with one stone.

When I got to know Craig, I figured that he wasn't so bad. His confidence and his little muscular body became a turn-on. He's tough at times, but overall he's good to me and the kids. In a lot of ways we're both changing. I used to be a total pushover, but that was definitely the old me. Craig used to be the type of man who cooked and cleaned and even put the toilet seat down when he was done. He was what I needed, someone to take me away from my pain, someone to take good care of me, and he showed me the kind of love that I hadn't received in so long. I had nothing and all of a sudden I was living in a nice, big house with a car, truck, jewelry, and a new wardrobe. Craig had a stable life with good credit and a good career at the textile mill. What more could I ask for. He swept me off my feet and sent me soaring and now I feel the momentum slowly shifting. Sometimes it feels like this roller coaster ride is headed downhill.

3

Naomi

I've been lying on the right side of my bed, completely entranced by the television for hours, precious hours that I can't possibly get back. I'm dressed in my favorite lounging gear, a pair of denim short shorts, a pink stretch T-shirt that reads, *Angel* across the front, and a pair of white Reebok classics. There's plenty of housework to be done, but I got caught up watching *The Young and the Restless* and *The Bold and the Beautiful.* Usually by the time *As the World Turns* comes on, I'm up and going full speed ahead, but not today. Something heavy is on my mind—I want Craig to respect me. I hate the way he talks to me.

I shift my body slightly and feel around the bed for the television remote. I find it a few seconds later under a pillow next to one of my favorite novels, *A Day Late and A Dollar Short* by Terry McMillan. I just finished reading it last night. I loved it. During the day all I have are my African-American novels and the TV to keep me company. Serena might stop by every now and then to chat with me for a while.

My eyes slowly drift from the television to the nightstand. The alarm clock reads 2:01 P.M. in big red numbers. I sigh, make a crooked little smile and think, *Good! I still have a couple of hours before the kids arrive from school and over three hours before Craig arrives from work.* All of a sudden the dreadful sound of Craig's truck momentarily steals my attention. I'm sure most of the neighborhood can hear his big ole beat down, O.J. Simpson-lookin' white Ford Bronco. Of all days, why did Craig have to come home early today? My sleepy eyes widen as a sense of urgency overtakes me. I know the deal, so I jump to my feet and scramble around the bedroom like a crazy woman in a hopeless attempt to straighten up the place.

Hours have escaped me and so did my good sense, because I know damn well that Craig Gaffney doesn't tolerate a messy house. I hear him enter the house, making his way around, surveying my day's work. I already know the damage—five loads of unfolded laundry, a kitchen sink full of dirty breakfast dishes, two dirty bathrooms screaming to be cleaned, and numerous pieces of furniture with a very noticeable coating of dust. With such a mess he probably won't even notice that I did get a little vacuuming done.

Craig calls out. "Naomi!"

The sound of his voice makes my blood run cold. I shake my head and softly ask myself, "What's the use?" I drop the clothes I was attempting to fold and simply climb right back in the spot on the bed where I've been most of the day.

Craig enters our bedroom with his five-foot, six-inch, one-hundred-forty-five-pound frame acting like he can intimidate somebody. "Surprised you, didn't I?"

I twist my lips a little to show him that I'm not the least bit affected and say a simple, "Hey. How was your day?"

When he sees the look on my face, he instantly tones it down a notch. He has this silly look that guys get when they're trying to figure a woman out. He kisses me in his usual fashion—nothing passionate, just a quick little peck on the lips.

Craig automatically starts undressing. "My day can be summed up with one word—*busy*." He sighs. "Aw man, I'm glad to be home. I've been at work all day and look at you, just lying there. I figured this was how you operated."

I mute the TV and turn over, lying on my left side with my elbow and left hand supporting my head. I look Craig dead in the eyes and say, "Boy, don't give me that crap. You better go on with that, spoiling my afternoon. I heard you come in. Heard your hunk-of-junk truck coming a mile away. I ain't thinking 'bout you, my workday ain't over yet, so save the drama for your momma. I've got plenty of time to get my chores done."

"Who in the hell are you talking to? Girl, *you* better go on with that. You don't understand what I've been through today."

"No more than I've been through, I'm sure."

"You better check yourself. I don't know who you're talking to in that tone."

"I'm talking to you, Craig Maurice Gaffney. I'm talking to you, Lil' Mo. Ain't that what your drinking partners call you?"

Craig doesn't say a word. He just gives me a mean look and plops his narrow behind down at the foot of our bed. He takes off his shoes, kicks them into the closet, and finishes getting undressed. Such an angry little man, cute in his own unique way. Always wants to be a little bad-ass. Guess that was another quality that initially attracted me to him.

Craig continues with the mean look. I can tell that I'm starting to get on his nerves.

I ask, "What's that look about? You ain't the boss of me. I run this. Nobody gave me a schedule."

Craig shakes his head in disbelief. "Same old excuses. You need to—"

I cut him off. "I know what I need to do. You need to go somewhere with that country-behind truck of yours."

He gets defensive because I'm talking about his pride and joy. "Oh boy, here we go again. You need to leave my truck out of this. I've told you time and time again that that thing is a classic, not to mention a good investment."

I laugh and say, "Whatever you say. Every time I see that big white Bronco coming down the road, it reminds me of that slow speed chase out in L.A." Craig doesn't look amused. "Look, I'm worn out. Besides, your day must not have been too busy, as you put it. You're home three hours early."

"Forget about that. It's not important anyway. This house is a mess."

Craig's comment makes me get a little defensive. "Damn! Can you ever come home without complaining? Always nitpicking. You do more bitching and complaining than a broke-down old woman."

Craig doesn't like my tone at all. "What did you say to me? Girl, you just don't know."

"You heard me. Now, stop complaining. That's all you know."

"I don't know what you've been watching on TV or reading lately, but this is reality." He looks over at the TV. "Watching those damn soaps got you just as stupid as you wanna be."

"Yep, the soaps do make me stupid, but what's your excuse? I'm sick of you complaining about what I do, how I do it, and what I don't do. You have a comment about every little thing I do around here. Do your thing and I'll do mine."

"I'm doing my thing. Every time I bring a paycheck home, I'm doing my thing."

"And keep doing it and stop complaining about what I'm doing. That all I'm asking."

"I always have a reason to complain, don't I? Stop giving excuses and I'll stop complaining. I can't believe your lazy ass."

"Oh . . . my . . . God, give me strength. I know you didn't just cuss at me, calling me a lazy ass. That's it!"

Craig continues on, but I completely block out his voice. He looks real stupid, standing in front of me butt-naked, fussing and cussing about housework. After a few seconds he wraps a towel around himself. I've known for a while that he hasn't been happy with himself and his job situation and now he wants to make everyone else miserable.

As Craig continues to fuss, my attention turns toward the bedroom window. I stand up and look out, watching as clusters of storm clouds slowly converge in the unsuspecting afternoon sky. A forceful wind rips through the trees. I begin to realize that there was already a black cloud over my house.

"You need to learn to appreciate this shit. I work hard to keep all this going. After all this time, you should be used to carrying your own weight. All I ask from you is to keep this house clean. Is that asking too much?"

All of a sudden I feel very anxious—I feel trapped, and a weird, suffocating feeling begins to take over. Without thinking, I open the window and rest my hands on the windowsill, then press my face against the screen, taking in a deep breath. I slowly exhale, feeling the refreshing sensations of the wind and rain against my face. It's somewhat liberating—I'm sick and tired of letting Craig get the best of me.

He yells, "I ain't made of money. Close that damn window, letting my air out. You know the AC is on."

For a second I forgot that I was married to a penny-pincher, the only man I know who goes around cutting off lights on his family and restricting us to two-minute showers. Once he even tried to limit the amount of toilet paper we used. That was just plain stupid, not to mention nasty. Another time I watched this fool as he cut the bottom out of an empty tube of toothpaste and stuck his brush inside trying to get the last traces out.

My frustration reaches its peak. I snap. "Shut up! Just stop it. I can't take this anymore. I'm sick of pretending. There's something wrong here and don't act like you haven't noticed. I've given you all that I have and I can't give anymore. I'm done trying. You take me for granted."

"And you don't take me for granted? What are you talking about? I'm good to you. Shit, I've been great to you. Where would you be without me?"

Hearing Craig say something like that really hurts. That's why I always liked doing for myself, so nobody could ever throw what they've done for me back in my face.

"Am I supposed to answer that?"

"Don't worry, 'cause you probably don't have a clue. The bottom line is that I get up every morning and go to work. Meanwhile you lay your lazy ass up in the bed watching TV or have your head buried in one of those books until it's almost time for me or the kids to come home. Then you come to life, acting like you've been working at a busy pace all day."

"Is that what you think? If that's what you think you can go straight to hell. You don't realize it, but I'm working right now."

"Yeah? Doing what?"

"I'm washing clothes."

"But the washer and dryer are doing all the work."

"Give me a break. You're off from work right now, but I'm never off. I work here 24/7/365. In other words, I'm a full-time housewife and momma working killer overtime. I'm not supposed to take a break, right? As the lady of the house I'm supposed to work constantly. What about my vacation and sick time? I guess I don't deserve any of that."

Craig pauses for a few seconds, letting my last statement sink in a bit. "You're right. We'll have to work on making a few changes around here."

"Oh, thank you *master*. I sure do appreciate the consideration."

"Stop acting silly."

"Yessum, master. You reckon a po' lil' slave girl like me can get a break."

"Funny, real funny."

"I'm serious. Something's got to change around here. If I can't get your help, at least respect me and what I do. I am your wife, remember? We don't even talk like we used to. When was the last time you kissed me?"

"I kissed you when I came in here."

"Huh, I mean *really* kissed me. When was the last time you told me that you loved me or told me that I was beautiful? How long has it been?"

He softens up. "Baby, I love you more than you'll ever know. And you know I think you're beautiful. Do I have to tell you every day?"

"Yes. I need to hear things like that every day. You always say that you love me more than I'll ever know. What does that mean? I need to know exactly how much you love me. I wanna know."

Craig gets this strange look in his eyes. He raises his eyebrow and says, "Hold up. You expect me to tell you that I love you and you're beautiful every day?" Within seconds he transforms back into his insensitive hotheaded self.

"Yes!"

"Then you have a real self-esteem problem. I don't need that type of daily confirmation."

"Well, I do. You're my husband and you should know me by now. I need to be held, not yelled at. I miss being cuddled and kissed like in the old days."

"I'm sorry. I'm under so much stress. Nobody knows what I go through on a daily basis. Sometimes it's a real struggle to keep going. For God's sake, I'm about to lose my damn job. I wish you could understand the stress and anxiety I feel."

"I can't begin to imagine, 'cause you never talk to me. There's no way for me to really know. I always have to hear about things second-hand or when they're out of control. Your momma knows more about your life than I do and that's sad. You can talk to me. Really you can. That's what I'm here for. What's happening to us?"

"I don't know, but we're gonna work it out, okay? We've come too far to start messing up now."

Craig pulls me in close to him and holds me tight. I feel his lips and a couple more things I haven't felt in a long time: his tongue and a little bit of passion.

4

Craig

My wife is the most beautiful woman I've ever seen in my life. I'm reminded of that as she stands here in my arms. I'm not sure where my mind has been lately. My job and other minor issues have completely consumed me and affected my ability to be me. Naomi and I haven't had sex—correction, made love—in a long time. This feels like the start of something good. I hope she feels the passion in my kiss.

As our lips part, I ask, "How was that kiss?"

Naomi gives me the cutest little smile and says, "Good. It was really good."

"Reminds me of how good things used to be. Do you remember how good it was?"

"Sure do—think about it all the time. I remember how you used to touch me. Makes me wet just thinking 'bout it . . . thinking 'bout you."

"Damn, I really fell off for a minute, but I'm back, baby. I'm back, okay?"

"Don't worry about that. Our love's still good. Let's work on making it the best it can possibly be."

"I hear what you're saying. We have to work on building, and not tearing this marriage apart. I love you."

"And I love you."

"I'm not just saying this because I think you need to hear it, but you're without a doubt the most beautiful woman I've ever seen in my life. You're a fantastic wife and an outstanding mom to all our kids. I appreciate that so much. I couldn't possibly ask for more in a woman. Thank you, baby."

"Thank you for saying exactly what I wanted and needed to hear."

Naomi and I kiss again. She's breathtaking, so beautiful in my arms. What was I thinking? I've been so blind, but now I see exactly what I've been missing.

"Look at us. This is nice. I hope the kids don't come home anytime soon." I laugh. "We really need quality time together. Wish they could stay at school all evening. What are you thinking?"

Naomi gives me a curious look. "Do you understand me now?"

"Yeah, I do. The blinders are off."

"Can't live life with blinders on, you know?"

"I know. I don't plan on living like that anymore. I mean, living for tomorrow and just letting today pass right by."

Naomi puts her index finger to her lips in a seductive manner. Her eyes and smile reveal her thoughts before she even speaks. She's got sex on her mind.

She says, "Shhh. Stop talking. We're running out of time. The kids will be here soon."

I begin to undress Naomi. Now, this is what I'm talkin' 'bout.

I love hard, giving everything I've got physically and mentally. I go all out . . . freefalling headfirst into love. No pain, no gain used to be my motto, but I stopped living by that a long time ago. Love hurts and that's what made me change. Seems whenever I love a woman too much, nine out of ten times I lose her. And I guess the same can be said when I take the one I love for granted. I've only truly loved three women in my life: Naomi, Debbie, and Khamia. I've cheated on every woman I've loved, except Naomi. This is my first committed relationship.

I was a straight-up dog, running around on my first wife like a natural-born fool with my old girlfriend Khamia. I like to call her Mia for short. Sometimes it's hard to give up on a good thing, even when you're married. Mia was my good thing. My first wife Debbie was out of my life quicker than I could blink an eye when she found out exactly what I was doing with my good thing. Mia was always in and out of my life since we first met on my job at the mill seventeen years ago. She was a wild thing and a real tease wrapped up in one. That girl was healthy, built like a brick house. She controlled me. Had me sniffing and chasing behind her like a dog in heat. She made me do things I had no business doing, like screwing her. Before long I was screwing her more than I was screwing Debbie. The whole thing came to an abrupt end when Debbie peeked in the bedroom window of Mia's trailer home and saw both of us butt-naked making love. Mia had me so sprung that I had become absolutely crazy and careless. It never dawned on me to pull the damn shade down. The fact that my truck was in her driveway in plain sight didn't help much, either. To make matters worse, Debbie had C.J. and Erika right there in the car and they've never forgiven me for what I did that night. That experience made me wake up and forced me to be a man and settle down for real with a special lady like Naomi.

Sometimes I hate love with all its heartaches and pain and ups and downs. In the past I brought a lot of that on myself. But don't get me wrong, I've known the joys and pleasures of love, too. That's what I'm feeling right now with Naomi. I fell off track for a minute, but now I'm just trying to reach a certain comfort level. Before long I'll probably be that kinder, nicer, gentler, and more sensitive lover Naomi wants me to be. I just can't give in to my wife like that too fast. She might mistake it for weakness. I can't let my woman make a punk out of me. She really should appreciate what she has because I could be a lot worse. God forbid, I could be like I was in the past.

Some men are naturally sensitive, but not me. I use so many different defenses to protect my heart and hide my real emotions. Fear of losing control is my worst enemy. Fear in general is my greatest opponent, but there's no quit in me. I'm working on self-improvement. In the meantime, I'll just keep pressing on, challenging and overcoming obstacles like a true warrior.

Why should I change? Every beat of my heart and every breath that I take is for Naomi. Everything I do is about loving her. And more than anything, I love giving her something she can feel.

I slowly guide Naomi to our bed and she knows what's next. I'm not really big on foreplay.

Naomi puts her hands up to my chest and says, "Hold on, slow your roll a bit. I know you're ready to slide inside quicker than a hot knife through butter and all, but I wanna try something different. You'll like this . . . I hope."

Naomi gets off the bed and heads straight to her underwear draw. She reaches deep in the back and pulls out what looks to be a long black toy snake.

I yell, "What in the hell! I thought you were about to put on some of your sexy underwear or something."

"Don't act like that. Be spontaneous."

"Be who? Girl, you better get—"

"Stop! It's just a sex toy."

"For who? Get that thing away from here. We don't need any toys to have the kind of fun I have in mind. What is that and where did that freaky-ass thing come from?"

"It's a vibrating dildo and I got it from Serena."

"I should've known. Something that freaky had to come from a freak like her."

"Leave my sister alone."

"You're damn sure not gonna use that on me."

Naomi laughs and says, "It's definitely not for you." She holds the toy up, letting it dangle. "All this is for me. If you don't wanna use it on me, then I'll just have to use it on myself. Just sit back and watch the show. If you want, you can slide that little chair right up to the bed and have a front-row seat. Do whatever makes you comfortable."

"What are you doing?"

"Being young, creative, and sexy for my slightly more mature husband."

I throw my hands up and say, "Go 'head and do it then."

"All right. You're gonna enjoy this. Look at you, sweatin' already." She wipes my forehead. "Relax, honey. Momma won't hurt you—not yet, anyway."

Naomi eases her way up the center of our bed, resting on her back with her knees bent and legs wide open. She's almost naked, except for her bra. That's her trademark. Naomi has always been insecure about her breast size and rarely exposes them. She's been like this so long that this is something that I've just grown to accept. The bra doesn't bother her and it doesn't bother me either. As far as I'm concerned, everything else looks so damn good that her bra is the last thing on my mind. At this point, it's invisible. Shapely hips and thighs are what I like most. Big breasts are nice, but a nice, plump booty is even better. I'm an ass man and my baby got back.

Naomi's eyes are focused directly on me, lookin' like some sinister sexual spirit has possessed her. She slowly seduces me with her stare. I don't know this side of my wife. Naomi brings her big, black sex toy up to her mouth and begins to lick it. She kisses it a little, then puts the tip in her mouth and sucks it like she used to do me back when she found me irresistible. This is shocking, bothers me in both a good and bad way. Part of me wants her to stop and the other wants to see just how much of the toy she can fit down her throat. Within seconds she begins to deep-throat her toy like a pro. I have a perfect view of what's happening between her legs and it's nice. She's getting so wet that her sweetness begins to glisten. We're both getting aroused. I lie back in my chair and stretch my legs out in front of me as much as possible. My hands are resting on my lap, right next to my right thigh and penis, not exactly touching it, but close enough to feel it rise and expand. Before long I'm damn near forced to touch myself in front of my wife for the first time in eleven years. My mouth begins to water. My heart races, beating a mile a minute. I want to masturbate so bad, but I don't want Naomi to see that side of me yet. I never realized how good she was at giving head, never seen her perform from this angle. I like what I see and hope she's pretending that's me in her mouth like that. Naomi closes her eyes and I'm no longer her focal point—it's just her and that damn sex toy. She does something I've never seen her do. She places her free hand between her legs and begins to touch herself.

In the meantime, she continues sucking away on her toy. The average man would have exploded by now, especially if she was performing oral sex on him like she's throwing down on that toy. I'm so hard that I'm about to explode, just from watching this. She's good, damn good.

Naomi finally finishes her oral escapade and lowers her toy down to her vagina. She taunts and teases herself externally, giving special attention to her clitoris. She moves her toy all around her vaginal area, sending vibrating sensations throughout her pelvic region. With great anticipation, she penetrates herself. She starts with slow, short thrusts, in and out. Naomi eventually increases the depth and speed. I watch as her juices lubricate her toy and she's able to accommodate almost every inch.

She hasn't looked at me for more than five minutes. I'm no longer an active participant. I don't know this woman. Her moans and groans are even different.

Naomi is in a zone, entranced by her own passion. This is a side of Naomi that I didn't know. Makes me wonder where this came from, all of a sudden.

I'm fully erect and on the edge of my seat. This is hard to watch. Naomi's toy makes me feel kind of inadequate. I'm a nice size, but let's be real for a minute. My ego is bruised and madder than a mother-fucker. Makes me wonder if I'm up to following a ten-inch vibrating dildo. I think that's a hard act for any man to follow. Something strange overtakes me. I want in on this, but first I wanna do a little experimentation. I approach Naomi from the right side of the bed, grabbing her hand with my right hand and forcing the toy deeper inside her. She begins to rock back and forth like she wants more.

She gives me this intense stare and screams, "Faster! Faster! Uh-huh. Uh-huh. Ooh, that's it. That's it, baby."

I'm really into this now. "Does it feel good? You like it?"

"Yeah! Yeah!"

"Want it harder and faster?"

"Yeah! Do it. Do it to me. I like that. Feels so damn good, baby. Yeah . . . yeah!"

"You like it rough? Huh? Answer me!"

"Yeah! Fuck me! Ooh! Fuck me! Fuck meeeee!"

"You're so fucking nasty. You're gonna make me come."

"Me too! Oooooooh! Ooooooh!"

"I can't take it. I'm 'bout ta come all over you. Oh shit!" I grab myself and come all over Naomi's chest and abdomen. "Aw, yeah, girl! That was good. Did you come yet?"

She moans. "Uh-huh. Uh-huh."

"How many times?"

She's damn near breathless. "Four. I came four times."

5

Naomi

Craig and I are lying in our usual spoon position, I'm the dip and
he's the spoon. We're both a bit exhausted from our little sexual
encounter. That was hot. Oh my God, I should be ashamed of myself,
but I'm not. Finally my wild side has been exposed and I think Craig
was able to tap into his wild side as well. Damn, what a release! My insides are singing and dancing. I'm not sure what got into me, but
Serena would have been proud of me.

This is the calm before the storm. I'm referring to the weather and
not me and Craig. As I lie here looking out our bedroom window, I'm
able to see the same ominous-looking clouds still looming overhead,
giving the sky a layered appearance. There's a small group of light
fluffy clouds with a hint of sunlight piercing through. Several gray
clouds add to this dramatic effect and then there are miles and miles
of huge black storm clouds as far as the eye can see. Other than a
cloudy, dramatic sky, everything else remains the same. No thunder
or lightning, not even a drop of rain.

I feel Craig come to life, out of his deep sleep. He runs his left
hand up and down my left thigh and buttock, then up my abdomen,
finally resting on my left breast. I feel his throbbing dick come to life
and try to find its way inside me. I'm still lubricated well enough
down there so he shouldn't have any problem pulling off his famous
hands-free penetration move. I knew Craig would eventually rebound

from his first ejaculation and be ready for round two. This just isn't the position I had in mind. Not really one of my favorites.

He's inside me.

I think, *This is so lame. Come on, brotha, give me a break. Is this the best you can do? After my sexy exhibition you should be ready to bust a new move. Be creative.*

As his hips gyrate, my mouth dictates. "Faster, deeper. Come on, you can do it. Come on. Harder. Give it to me."

"I'm giving it to you."

I'm getting heated and caught up in this brief moment of passion. "Do me like you did earlier."

He slows down a bit and his rhythm is thrown off. "What? Like I did earlier? That wasn't me." All of a sudden his off-beat sexual rhythm comes to a complete stop. "That was your toy, remember?"

Oh shit, I forgot for a minute. I think I'm in trouble. Somebody's ego just took a powerful blow. Hope he's not down for the count.

"I know, but you provided the force behind it. That was your rhythm, sweetie. That was you."

I feel his hot breath on my neck as he yells in my left ear, "Bullshit! Do you like that thing more than you like me? You don't even need me now. How long have you had that thing, anyway?"

Uh-oh, my man's thing just went limp and I'm not sure what to say. "That was my first time using it. What's going on? I know you're not getting jealous of a toy."

"I ain't jealous. Man, I don't want you using that thing again, especially if I'm not around. You hear me?"

I laugh. "I promise."

Craig moves away from me. He's lying on his back, talking to me but eyeballing the ceiling. "What in the hell are you laughing at? I'm serious."

I turn to my opposite side, facing him. "I know, but you're funny. You're so much better than that stupid toy. Come on, that can't possibly compare to the real thing. And you got the real thing." I grab a handful of his limpness and flip-flop it from side to side. I'm trying to keep a straight face because I'm lying my ass off. That toy ventured into no man's land, a place where no man has ever been and probably will never go. Lord, have mercy! Whoo! I'm still feeling it. "Boy, stop acting crazy. You know you can move. You be working it, I swear. Now come on and let's finish before the kids come home."

Craig's confidence slowly emerges as a mischievous grin begins to appear. "Okay. I was trippin' for a minute. Ain't nothing like the real thing, huh?"

I wink and say, "That's right. Work it, baby. You wanna do it doggie-style? Want me on top or you on top with my legs in the air? Whatever makes you happy."

He smiles. "Nah, girl. Turn around and lay on your other side." He motions me over on my right side with both hands. "Yeah, just like I like it. I'm gonna spoon you to death."

Here we go, right back to lying in a damn spoon position, the lazy lovemaking position. To make it a little more exciting, I start bouncing my ass back and forth and grinding a little. Next I grab my leg close to my ankle and raise my leg in the air for deeper penetration. Craig is into this, pumping back and forth faster then a jackrabbit running away from a pack of angry hounds. I'm tired of the same old thing, but with some creativity, this position ain't that bad.

After about five minutes or so, Craig is done and I mean that literally. He's breathing all hard. "Baby girl, that was good. You like that?"

"Yeah, it was good. I wanna try some new positions, though."

He laughs. "Whatcha talkin' 'bout? Don't you know you can't teach an old dog new tricks?"

"Huh? What are *you* talkin' 'bout? You better go on with that old-dog stuff. Shucks, I'm still in my twenties. We gotta keep this fresh and exciting. I ain't asking for nothing too difficult. Come on, do something new, anything. Tickle my ass with a feather. Put some ice cubes on my nipples."

Craig laughs. "Yep, just as soon as you take off that damn bra." His demeanor quickly changes. "You know what? I just realized something. You're too damn hard to please. I don't know where this bull-shit is coming from, but it better stop. Is another man filling your head with stupid ideas?"

"What man? Give me a freakin' break. Serena suggested that I surprise you by doing something extra special. Anyway, you're the only man I'm allowed to interact with, Mr. Insecure."

"Why am I the only one with faults? Look at you, little Ms. Perfect with your holier-than-thou attitude. You need to learn how to please your man and stop concentrating so much on pleasing yourself. So damn selfish. Me, me, me, my, my, my, that's all you know. Better pick up a book on How To Please Your Man or ask somebody besides your damn sister how to make a man happy. You've been misinformed."

I asked for this and now I got it. Boy am I ever getting it. This fool is giving it to me like never before. What did I do to deserve a crazy man like this? Nothing I do or say makes him happy.

A loud clap of thunder echoes all around us, sending vibrations throughout the house. A couple of quick rounds of thunder go off. The storm clouds can't hold back any longer. The sky opens up. Here comes the rain, beating down on the rooftop. At the same time I feel my eyes begin to water because I just realized that love isn't enough to keep our relationship or intimacy going. I want out of this because I'm not in love with this man. Loving and being in love are two very different things. What am I doing here? I know I deserve better then what I'm getting right now. Yeah, Craig *was* good to me, but what he did for me in the past is in the past. The fact that I'm not in love with him is completely ruining what we have or had. That's the root of all of our problems.

I watch the rain as it trickles down the glass of our bedroom window like a thousand lost tears.

My eyes are back to normal. No tears for me. I begin to toughen up a bit because I know that crying won't change a thing and knowing is half the battle.

I think, *Love don't live here anymore.*

Next comes my favorite saying, *You live, you love, you learn.*

Finally, I hear the kids arrive from school, complaining of being soaked. C.J. and Erika enter the house first, and then, a few minutes later, Morgan arrives.

6

Craig

We live in Eden, as in the Garden of Eden, just not as peaceful and undisturbed. It's a wonderful town based on southern comfort and hospitality, a place where you can enjoy a moment's peace while sipping a cold beer, or a refreshing glass of my momma's sunbrewed sweet tea. Can't get enough of Eden's down home atmosphere and old-fashioned goodness. This place is changing, but don't get me wrong—it's still a great place to live, with its traditional country houses, manicured lawns, and rows and rows of assorted mailboxes along the roadside. You might come across an occasional lawn jockey, but you can bet it won't have a black face like in the old days. I haven't seen one those things around here in years. You still might find a rocking chair or porch swing here and there, but you won't find any snobbish people. Maybe a cutthroat, but no snobs. For the most part, this is a blue-collar town with a population largely composed of whites and a small, close-knit African-American community, where just about everybody knows everybody else.

Our biggest employers are Morehead Memorial Hospital, Duke Power Company, Miller Brewing Company, and the textile plant where I work that we all refer to as the Mill.

If you do something wrong around here, you can be sure to find your name, address, and all kinds of personal information, maybe even your momma's name, in the *Eden Daily News* the next morning.

That's how it is in a small town like this, and we do have our fair share of crime. Back in the day, we never had to lock our cars or front doors. The influx of crack cocaine in the late Eighties changed the landscape and introduced us to shoplifters, break-ins, and armed robberies. Even with all that nonsense going on we're probably most famous for our crimes of passion. That's what happens when it gets real boring around here and everybody starts sleeping with everybody else's mate. There seems to be a memorable crime of passion committed almost every year, usually a senseless stabbing or shooting. But none of those cases are as popular or as well-known as the one committed over twenty-one years ago. The headline read: LOCAL BLACK POLICEMAN MURDERS WHITE WIFE. That was Naomi's parents. There was a small headshot of Mrs. Goode's pretty face in the bottom right-hand corner of a larger photograph of Mr. Goode in handcuffs, standing next to two deputies from the sheriff's department outside of the Rockingham County Jail. The article went on to describe the details of the murder and how Mr. Frank Goode had allegedly stabbed his wife thirty-two times in the chest, neck, back, and arms. The autopsy was performed at the North Carolina Medical Examiner's Office in Raleigh. The whole ordeal sent shockwaves throughout Eden.

I was born and raised here. I promised my parents a long time ago that I'd live here for the rest of my life, and that's a promise I won't renege on. My daddy's name is Maynard and my momma's name is Georgia. They own and operate a little grocery store down in Draper. It's the oldest grocery store in this community.

I'm the youngest of five kids and the only one of my siblings who decided to start a family here. Two of my brothers, Maynard Jr. and Chester, live in New York with their families. Another brother, Bobby Ray, lives in Dallas with his wife, and my sister, Ida, lives in Atlanta with her family. They can have those big cities with all the noise and air pollution. Terrorists are drawn to big cities and that's another reason why I'm fine with a small town like Eden. I don't need all that chaos and confusion. But still more and more young people are moving away from here, because of layoffs, the sluggish economy, and Eden's delayed development. Most of them feel like there's no future here— there sure won't be any future if everybody falls for that bull. Some development plans are in the works right now to turn our Wal-Mart into a Wal-Mart Supercenter Store and we should be getting a Ruby

Tuesday soon. That's the best news this town has heard in a long while. The only bad thing is I'm not sure what's going to happen when the Wal-Mart Supercenter Store comes. Hope it doesn't run Winn-Dixie or Food Lion out of business. That's exactly what happened to poor old Kmart and a bunch of stores in the Eden Mall when Wal-Mart first came here. I don't have nothing against Wal-Mart because I love a place where I can shop for clothes, tools, electronics, and have meal all under the same roof. Momma and Daddy's little store will be just fine because it's the only place that allows customers to buy anything and everything under the sun with food stamps. When I say anything and everything, I mean beer, liquor, cigarettes, and anything else our people around here need. People respect that and keep it on the hush.

I'm determined to stay here and make the most of this place, where traces of my ancestors' blood, sweat, and tears still make up this fertile and sacred ground. You have to know their story to understand where I'm coming from. I love the South in general for its rich but tainted history. Most people don't understand or are ashamed of slavery, but I'm not. I'm proud of slavery because it made us strong and more resilient. What didn't kill us truly made us stronger. My ancestors worked this land for free, from sunup till sundown, six to seven days a week. Most slave masters recognized Sunday as God's day, which led to some slaves getting the day off. Even though slaves were forbidden to touch the Good Book, they still found a way to get God's word. Slaves were also able to turn table scraps and the most undesirable animal parts into delectable meals. After a while those same modest meals began to look and smell so good that they made the slave masters' mouths water. That was the origin of soul food. My ancestors turned pieces of wood and metal into ingenious inventions and mighty machines. They made something out of nothing, always knew how to make a way out of no way. That's the strength of our people.

Black men and women cut down trees, built houses and barns, plowed endless fields, picked and harvested crops, cared for farm animals and their slave master's kids as well as their own. Black women have always been the true nurturers. Mammy cared for the white babies in the "Big House" while her counterpart, Aunty, cared for the black babies in the slave cabin.

The South is growing and probably is more popular then ever, thanks to so many rappers talking about "The Dirty South" and getting "Crunk" in their songs. I love it 'cause I was country when country wasn't nowhere close to being cool. My daddy raised us to be proud of our southern roots. Since I was the smallest of my siblings, he raised me to be tough as hell. Just had to be 'cause he wouldn't have settled for anything less. That man loved to hit me. Sometimes I thought my daddy hated me for being so small because he and my brothers are all well over six feet tall. He didn't cut me any slack for being premature. I'm five-foot-six-and-three-quarter-inches, but you can't tell me that I'm not seven feet tall. I was always small in stature and had a big mouth. I talk a lot of shit, but without a doubt I can back it up. I've been fighting all my life.

Naomi and I are lying here in silence, mad as hell at each other. If this ain't love, then I don't know what love is. What else can I give Naomi? I've given all that I have and more and now I have nothing else to give. I bought her a brand new Toyota Camry a month ago as kind of an early birthday present. It sure beats the hell out of her old Toyota Corolla.

I'm an average, hardworking black man, but I like nice things for my family. We live in an eighteen-hundred-square-foot, four-bedroom, two-and-a-half-bath rancher. Part of the eighteen hundred square feet includes two room additions we added over the past eleven years. I transformed our old garage into a recreation room with a bar, nine-foot pool table, an air hockey table, and a couple of video arcade games for the kids. There's a large stone fireplace in our rustic but cozy family room. We have an eat-in kitchen and formal dining and living room. This house has all types of modern amenities and is actually one of fanciest houses in this area, especially among the African-Americans. We're blessed to be in a place like this. It's just too bad that not all of us can appreciate living here. Within a couple of months I took Naomi from a dirt-poor household to a middle-class household and she repays me by acting like this, being disagreeable and ungrateful.

Naomi's aunt was a cruel woman when it came to raising her. People around here used to say that she was as crooked as a barrel of snakes using God's name as a front for her corrupt ways. I've never understood how somebody could preach to a congregation about how God will pull them out of all their financial hardships and then turn around and ask that same bewildered congregation for an outrageous amount of money in order for their prayers to be answered. I was a member of that church until I couldn't stomach Momma Pearl's disregard for people's well-being. Plus, it was strange being part of a church where the congregation referred to the pastor as Momma. She wasn't my Momma. More than anything, I didn't like the way Naomi was, so I decided to make her life better by making her part of mine. That definitely seemed like a good thing for both of us.

In the beginning she was as plain as a slice of cheese pizza and now she's a slice of deluxe with the works. At the same time she's added a lot of spice to my life. I'm blessed to have a woman like her. I love her, even though it might not seem like it all of the time. Things change and that's no excuse. As a man and sole provider, I sometimes get my priorities screwed up. I'm only human. At times sex and romance may be low on my list because things like keeping the lights on and keeping food on the table and a roof over our heads head my priorities. Why is it that women can't understand that? Men don't intentionally ignore the needs of our women—it's just that we have more pressing issues to deal with and maybe we're not equipped to handle multiple tasks like women. That's definitely something to think about.

The sound of the rain pouring down hitting the roof and being blown against our bedroom window has my attention. The television is off and the storm serves as my entertainment. I hear the sound of puddles as the rainwater runs down the roof into the gutter, then down the drainpipe. Next I hear footsteps—loud, quick footsteps.

I yell, "Stop running in the house!"

C.J. yells out, "That's Morgan running around in here."

A little voice says, "That wasn't me, Daddy."

I'm sure it was Morgan. My kids are habitual liars and the bad thing is that they know I know they're lying, but they continue to lie with straight faces. I guess that's typical.

There's a knock at our bedroom door. I readjust myself in bed and Naomi does the same.

I say, "Come in."

C.J. steps inside and says, "Hey, Ma. What's up, Dad?"

My son is a six-foot-two, seventeen-year-old senior at Morehead

High School. I'm sure he gets his height from my daddy and my brothers. C.J. has had his problems, but overall he's a good kid. He swears up and down that he's going to graduate on time. I'm not too sure about that because he spends too much time playing PlayStation 3 and running behind his silly friends. We made an agreement that if he played basketball and kept his grades up he wouldn't have to get a job during the school year and on top of that I'd buy him a car. Well, things didn't quite work out like I'd hoped. C.J. didn't keep his grades up and as a result he wasn't allowed to play basketball. He's still catching the bus to and from school every day and has a stack of fast food applications on the desk in his bedroom right now. More than anything, I wanted C.J. to do well on his S.A.T. and get any type of scholarship. To be honest, I just want him to go to college so he can have a better life than mine. I used to see him as a reflection of me, but not anymore.

C.J. and I don't have the best father and son relationship. My infidelity has never been much of a secret and he blames me entirely for his momma leaving us when he was a kid. I'll never forget that cold, heartless stare he gave me that night outside of Mia's trailer. I'm not sure what hurt me more, C.J.'s stare or the fact that Erika refused to look at me at all.

Debbie got fed up with me messing around on her. She left one morning without a word, and just like that we never heard from her again. She abandoned us, but I abandoned her way before the day she left. Debbie always talked about moving to Washington, D.C. with some distant relatives. For years I tried to track her down, but my attempts were all in vain. Guess she doesn't want to be found and I don't blame her because I really put her through a lot of unnecessary heartaches.

One good thing is that C.J. and Erika were able to establish a quality relationship with Naomi.

I say, "Hey, C.J."

Naomi goes, "Hi, honey. How was your day?"

"It was okay. What's for dinner?"

Dinner? That's exactly what I was thinking, but I don't say a word because I know it'll just start an argument.

Naomi looks puzzled. "Don't worry. I'm working on it."

Morgan comes into our bedroom, all happy with tons of energy. "Hi, Mommy! Hi, Daddy!"

Morgan is a ten-year-old going on thirty-five. Sometimes she can be sassy as hell, but she's still a very affectionate little girl. She's really good at caring for younger kids like her little cousins and that's why I call her Lil' Mama. Morgan's the type of kid that spends most of her time reading, doing homework, or watching something educational on television. The worst thing about Morgan is that she likes to join grown folks' conversations and to have the last word.

Naomi says, "Hi, Morgan. Come give me some sugar."

Morgan hops up on our bed and kisses her momma on the cheek and says, "It's raining cats and dogs outside, Mommy." She laughs, "I like saying that."

I give her a hug and say, "What's up Lil' Mama?"

She climbs off of our bed and says, "Nothing, Daddy."

"Nothing? Did you have a good day at school? Hope you actually learned something." I lower my voice to a whisper. "And didn't waste your time in school like your brother. That big dummy."

Naomi nudges me. "Shhh. Don't do that. He might hear you."

C.J. says, "I heard that. It's cool 'cause I know I'm gonna graduate next week."

"I'm just kidding, but I wanna see it in writing."

Morgan laughs, "I'll believe it when I see it, too."

C.J. looks at Morgan and says, "Shut up, big head."

Naomi comes to the rescue and says, "C.J., don't listen to them. I know you can do it. I'm proud of you."

He smiles as if he just received confirmation from his guardian angel that everything is gonna be okay. "Thanks."

"I'm proud, too, son, but I'll be even prouder when I hear them call your name and see you walk across that stage, all tall and proud."

"They'll call my name—don't worry."

Morgan asks, "Can I talk now?" She turns toward me. "Daddy, I did learn something. In math I learned. . . ." She pauses. "Oh, I almost forgot. Sorry to change the subject, but this girl in my class named, Brea, said that her momma is missing. They called her to the office and I think she went home early. Some of the teachers said her daddy must have realized that he made a mistake sending her to school. She was sad all morning. I think something bad must have happened to her momma."

Naomi says, "Oh my God, I hope everything is okay."

I say, "Me too. We'll have to watch the news in a little while to find out what happened. A few people at work mentioned that a woman was missing. I heard something happened to her on the way to work."

Morgan sits her little butt on our bed. She turns on the television and switches the channel right to Nickelodeon. This show appears to be too silly and juvenile for her taste, so she quickly turns it to The Discovery Channel.

I ask, "Where's your sister?"

Morgan has her eyes fixed on the television, but she's still able to answer me quicker then C.J. "She went straight to her room. I think she's on the phone. That's all she knows, being on the phone all night. I bet she's talking to a boy."

C.J. smiles and says, "Yeah, I think she's dating this white boy from our school now."

I say, "I'm not really surprised. In an area like this it was bound to happen. I thought C.J. would be the first to date outside his race."

"No sir, I'm just fine with my own kind."

"White is all right, but black is beautiful."

Naomi goes, "You remind me of my daddy, saying stuff like that."

We still make all kinds of comments, even though we know Naomi is biracial. Sometimes I think she forgets her white roots, maybe because she's only used to being around black folks.

Naomi says, "Tell Erika to come here. That girl doesn't know what to do with herself. She goes from one dating extreme to the next."

Within seconds, C.J. returns with Erika. She's on the cordless phone talking to somebody. Dating the wrong type of guys and that damn telephone are her two biggest downfalls. I came close to killing my daughter back in February when I found out she was dating a twenty-four-year-old man named Jerome. Erika looks and acts mature, so I didn't place all the blame on the guy. She lied to him and said she was an English teacher at Morehead and she didn't have a car. The guy was either stupid or horny enough to believe her. He started picking her up from school every day until C.J. told me what was going on. I hid out across the street from the school, waiting for Jerome to make his daily pickup. Let's just say I brought their relationship to an abrupt end.

Erika is the spitting image of Debbie. Momma used to say she looked like she came right outta Debbie's face.

Naomi says, "Hey, Erika."

Erika pulls the cordless away from her ear and covers the receiver. "Hey, how y'all doing?"

I say, "I was about to ask you the same thing. Hang up the phone for a minute. I wanna talk to you."

Erika says, "I'ma hafta call you right back, all right? Okay, 'bye." She hangs up the phone and asks, "What's on your mind, Daddy? What are y'all doing in bed so early?" She frowns a bit and waves her hand in front of her face. "It's kind of hot and musty up in here." Her eyes widen and her jaw drops. "Oh, I know what it is. That's disgusting. Smells like sour sausage in here."

C.J. doesn't say a word. He just laughs.

Naomi says, "Watch yourself, Erika."

I add my quick two cents. "Yeah, stop being disrespectful."

Erika says, "Yes, sir."

Morgan has this curious look. "What? What's disgusting? Tell me. What's she talking about?"

Everybody ignores Morgan.

I say, "Erika, cut that nonsense out. You got a problem? You don't know how to speak to us when you first come home?"

"Sorry. I had to call my friend, Terry, right away."

I ask, "Is Terry a male or female?"

"Female. Why?"

"Just wanted to know. You and your brother are so secretive and distant lately. The two of you hardly want to be around the family."

Naomi turns to me and says, "They're growing up. You know that's how teenagers do."

I turn back to her and say, "You're not helping."

C.J. shrugs. "You can ask me anything. For real, I don't have anything to hide."

C.J. might not have anything to hide now, but he experienced his biggest problem last year. For about a month I kept complaining about smelling this strange odor. Before long, I narrowed down the suspects to C.J. I noticed that all of our air fresheners and scented candles were in his room. His clothes reeked of smoke, but he denied he was smoking. Claimed he had been around a few smokers at school. Then he started to get a little careless. During one of my search-and-seizure missions I found a lighter in his bedroom. A few days later I found ashes on his windowsill and the screen smelled like reefer smoke. I didn't confront him because I wanted some hard evidence. I was closing in on him. One evening he must have been in the bathroom for two hours, no flushing or water running. I waited for him to come out and when he did I could see it in his eyes. The redness and glassy appearance confirmed one of my worst fears: he was getting high.

I asked, "What's wrong with you, boy? You been smoking weed, haven't you?"

"Nah, Dad. It's my allergies again. I told you I don't smoke. I haven't been smoking nothing, cigarettes or weed. I'm serious."

"You're lying. And I know it, but you're slowly telling on yourself. If you're messing with drugs you can tell me right now and I'll get you some help. I'll get you all the help you need."

"I swear, I'm not getting high. Look at me." In a weak attempt to look pitiful, he pointed to his eyes and said, "This is just my allergies acting up. The Benadryl has me drowsy and light-headed. I wanna go lay down now."

"Go 'head and keep doing what you're doing. It's gonna catch up with you. Marijuana is a gateway drug. Weed today and crack tomorrow."

I told Naomi what was going on and she said I should stop worrying and just believe my son. The next day I got an emergency call from Naomi telling me to come home right away. When I arrived on our street I noticed that traffic was stopped in both directions. I had to walk halfway down the block—I could see that two police cars and an ambulance were at my house. Naomi rushed over to me. She said that C.J. was having some type of breakdown. When I approached him my first thought was that we had lost him forever. He was in the middle of the street, sweating up a storm, singing and dancing like a crazy man. He looked like he was in fast-forward mode, singing the Jackson Five's *Dancing Machine.* He was doing the robot, Bankhead bounce, Harlem shake, Crip walking, Poppin' and Lockin', and every other stupid dance he knew. Naomi and I laughed to keep from cry-

ing. I grabbed C.J. by his shoulders and when I looked at him he was
tore up. He could hardly keep his eyes open, but he was so revved up
that he could hardly stand still. Somebody had given him some bad
stuff. Later that night at the hospital, C.J. admitted to smoking weed
and taking ecstasy. He said the song "Dancing Machine" was stuck in
his head because he had watched the Jacksons' movie on VH1's
Movies That Rock the night before.

Erika makes her typical lying face and says, "I don't have anything
to hide, either."

I usually can tell when my kids are lying, because facial gestures like
nasal flaring and twitching of their eyes or mouths gives them away.

Naomi says, "Well, who's the white boy you've been hanging out
with in school lately?"

Erika turns to C.J. and hits him in the arm. "I hate you, C.J., always
running your big mouth."

I ask, "Who is he?"

"He's just a friend."

"His name?"

"His name is Brad and like I said, he's just a friend."

C.J. says, "He's some rich kid who drives a Lexus and likes black
girls. That's all he ever dates."

Erika turns to C.J. and asks, "Who are you dating? You big, nappy-
headed weirdo. Let's talk about your love life. Oops, I forgot—there's
nothing to talk about. Now look how quiet you are. Bet you're still
crying over Ginger breaking your heart."

"Yeah right, forget Ginger. I got other girls."

"Who? Name one."

C.J. was in a long-term relationship with this girl named Ginger
Davis. She started dating another guy and it damn near killed my son.
He still hasn't gotten over her completely and probably never will.
For a while he couldn't eat or sleep. He'd given up on himself over a
little skinny-behind, flat-chested girl named after a character from
Gilligan's Island. C.J. stopped going to the barbershop and let his hair
grow into a wicked Afro. Naomi felt sorry for him and braided his
hair and that's when other girls started thinking he was cute again. I
guess he had to go through something to get to the next level. Now
girls love him to death and guys envy his style.

Naomi is so protective of C.J. She says, "We know C.J. has plenty of girls, but we're more concerned about you right now, Erika."

Erika says, "I don't understand this. What did I do?"

I say, "Nothing. It's just that we wouldn't be good parents if we didn't communicate with you. We're a little concerned because you act like we get on your nerves and you don't want to be around us."

Erika seems to get an attitude and acts as if we're keeping her from something more important. "See? You said that, not me. Trust me, everything is okay. Is that it? I have a lot of stuff to do."

"I can't stand a little smart-ass and that's just what you are. Yep, that's it. Go 'head and learn life's lessons the hard way. You can go now, but don't tie up my phone line all evening."

Morgan says, "Yeah, because I need to go online to do my homework."

The longer this goes on, the more irritated Erika gets. "When can I get my own phone line? It's hard living like this. I need a cell phone or something. All my friends have cell phones."

Naomi says, "Your father is too cheap to get an additional phone line and you can definitely forget about a cell phone. I keep telling him that we can get a good deal on a family plan."

Somebody's asking for an argument. I turn to Naomi. "Don't you get started again. I was trying to ignore you as much as possible and just talk to the kids. You get on my damn nerves."

With a concerned expression, Morgan asks, "Are y'all having an argument?"

C.J. yells, "No!"

Erika is no help whatsoever. "Yes, they are."

C.J. says, "No, they're not."

"Are y'all gonna break up? Thomasina's parents used to argue all the time and now they're divorced."

Erika says, "Morgan, you're so silly. Ma and Dad will never break up—they'll just stay together for the kids, like most unhappily married couples."

I'm not too sure about Naomi, but I'm not the type to stay together for the kids' sake.

I reply, "Shut up, Erika. Keep your silly comments to yourself and go back to doing whatever you were doing in your room or just get back on the phone and talk to whoever you were talking to."

"All right, but it's not my fault that y'all talk so loud in the morning. And one last thing—you do need to consider getting another phone line in this house. I'm the only one of my friends who doesn't have a cell phone."

With a serious look, I say, "Good, and you should be proud to say that you're the only one who doesn't have a cell phone *bill*."

"That's mean. I'm leaving."

Naomi says, "Freeze! Where did you get that outfit?"

"Jerome bought it for me before we broke up."

Naomi and I have good memories. We know everything we buy for our kids and Erika's outfit sent up a red flag. That was a good pickup.

I say, "Just gon' 'bout your business. We know that new boy done went out and got you some new clothes. Always thinking somebody's stupid. We were teenagers once, too."

"All right, Daddy, I'll keep that in mind."

Erika leaves our bedroom.

I guess mentioning clothes must have sparked something in C.J. Out of nowhere, he asks, "Dad, can I get a jersey?"

"Didn't I just buy you a NBA and a NFL jersey? That was two in one week."

"Yeah, but those were replica jerseys and I'm trying to get an authentic."

"Don't make me laugh. I got news for you. You better take your replica ass and get an authentic job."

Naomi shouts, "Craig! Don't talk to him like that."

I turn to her and say, "What did I tell you?"

C.J. interrupts, "That was funny, Dad, but it didn't make any sense."

"You understand what I'm saying, don't you?"

Naomi and her accommodating ass says, "C.J., we'll talk about the jersey issue later when I rebraid your hair."

"Didn't I ask you to stay out of this? I'm the one with the money. Those damn jerseys cost a hundred and fifty dollars and up. If he wants an authentic jersey, then he needs to go play for a damn professional team. Bet he'd get an authentic jersey then. Black people kill me, especially poor ones like you, boy. These people are making all kinds of money off stupid young boys spending money on useless shit. You need to save your money for a rainy day."

Morgan says, "Mommy, I'm hungry. Can we go to McDonald's?"

I cut in, "No! You can eat right here at McGaffney's. Your momma can fry you a hamburger and put you some of those frozen fries in the oven and season them real good."

"Aw, man. You say that all the time. That doesn't even taste like McDonald's."

"Watch your tone with me. We need to have a family meeting tonight, so I can explain to all of y'all that I'm not made of money. Cut some of these lights out around here—it ain't Christmas."

"Okay, everybody out so I can get up, get dressed, and get dinner going," Naomi says.

C.J. and Morgan don't budge. The two of them just stand still as if no one asked them to leave. Momma always told me that a hard head makes a soft behind, and these kids ain't too old for whippings.

"Why are y'all still standing around? You heard your momma—get outta here."

Morgan says, "You're mean, Daddy."

"You're about to see exactly how mean I can be. Now, get!"

The kids damn near fall over each other trying to get out of our bedroom.

7

Naomi

Music softly filters in from the background. A woman's voice cries out over this mellow but haunting track. I'm too busy with my current task to be moved.

I swear this damn oven is a beast. Although dinner smells so good I can taste it. The sight of the food makes my mouth water and quenches my thirst. The aroma alone sustains me, calms my hunger for the moment.

Although I've been moving at a snail's pace, dinner is almost done. I just took a quick look at the marinated chicken breasts I have on the George Foreman Grill and dashed them with some lemon pepper seasoning. There's a pot of string beans with cut up potatoes and a piece of fatback simmering on the stove. My biscuits are golden brown and now all I have to do is top them off with some butter. My macaroni-and-cheese casserole is thick, rich, and flavorful, making it delicious and satisfying enough to be a meal by itself.

I'm tired of Craig trying to control what I do and say. I can't even comment on our kids without him getting offended. I'm trying my best to stay busy to keep from getting too stressed out. There's no real way to measure the intensity of my emotions. I'm about two steps away from being an emotional wreck. This is what I do to myself. So much is weighing on my heart and mind that I feel like I'm about to explode. It makes me even madder that I'm in the kitchen, boiling over with frustration, while Craig's in the family room relaxing. He's in there listening to his Etta James CD as if he doesn't have a care in the world. He loves the blues so much that I bet he's about to get up and start dancing by himself.

Who am I fooling? I can't get that simple little nigga off my mind. He owns me and there's nothing I can do. What have I gotten into?

All of a sudden I feel someone come up behind me dancing. It's Craig and his simple self. He's dancing and humming while Etta James sings her heart out. Craig surprises the hell outta me by kissing me on the back of my neck. I almost jump out of my skin as chills run up and down my spine. I'm not used to this. That felt nice, so nice that I'm almost ready to give in to him. I have to remind myself that he's not the enemy and it's okay. Confusion floods my mind like the swelling muddy waters of the Dan River during this prolonged rainstorm.

Craig moves in even closer, holding me from behind. He does this sexy little slow grind. Here I am, trying to control the floodwaters. Within seconds this song and Craig's passionate burst of energy become too much for me. I surrender to him completely. He controls my ability to resist him. This is one of my weak moments.

He kisses me again from behind, but this one's on my cheek. He drags his lips across my face, stops at my ear and says, "Dinner smells good. Whatcha making, grilled chicken sammiches?"

He makes me smile. "Stop being silly, talking 'bout sammiches. No, I ain't making no sandwiches. This is a miniature feast. Have a seat and I'll make you a plate."

"I ain't ready to sit yet. I should be, 'cause it's hot as hell over here. I'm about to pass out."

"If you can't stand the heat then stay your butt out the kitchen."

"Don't worry 'bout me. I can stand the heat. It's you I'm worried about. Why'd you jump like that when I kissed your neck?"

"'Cause I ain't used to being kissed back there like that. One of my sweet spots, you know? You don't play fair. I'm supposed to be mad at you."

"Is that all it takes to soften you up?" He lowers his voice and whispers directly in my ear. "One little kiss? I figured an unexpected kiss on the back of your neck might do the trick."

"Maybe, maybe not. And who said you softened me up?"

"No need to say it, just look at you. Your body temperature is rising and it's not the oven doing it. I know when I'm on to something and I know all your sweet spots, too." He kisses my neck in the same spot. That same sensation races up and down my spine again. "And I ain't supposed to play fair, either."

I smile and say, "So, you think you know all my sweet spots, huh? Find another one, then. I dare you."

Craig turns me around toward him. Etta James is still singing to us in the background. Seems as if the lighting in here has gotten dimmer. It's moments like this that make me wish we didn't have kids, so we could do it anywhere around the house without hesitation. Craig looks me up and down with this sly expression, then grabs my right arm and slowly lifts it in the air. He gently kisses the inner part of my upper arm. He begins to nibble on my skin and the moistness and texture of his lips drive me crazy. Ooh, it sends tingling sensations throughout my body, causing me to get even more heated. I want to hate him so much, but I can't.

"See, you're not playing fair."

He pulls his mouth away and says, "I know, but this ain't a game. I was in the other room thinking, and I know I'm on to something. You're at a real vulnerable stage. You're one of those kind of women now."

"What do you mean by, one of those kind of women?"

The lighting in here seems to have returned to normal and Etta James just finished singing her last song for the evening. The CD ends.

Craig continues. "You're one of those kind of women I used to prey on when I was out there being bad, being a dog. Whenever a woman's husband or boyfriend would mess up, I was right there to pick up the slack. A real smooth operator like me could sense your vulnerability a mile away. If we were strangers," he laughs, "let's just say we wouldn't be for too long. One touch and you'd be all mine. One kiss and you'd be in my bed. After one night you'd be begging me for more. I'd be like, gotcha! And just like that I'd be gettin' all your good lovin'. As easy as I said that, is how easy one of those young dogs out there could get you." Craig shakes his head. "And you know goddamn well I ain't having that."

Craig is absolutely right. I am at a vulnerable stage, thanks to him not doing his job in the bedroom. The thought of a new man, new hands, and new lips all over me sounds so good.

Although I'm hot as ever from that vivid image in my head, I'm still able to play it cool.

"You called yourself a smooth operator." I laugh. "I haven't heard anybody say that since Big Daddy Kane or Sade from way back when."

"Don't laugh, I'm old school. Call it whatcha want, a smooth operator, a playa, a P-I-M-P, or a dog. But just remember, I gotcha. I'm gonna have to keep my eyes on you. You're vulnerable. Tell me I'm wrong."

I'm still thinking about those new hands and lips all over me. I'm good at playing dumb, but I'm no fool. This is nothing more then a test of Craig's EIS (Emergency Insecurity System). Every man has one.

"What? You're wrong. But if you know all this, then why don't you just give me what I need all of the time?"

"The same reason why you don't do certain things for me. We're comfortable. You ain't goin' nowhere and neither am I."

"How long did it take you to figure this one out, Sherlock? And check you out, sounding all certain. I ain't goin' nowhere?"

"That goes for both of us. It took just a few minutes for me to figure this out and I'm right. Shit, I'm the best thing that ever happened to you." I give him this look that just expresses everything I'm thinking without saying a word. Craig instantly gets the message. "Oh, baby, and you know you're the best thing that ever happened to me."

"And don't you ever forget it."

"Come on, let me make you a plate. Hopefully dinner's still hot."

"Let me get the kids so we can all sit down at the table together like a family is supposed to." Craig looks at me and says, "I love you. You know that, right?"

"Yeah. And even though you make me sick, I love you, too."

Craig has the type of personality that makes a woman give in to him. He's good. How can I stay mad at a man like this? I'm at the point where I'm just looking for something wrong with him so I can have an excuse to go outside of my marriage and do something crazy and totally out of character that I'll possibly regret for the rest of my life.

8

Naomi

It takes more than four walls and a roof to hold a house together. A family is what adds stability to a house, making it a home. Here we are, sitting at the kitchen table for dinner as a family. I love this and I think everybody enjoyed dinner. That means a lot to me. It'd be nice to eat in the dining room, but it's a little too formal for common folks like us. We usually reserve the dining room for holiday feasts or whenever we have special guests. Otherwise, the kitchen table is the norm.

C.J. looks me square in the eyes, smiles a bit, and says, "Thanks for dinner—it was really good."

Erika adds, "It was good, especially the macaroni and cheese. Thanks, Ma."

Morgan breaks her silence. "Thanks, Mommy. Everything was good."

Craig follows the kids' lead. "Baby, you sure put a hurtin' on dinner tonight. Thanks."

I can't help but smile. Receiving praise from my family is really gratifying. Lets me know that all my hard work in this hot kitchen wasn't in vain.

I smile as a lump forms in my throat. "Glad y'all enjoyed dinner. That means a lot to me." I pause for a few seconds, looking each of them in the face. "Now, who's gonna help me clean up the kitchen?"

No one says a word, nor do they give me any eye contact. They all just pass silly grins around the table. It's not like there's a lot to be done. We used paper plates and plastic utensils. The kids and I drank straight from our pop bottles and Craig drank straight from his two 12-ounce cans of Miller's Genuine Draft before crushing them into compacted aluminum recyclables with his bare hands.

This is where a major part of my frustration stems from. No help in this house whatsoever. I'm nobody's maid. Dammit, I'm not sure what holds this house together. I need to give these four walls and this roof more credit for holding this house together and less to my inconsiderate family.

A woman should always know how to take charge and delegate. "That's okay. Don't strain yourselves. I'll take care of the pots and pans. But, C.J., you can take out the trash. Erika, you can sweep the floor. Morgan, you wipe off the table and countertop. And Craig, you can go do whatever you usually do after dinner."

"What's that supposed to mean?"

"You don't do housework so you can just go relax and prepare yourself for work tomorrow."

"'Nuff said. Sounds good to me."

I think, *Not the response I was looking for. What a freakin' idiot.*

I'm tired and more than ready to hit the hay. I haven't had a good night's rest in God only knows how long. It's been a while since I've been able to shut my eyes for more than a few minutes and when I do fall asleep for those brief moments, my mind is blank—not even a sound, just crisp silence. That's when I realize that something's wrong, really wrong. Too much time has passed since my last dream. I'm so empty inside that I don't even have nightmares, and that's pathetic because I'm starting to realize that I'm actually living a nightmare. Someone has stolen my dreams. If I died tonight, what would my obituary say? I'd be lucky to have one decent paragraph and over half of it would describe my role in this family as the devoted wife and mother of three. The bad thing is that little would be said about Naomi Leslie Goode-Gaffney, the individual. I haven't lived, haven't seen or been anywhere. I haven't done anything significant and that bothers me. This feeling or thing that I'm not sure about rides me all day, every day—it just gnaws away at me, and it hurts.

I've only known the pleasure of being with one man my entire life. My husband has had many lovers, and in a way I resent that. My life is so humdrum, and living vicariously through my sister's sex life is just plain pitiful. Everything I am, from my likes to my dislikes, is defined by my family and not me personally. I wanna scream, *What about me?* I need an outlet, a stress reliever, a nice dose of sinful pleasure, and then a harsh dose of reality to wake my dumb behind up.

From the kitchen table we have a clear view of our high-definition, wide-screen television in the family room. C.J. and Erika reluctantly rise from their seats to start their chores. Meanwhile, Morgan and her trifling daddy remain seated. These two are so much alike. Craig picks up the remote sitting on the table next to him and turns on the television.

I turn to C.J. and Erika. "Thanks for helping out, you two. And I only had to ask once. At least somebody's trying to do something to help me." My eyes shift over to the wide screen. "Cut that off!"

"Aw, babe, the evening news is on."

Morgan begs me. "Please, Mommy. We have to watch. They're talking about Brea's mom. Turn it up!"

Craig goes, "Shhh."

All of my undivided attention goes toward the television as Nolan Pollard, a local news anchor, gives a full update about Brea's momma's disappearance. A familiar sadness comes over me, makes me bite my bottom lip and shake my head in disbelief. Morgan appears to be saddened and somewhat frightened by the news report, so I take her by the hand and she sits between my legs. We hold on to each other tightly, as if to say that nothing can separate us. No child deserves to lose their momma. My heart goes out to that little girl and her family.

A highway patrolman discovered Carolyn Tinsley's late-model, blue-and-gray Ford Explorer abandoned in a ditch along N.C. 135 at 12:45 A.M. this morning, shortly after she failed to report to work for her midnight shift at Morehead Memorial Hospital. The segment switches over to taped footage from the scene where the truck was found. They actually show Carolyn's truck blocked off with yellow crime-scene tape as the patrolman describes the scene. The truck was found with the headlights on, engine still running, radio blaring, and the driver's side door left open. Carolyn's purse was found inside of her vehicle with her money and personal items intact. Authorities found no blood evidence or signs of foul play. Although the vehicle was found, Carolyn remains missing. The victim's husband, Mr. Wayne Tinsley, was brought in for questioning, but the police reiterated that

Mr. Tinsley is not a suspect. A large search party composed of police and local volunteers has been assembled to comb the area along N.C. 135. A recent photograph of Carolyn flashes on the screen, along with a phone number for anyone with information about her disappearance. The sight of this missing woman's young innocent face gives me an eerie feeling that penetrates to my core. I know Carolyn. When I look at her face again it somewhat reminds me of my momma. The thought of a predator on the loose in this area is frightening. Makes me wonder if her attacker was someone Carolyn knew or if this was just some type of random crime. Regardless, I'm sure no one around here feels safe. Although details are still sketchy, Carolyn's family anxiously awaits her safe return.

I take a deep breath. "It's always something. God only knows what's next. I just saw Carolyn last week at your school's bake sale."

"I feel sorry for Brea. Hope they find her momma and she's okay," Morgan says.

Craig offers a bit of comfort. "Don't worry, baby, they'll find her momma. I'm sure they will. C'mere and give me a hug."

Morgan says. "I feel sad. Is this how it was when Grandma was missing?"

"It's kind of similar." My eyes begin to water. "Let's talk about something else."

The phone rings and scares the heck outta me and Morgan. We jump, then look at each other and start to laugh.

Craig says, "No need to jump like that—it's just the phone. I'll get it." He heads over toward the phone and picks it up. His expression quickly changes. A frown appears.

"It's your sister."

I twist my lips up at him and say, "Hand me the phone and wipe the silly look off your face."

Morgan says, "Tell Aunt Serena I said hi."

"Hello."

Serena says, "Hey, Nay. Girl, I need a big favor. Darryl is over here acting a fool again. I'm about to call the police."

Morgan motions her hand in front of me. "Tell her I said hi."

"Your niece says hi."

"Tell her I said hey."

I lower the receiver away from my mouth. "Your aunt said hey." I resume my conversation with Serena. "What do you need me to do? You okay? Did he put his hands on you again?"

"No, he ain't put his hands on me." Serena pauses. "Well, not really."

"Either he did or he didn't. I'll take that as a yes."

"It was me. I started it this time."

"You started what—and how?"

Serena ignores me. "Is it all right if me and the kids spend the night at your house tonight?"

"I guess so. I'll have to ask Craig. I asked you a question. How'd you start it?"

"I heard you. But first, why do you have to ask Craig?"

"'Cause this is his house too. How'd you start it?"

"Blood is thicker than water. You shouldn't have to ask him a damn thing in my time of need."

"True, but that's my husband. And how'd you start it?"

"I'm your only sister. Momma's gone and Daddy can't help me. You're all I got."

"I know and I'm here for you. Now, are you gonna tell me how you started this mess or not?"

"Remember that movie, *The Burning Bed?*"

The Burning Bed is a movie from way back, based on a woman who was being abused by her husband. She got fed up and set the husband on fire while he was asleep.

"Oh my God! I'm on my way over there right now."

9

Craig

In every family there's at least one or two people with good sense, and right about now, that's us. I'm supposed to be in bed relaxing, but instead I'm in my truck barreling down a wet road on a stormy night with my distraught wife. We're on Van Buren Road on our way to Serena's house to see what kind of damage she's inflicted on Darryl, her useless, good for nothing husband. Those two have been at it for years, fussing and fighting. They shouldn't be together in any way, shape, or form, but no one can keep them apart. Naomi tries to act like her sister's too good for Darryl. In my opinion, one's about as bad as the other.

We're passing through the busiest part of Eden and there's hardly anyone out here. Wal-Mart's parking lot is about as empty as I've ever seen it. Food Lion and the entire shopping center are a ghost town. There's only one car at the Sonic's drive-thru, three at McDonald's, Arby's and Wendy's are completely empty. Business at the Burger King and Hardee's on Kings Highway is probably about the same. There's not a lot to do here in Eden, but there sure is plenty to eat.

An unusually large number of cars are parked outside of the Hampton Inn. The Inn Keeper and the Jameson Inn are both busier than usual. I bet these people are from out of town and are here for Morehead's graduation next week or a big annual family reunion. Local people are feeling uneasy about the disappearance of Carolyn

Tinsley and are lying low. Naomi and I are the only ones foolish enough to put our lives on the line for nothing. As we pass Morehead Memorial Hospital, I think of the real reason we're out here. Hope Darryl doesn't have to go to the hospital because that will be another inconvenience. I'd sure hate to be up all night waiting in the damn ER.

"So what did Serena say about Darryl's condition? Is he still breathing or what?"

Naomi appears to be very nervous, bouncing her left leg up and down. "I didn't really ask. Once she said something about *The Burning Bed*, basically I hung up just after telling her that I was on my way. Evidently, Darryl's still alive because she said he was acting a fool again and she was gonna have to call the police."

"She ain't crazy enough to call the police 'cause they'd lock her ass up for starting a fire. Then again, maybe she is simple enough to do something like that. What she did is attempted murder."

"I know. She's not in her right mind. I hate to see my sister make a fool of herself like this over a man."

"Shit, she's making us look like fools, out in this storm. Come to think of it, *I* must be a fool. I'm not even sure why I'm out here. I'm not trying to catch an aiding-and-abetting charge."

"You're here for me and nobody's catching any charges. I don't know what we're gonna find when we set foot in that house and I'm not about to face it alone. That's why you're here—to support and comfort your wife." She pauses for a second. "Slow down a bit, this road looks slippery. There's enough going on and the last thing we need is an accident."

I turn my wipers on high and adjust the defogger. "Usually I'd tell you to shut up and stop complaining about my driving, but this time you're right."

"Sorry. I'm just anxious. I can't lose my sister. We're all we've got."

"You've got me and the kids."

"You know what I mean. My parents are gone. I refuse to turn my back on Serena."

I hate to hear Naomi say that her father's gone. He's alive and doing about as well as expected for a man who's already spent over a third of his life behind bars. I'm sure if he could help out in a situation like this, he would.

"Is that guilt I hear, because if it is, you need to silence it. You've done all you can do for Serena. I've done all I can do for her. She lived with us for over a year when we first got married. We helped her get on her feet and it's not our fault if she's only attracted to sorry-ass men. Remember when I tried to hook her up with that guy named Wilbert? And what did she say, 'He ain't my type. He's too quiet and too into books and politics. Plus, he's country.' I told her that it was time to switch to a new type of man 'cause her type was the wrong type for any woman trying to get something real or meaningful out of life. She's too old to be so stupid."

"Wilbert was just as ugly and homely as he wanted to be. Him and his made-up words. His intellectual conversation and distinguished mannerisms intimidated Serena. Where was he originally from, anyway?"

"I can't remember exactly. Maybe Maryland. I know he went to college somewhere in Georgia or Alabama."

"Just say you don't know. What's all the guessing about? I know he needed to go somewhere, with that old-timey bald on top with the nappy-as-a-sheep's-ass lookin' hair on the sides. My sister likes nice-looking young men."

"Yep, Darryl looks real nice when he's whipping her ass."

"Don't say that."

"Don't get me wrong. I don't have any respect for a man that puts his hands on a woman. That's a real coward, in my book. I've never put my hands on you."

"You know better. Shoot, I don't play. I never tolerated that at all and she shouldn't, either. Hit me? I don't think so. If you ever hit me, you'd find yourself in jail."

"Calm down. Nobody's trying to hit you."

She laughs. "I got mad real quick, didn't I? That just goes to show you how serious I am about a man putting his hands on a woman. Daddy used to hit Momma and you see what that got her."

"I knew that was what this was all about."

"The last thing I wanna do is sit back and watch my sister end up in an early grave because some stupid man didn't know how to treat her. That's why I wanted to know if Serena and the kids could stay with us for the night or until she's able to work this situation out with Darryl."

"Stay with us? Definitely sounds like aiding and abiding to me. I don't know about that. Plus, that's three more mouths to feed. We can't afford that. And where in the hell are they supposed to sleep? Your sister ain't wrapped too tight, and I don't wanna see birth control number one and two running around the house all day messing up our stuff. We've got too many nice things made out of glass around our house for toddlers."

"Stop talking about my family like that. Serena is a little off, but my niece and nephew are cute."

"They're cute if you look at them sideways with one eye closed. Poor little babies look like they fell out an ugly tree and hit every branch on the way down."

"Stop!"

"I'm serious. Goddamn Bebe's kids. I can't tolerate ugly, bad kids and shitty diapers together. That's too much."

"Ummm, you do have a point there. How does one night sound?"

"Sounds like an invitation to hell, if you ask me. But I guess we can do it. One night, remember?"

"Okay!"

When we pull up to Darryl and Serena's little run-down white house, the first thing I notice is that the mailbox is beat up and leaning to the side. Somebody didn't maneuver their vehicle properly while making a right turn into the driveway. Darryl probably hit it while returning home from a bar all tore up. I notice that the siding on the house is buckled and hanging off in some spots. Every window in the front is up and I assume the ones in the rear are up, too. The front door is standing wide open and the screen door is propped open by a broom. The front yard is littered with toys and little bikes. Serena used to run a home daycare here and never got rid of the excess toys. Darryl's red Ford Escort is parked in the driveway, while his old black Monte Carlo sits off to the side of the house. It's been needing an engine and God only knows what else for years.

The best thing about this house is that it sits off in a secluded area surrounded by woods. The fact that it's secluded probably isn't so good for Serena because no one can hear her screams for help. This was originally Darryl's parents' house. He's lived here all his life and flat-out refused to move out. He knew that one day this house would be his, so he literally sat around watching and waiting like a vulture for his parents to die. First his momma died from pancreatic cancer and then his father died either from a broken heart or cirrhosis of the liver. More than likely a combination.

It's still raining hard. I grab Naomi's umbrella and make my way around to the passenger side to escort her up to the house. Serena must have heard my truck when we pulled up because she's at the front door watching me and Naomi struggle as the wind tries to take the umbrella away from us.

Serena greets Naomi with a hug.

"Hey, y'all. Thanks for coming out in all this rain."

Serena even has a hug for me, which is highly unusual considering the fact that we hardly get along. We have a tendency to exchange insults. This time we act real cordial, and Serena hugs me tight. She's afraid, and I can see the fear in her eyes. Funny how people reach out to just about anyone in their time of need.

I put on a cheap smile and say, "Hey, Serena."

Naomi asks, "Girl, you okay? Got me all upset. Where's Darryl?"

"He's in the bedroom." Serena frowns. "Him and his stupid-ass self."

The house must have been enveloped by smoke because a toxic smell still lingers. The ceiling is leaking. A big metal pot sits halfway across the room, catching large drops of rainwater. Each drop in the pot is timed perfectly, reminding me of a ticking clock. *Drip . . . drop . . . drip . . . drop . . . drip . . . drop . . . .*

We're in the center of this small, cluttered living room with worn-out, mismatched furniture. The slipcovers and throw pillows don't do a thing for this decor. Old, lint-filled gray shag carpeting covers the floor. The walls are bare and scuffed up with tiny handprints. No artwork or family portraits, just the kids' original crayon markings from the baseboards up to as high as their little arms can reach. More of the kids' toys litter the inside of the house than the outside. There's a playpen sitting in the middle of the floor in front of an old-fashioned RCA floor-model television that serves as a light for the room because the double light fixture on the ceiling only has one working bulb. There's a lamp with a crooked shade on one of the end tables, but it's obviously broken. A highchair with orange and green baby food caked on the tray sits off to the right side of the room. I hear a television and see a dim bluish-white light coming from one of the two bedrooms on the left side of the house. The other bedroom door is closed. From where I stand, I have a clear view of almost the entire house. What a mess. I'm not sure where to step, where to sit, or what to do.

"Is Darryl still breathing?" I ask Serena.

"Unfortunately. I told you where he is." Serena points toward the bedroom. "He's in there pretending to watch TV, but he is probably listening to everything we're saying out here."

"You better be glad he's still alive. You still might be facing a few charges," I say.

She rolls her eyes and says, "Here he goes."

Naomi asks, "Where are the kids?"

"In their bedroom. I guess they're asleep."

"I doubt it. They're probably in there getting official instructions from the devil on how to take over the world."

"No, he didn't. Don't stand up here talking bad about my kids like that. You should be ashamed of yourself, a grown-ass man picking on toddlers like that." She pauses for a second. "Do me a favor and ask C.J. where I can get some of that good weed he used to smoke. I heard that shit'll have you singing and dancing for days."

"That ain't right. That ain't right at all," I retort.

Her face softened. "You're right. I'm sorry."

"I'll admit you got me. That's one point for you. Y'all know I was just joking about the kids. I love both of them," I add.

"Now he's lying," Serena says.

I'm kind of reluctant to sit, but I take a seat on the sunken sofa. The dust on the coffee table is so thick that I'm able to write, Dust and Polish Me, on it with my index finger.

"Looks like your housekeeper has been off for the past few weeks."

"Forget you. Nay, your ignorant husband is writing on my table."

"Stop, Craig! That's not funny. You know you're wrong for doing that."

"No, I'm not. This poor table is dying to be cleaned along with the rest of the house."

"Don't pay him no mind, girl. I can't take him nowhere."

"Huh, I clean my house whenever I get a break. You try raising a two- and a four-year-old in a little house like this and you'll see that it's not easy. The more I clean up, the more they mess up."

I feel like being sarcastic. "I never thought about it like that. I can

see how the amount of kids and the amount of space you have corre-
lates with your inability to perform effective housekeeping."

Serena says, "I hate you."

"I know. The feeling is mutual. I wanna walk around in here, but
I'm scared that I might trip on something. You wanna escort me back
to the bedroom so I can check on Darryl?"

"No. You'll be all right. Just watch your step and follow the trail of
smoke and you'll find Darryl."

Naomi says, "Wait, I wanna go back and see him, too."

When we get back to the bedroom, Darryl is sitting on a box
spring, drunk as a skunk, sipping on a can of Miller's beer with a plastic supermarket bag filled with ice duct-taped to his left arm. Darryl is
the most worn-out thirty-year-old I've seen in a while. He has on a pair
of muddy black boots. His dingy jeans, Winston cigarettes T-shirt, and
baseball cap that he probably picked up from a truck stop all make
him look like a real hick. As I glance around the room I notice the top
mattress with a black hole burned in the center propped against the
wall. Naomi and I stand here coughing up a storm as Serena sneaks
up behind us.

Darryl looks at us and says, "Well, well, well, if it ain't Mr. President
and the first lady herself, Mrs. Gaffney. To what do I owe the honor of
this visit?" He laughs. "Sike, I'm just playing. What's up, Mo? Naomi?
How y'all doing?"

Naomi answers, "We're fine. How's it going, Darryl?"

I say, "Hey, Darryl. Are you okay?"

"I'm fine, but my arm, it's kinda hurt. Take a look, Mo. Think it's
gonna make it?"

"Damn, I bet that hurts like a son of a bitch. You might wanna get a
doctor to look at that. There's some blistering. Looks like a second-
degree burn to me."

"I'm just gonna keep icing it."

Naomi asks, "What happened here? What are y'all trying to do kill
each other?"

Darryl laughs as if Naomi told a joke and then takes a quick sip of
his beer. "Look at me. I'm being all rude and shit. How 'bout something to eat or drink? These Bar-B-Q pork rinds and beer are saying
something." He holds up his beer and bag of pork rinds with one
hand. "See, this is the kind of stuff I'm forced to eat for dinner 'cause

my wife doesn't cook. It's either this or a goddamn happy meal from McDonald's. Ain't that pathetic?"

I say, "Yeah, it really is. I thought I had it bad." I look at Naomi and then at this messy bedroom. I think about the dinner Naomi made earlier and say, "I'll never complain about you doing housework or cooking again."

"Good. Told you I was a good wife." Naomi looks at Serena and asks, "Why don't you cook?"

All of a sudden the momentum shifts to Darryl's side. It isn't that we're favoring a wife-beater. It's just that Serena needs to do more around the house, at least for the kids' sake.

"I do cook, just not every night. He can cook too."

"No, I can't. That's your job."

Darryl sounds a bit like me, chauvinistic.

"What's *your* job? I don't consider laying around all day playing PlayStation 3 and getting drunk a damn job."

"'Cause those are hobbies. My main jobs around here are security and taking out the trash. I vacuumed last week, now say I didn't."

I know this look of frustration. Serena is definitely Naomi's sister. "That's right—you did, baby, and you did a good job." Serena turns toward me and Naomi. "See, that's how he wants me to treat him. I don't have time for that shit. Big dummy."

"Oh, but you got plenty of time to try and kill me. Naomi, you asked and I'ma tell y'all what happened. I was lying in bed minding my own business, sipping on a bottle of Jack, and then I drifted off to sleep. That wench over there must have poured my liquor on the bed and threw a match on it. I thought I was dreaming till I realized the pain in my arm was real. So I jumped up, ran in the bathroom, filled a basin with water and threw it on the bed. The house was full of smoke. I thought the whole thing was 'bout to burn down. I rushed through the house like a fool, looking for Serena and the kids. Something told me to open the front door. I looked and bingo, there she was with the kids, sitting in the car looking at me all crazy."

Naomi says, "Lord, lord, lord. What is wrong with y'all?"

Darryl continues. "I should press charges for 'tempted murder."

I'm fixin' to correct his English, even though we all pronounce things wrong from time to time. Southern dialect is one thing, but ignorance is another. "Darryl, that's *attempted* murder."

"That's what I said, 'tempted murder." He turns to Naomi. "What's wrong with your husband's ears? Is he deaf or what?"

Naomi doesn't say a word. She just smiles and shrugs.

Serena gets fired up. "I should charge you with attempted murder, too. Every time you hit me, that's attempted murder. See y'all, he left out the part about him yelling at me about dinner and hitting me in front of my kids."

"Don't be stupid all your life. They're babies—they don't know what's going on," Darryl retorted.

"Oh, they know, all right, they know. They know, don't they, Naomi? We remember, don't we?"

A sad expression falls over Naomi's face. "They know. I knew when I was a kid. Y'all need to stop and take a good look at what you're doing to yourselves. Look at what you're doing to Travis and Taylor. Please! There's enough going on 'round here without this unnecessary stuff happening. This is something that y'all can change on your own and if you can't, then you don't need to be together."

Darryl looks angry. He and Serena both get highly offended when anybody advises them to break up. "Naomi, do me a favor and answer one question. Who the hell do think you are? You and Mo, coming up in here acting all superior and shit. Y'all niggas kill me. You ain't no better. Get off your high horse and come back down to earth with us common folk. What makes y'all so special? When the rain comes down it hits your house, too. Just be prepared 'cause a storm's gonna be coming your way soon."

Now I'm mad. "Ain't that some shit to say? At least I'm a man and I know how to protect my family from a storm."

Serena tries to calm things down, but it's too late. "He's drunk and doesn't know what he's saying."

"I'm sober and I meant every word I said."

I'm pissed. "Okay, that's it! Let me get outta here before I do or say something I'll regret. That's exactly why I don't get involved in shit like this. With my luck, I'll end up being the one to go to jail."

"Say what's on your mind, Mo." Darryl stands up, looks me up and down, and then smiles. He's four or five inches taller than me. "What you gonna do, little nigga?"

I throw my hands up out of frustration and back up. "Serena, if you're going, you better get the kids and come on."

Serena says, "I think I'll just stay here."

"Fine. If you wanna stay here like this, then be my guest."

Darryl yells, "That's right, she ain't goin' nowhere!"

I say, "Naomi, I don't have time for this. Let's go."

Naomi makes one last attempt to get Serena to come with us. "Come on, Serena. Grab the kids and let's go."

Serena thinks for a second. She looks at Darryl and says, "Okay, Nay, give me a minute."

Darryl grabs Serena by her right arm and slams her against the wall. "I said you ain't goin' nowhere!"

I yell, "Darryl, don't grab her like that, man! Don't you ever put your hands on her like that in front of me. Let her go. You better gon' and sit down somewhere!"

Serena looks at me and says, "Craig, it's okay. You don't have to talk to him like that."

Naomi asks, "What are you talking about?"

"I do have to talk to him like that. I'm defending you."

Darryl yells, "Defend this!"

He lets go of Serena, turns around, and throws a sucker punch at me. I'm able to move out of the way in time. His drunk ass misses me by a mile. I quickly counter with a punch of my own, hitting Darryl dead in his mouth and knocking him to the floor.

"Aw, man. Why'd you have to go and do that? He done hit me in my damn mouth and made me hurt my arm even more."

Serena yells, "Don't you hit him no more, Craig! Now, that's my husband and my babies' daddy you hit." She looks down at Darryl. "Oh my God, look at his lips. I loved those lips and now they're all swollen."

"I'll hit him again if he raises his fist at me. Serena, you're outta your mind."

Naomi says, "Don't worry, baby, I got this. Serena, wake up and stop being a fool! We're here to help you. That idiot right there is the one that's trying to hurt you."

Darryl slowly gets up, dusts his hands off, and walks over to the other side of the box spring to his nightstand. "That's okay. I'm gonna fix all y'all. Don't go nowhere. I got something for y'all."

Naomi yells, "Oh my God, that fool's going for a gun."

"No, I ain't. I'm going for the phone. I'm calling the police to come and lock y'all asses up, Serena for 'tempted murder, Mo for hitting me in my damn mouth, and Naomi, you for trespassing."

I yell, "Let's go, Naomi! There's nothing we can do. These two belong together."

Serena says, "No, wait. I can't stay here now. He's talking to the police. I can't go to jail."

Darryl has the receiver up to his ear. "Hello, I need the police. My wife tried to kill me and my brother-in-law hit me in the mouth with his fist. His wife is standing here harassing me and won't get out of my house. I want her arrested too. My kids are all right. They can stay here." He pauses and the person on the other end asks him a question. "No, I ain't drunk. Yeah, I been drinking, but I said I ain't drunk. Okay, five minutes. That's fine. Appreciate it—God knows I do." Darryl slams the receiver down. "Police are on the way."

"I'm outta here," I say.

"No, just wait. I'll fix you for hitting me. Nobody hits Darryl E. Broadnax in the mouth and gets away with it."

"Can y'all please wait for a minute while I get the kids and a few things together?"

Naomi says, "We'll wait."

"They're on the way. Three and a half more minutes!" Darryl yells.

Serena mumbles, "Don't listen to him."

I say, "Come on, Serena, and do what you have to do."

I'm back out in the living room sitting on a raggedy, sunken sofa. Naomi and Serena are in the bedroom getting the kids together. Serena's only supposed to be packing enough clothes for an overnight stay, but as long as it's taking, she must be planning to stay for a week or more.

The five-minute arrival time for the police is up. There's no sign of them, and Darryl grows more and more agitated as the seconds pass. He paces back and forth around the entire house, fussing to himself. Over the years I've watched this man slowly deteriorate and this is truly his breaking point. Darryl has *alcoholic* written all of him. He's desperate for a drink and has to reach under the kitchen sink for his private stock.

Darryl sips a shot of corn liquor, then yells out, "Where the hell are the police? See, I'm trying to do things the right way and look how they're treating me. I can't take it."

"They're just doing this 'cause you're black," I say.

"I know." He staggers for a few steps, stops dead in his tracks and thinks for a second, then quickly turns back in my direction. "Don't talk to me! I wasn't talking to you. I'm telling y'all, if the police don't hurry up and get here, I swear somebody's gon' die in here tonight and it ain't gon' be me."

"Relax, Darryl. It doesn't have to be all that. Naomi and I will be outta here in a minute or so. We're just trying to help out. I don't wanna be here no more than you want me here."

"Y'all trying to take over my damn house—that's what you're trying to do."

"Call the police back and see what the holdup is."

Darryl looks like he's about to self-destruct and possibly take us down with him. The only reason I'm sitting here is to make sure he doesn't do anything to hurt his family or Naomi. If Darryl's parents could see him now they'd probably turn over in their graves. Then again, they already knew what kind of fool he was when they were alive.

I yell, "Naomi, c'mon. Let's go!"

Darryl goes, "Okay. Okay, I'll call the police back, but if they take me for a joke again, I'ma kill everybody in here."

This time I stand up and yell, "Naomi! I mean it, c'mon!"

She responds, "We need another minute."

"Hurry up!"

Darryl goes over to the phone. Before he even picks it up, two police cars arrive in front of the house. Within seconds a third police car pulls up, blocking the driveway. Darryl looks up and gives me a big smile. There's a look of revenge in eyes that lets me know that he thinks he has the upper hand. Darryl seems relieved to see the police. On the other hand, my stress level is at an all-time high because I'm guilty of hitting him. Guess Darryl does have the upper hand now. He heads to the front door to let police in and to tell them what happened. Darryl starts running his mouth before the police even set foot in the house. All three policemen are big, no-nonsense-looking white officers.

The first thing Darryl says is, "I want this man and his wife arrested right away, Officers."

One of the officers holds his hand up and says, "Calm down, sir. Let us get inside and then you can tell us what happened."

Another officer says, "This is my third time here this week."

The third officer says, "Yep, looks like Mr. Broadnax is up to his old tricks again."

I remain seated and wait for the policemen to say something to me. One black man acting like a fool is more than enough for the moment. I scan the room quickly and then look the three officers up and down. Their guns, badges, and nametags stick out most. For some reason I make a mental note of their names, Officers Powell, Hartwell, and McClain.

Darryl says, "Nah, see, it wasn't me this time. This man right here hit me in the mouth and his wife is guilty of trespassing and instigating in my business. Not only do I want you to tend to them, but I want my wife arrested for 'tempted murder."

Officer McClain asks my name and if what Darryl said about me hitting him was true. I tell him that it was self-defense and explain why I'm here. He asks me for identification and tells me to remain seated.

Officer Powell looks at Darryl and asks, "Where's your wife, sir?"

"She's in the bedroom. But first, do you smell that odor in here."

Officer Powell asks, "Yeah. What is it?"

Officer Hartwell says, "Smells like smoke to me. What is or was burning?"

"My wife set the bed on fire with me in it. That little wench tried to kill me."

Officer Hartwell says, "If that's true, she's in big trouble. We need to talk to her right away."

"Serena, get out here! The police need to talk to you." Serena peeks her head out the bedroom. "There she is, Officers."

Serena says, "Evening, Officers. My sister and her husband are here helping me and my kids pack. We're just trying to get outta here that's all. My husband is the only person looking for trouble. And I'm sure you all can see that he's had way too much to drink, as usual."

Officer Powell says, "Ma'am, can you please stop what you're doing and step out into the living room? Please, I need everyone else in there to step into the living room as well."

"Sure, Officer."

"Thanks."

Naomi and Serena come out, carrying the kids and trying their best to look pitiful. It's obvious that Travis and Taylor can walk, but carrying them is a nice touch. Makes it appears as if the women and kids feel threatened. Serena begins to explain everything just like it happened. She tries to get me and Naomi off the hook first. She tells the police that I was just trying to defend her from Darryl's attack and Naomi was simply offering advice. We were basically there to ensure that she and the kids got out of the house safely. I had no idea Serena could be so articulate or savvy. She explains the part about the fire last and, to my surprise, adds a twist to it.

"My husband was drinking as usual and fell asleep with his bottle of Jack Daniel's in his hand. He gets very careless when he drinks. That liquor impairs his judgment and you can see what I mean by looking at the front bumper of his car and the condition of our mailbox. The liquor must have spilled in the bed. I'm not exactly sure what happened after that. My son is famous for playing with matches and had to have been in there with his daddy. What I'm trying to say is that my son must have started the fire. Lord knows I asked this child to stop playing with matches and he didn't listen. I'm just glad no one was seriously injured or killed."

"That's bullshit! She's lying!"

Officer Powell says, "Calm down, sir. If I have to ask you to calm down again, that's it—I'm arresting you. Do you understand me?"

"Uh-huh."

Officer Powell says, "Ma'am, I find it awfully hard to believe that a little kid like this could even strike a match."

The other two officers agree.

Serena says, "Oh, he can do a lot more than strike a match."

I say, "Yes sir, that's a bad boy right there and the little girl's no angel, either."

Officer Powell asks, "Can I talk to your son, ma'am?"

"You sure can."

"What's your name, son?"

"My name Travis."

Officer Powell smiles and says, "Well, he said that clear enough. How old are you, Travis?"

Travis holds up three fingers and says, "This many. I'm this many."

He's actually four. I'm not sure if Travis is confused about his age or if he's trying to confuse the officers. The look in his eyes tells me that he wants them to underestimate him. He's a little devil in disguise.

Darryl knows his son well because he yells out, "He's four!"

Officer Powell says, "I'm talking to Travis, okay? Now, Travis did you set the bed on fire?"

"Yeah. I burned it up, but I didn't mean to hurt my daddy's arm. Wanna see what I burned up?"

"We sure do."

Officers Powell and Hartwell go into the bedroom to investigate. Meanwhile, Officer McClain stands guard over the rest of us in the living room.

When the two officers return from the bedroom, Officer Powell says, "I still don't believe it. I can't see how this little boy could have done all that."

Darryl laughs and says, "That's what I'm saying. Get him to strike a match. He don't even know how to strike a match, much less start a big fire."

Serena hands Travis a book of matches and says, "Here you go, Man-man. Now show Mommy how you lit the match when you set the bed on fire."

Darryl marches his drunken ass around in a small circle, laughing and clapping his hands. "Go 'head, Travis, and show us. Light it up, Man-man." He laughs even louder. "That boy can't light no match 'cause he ain't set that bed on fire no more than me and I damn sure didn't do it. Next thing you know, that wench will be telling y'all that Taylor hit me in the mouth."

Officer Powell says, "Sir, I'm not gonna ask you again. Your mouth is gonna get you in some big trouble."

"You're right. I'm sorry."

Travis holds the matchbook in both hands and looks around at everybody with a puzzled look.

Darryl bursts out laughing. "I told y'all that baby can't strike a match. I ain't never seen a four-year-old strike a match."

All of a sudden Travis opens the matchbook and tears out a match. He looks at Darryl and squints his eyes with an evil expression, then smiles at the rest of us. He places the match on the black strip on the back of the book. He pauses for a few seconds and then folds the book in the opposite direction over the match. Travis's little sister Taylor looks on in amazement, taking note of every move he makes. She smiles at him like he's the greatest thing since Barney.

Travis holds the match in place and says, "Watch this, Daddy." He pulls the match away quickly and a spark of fire appears, igniting the match.

Darryl completely loses it. He jumps up and down, yelling, "That's bullshit! That's bullshit! That wench just taught him that shit in the bedroom. That boy didn't know how to do that. Awww! I'ma kill her! I'ma kill all y'all for lying on me!"

You can get away with saying a lot of words around policemen, but you can't get away with saying the word *kill.* It's a magic word that sets them off. All three policemen go into attack mode in an attempt to restrain Darryl. The rest of as grab the kids and get the hell out of the way. In the process of getting to Darryl, Officer Powell hurdles the coffee table while Officer Hartwell accidentally bumps into it, knocking over a small flowerpot and Darryl's bottle of corn liquor. Officer McClain accidentally knocks over the end table where the old lamp with the crooked shade sat.

Darryl goes berserk. "Get off me! Y'all can't treat me like this! I'ma call the NAACP!"

Serena yells, "Please don't hurt him! Darryl, stop it. Don't resist or fight back."

The policemen eventually wrestle him to the floor with brute force, placing him under arrest. Officer Powell reads Darryl his rights.

Darryl cries out, "I don't believe this shit! I called y'all and now I'm goin' to jail. They set me up. My wife tried to kill me, he hit me in the mouth, and this other one over there was trespassing on my property, and they're getting off free. Damn! Even turned my son against me. What kind of evil is that?"

Officer Powell says, "You just need some time to sober up and I'm sure everything will be right back to normal in a few days. You'll be laughing about this in no time."

Darryl says, "Serena, you know God don't like ugly and that was ugly what you just did."

Officer Powell says, "Get him outta here!"

Darryl continues to mouth off useless information and excuses as Officers McClain and Hartwell escort him out to one of the police cruisers. Serena stands off to the side, discussing something with Officer Powell, and Naomi plays with the kids, trying to keep their minds off the fact that their daddy was just beaten down, handcuffed, and arrested in front of them. I hate seeing Darryl and Serena go through this. And more than anything, I hate seeing Travis and Taylor involved. Serena is a mess, but all of the blame can't be put on her. If Darryl could just step up to the plate and be a man instead of a sorry excuse for one, then things would probably go a lot smoother around here. They definitely need some type of counseling. Individual counseling would do wonders for Darryl because he needs help redirecting some of that aggression. Trying to escape his problems with a bottle is the absolute worst thing he could do. Drinking only intensifies problems. I'm speaking from personal experience. I tried for a while to be a friend and mentor to Darryl, but every time I offer advice he thinks that's my way of saying that I'm better than him.

Officer Powell says, "Mr. Gaffney, I'm sorry if there seemed to be any kind of misunderstanding between you and me or the other officers earlier. We do appreciate you and your wife coming over and trying to defuse this situation. Who knows, the two of you may have saved a life tonight."

"I'm not sure about that, but we're family and we're supposed to look out for each other."

"You and Mrs. Gaffney are mighty good people, letting your sister-in-law and her kids move in with you. Mrs. Broadnax plans on separating from her husband and I think that's the best thing for the two of them. Her living here is nothing but trouble. What do you think?"

"Well, now that Darryl's outta here she probably won't even need to stay with us." I look over at Serena. "Ain't that right, sis?"

"Actually, I don't feel safe in this house with or without Darryl. I think a change of scenery would do me and the kids a lot of good."

"I don't blame you, ma'am. Things aren't the same around here anymore."

I say, "Sure aren't."

"Besides, Mr. Broadnax could be home as soon as tomorrow. I hate to say it, but we'll all probably end up back here again within twenty-four hours or so. I don't want that, and by the look on your face, I'm sure you don't want that either, sir."

I look over at Naomi and she offers this empty little grin. My eyes move over to Serena as she smiles from ear to ear. My attention goes back to Officer Powell. "I guess you're right. We can't have that."

As if my problems aren't already enough. Here comes three more. A real man's work is never done. Along with God's help, I guess I'm strong and wise enough to help bare the weight of another man's burden.

10

Naomi

I'll call this the quiet after the storm. That seems appropriate since the rain has finally come to a welcome end and there isn't much being said around here, especially between me and Craig. I think he's mad about the way things unfolded earlier. All I can say is that Darryl and Serena are both full of surprises.

C.J. is in his bedroom playing PlayStation 3 and listening to 94.5 The Beat, while eating an oversized bag of smelly Doritos and drinking a two-liter bottle of Coke. It doesn't take much to entertain him. Erika is in her bedroom relaxing on her bed wearing a pink robe and a pair of pink fuzzy Betty Boop slippers, while talking on the cordless phone. Morgan had her hands full earlier, looking after Travis and Taylor. That girl earned her nickname, Lil' Momma. She likes taking care of younger kids because it makes her feel more mature and responsible. Morgan got the kids ready for bed by washing them up and helping them put on their pajamas. Of course those little heathens weren't ready for bed, so Morgan set their little butts in front of the TV in the family room with a bag of microwave popcorn. Travis and Taylor watched Cartoon Network on the wide screen while Morgan sat next to them watching *ER* on Craig's portable black-and-white TV. Eventually they all fell asleep with the TVs on.

Serena is making herself at home. She's in the laundry room trying to get caught up on her chores by knocking out a huge pile of dirty clothes that belongs to her and her kids.

Craig and I are in the bedroom, fully dressed, watching TV. He has the remote, surfing the same channels over and over. Craig is too hypnotized by the TV to realize that there's nothing on. Sometimes I wonder what's up with cable TV because there's hardly ever anything good on, but we continue to pay outrageous amounts of money for inferior programming.

I ask, "Baby, are you mad at me? If you are, I'm sorry. Who knew Serena and the kids would end up here? Things are just so unpredictable."

"I am kind of pissed off still, but I don't blame you. Everything happens for a reason. I'd just like to know how long Serena's planning on being here and what's with all those plastic trash bags."

I laugh and say, "You mean her luggage?"

"They looked and smelled more like trash to me, big heavy sacks of trash. Why so many?"

"We packed everything. All types of clothes, both clean and dirty."

"That's nasty. Hell, y'all could have left all that nastiness where it was. Our house is finally in the shape and proper order it belongs in, and now this."

"I know. Serena is in the laundry room right now washing her clothes."

"This is starting to sound expensive already. Damn, just think of how high our water bill is gonna be. I hope she brought her own detergent."

"Maybe in a perfect world everyone has responsible relatives with real luggage and their own supply of laundry detergent, but unfortunately we live in an imperfect world and occasionally we have to help out our less fortunate relatives. God'll bless us, you'll see."

"I'm okay with this mostly because that's your sister. You're right about being blessed. God has constantly made a way for us, and I'm committed to uplifting other people, especially family. Regardless of how I appear on the outside, on the inside I'm with this one hundred percent. I just pray that our houseguests didn't bring along any little unwanted critters in their so-called luggage."

"Oh God! That's so gross. Roaches. I didn't even think about that. Yuck, gives me chills just thinking about it."

"If I see one roach I'll know exactly where it came from. That's the bad part about bringing people in your house—you never know what else you're getting. Travis and Taylor seemed kind of sniffly and sneezy, too."

"Can we please change the subject?"

"Fine, but you'll get the blame for anything that goes wrong during your sister's stay."

"Well, that's no different from the norm. I usually get blamed for everything that goes wrong around here."

Craig smiles and says, "True. Some things never change."

"Okay, I see that I'm not getting anywhere here, so I'm going down to the laundry room to talk to Serena."

"Gon' then. I'll be right here when you get back."

As I make my way down the hallway and through the kitchen I hear the sound of my little boom box blaring a rap song by the Ying Yang Twins. I can't believe my eyes when I open the door to the laundry room. My crazy sister has stripped down to her underwear. She has on a light blue bra and panty set, dancing around, shaking and bouncing her ass like a video ho. And the mini blinds of the laundry room are open. I pray to God that my neighbors haven't peeked inside.

I rush over to the window and close the mini blinds. "Ugh-uh! Girl, you're dead wrong. Where are your clothes?"

Serena continues dancing as if everything is all right. "Hey, Nay! My clothes are in the washing machine. Come over here and let me show you how to drop it like it's hot."

I hold up my fist and say, "I'ma drop you like *you're* hot if you don't put on some clothes. There's a robe right there. Put it on."

I think I'm a little jealous because her boobs are two cup sizes larger then mine.

Serena laughs at me and says, "You need to stop."

"No, you need to stop. I mean it. Stop all that bouncing and put something on."

"I got something on. The bikini I wear to the beach is more revealing than this."

"Well, this ain't the beach and that ain't a bikini. What if Craig or C.J. would have walked in here instead of me and seen all that?"

"Please, you're the only one complaining. Who else would have a problem with this?" She runs her hands up and down her body in a provocative manner. "Most people actually appreciate a sexy well-proportioned woman."

"Well, I'm sexy and well-proportioned too, but I don't walk around like that."

"Who's walking around? I was just standing back here with the door closed having fun by myself. Don't hate, celebrate."

"It's not about hate. Anybody could have walked in here. Thank God it was me. I wouldn't even want one of the girls to see you like this. You're supposed to be a good role model to your nieces. I hope my neighbors didn't look in here."

Serena grabs the robe and puts it on. "You're right. God forbid if the neighbors saw me and thought it was you. They'd say, 'Naomi finally let her hair down and isn't so prim and proper anymore. She musta got laid by a young stud.' That's exactly what you need so you can stop acting so stuffy."

I disagree and shake my head, but out of nowhere a little grin appears on my face. "You are so dumb. All I need is who I have right here in this house."

"Uh-huh, look at you smiling. You know you need a spark in your life. That's exactly what you need and you're ready." She starts dancing again. Now an old song by Too Live Crew is on. "C'mon. *Don't stop, get it, get it.*"

"Stop. I'm not even listening to you. I thought you'd be back here kind of down in the dumps about Darryl. Your man's in jail."

She twists her lips and says, "Please, I'm not like you. I don't let no man get me down." Serena starts dancing again. "I got this little song that I sing called, *Fuck him, girl. Fuck him.* I ain't thinkin' 'bout Darryl. You and a lot of other women should try singing my song sometime."

"I'm trying to build on what I have here, not destroy it."

"I used to say the same thing. You'll change. We all do, and Craig will give you a reason to change. Just wait and see. He's probably already given you a reason to go out there and do your thing, but you just won't admit it."

"I don't know what you mean."

This mischievous expression comes over her face. "Oh, you know. I was just joking when I said I wasn't like you. We're just alike. Shit, we're sisters. We've got the same hot blood running through our veins. Look at who our momma was and how she did things. I know you've heard all the rumors."

I don't care if Serena is my sister, I get highly upset hearing Momma talked about in a negative way.

"Serena, I swear, I will smack the taste out of your mouth if you talk about Momma like that again."

"You can get mad if you want, but you know the truth better than anyone else. Remember that night just before Daddy came home? There was another man in the house. That was her boyfriend and you know it."

"You only know what I told you."

"I rest my case. You know the truth, then. It's in us. We were born to be wild. If somebody wrote a book about us, it'd be called *Goode Girls Gone Bad*."

"It'd be called *Goode Girl Gone Mad*. Girl, you're crazy as shit, and you know it."

"I'm far from crazy. Remember Dr. Easley?"

Dr. Timothy Easley was and still is a black child psychologist from Greensboro that Serena and I used to see after Momma was murdered. We saw him from the time we were in elementary school up until we finished high school. Visits to his plush office were a welcome escape from Momma Pearl's dump of a house. I loved that man, loved the smell of his Lagerfeld cologne. In the beginning, he was the only person that helped me and Serena cope with our loss. As time passed, we were able to confide in our spouses, but I'll never forgot what a remarkable man Dr. Easley was. Makes me smile just thinking about him and his handsome self.

"Yeah, how could I forget Dr. Easley? What about him?"

"He said I was normal." Serena laughs. "Shoot, he said a whole lotta stuff about me, stuff I never told you about."

I get a look of suspicion in my eyes. "Like what?"

"Promise you'll never repeat this. I'm not trying to ruin anyone's career or happy home after all these years."

Automatically, I think the worst. I get a pain in my chest because I'm not sure if my heart can bear any bad news about Dr. Easley. "Oh God, no. Please don't tell me he molested you. Aw, that's all I need to hear."

"No, it was more like I molested him." Serena smiles with a love-struck expression. "It was all consensual."

"It couldn't have been. You were just a child."

"I was sixteen and far from a child—or a virgin. Me and Dr. Easley were sweethearts for years, right up until the time I first moved in with you and Craig. Tim used to tell me how beautiful I was, how sexy he thought I was, and how good I made him feel. I did things to him his wife never dreamed of doing."

"Please tell me you're lying," I begged.

"I swear to goodness. If I'm lying, I hope God'll strike me dead where I'm standing. I was just a girl around the boys I dated, but Tim is the one I credit for making me into a real woman."

I know Serena is telling the truth, no matter how shocking or un-believable this sounds. I'm angry and disgusted because this was a man that I respected and confided in for years. All those so-called happy memories of him have been tarnished now and suddenly slipped far away in the back of my mind where so many of my bad memories lie. I held him in the highest esteem, but now he's at the top of my shit list.

I say, "That's extremely disgusting."

"There was nothing disgusting about us. I loved him and he loved me. I ran into him a couple of years ago and we got a room at the Hampton Inn."

My eyes are burning and the corners of my mouth move in a down-ward motion, forming an involuntary frown. "Please tell me you're making this up. I thought the world of that man. For a while he was all I had. He made me believe in myself."

"I'm sorry, Nay. You look hurt. Did he ever come on to you?"

"Never. He was always a gentleman, very professional with me."

Serena sighs. "Good! I was worried for a minute. I feel much better now."

"Why do you feel so much better now?"

"'Cause now I know for a fact that what Tim and I shared was real. I was special to him."

"Damn, I thought you were worried about my safety or something."

Serena's face displays a false look of concern. "Yeah. I was thinking about that too."

"I bet you were. I'm scared of you and I mean that. There's something seriously wrong with you. You should have kept your dirty little secret to yourself. That man took advantage of you, but you can't see it."

"So what if I slept with our doctor? What's the big deal?" she said defensively. "He didn't take advantage of me. If anything, I took advantage of him. *I* made the first move. I take all of the blame for what happened between us. I'm not the type of woman who can share so much of myself mentally and emotionally and not become physically attracted to a man, especially one so fine and so rich."

"He was intelligent and stimulating. Funny you left those out. That was what I liked most about him. Intelligence goes a long way."

"Intelligence is good, but let's just be real. Most intelligent men are nerds. I'll take a fine-ass illiterate stud over an intelligent, geeky dude any day. Why would I want a man who's smarter then me? When I was younger that was okay, but now that doesn't go along with my personality. I like to manipulate a man like a puppet on a string."

"I guess you're right. Now I understand why you like dumb guys. You know, we attract what we are."

I hope she caught that bit of sarcasm. The look on Serena's face instantly tells me that she got the message.

"Uh-oh, somebody's catching feelings."

"No, I'm fine."

"You can't fool me. We've been through a lot together. I know you like the back of my hand and you're not fine. I'm sorry if what I told you about Tim hurt you."

"It did and you'll never understand why. It's even more sickening when I think about you having sex with a grown man at the age of sixteen. What do you think that did to you? It had to have affected you in some way."

"No. It did nothing but give me more confidence when it came to men. Don't feel bad for me or Tim. My relationship with him didn't have a negative impact on my life at all. Shit, by sixteen I was already doing what I wanted and was the person I was meant to be. I'm just a very sexual type of woman and I can't change. Don't wanna change, either. That's just who I am. There's a little slut who lives inside both of us. Set her free and you'll enjoy yourself."

"Momma Pearl could sense that something was wrong with you and I caught a whole lot of flak 'cause of you being too grown and freaky."

An angry expression comes over Serena's face. "Fuck her. I can't even believe you mentioned her name. Outta site and outta mind. That evil bitch doesn't exist in my world anymore."

Serena must have had a flashback of a bad memory. She plays it off by switching her attention toward the clothes in the dryer. The dryer stops just as she reaches to open the door, making her timing seem perfect as if she naturally intended to do that. There's a moment of silence between us, which gives my idle mind time to wander. I think back to all the countless hours of intimate sessions with Dr. Easley and how many times I dreamed of reaching out to him, wanting to touch or kiss him. We hugged after every session and I never wanted to let him go. I had stupid fantasies about him marrying me and taking me away to live in a big white mansion.

Serena was bold enough to pursue what she wanted and that's probably the biggest difference between us. I'm not a risk-taker and she's daring enough to put everything, including her life, on the line.

An idle mind is the devil's playground. I say, "Damn, Dr. Easley was fine. I loved that man, thought the world of him. I dreamed of finding a man like him." I pause. "How was he?"

Serena smiles. "In general, or sexually?"

I put my hands up to my mouth as if I'm ashamed of what I'm asking. "Both."

"He was everything a woman could ask for in a man."

"That's all I need to know."

"I hope you don't hate or think bad of me in any way," she said softly.

"I don't. Like I said, he took advantage of you. I don't blame you for what happened."

"Good, because I don't want you to hate me." Serena pauses, then says, "I've done some wild stuff in my life."

I knew for a long time that Serena was a freak, so I shouldn't be shocked by anything that comes out of her mouth.

"Are you proud of the things you've done?"

"I don't have any regrets, but being proud of certain things I've done is another story."

"What's the wildest thing you've ever done?"

Serena twists her lips. "No, I'm not sharing. I've already let out one of my biggest secrets. You tell me the wildest thing you've ever done."

"There's nothing to tell. Let's see. Oh yeah, I used that sex toy you bought me with Craig earlier this evening and it was unbelievable. Girl, let me tell you. Whew!"

"You can't be serious."

"I am serious. I did exactly what you said."

"I don't doubt it, but if that's the wildest thing you've even done, then you need to keep trying. Live a little, then come back with the dirt. I can't stand squeaky-clean broads like you."

"What do you expect? I don't go anywhere. I've only been with one man my entire life."

"That's sad. Let me stop, that's good. More power to you. Keep up the good work. Not many women can count the number of men they've been with on one finger, but you can. Be proud. I can't even count the number of men I've been with on two hands."

The look on Serena's face reveals a hint of regret. Whatever she's thinking right now seems to have stolen a large portion of her energy. I decide to revive her a bit with a question.

"All right, what's the wildest thing you've ever done?"

"God forgive me." Serena closes her eyes and pauses. She continues with her wild story a few seconds later. "I had a threesome with a friend of mine and her sexy-ass husband."

I blush. "How was it?"

Serena's energy returns. "It was a lot of fun."

"The excited look in your eyes tells me that it was more than just a lot of fun. How did it happen?"

Serena sucks her teeth. "*Now* you want details. I guess it's okay to tell you. Well, my nameless friend and her husband sell sex toys. They do these parties every now and then. One day I was at my friend's house—and keep in mind that I was under the impression that her husband wasn't at home. She asked if she could demonstrate one of her new toys on me and I automatically said no. She tried to make this seem as innocent as possible. After a half hour or so, I eventually agreed because she said I could remain clothed. The toy was similar to the one I gave you, but this one had a remote and the catch was that my friend would control the intensity of the vibrator. That was some kinky shit, but the toy looked so interesting that I wasn't about to say no."

Serena pauses for a second.

I say, "Go 'head—I'm listening."

"Okay, okay. I had on a skirt that day and that made it even easier. I took off my panties and inserted the toy inside myself and it felt nice without the vibration. When my friend turned the toy on, that damn thing drove me crazy. I screamed, 'Oh God!' 'cause I never felt anything like that in my life. The whole experience really took me outside of myself. My friend turned up the vibration even more. The next thing I knew she started touching my breasts and kissing my neck. The whole time I was thinking, this chick is trying to turn me out. But everything felt so good that I couldn't stop her. Then her husband appeared out of nowhere butt-ball-naked with a long, strong hard-on and then one thing led to another. That's all you need to know about that experience."

"That's hot, but I didn't know you were into shit like that."

"Like what? Threesomes?"

"No, girls."

"I'm not, they're into me. I don't touch them. They touch me."

"I shouldn't ask, but what else happened?"

"Look at you, getting all excited."

"What? It's not like that. This is strictly for entertainment purposes. Go 'head and finish."

"Yeah right. Anyway, my friend continued to pleasure me with her mouth, hands, and toy, while her husband came up from behind and started pounding away on her ass like a maniac. All three of us were extremely turned on. The whole time my friend's husband was inside her, he kept his eyes on me, and my friend knew he wanted me. She asked me to have sex with her husband and I agreed. She just sat back and watched me and him get busy. We fucked for a couple of hours."

11

Craig

The television was doing a poor job of keeping me company. The same old predictable movies, sitcom reruns, celebrity gossip shows, music videos, reality TV shows, and news magazines night after night. It finally dawned on me that I had been channel-surfing for over an hour. I was lying in bed fully dressed with both my soggy pant legs and Nike Shox hanging off the side of the bed. Although I was too tired to move, I was able to muster up enough energy from somewhere to peel off my clothes and hop in the shower. I began to crave my wife's attention, missed her smile and her touch. That's what usually happens when I'm standing around the bedroom naked and she's not around. I got in the shower without Naomi because it was a shorter distance to the shower than having to leave our bedroom to track her down.

After one of my usual lukewarm two-minute showers, I figured I could find Naomi out in the laundry room or somewhere else in the house wasting time running her big mouth gossiping with Serena, who doesn't have room to talk bad about anybody. Momma always said people who live in glass houses shouldn't throw stones. Spreading gossip is all Naomi and Serena know. Well, at least that's all I thought they knew, until I got an earful and heard for myself what they were really talking about. I was about to knock on the laundry room door until I heard all this sex talk that nearly knocked me off my feet. Women are bigger perverts than men.

I know I'm wrong because I've been standing outside of the laundry room with my pajamas and robe on, eavesdropping for at least ten minutes. It's not my fault that these two are speaking so loud and carefree about themselves. I wasn't tiptoeing around or being sneaky, pressing my ear against the door or nothing. Naomi and Serena should be more careful of the secrets they reveal, where they reveal them, and how loud they speak. Just because they're behind the door of the laundry room doesn't mean that sound doesn't travel. It's not like the laundry room is soundproof. Anyone could have overheard the nonsense they're talking about. Thank God the kids aren't hearing this.

Serena is a goddamn nympho and the bad thing is that she's trying to persuade my wife into thinking she's one, too. All evening long, Serena has been smiling in my face and stabbing me in the back at the same time. I tried helping this woman, but some people are beyond help. For God's sake, sleeping with her doctor was an obvious sign that something was wrong from the get-go.

I'm not too sure how Naomi and Serena are positioned in the room. By the sound of their voices, I assume that Serena is farther away from the door.

Serena goes, "Girl, you sure you're all right with just one man in your life?"

"I'm sure."

"You ever fantasize any?"

"Not really."

"C'mon, everybody has some type of erotic fantasy or fetish."

"My fantasies are about Craig."

I think, *That's my baby!*

Serena gets loud. "Get real! I could see if you were in *The Wizard of Oz* and had a munchkin fetish, then I'd understand. I never understood what you saw in his short ass, anyway. You could have had just about any man you wanted. Why him?"

After that comment I'm tempted to kick the door open and go upside Serena's big apple head. It's so wrong for her to sit her freeloading ass up in my house, trying to change my wife's perception of me, the man Naomi loves.

"You know exactly why I chose Craig. Actually, he chose me and I wasn't about to turn him down. There's nothing wrong with my man. I love his height."

That's right, defend your man and tell that nasty wench where she can go. Naomi should ask Serena why she chose *her* sorry-ass husband. I shift my weight from one side to the other because I'm getting tired of standing. I'm tempted to grab a chair from the kitchen because I have a feeling that these two are going to be in there going back and forth like this for a while. I don't want to miss out on something important.

"Do you love when Craig wears those pointed-toe, high-heeled cowboy boots of his?"

Serena's really picking now. My boots are expensive and go just fine with anything, especially my jeans and a nice dress shirt.

"Craig wears them so he and I can see eye to eye. That's his way of compensating for our height difference. That's sexy. Prince does it, too. That's why he wears heels."

No, Naomi didn't just compare me to Prince. To be honest, maybe that's where I got the boots idea. I dunno.

"I can't win. You've got an answer for everything I throw your way. Forget Craig's little short ass. He sounds like a fake fantasy to me. What's your real fantasy?"

"I don't know. Leave Craig alone. What's your fantasy?"

"Here we go again. It's always about me." Serena pauses. "Well, I've been messing with Walter Jefferson for a while now."

Walter Jefferson and I work for the same textile plant. As a matter of fact, I'm his supervisor. No wonder he's always asking me about Serena. He's a tall slim older guy, married with two kids. A vision of Walter's wife Henrietta's face just popped in my head. She's sweet as can be, but she's one hideous beast of a woman. Guess that's the reason why Walter had to get him a little something on the side.

Naomi says, "Walter's cute, but his wife, yuck."

"I know, girl. I call her big ugly ass, Sasquatch, or Big Foot."

Naomi and Serena burst out laughing. I fight to keep my laugh inside.

Naomi says, "That woman would crush you and swallow you whole if she found out about you and Walter. I wouldn't blame her, either, 'cause I'm sure he's the only man she ever had in her whole life. You better watch out."

"Chile, I ain't thinking 'bout Bigfoot. I feel sorry for Walter for being forced to look at a beast like that every day. Could you imagine waking up to that every morning?" She pauses for a second, and then lets out a laugh. "Maybe you can—I almost forgot about Craig. You're forced to look at that face every morning. You poor thing."

"Don't even try it. Craig is fine. As a matter of fact, Craig is finer that both of your men."

"Who?"

"Darryl and Walter." Naomi laughs. "That's why you've been kissing and doing it to Walter after he's been with Sasquatch. Look at you, got me calling Henrietta out of her name."

"Whatever. Don't mention her name around me. And for your information, Walter don't put his lips on her and he damn sure ain't having sex with her ugly ass. Like I said, I feel sorry for that man. He deserves a treat like me every now and then."

"Aren't you afraid Darryl's gonna find out 'bout you messing 'round behind his back like you do?"

"Forget Darryl. So what if he finds out. We're talking about my fantasy and not my husband. Back to the subject at hand—my fantasy would be for me to please Walter and his brother Dave at the same time."

"Tramp! You're too over the top with that one."

"Come on. I told you a long time ago, you better get real. You've got enough equipment and maybe enough skills to please a few good men at the same time. Women are blessed like that."

"I guess you're right. You're still a tramp, though."

Oh my God, I can't believe Naomi just agreed with that bullshit. I don't know whose neck I should wring first, hers or Serena's.

"I said you're right, but I'm not that freaky. One man is enough for me. I don't see the point in cheating."

"It's exhilarating. I get a rush every time I have a different man inside me."

"Sounds mighty whorish if you ask me. I love my husband, I really do . . . but."

"But, what?"

My eyes widen and buck out my head like one of those old Negro actors forced to play servants in those racist movies from back in the old days. I think, *Yeah, but what? But what, my ass. You better keep it to yourself.*

"I'm just not in love with him, not the way I should be."

My heart stops and then shatters like a glass figurine that was intentionally slammed to the floor.

Naomi continues, "I'm not sure if I was ever actually in love with him. Sometimes I wonder if simply loving him and not being in love with him is enough to keep us together."

I've been reduced to *him.* I don't think Naomi said my name once in any part of her last statement. It's as if *she* no longer knows my name or knows me. I sure don't know *her.* I'm hurt. I knew that my heart was an easy target for a long time and Naomi's words just hit directly where it hurts the most. Her comments wounded my heart and left a bitter taste in my mouth.

How did we get here? It goes way back to the day I first laid eyes on her. Naomi had just about everything I could ask for in a young bride. She was a precious young thing and a virgin with a trusting heart. That was my chance to prove that I could commit to one woman and erase the mistakes of my past. Maybe I forced myself on her, coming along at a time when I thought she needed me most. Naomi was just as beautiful and vulnerable as she could be, and her life was in need of a serious change. I tried to make her love me, but instead I think she fell in love with all the material things. We hooked up for all the wrong reasons and now time has exposed a weakness, a major flaw in our relationship. Everybody has problems, but what I thought was real and everlasting has finally worn out or been revealed as an ongoing lie. It seemed as if our love was strong enough to stand the test of time, but I dunno. That's what I get for eavesdropping.

"You probably feel sorry for Craig, but don't. He's had his fun. Live your life, do your thing, and keep him. Nobody said break up. I'll admit, you got a good thing going here."

"I know. I'm just not happy. It bothers me not truly knowing whether I'm in love with him or not."

There's a new energy in Serena's voice. She says, "I knew you weren't as happy as you pretended to be. Nobody's that damn happy and no marriage is perfect. I knew it!"

Naomi must have been sitting on top of the washer or dryer because I hear the impact of her feet hit the floor when she jumps down and says, "That does it for me. We've said enough tonight, maybe a little too much. I'm going to bed to be with my husband. Good night."

"Go 'head then. Gon' and tuck his little ass in and kiss him good night. Don't forget what I said. You know what you need to do."

"Uh-huh."

Just before Naomi opens the laundry room door I'm able to dart into the kitchen and head over to the refrigerator. Naomi steps into the kitchen. Neither one of us says a word. When she looks into my eyes I'm sure she can see the hurt. I disguise it as frustration before she senses my pain.

"You seen my lemonade? Don't make me hurt somebody in here, 'cause I will."

"Calm down. I'm sure there's some Kool-Aid in there."

"I don't want no damn Kool-Aid. What do I look like, a kid?"

Serena steps into the kitchen, looks at me, and says, "I know you don't want me to answer that, do you, junior?"

"Don't talk to me! I swear, you're two steps from a homeless shelter. Say another word and you'll be another step closer. You and your little pests."

"I know you're not talking about my babies like that. You and those big, stupid kids of yours."

Naomi says, "That's enough, Serena."

"He's threatening to put me out."

"Nobody's going anywhere. We all have to learn to get along until we can work through this crisis."

"We ain't gotta learn to do shit." I look at Naomi and say, "If you and your sister need to be together so bad, you can go with her. Share a room, for all I care, and it can be just like old times."

"What?" Naomi gives me a strange look and ignores me. She continues looking for my lemonade. She reaches in the back of the refrigerator behind the milk jug and a stack of Tupperware. "Here's your lemonade. You never look for anything. Thank God nobody drank it."

"I don't even want it now. You can stick it back in there for later. I'm going to bed."

"Good—you need to sleep that anger off. Gon' in there. I'll be in there in a minute."

"Take your time."

"Craig, you shouldn't even act like that."

"I'm not acting. And don't wake me when you come to bed."

Hours later, I wake up thinking about my carton of Minute Maid Premium Lemonade in the refrigerator because my throat and mouth are dry as hell. My tongue feels like a piece of sandpaper topped with thick cotton balls. That lemonade in the fridge is the best thing, next to fresh-squeezed. Somebody probably poisoned it by now. Little Travis probably laced it with cyanide or antifreeze. I'll still take my chances and drink it. Might help alleviate my problems.

My eyes focus on the alarm clock that reads 3:27 A.M. I notice that it's hot in here. My house usually has a slight chill in the air because I keep the thermostat at sixty-eight degrees.

I feel groggy as I sit up on the side of the bed. I kick my feet around to locate my slippers because I never like to walk around barefooted like Naomi and the kids. And they call *me* country. Moonlight shines through the bedroom window as I make my way into the master bathroom to wash my hands and splash some water in my face.

I hear music and see a bluish-white light coming from the family room as I open my bedroom door and make my slow approach down the hallway. From here the music is barely noticeable, but to a grumpy person like me, it might as well be blasting to the top of the house. I'm sure it's Serena. Either she's watching a music video or she's gone through my CD collection and is playing one of my old Tribe Called Quest CDs. I glance over at my entertainment system and everything is lit up, my stereo and home theater. This is an unnecessary waste of money and electricity. When you don't have to pay, you don't care. It's hard not to let this bother me. I'm even madder when I notice that the sofa bed in the family room is empty. Serena and birth control number one and two should have their asses in bed this time of night. I look to my right and see Serena standing in front of an open refrigerator in her underwear, pouring herself and her kids three tall glasses of my lemonade.

I think, *Why? Why me, Lord? Why tonight? Why my lemonade?*

I close my eyes and count to ten, just like it says to do in this anger management brochure I picked up at my doctor's office a couple of months ago. Serena just wants to start some shit with me in the wee hours of the morning, but I'm not about to give her what she wants. First of all, she's wrong for drinking my damn lemonade, and second, I don't even drink out of glasses. For the most part, my family and I use disposable Styrofoam or plastic cups. Here these three refugees come, making me mad, doing things their own way in my home.

I don't say a word—I just stand here looking at Serena with a very disgusted expression on my face.

"What? Why are you looking at me like that? See something you want? I'ma tell your wife. What's wrong with you? Act like you never seen anybody in their underwear."

"It's not even that. Trust me, I hardly even noticed. I'm standing here trying to figure out why in the hell you and your rug rats are drinking my last bit of lemonade. Why'd you have to pour those big-ass glasses? Those are small children and they shouldn't even be handling glasses. They're barefooted. What if one of them dropped a glass and it shattered all over the floor?"

"Then hopefully they'd have enough sense not to step in the broken glass. I'm sorry if we took your last bit of lemonade. I'll just have to buy you some more later."

"Later? What about right now? I'm thirsty like you wouldn't believe."

"I'll grab you a cold beer out of the fridge in the rec room."

"Forget it."

"How 'bout some ice water? Bet some Kool-Aid sounds real good right about now."

"I'm about to just go back to bed. Forget it and forget you, too."

"How 'bout if we give you some lemonade out of our glasses."

I look at Travis and Taylor's snotty little noses. I watch as they slurp my lemonade and drool into their glasses. God knows I wouldn't drink after Serena because there's no telling where *her* mouth has been.

"Hell, no! I'll be just fine. Consider that premium lemonade a treat 'cause I know your broke ass ain't used to nothing but Kool-Aid and water."

"Forget you." She turns to the kids and says, "That's enough. Put those glasses down. Put them right on the table."

Travis continues drinking the lemonade as if it's the best thing he's ever had. Taylor struggles to place her glass on the table because she isn't tall enough.

Serena yells, "Travis!"

His little bad ass answers. "What?"

"Don't say what, say *huh.* What did I teach you? Put that glass down and get your lil' ass in bed 'fore I knock you down. You too, Taylor."

"Sorry excuse for a mother."

"Sorry excuse for a man." She giggles. "I know shit about you, Craig."

"I know shit about you that you don't even know about yourself, freak."

She smiles and says, "I like you, Craig. I'ma tell you 'bout me one day and maybe a little sumthin' 'bout yourself one day, too."

Travis and Taylor never moved. They're just standing still, looking and listening.

"Y'all c'mon and go back to bed. Oh, Craig, if it's a little warm in here, don't worry. We were cold so I turned the AC down some."

"I'd appreciate if you'd ask before you decide to do so much on your own."

"This is my sister's house, too, and I shouldn't have to ask your permission for everything."

"Well, you do. I'm not about to argue with you this time of morning. We can pick this up later."

"We sure can. You don't put any fear in my heart."

"And I ain't scared of you and nobody else. Have a good night, freak."

Serena walks past me real plain and natural, as if she's fully dressed. I'm a man and I can't help but take note of her body. The sista is stacked. I only take a quick look because this sista is my wife's sister. Travis and Taylor get in bed first, then Serena gets in. She lies down and covers the kids, then covers everything except her butt, which is poked out toward me. I'm not sure if that's supposed to be sexy or if that's her way of telling me to kiss her ass.

When I return to my bedroom, the first thing I notice is how stunning Naomi looks as she bathes in the moonlight. It caresses every inch of her exposed skin, making me stand still. It sounds strange, but my eyes don't lie, especially when I see with my heart. Maybe I'm blinded by love. There's a gentle, yellowish-white light flowing down on Naomi that makes her glow. Beauty beyond reason is what I see.

Naomi is extremely peaceful when she's asleep. No tossing or turning, just stillness. The moonlight is soft and subtle and heightens the perception of peace unlike the sun's forceful and harsh rays. That's how my love is, forceful and harsh. At least that's what Naomi leads me to believe, but I know better.

For the moment, I'm lost in thoughts of her. Then visions of us touching and sharing passionate kisses come to mind. The way we used to make love seems like a distant memory or a dream, but at least I still remember. Yep, I remember.

Naomi is in front of me for the taking, but part of me has no desire to even touch her. I'm stubborn like that sometimes, too much pride to give in. On the other hand, the other part of me wants to ravage her body like a wild beast fueled by desire and anger. The anger I felt earlier has somewhat subsided. It's called acceptance. Is it important that my wife be in love with me? What percentage of married couples are actually in love, anyway? Not a whole lot, I bet. The fact that she loves me is enough to keep us together. The only thing that bothers me is that if my wife isn't in love with me, then there's a strong possibility that she could fall in love with another man. That really bothers me. Maybe this is all my fault for being such a run-of-the-mill type of lover. Shit, I can't even put that on myself. None of my other women from previous relationships ever made me feel like a mediocre lover.

I'd probably scare Naomi half to death if she woke up and found me standing here staring at her like this. I decide to lie down in my usual spot on the right side of the bed. As soon as I close my eyes, a vision of a nice, plump, round ass pops in my head. It excites me beyond any fantasy I've had in a while. I feel the blood rush down there and it becomes erect. Soon I realize that the ass I've envisioned doesn't belong to Naomi. It's Serena's. I'm dead wrong for thinking about her, and believe me, I don't want to. I can't stand Serena and would never, ever consider doing anything with her. These lustful thoughts frustrate and irritate me more and more, causing my erection to grow longer and harder. Before long, I'm forced to touch myself. Naomi's bottle of Lubriderm is next to me. I reach over and hit the pump a few times. Her bottle is thirty percent larger than the usual and I really appreciate that because I'm about to use at least ten percent of this pleasing myself. As I begin to stroke myself, I'm reminded of the warm body lying next to me. All that moonlight and sunlight bullshit or whatever else I was thinking about earlier is soon forgotten. I reach over, feeling between Naomi's legs, and all I feel are panties.

As Naomi sleeps, I whisper, "What I tell you 'bout wearing panties in my bed? What's wrong with you, girl?"

Naomi's about to get a rude awakening. I'm gon' show her what this country boy's about and do it to her old-school style with me on top. I slide her panties down, past her knees, past her ankles, then completely off. She's asleep, but not for long. I climb on top, kiss her lips, neck, and do a quick something to her breasts with my mouth and tongue. And then I slide inside with ease. The lotion did the trick. Saved me some time instead of drawing things out with unnecessary foreplay.

I forgot how good the missionary position felt. I can hardly contain myself. "Oh God. Naomi, you feel so good. Too good. Oh God!"

Naomi gradually awakens with each thrust. She moans. "Mmmm. Mmmm. Yeah! Oh yeah!"

I go, "Oh damn. Oh damn. Awwww. Feels good. Awwww. That's it! Yeah, gurrrrl. Awwww. This it!"

I'm done.

Naomi goes, "That's it? That's it? Shit!"

"I'm sorry. Sorry. You felt too good. That just goes to show how good your stuff is. You made me come fast. You should take that as a compliment." I give Naomi a kiss, climb off, and roll away from her. "Good night. See you in the morning. Love you."

She repeats, "*Good night. See you in the morning. Love you.*"

Finally I can get some rest. What a day, what a night, what a life. I've got to get up early and go to work. I'm at ease, feeling good. I had a lot on my mind earlier, but right about now, I don't have a care in the world, nothing matters but sleep. If I were any more relaxed, I'd be dead. Within seconds I'm fast asleep.

12

Naomi

No, Craig didn't just wake me up for that. I was sleeping good, like it was the weekend or something. That was the first real sleep I've had in weeks, and Craig decided to wake me up for nothing. When I say nothing, I mean nothing, absolutely nothing! If you're gonna wake me up, disturbing my rest, it better be worth it. Don't leave me wanting and needing, because that does nothing but frustrate the hell out of me. Craig's sorry behind is fast asleep, already snoring, sounding like a miniature lawnmower. Men have it made, for real. They're guaranteed to have an orgasm every time they have sex. Must be nice. Makes me wonder what the world would be like if women had orgasms first and fell asleep, leaving men disappointed and sexually frustrated. How would men deal with that? I guess the world would really be a much more violent place.

I thought I was in for something good tonight, something different. I was all laid back, thinking, *Oh my goodness, a new position.* It's pretty sad when a woman is excited about being in the most common sexual position in the history of the world. For a minute it took my mind off the fact that Craig was doing his predictable abbreviated foreplay. He had the nerve to lube his thing up with lotion so he wouldn't have to expend too much time or energy getting my natural juices flowing. I hope he didn't think I couldn't smell the lotion he used on himself. Craig can't seem to comprehend when I try explaining the purpose of foreplay. When it's good for me, then it's good for him, period. But no, he has to rush and be predictable. I know where he's going to touch or kiss me before he even makes a move. He takes the same route every time. If he wants to be quick about something, then he can always take the expressway downtown, if you know what I mean. The midline of my abdomen bears a light brown line, which is the mainline en route to my pleasure zone, and all Craig has to do is let his tongue ease on down that line. Instead, I get a kiss to the lips, then the neck, a quick grope to one of my breasts, a quick lick to my nipple, and if I'm real lucky that same nipple might get sucked. Selfish bastard. I feel so cheated right now. Oh, I'm pissed. It's hard to feel any other way when I'm left lying here in a damn wet spot, feeling angry and disgusted. In addition to that, I feel nasty between my legs. Feels wet, goopy, and sticky, all at the same time. When a woman gets fed up, somebody's gonna have hell to pay.

I feel real nasty lying here like this and decide to get out of bed and head straight for the shower. Thank God, I can finally use all the hot water I desire because nobody's awake to complain. Sometimes Craig and I shower together, but that's just a waste of time because he doesn't like hot water like I do and he's too cheap to use much. When Craig and I shower together he usually stands directly in front of the shower-head, blocking the water's flow. He leaves me standing in the rear of the shower, complaining like a maniac with soapsuds running down my freezing body.

A hot, soothing bath sounds even better than a regular ole hot shower. This is a little out of the ordinary for this time of night, but what's the worst that can happen? Craig might wake up, see this as a cry for help or some type of distress signal, and realize that something's really wrong. I doubt that very seriously. As the bath water runs I pour a mixture of body wash and baby oil into the tub, adding bubbles, a silky texture, and a pleasant aroma.

My body is submerged into relaxation, a sweltering stress reliever. I know exactly how to bring the heat, even if Craig doesn't. As my husband, he should. You'd think that after all these years he'd know me inside and out. The water temperature is about as hot as I can stand it. Stress and tension seem to be released from my body with the rising steam like evil spirits. Thanks to the bathwater's ingredients, my skin feels sensitive and silky smooth to the touch, my own touch. Just that quick, wishful thinking and a naughty fantasy about pleasing more than one man at a time takes over, courtesy of my wild and crazy sister. I soon forget that these hands caressing me are my own because they seem to have a mind of their own. Now they're massaging my breasts and inner thighs. I don't have a problem taking care of myself. I know exactly what it takes to please me and no one I know can do it quite as good. I make small circles between my legs with my fingertips, adding just the right amount of pressure against my clitoris. Before long I penetrate myself with one, then two fingers. My other hand explores a little lower and soon I find myself lost in a double penetration fantasy. I tell myself that I'm a cheap little slut for liking this type of thing, but it turns me on even more.

I climax, relax, and then return to bed fully satisfied.

A couple of hours later I wake up and see Craig staring out of our bedroom window with the same bewildered expression I usually have when I look out that same window. Something's troubling him. As he stands there, I wonder if he sees what I see and thinks the same thoughts I do when I look out at the world. Maybe he's bothered by the fact that I overslept. If the alarm clock went off, I sure didn't hear it.

I say, "Good morning, sweetie. You all right?"

Craig gives me a quick, empty glance. His mind is definitely somewhere else. Now I sense sadness. Craig's focus somewhat shifts away. He's more concerned with whatever is going on outside our bedroom window.

He turns away from me and says, "Good morning. I guess I'm okay."

Craig doesn't seem okay, because he's not even looking at me. A suspicious look comes over my face. "Are you sure?"

With caution he says, "Not really, but I'll be okay."

Guilt makes me say, "Sorry I overslept. Did you wake the kids already?"

"Don't worry. I took care of them. They're up already. It's my fault you overslept. Sorry for disturbing you last night."

"It's okay. You don't have to apologize. C'mere."

Craig walks over to my side of the bed. He scoots me over and lies down next to me. Here we go spooning again.

He says, "You can sleep in today. The house is in pretty good shape and I already put something together real quick for breakfast."

The kids yell out their good-byes, letting us know that they're on their way out the door. Craig and I yell good-bye and tell them to have a good day. Morgan's bus has arrived. C.J. is walking down the road to his friend Ryan's house to wait for the school bus. Erika is catching a ride with her new boyfriend.

For the moment I'm more concerned about Craig than anything, because of the depressed look on his face. I grab his hand.

"Baby, what is it? I know when something's bothering you. You can talk to me. You know that, right?"

"Yeah, I know. It's just that I was standing over there, looking out at the backyard, and it made me think."

I smile and say, "Isn't it beautiful? I mean, the sky, the trees, and the grass."

Craig lifts up. To my surprise a smile appears. "What in the hell are you talking about? I'm talking about Chop-chop. Poor girl, all caged up in that pen like that, day in and day out. It bothers me to think that I've taken her freedom away. Plus, I haven't been giving her much attention lately." He laughs. "I'm talking about my dog and you're talking about the sky, trees, and grass. You're silly."

I throw his hand away. "I should have known."

Craig continues to smile and then he kisses me. "You should've known what? That I'm not the sensitive type to look out of the window and see the same things you see and express myself the same way you do?"

"No. Whatever, Craig. It's a shame. You've got more empathy for that damn dog than you have for me."

"Oh my God, stop being jealous. Look at you, jealous of my dog. You need to stop. Anyway, I gave you a bone of your own last night."

"That's not even funny. See, you're joking, but I'm serious. You need to concentrate more on me before you find yourself in the doghouse with Chop-chop."

"I hear you. I'm just playing around with you. Wish I could lie here with you all day, but I gotta go. You want me to bring you anything from the kitchen before I leave? I made some bacon and eggs with fried apples."

"Sounds good, but no thanks. I'm fine. I'ma let you go now. Have a good day and be careful."

"All right. I love you."

"I love you too."

"Uh-huh. Yeah, right."

"What?"

"Nothing. I'm just kidding."

In a playful way I say, "Get outta here!"

"Before I go, what do you think of me getting one of those long chains for Chop-chop? That way she can have a little more freedom."

"I think it'll work for both of y'all. She'll have a little more freedom and you can limit how far she goes. The important thing is, you'll still be in control."

"You know that's important to me. Thanks, babe, I'll see you this evening."

I was being sarcastic and Craig didn't even notice. He grabs his keys off the dresser, then exits the bedroom. Within a couple of minutes I hear him yell out Serena's name. His voice echoes loudly down the hallway and through the ventilation system. Craig yells Serena's name so loud that it makes me sit up in bed like he just called my name. He's in the kitchen when he explodes, using curse words that I haven't heard him use in a long time. For a minute I forgot Serena was still here. After my bath last night I went out to the kitchen for a bottle of cold water. On my way to the kitchen I stopped in the family room for a minute or so and watched Serena and her kids as they slept. Seeing them lying there, safe and sound, gave me a good feeling inside. I felt proud that I was able to get them away from all the unnecessary madness and confusion that they had been subjected to all these years, thanks to Darryl's crazy ass. As I watched Serena and her kids I said a quick prayer for them, and then I looked around my house and realized how blessed I truly am. Material things are nice, but I really appreciate the atmosphere around here. It's organized, comfy, and cozy. I ask myself, as much as Craig and I try to help Serena, why does she want to come here and cause chaos and confusion? For some reason there were three glasses of lemonade on the kitchen table. I hope that's not what they're out there arguing about.

I grab my pink terry cloth robe and rush out to the kitchen. Craig and Serena are yelling obscenities back and forth at each other while Travis and Taylor sit Indian-style in the middle of the sofa bed like they're watching a tennis match.

I ask, "Why are y'all out here carrying on like this?"

Craig appears to be boiling over with anger. "Take a good whiff and you can smell what I'm talking about."

The pleasant aroma of Craig's breakfast is all I smell. All of a sudden a funky odor attacks my nose, forcing me to become a mouth breather. It's so bad I can taste it.

"Whew! I can smell that." I look at Serena and say, "Please don't tell me you put a shitty diaper in the kitchen trash can."

Craig says, "She did, and I asked her nicely to get it outta here. As a matter of fact, there's two of them in there. One is small and the other looks like an adult diaper. That big-ass boy over there is still wearing pull-ups."

Taylor laughs out loud while Travis gives Craig a mean look and curses under his breath.

Serena says, "So what? I've never seen a man make such a big deal outta everything. You ain't a real man."

"You wouldn't know a real man if you were standing face-to-face with one, because all you're used to dealing with are good-for-nothing bums like your husband."

"He's more man than you'll ever be. He keeps me satisfied."

"That's a lie."

"You should try satisfying your wife once in a while. Too bad you can't make her happy—I mean, *really* make her happy."

Craig has this what's-that-supposed-to-mean kind of look on his face.

I'm so embarrassed right now that I want to run and hide. I forgot that I couldn't trust my sister with my innermost secrets because she's stupid as shit. Now she's going to stand here and turn everything around that I told her about Craig in hopes of hurting him.

Craig never looks in my direction and I'm glad, because the expression on my face would automatically tell him that I told Serena that he doesn't satisfy me. But that was a while back, and that's when she recommended that stupid sex toy.

Craig yells, "You should stay the hell out of our business. I want you outta my house right now! Get out, Serena, and I mean it!"

"This is my sister's house too. I'm not leaving till she tells me I have to. Don't forget, blood is thicker than water."

Blood is thicker than water, but Serena has no idea how thin her blood is running. If she had any idea, she'd shut her big mouth and quit while she's ahead. Craig is my husband and she needs to respect him.

"Go back to where you belong," Craig shouted.

"What, you think I'm not good enough to live here? Shit, you ain't livin' large. Everything you have is because of your parents. Your daddy helped you get this house and it ain't all that."

"Don't forget who helped *you*. Can't be nice to you, though. 'Cause you don't appreciate shit. I've tried my damnedest to get along with you, but I'm done trying. At first I used to feel bad for you and wonder why Darryl likes to kick your ass so much, but now I know. You deserved every last ass whippin' you ever got. You're miserable and you don't wanna see anybody else happy. It's a doggone shame."

Serena looks surprised. "How could you say that to me? No woman deserves to be beaten by a man, no matter what."

I've been quiet long enough. Craig is out of line now. I turn to him and say, "She's right. He didn't mean it, Serena. Did you, Craig?"

"I don't know."

"I need help and he's turning his back on me. Y'all just don't know what I've been through."

Craig says, "You're right. Tell me what you've been through."

"I'm trying to support my family, but I can't even do my daycare anymore."

"Why not?"

"I might not have a house much longer. They're about to foreclose. Plus, Darryl ran all of my daycare families away. Nobody wants their kids around a drunk every day."

"You're lying about the foreclosure. Everybody knows that Darryl's parents paid that house off way before they passed away. You need to come up with a better lie."

"I ain't lying. Does everybody know that Darryl took out a second mortgage and that's how we've been making it all these years? Darryl hasn't made a payment in months and now we're facing foreclosure. He doesn't work and the daycare was our only real source of income."

"Well, that's the bed you made and now it's time to lie down in it. You're an adult and so is your husband. We all make certain bad choices in life—they're called *mistakes,* and you need to learn from yours. Like I always say, nobody wants to deal with the consequences of poor-ass planning. Too bad."

"You're a heartless son of a bitch. That's why I hate you! You're not perfect, not by a long shot." Serena looks down at the ground and within seconds she has a new burst of energy. "Nay, you should have seen how this bastard was looking at me last night when I was in the kitchen with the kids. I made a mistake and went to the kitchen in my underwear because I didn't expect anybody to be up that time of night. I'm sorry for that, but you better watch him."

Craig turns toward me and yells, "She's sick in her damn head! I swear, this girl ain't got a bit of sense." He turns to Serena and shakes his head in disgust. "I wasn't lookin' at you. Don't nobody want you, gurl."

I'm at a loss for words, and then I'm quickly reminded of what's going on here. Misery loves company. Serena is trying her best to bring chaos and confusion into my life. She wants to divide my household, but that's not gonna happen. Her back is against the wall and she's just digging deep to come up with something bad enough to make me mad at Craig.

"Stop it, Serena. Don't even try that with me 'cause it's not gonna work." I look at Craig and say, "C'mere, we need to talk."

"Baby, I swear I wasn't looking at her. I swear in a stack of Bibles."

"Shhh. I know. C'mere and keep quiet."

I decide that we're going to help Serena instead of going along with her wickedness. I'm not going to give her what she wants, and that's an argument. She'd love to see me and Craig at each other's throats. I'm going to give her what she needs—financial help to keep her from losing that house.

I ask, "Serena, how much do you need to get caught up on your mortgage payments?"

Craig gets a wild look in his eyes because he can kind of sense where I'm going with this. "Why? What difference does that make?"

Serena is clueless. "Yeah, Nay. What difference does it make?"

Craig's trying not to hear this at all. "None!"

"Craig, shhh. Just answer my question, Serena."

"Including late fees, we must owe about nineteen hundred and fifty dollars. We're supposed to have it paid in full by Thursday of next week."

"Jesus Christ!"

"Craig!"

"Sorry. I know. Y'all got me using the Lord's name in vain. But that's a whole helleva lot of money." He calms down a bit. "So, Serena, how are you gonna come up with a large amount of money like that in such a short amount of time?"

I answer before Serena can even process Craig's question. "We're gonna help."

"Shit! I thought we were already helping her. That's how she ended up here in the first place. On second thought, if it means gettin' her and those shitty babies outta here, I'm all for it."

Surprisingly, Serena just stands in front of us as quiet as a church mouse with a puzzled look on her face.

I turn to Craig and say, "Now you're starting to see things my way."

He goes, "Uh-huh. Serena, how much of the nineteen-fifty do you and Darryl have?"

"I don't know. Let me see . . ." She looks up at the ceiling for an answer. "Well, probably about fifty."

Craig asks, "Dollars?"

I say, "You can't be serious."

With much attitude, Serena says, "Well, I am."

"Okay, let me ask one question. What in the hell have y'all been doing with all your bill money?" Craig asks.

"What you think? Spending it. Might as well have spent it, 'cause we fell so far behind with our payments. It's like trying to climb out of a thirty-foot hole using a stepstool."

"I shouldn't have asked," Craig exclaimed. "I know all those trips to McDonald's, Wal-Mart, and Blockbuster Video can add up to thousands in no time. Serena, I swear. Girl, y'all are gonna be the death of me. Even if we help them out, they'll just be right back in the same situation within a month or so. It's like trying to use a Band-Aid to stop a major hemorrhage."

I look over at Serena and she looks even more puzzled than before.

"Don't say anything else, Craig, because you might just make things worse."

"I'm about to head off to work. See you this evening."

Craig and I kiss, a quick peck on the lips.

Craig says a general, "Okay, have a good day."

Serena yells, "Craig!"

"What?"

She gives him an emotionless, "Thanks."

Craig nods his head. "No big deal. Sorry I yelled at you." He walks out the back door.

My plan worked out better than I thought. I'm slicker than the average housewife. I know my husband and I'm sure he was looking at Serena in her underwear. As much as he loves to see a phat ass, he was looking. That's probably what got him so excited and made him wake me up in the middle of the night. I got him in the end because he's literally going to pay for that.

13

Craig

My director, Tom Raymond, paged me to his office less then a minute ago. I knock on his door and wait patiently for him to answer. I'm sure he knows it's me, and he's in no real hurry to open his door. Although I know he's about to hit me with some bad news, I'm about as cool as can be, cool as a cucumber. I'm a rock—somebody's gotta be. Tom is supposed to give me a hit list of over 250 employees that will be affected by the first round of layoffs. As soon as I arrived here this morning, I heard rumors buzzing around about which employees would be the first to go. The employees were all standing around speculating over hot cups of coffee. They kind of quieted down a little when they saw me. I'm a supervisor, so naturally I'm the enemy in situations like this. A few of the brown-nosers approached me without hesitation in hopes of getting an inside scoop, but unfortunately, I wasn't much help because I was in the dark just like them. When they heard me paged to Tom's office, a hush came over the crowd. All eyes were on me.

The tension around here is thick as molasses and morale is at an all-time low. Now it's finally time to get confirmation of the layoffs.

I've worked for this textile mill for eighteen long years and I've seen my fair share of strikes and layoffs, but this time's different. There's nothing the union or upper management can do. I finally got a little recognition for my hard work, and now this shit. They made me a supervisor because people looked up to me and now I've got to be the bearer of bad news.

Tom's office door opens. He's a tall, thin white guy with a buck-toothed smile, a bad case of acne, and a ridiculous-looking mullet haircut. Even with all that going on, he's still able to have an affair with Priscilla, one of the hottest young girls around here. Just one privilege of being the big boss man. Tom's a good ole boy, just one step up from a redneck. He has on a pair of Wrangler jeans, the same ones he wears every day. He wears them so much that the damn things can probably stand up and walk around this office on their own. God knows they've had enough practice, day in and day out. The long sleeves of his white dress shirt are rolled up to his elbows. Tom has on a black Harley-Davidson T-shirt under his white button-down. The armpits of his shirt have perspiration stains the size of grapefruits and there are beads of sweat forming on his forehead. Tom looks about as comfortable as a slab of prime rib at a Weight Watchers meeting.

Tom gives me this shit-eating grin and says, "Good morning, Craig. Come on in."

"Good morning, Tom. How's it going?"

"Have a seat. Not too good, buddy. Not good at all. I'm sweating like a pig. My hands are tied, that's all I can say. I had an important meeting with corporate yesterday and here's the list of layoffs. This is just the first round. Round two is coming in two weeks. I need you to announce the layoffs today after lunch—you'll have to call an emergency meeting."

"I knew it. Why me?"

"I think it might soften the blow, coming from you."

I guess he's asking me to do this because he sees me as a simple black man and the employees are supposed to relate to me better or something.

Tom starts giving me stupid reasons why I should drop the bomb on our employees. I'm starting to feel like a flunky. I'm nobody's fool. I know when the man and the establishment are trying to use me. My attention is drawn away from the list for a few seconds.

Tom's office is like a tribute to NASCAR's finest. He has posters and plaques on the walls and model cars on his desk and shelves. This guy has all types of NASCAR memorabilia. He even has a picture from the early Nineties of himself and the Intimidator, Dale Earnhardt, standing side by side at Martinsville Speedway. As I look around, I notice even more memorabilia. There's a ten-pound glass jar of jelly beans on top of his file cabinet behind me with checkered flags and the number three plastered all over it. This reminds me of a confused adult trying to relive his childhood. If his office looks like this I'd hate to see what his house looks like.

My attention goes back to the list, and I can't believe my eyes. I yell, "Damn, Tom! I'm on here, too, and you knew it. My name is the one hundred and twentieth name on the list. And you want me to make the announcement? Man, you must be out of your damn mind."

"Sorry buddy, but we'll all be on there sooner or later. The good thing is that corporate has put together some nice severance packages for everybody." He shrugs like it's no big deal. "This mill is gonna shut down completely within the next two to three months. We can't compete with the cheap labor overseas. It's killing us."

I'm pissed, mad as hell. I'll be the first to admit that I have anger management issues, but right about now I couldn't care less about cheap overseas labor.

"What kind of fool do you take me for? I'm not about to let you throw me to the wolves like this. Those people respect me."

"And they'll still respect you whether you're here or in the unemployment line."

"Yeah, they will, 'cause I ain't doing it. Your name isn't on this list, so I think you should make the announcement. That's the right way to do this."

"Be a leader. You should be willing to go down with the ship. Go the extra mile one last time, regardless of the circumstances. Great men are made during crisis situations."

"Don't give me that psychological mumbo jumbo bullshit. I was at the same two-day workshop with you, remember? As a matter of fact, I was sitting right next to you. I took notes for both of us."

"You're right, buddy. I'll do it. It's only right since I have to do your job tomorrow, anyway. The layoffs are effective as of the close of business today."

"Aw man, what are we 'posed to do?"

"I don't know about all y'all, but I'm moving back to Arkansas. My brother-in-law helped to line up a job for me out there. My kids are grown and my wife is about to retire in less then ten years. We plan to keep the house we have here and use it as a summer home or for rental property."

"You've got it all planned out, huh? Damn! What about these employees?" I wave the list in front on Tom's face. "I've got a little savings to fall back on, but these people are *po'*. I don't mean *poor,* I mean they're P-O *po'.* The only rich people I know of is upper management. Middle management and below are screwed."

"You're right, but that's beyond my control."

All I can do is take a deep breath and shake my head in disgust. There's a knock at the door and before Tom can say come in, Russ Peterson steps inside, smiling from ear to ear. He's only been employed here about a year. The kid's about as dumb as a doornail.

Tom whispers, "What's this dip-shit want?" His voice returns to its regular speaking volume. "How can I help you, son?"

"I need to talk to you." Russ looks at me and says. "Oh good, I see both of my favorite people are here."

I say, "Hey, Russ. What's up?"

Tom says, "Doesn't matter what's up. We can't talk to him right now. Russ, you'll just have to come back, because we're in the middle of an important meeting. And next time wait for me to tell you to come in before you just barge into my office like a maniac."

Russ's smile slowly dissipates. I'm paying close attention to this weirdo. Something isn't quite right with him because it's damn near summertime and this jackass has on a long, dusty black trench coat. I'm having flashback of Columbine High School. I'm still a rock, but I swear this redneck is about to go postal. I look down at the list and Russ Peterson's name stands out boldly printed on the last page.

I think, *Oh shit!*

Just as that thought crosses my mind, Russ politely closes Tom's office door and pulls out a 9-millimeter handgun. I'm no psychic, but I know these employees like I know these country back roads at night.

Russ's hands are shaking, but still he aims the gun at Tom and says, "Tom, I think you might wanna make time for me right this minute and you, too, Craig. Stand up, both of y'all!"

Tom stands and says, "Calm down, Russ!"

I stand and say, "Yeah, man, please don't do anything we'll all regret."

"I won't regret a damn thing. I wanna do this so bad. Been wanting to do something like this for a long time."

Tom asks, "Why?"

"Respect. Nobody respects me. This is the first time I've ever heard Tom use my name. Usually I'm just 'son' or 'kid', but not today. Call me Mr. Peterson, Tom. You, too, Craig."

Tom whines, "I'm sorry if I disrespected you in any way, Mr. Peterson. Please accept my apology."

I can hardly speak, but I manage to say, "I never disrespected you, Mr. Peterson. You're a valued employee and I mean that from the bottom of my heart. Hope you know I'm not just saying that because you have a gun in your hand."

Russ laughs, then yells, "I love it! I wanna hear you two beg for your lives."

I say, "Look Russ, I mean, Mr. Peterson, why us?"

"'Cause my life is all fucked up, that's why! And this is a good time for us to die." He pauses. "Plus, I'm about to lose my job. I know I'm on that list, right?"

As much as I want to lie, I can't lie to this idiot. Without hesitation, I say, "Yeah, you're on here and so am I."

Tom yells, "Dammit, Craig!"

"What? How can I lie? Mr. Peterson can read his own name. It's not rocket science, it's a list of names."

Russ, a.k.a. Mr. Peterson, snatches the list out of my hand and says, "Let me see your little shit list. Whoo-wee! Looka here, boys, I was right—my name is on here. I'm about to make us famous. Who's first?"

In the back of my mind I'm hearing news reports from the local news, BET Nightly News, CNN, and Headline News about how a crazed redneck shot and killed a good ole boy and stupid black flunky at a textile mill in Eden, North Carolina.

I yell, "Hold up, Mr. Peterson! I'm your friend and so is Tom. Let's talk about this. We can work on getting you an extension and possibly a full-time position somewhere else if you'll just give us a chance. Anything's possible. C'mon, let's talk about it."

"Ain't shit to talk about! I told you, my life is fucked up with a capital F. I'm two months behind on my rent. My truck was repossessed last night. All that happened while I was getting a paycheck. Imagine what my life will be like without this job. Think about it! And that ain't all of it. I just found out that my brother's sleeping with my girl. They don't even know that I know." He laughs. "But I do!"

Tom says, "That's messed up. Why don't you go kill them and leave us alone?"

Russ starts trembling all over. "Shut up, goddamit! I'm tired of talking. I'm ready to start shooting and since shit rolls downhill I'm gonna start with you, Tom. Watch this Craig."

I'm a rock. I'm not moved, nor am I shaken by this jackass. I'm one of three sons raised by a strong black man. My older brothers used to whip my ass almost every day, but I never stopped fighting. I was born premature and wasn't expected to live beyond twenty-four hours. I've been fighting all my life and I'm not ready to be taken out at work by some crazy-ass, gun-toting redneck. This boy has no idea who he's fucking with.

Russ aims the gun directly at Tom. Russ closes his eyes and it looks as if he's meditating, saying a silent prayer. This is it. He's about to squeeze the trigger.

I ask, "Mr. Peterson, are you okay?" Russ doesn't respond, so I ask again. "Mr. Peterson, are you okay?"

Tom looks at me with a puzzled expression and shrugs. He's so scared that I can see tears in his eyes. Instead of breaking down, I shift into survival mode. Without even thinking, I grab Tom's jelly bean jar and slam dunk it right on top of Russ's head, knocking him out cold.

Tom yells, "Craig! Aw buddy, you did it! You saved our asses!" His expression quickly changes as he looks down at Russ. "I think you killed him. Security was on the way. I hit this panic button over here."

"He ain't dead yet." I take my foot and kick Russ right in his ass for what he just did.

Tom goes, "That's enough! He's done! Good enough! Stop it!"

I reach down and pick up Russ's gun, and the next thing I know, these two Andy Griffith and Barney Fife-lookin' security guards come crashing through Tom's office door with guns aimed directly at my head. This ain't exactly the best scenario for a brotha to be caught in. I've got a white man lying unconscious in front of me, a gun in my hand aimed at him, and another white man standing in front of me, scared shitless, yelling at me.

Tom yells, "Drop the gun, Craig! Please!"

Andy Griffith yells, "That's right. Drop the damn gun, boy, or you're about to meet your maker!"

I turn toward the security guards and yell, "Don't shoot! I'm dropping the gun. It's not mine. Tell 'em, Tom. Please tell these motherfuckers something so they can stop aiming those guns at me."

Tom laughs and says, "It's okay, fellas—he saved my life. That's the real gunman on the floor. Craig's a hero. I can thank my lucky stars for him."

I say, "Forget your lucky stars—you better thank God."

After an hour or so, Tom said business still had to go on as usual. He went ahead and announced the layoffs. He gave me a simple handshake along with my severance package from our human resources department. He even let me get off early. Ain't I lucky? I guess Tom did all that as some kind of repayment for me saving his life, and now I'm supposed to go home just like any other day. After eighteen years I end up putting my life on the line during my last day of work and that's all the thanks I get. Well, at least I'm alive. Everybody can read about what happened in tomorrow's newspaper.

Before I go home I need to stop by the ABC store for a case of beer and a bottle of Jack Daniel's.

14

Naomi

I'm in Greensboro, about twenty-five minutes or so from home. As I step through the doorway, I notice this well-dressed, barely legal-looking black girl sitting behind a big, fancy wood-grain desk. She looks directly at me, gives me a fake smile, and says with a southern twang, "Good afternoon, ma'am. How can I help you?"

She uses proper office etiquette and all, but she's not fooling me, because I can tell that this little hoochie thinks she's somebody real important, sitting up here all full of herself. The old receptionist never wore this much makeup or showed so much cleavage. She shouldn't be around Dr. Easley looking like this.

For the first time in my life, I think I'm jealous of another female besides Serena. Must be this girl's youth and beauty that's got me feeling like this. The simple fact that she has a nice job and I'm a plain ole housewife doesn't help much, either.

I don't know why I'm here. I hesitate for a few seconds, looking toward the ceiling for strength while fiddling with my purse strap at the same time.

"Hi. I'm here to see Dr. Easley."

I can't believe I'm actually here doing this. It takes a lot of courage for me to confront the sick bastard who took advantage of Serena. Seems like a long time ago, but no matter what, his deeds had a lasting affect. I must have stood outside of this office for a good ten minutes or so, just staring at Dr. Timothy Easley's mahogany-and-brass nameplate.

As I stand here, the air conditioning blows cool crisp air and circulates the smell of Lagerfeld cologne, new carpeting, and fresh paint. Behind all the extravagance of this two-story office building hides a sick, disgusting bastard who performed sexual acts on my little sister and probably a bunch of other young girls. There's a chance that I'll actually accomplish something positive from this meeting, and then again there's a good chance that I'll make a complete ass of myself.

Little Miss Prissy asks, "What's your name, ma'am? And is your child a patient here?"

The office phone rings and the receptionist excuses herself for a second to answer. Thank goodness the phone rang. I was too distracted to process anything this girl was asking me because of being caught up in a flashback of my very first visit here. I was eight years old back then, standing in this exact spot, shaking like a leaf on a tree. I was as skinny as a pole, wearing a white tube top with a pair of navy blue jogging shorts, the real short ones with the thin white stripes on both sides. I looked cute even with my little blue-and-white Bo-Bo tennis shoes.

Momma Pearl knew that I was so nervous that I could hardly think straight. She knelt down, looked me dead in the eyes, and said, "You better get your little flicted-minded ass self together. When that doctor asks you questions, you better answer him like you got some sense. You understand me, chile?"

In a low, fragile tone I answered, "Yes, ma'am."

I was anxious then and that same anxious feeling still lingers with me.

The receptionist concludes her phone call, then asks, "Ma'am, is your child a patient here?"

Although my mind is back, I sound like a scared little girl when I say a soft and emotionless, "No." I repeat myself in a regular speaking tone, "No. And thank God none of my children are patients here."

The receptionist looks at me as if she doesn't have a clue as to what the hell I'm talking about or why I'm even here.

"Well, is the doctor expecting you, ma'am?"

This girl is killing me with all this ma'am stuff. She forgot to ask me my name again. "No, but I was a patient here years ago. Dr. Easley knows me. I'm sure he remembers me."

"I'm sorry, but this is strictly a child psychology practice." She pulls out a business card and says, "Let me recommend one of Dr. Easley's associates, Dr. Dandridge. Here you go. He's an excellent psychologist."

"Miss, what's your name?"

"My name's Lashawn, Dr. Easley's secretary."

"Lashawn, I'm not interested in that card, nor am I interesting in seeing Dr. Dandridge. I'm here to discuss an important matter with Tim. Could you please tell him that Naomi Gaffney, I mean Naomi Goode, is here to see him? He knows me by my maiden name."

"Mrs. Goode, you don't understand."

My eyes widen. I have to show this girl that I mean business. "No, honey, *you* don't understand! I need to see him right away." I look around the empty waiting room. "Is he with a patient?"

She appears stunned. "I'm not sure, but his one o'clock appointment will be here any minute."

All of a sudden Dr. Easley's office door swings open and I feel him emerge. For some reason I don't even want to look in his direction. His baritone voice gives me chills when he asks, "Lashawn, is everything okay?"

At this point I know Dr. Easley hasn't noticed me.

"Yes sir, everything is fine. I was just trying to explain to Mrs. Goode that you don't see adults."

Dr. Easley's eyes are on me. I know because I can feel his stare, the stare of a predator. Instead of giving him the eye contact that a man of his stature usually commands or is used to getting, my focus is drawn toward the floor as if I'm the same scared little girl who stood here for the first time twenty-one years ago. Within seconds my eyes are drawn toward Dr. Easley, but not to his face. Oddly, the soles of his soft black leather shoes are the first thing to capture my attention. I'm not big on designer fashions, but his shoes look expensive and comfortable. There aren't any visible signs of wear. My eyes slowly venture up to the cuffs and creases of his neatly pressed brown slacks. Without even thinking, I take a quick glance at the crotch of his pants and the print of his semi-hard dick, noticing the length and width. Disgusting of him to walk around turned-on in a practice like this. My eyes move up to the matching vest of his tailor-made suit. I imagine that his suit jacket is hanging up somewhere to prevent unnecessary wrinkling. His cream-colored dress shirt appears to be tailor-made as well because of the perfect way it shows off his masculine physique. Dr. Easley's chocolate-colored silk necktie is tied in one of those exquisite double Windsor knots that only a man who wears a tie on a daily basis could create. His gold cufflinks are a nice touch.

There's nothing else to look at, except his face. I'm almost reluctant to make eye contact with Dr. Easley. My God, it's been so long since I've seen him. When I focus on his face, I soon realize that he actually looks much more handsome then I remembered. He looks good for an old man, very mature and well kept. Still has a full head of hair. Only difference is there are a few strains of gray here and there. His beard and mustache appear so neat that they almost look drawn on. I swear, this man is so attractive that he has an aura like he's been anointed by God or one of His angels.

I'm quickly reminded that he's nothing more than the Devil in disguise. Arrogance and elegance best describe the appearance and attitude of this man, who's originally from New York. Maybe he moved down south because he thought he could come down here and take advantage of us. Somebody needs to prove him wrong. He has always struck me as one of those uppity black northerners who viewed black southerners as slow and dumb and easily taken advantage of by his type, the smarter and flashier northerner.

Dr. Easley and I make eye contact and he shouts, "Naomi! Oh my God! My sweet little Naomi. C'mere and give me a hug."

Dr. Easley wraps his arms around me so tight that I can hardly breathe. I'm not in the mood for all this Mr. Nice Guy stuff. Not even the wonderful smell of his Lagerfeld cologne softens my mood. He feels my arms loosen from around him and realizes that it's time for our hug to end and slowly it does. Dr. Easley grabs me by both of my shoulders, takes a step back, and says, "Look at you. My . . . my . . . my."

Lashawn appears to be the jealous one now. The expression on her face alone softens my attitude and makes me act out a bit with Dr. Easley.

Like a big phony I say, "Look at you, Doc. You look nice. Still as handsome as ever."

I'm going to kill him with kindness and as soon as he lets his guard down I'm going to let him have it. This is the exact approach you have to take with a man like Dr. Easley.

"You really think I still look handsome?"

"Yeah. You really do."

"So Naomi, what can I do for you?"

"I just need a minute of your time."

The predator in Dr. Easley comes to life even more. He thinks he's about to get somewhere with me. "By all means. Come right this way."

Dr. Easley stands in his doorway and directs me to a seat in the middle of his office. He quickly closes the door behind him and tells me to make myself at home. He probably senses that I'm a little uneasy about this whole scenario because I keep staring at the closed door.

Dr. Easley makes his way over to his desk, picks up a remote, and turns on some annoying elevator music. I frown. Instantly he reads my facial expression and advances to the next CD in his changer. Relaxing environmental sounds begin to play. We're listening to the ocean.

Sunlight floods the office and that's fine with me. Evidently it's a problem for Dr. Easley, because he closes his vertical blinds completely, blocking out every trace of natural light. Instead of expressing myself, I just sit back in my chair, cross my legs, and allow my mind to slowly adjust to the altered but acceptable atmosphere. I look around and notice Dr. Easley's suit jacket hanging from his coat rack on a big wooden hanger. He's predictable.

I find myself admiring the brown-and-black contemporary cabinetry, shelves of thousands of books, and abstract paintings around the office. The furniture is different from years back, but the same basic setup still remains. I remember hundreds of sessions lying on Dr. Easley soft leather couch. I'm almost tempted to lie down on the new one, but then I'd be in a vulnerable state and that's definitely not happening today.

Dr. Easley sits down across from me in a matching armchair. His couch is the only thing between us. Then I feel it—a strange sexual tension is starting to build.

Dr. Easley looks at me with this I-wanna-fuck-you-expression. He gives me a smile and then asks, "How have you been, Naomi?"

"Just fine. And you?"

"Things couldn't be better."

"I see all the changes around here."

"This has always been a pretty fancy place, especially down here in Greensboro. But it was time for even more upgrades. What can I say? God's been so good to me."

I hate it when heathens mistake God's deeds for personal blessings. This man probably doesn't even know God, because if he did he would never have put his hands on Serena.

My facial expression throws Dr. Easley off because he quickly changes the subject. "You enjoying this weather? Nothing but sunshine today."

"I am. Glad the rain has finally stopped."

"We needed it." He pauses. "So what's really on your mind?"

"This visit isn't really about me. It's about Serena."

"How is she? I ran into her a couple of years ago."

"I heard."

I'm not easy to read. Dr. Easley can't figure me out. He changes, becomes even more seductive with his stare and body language. He crosses his legs and begins to wiggle his top leg, stimulating himself. He reminds me of an excited dog wagging his tail.

"Oh really. I thought she looked great, but damn, look at you. You're as fine as can be. If you were a song, you'd be a beautiful love ballard. I'd listen to you for a lifetime doing nothing but simply loving your sweet melody."

I think, *Oh brother, give me a break.*

"I appreciate the compliments, but I'd really appreciate it a whole lot more if you'd cut it out. Please!"

Dr. Easley appears stunned. His eyes widen with surprise. I'm easy to read now. He senses that I may be immune to his charm. A look of caution comes over his face.

"I'm sorry, Naomi. I didn't mean any harm." He appears slightly distracted. His ego is bruised. He closes his eyes and plays with his beard. Within seconds he comes back to life and asks, "So, tell me, what's up?"

"I'll tell you what's up. My sister is a mess. I'm not trying to blame you completely for the way she turned out, but you had a lot to do with it, whether you know it or not."

"Is that right? You really think so?"

I'm real short with him. "I know so."

"I'm not really following where this is going. Let me just say that I did my best to help you and Serena. Psychotherapy isn't one hundred percent foolproof, you know. You seem to have benefited from coming here all those years. So, what about now? What do you do for a living?"

"This is sad. You have no idea what this is really about, do you?"

"I'm sorry, sweetheart. You lost me as soon as something about Serena came out of your mouth. In addition to that, you never answered my question. Still using avoidance as a defense mechanism."

"I'm a housewife and please save the psychoanalysis for someone who needs it. I don't have time for bullshit, so let me get right to the point. Why in God's name would you molest my sister? She was sixteen years old and you had no right to put your filthy, disgusting hands on her, you sick bastard."

"Excuse me! What on earth are you talking about? I can't believe you'd sit here and accuse me of something so horrible. Those are false accusations and you know it. Come on, Naomi! I'd never put my hands on a patient. You've got me all wrong. I swear to you that I didn't do anything like that. And if Serena said I touched her in an inappropriate fashion or did anything sexual with her, she's lying. Think back for a second—did I ever touch you in any way other than with genuine affection?"

"All I remember were hugs," I confess.

"I hug all of my patients and if hugging someone is a crime, then all I'm guilty of is simple human contact. Your sister has so many unresolved issues that she's bound to say just about anything. Accusing me of molestation is completely over the top even for her. I'm offended that you would even entertain such appalling thoughts about me. Do you have any idea what an accusation like this could do to a man like me? My life would be over and I've worked too hard to have it all taken away over a bunch of nonsense. I'll have to contact my attorney right away. Are you willing to ruin the lives of hundreds of innocent people?"

"What are you talking about?"

"I'm talking about my family, friends, and patients. Promise me that this is the end of this foolishness."

"I can't promise you nothing. What about the time you spent with Serena at the Hampton Inn in Eden. Is she lying about that?"

"I'm not even going to dignify that with a response. I have absolutely nothing to hide."

"Maybe I should ask some of your current patients if you ever touched them inappropriately. I'm sure there are more than a few pretty little misguided teenage girls who would be more than willing to confess to the sinful acts you've performed on them."

Dr. Easley closes his eyes and shakes his head. "I need to ask you to leave my office at once because I can't believe you have the audacity to accuse me of violating my patients."

"I'm sure most child molesters have the same attitude. You never thought that someone would confront you, but this is it. Every dog has his day."

Dr. Easley jumps to his feet. "Get out!"

I remain seated. "I'll leave, but I promise that this is far from being over. I'll go to the local news, and *The Eden Daily News.* I'll e-mail everybody I know until you're put behind bars where you can't ruin the lives of any more innocent girls. You turned my sister's world upside down. Her life is a shambles because of you and what you did to her. She can't even give her family the attention they deserve because of you. She's a complete mess."

"What do you want from me?"

"I want to hear you admit to what you did to Serena."

"I can't do that because I didn't do anything. Is it money you want?"

A light goes off in my head. My mind begins to wander as I sit here deep in thought. I begin to block out the sounds of this stupid, monotonous CD, the sound of Lashawn's phone ringing from the other room, the roar of traffic and an ambulance siren.

Out of nowhere I say, "I didn't come here for money, but I'll tell you what—you can write me a check, made out to Naomi Gaffney, for two thousand dollars to keep Serena and her family from getting put out on the street."

He smiles. "So, that's what this is about. It's so clear. Neither of you have really done anything with your lives and now you think you can come here making false accusations against me and force me to dig into my pockets. I don't think so. Let me tell you something. That's nothing more than extortion. I could have your ass thrown in jail for this."

"Well, call the police. I'm waiting. Call 'em. Go right ahead 'cause I can't wait to explain all this to them, and then to the media. You already know who they're gonna believe."

"You win."

"That was fast."

"I'll write your little check. That's chump change to me, anyway."

"In that case, I'll be back every month to collect from you. If other families get wind of this, then I don't think you'll have enough hush money or, as you like to call it, *chump change* to keep up."

"I know my rights. This is defamation of character and extortion. I'll sue the media for slander if I see one word about these accusations in print. I'm going to give you this check for now and we can discuss any future payments. Here you go." He hands me a check for two thousand dollars.

On my way out of Dr. Easley's office, something inside me tells me to stop and question Lashawn for a minute. When I look at her, she appears different. She's no longer the little irritating hoochie I saw when I first stepped into this office. Now I see her as a young, troubled, confused, and naive girl trying to act out the role of a mature and seasoned receptionist.

"Excuse me, Lashawn. How old were you when you had your first visit with Dr. Easley?"

"I'm sorry, but what do you mean?"

"You know, when you were a patient here. It's okay. You can talk to me. I was a patient here myself and so was my sister. We know all about him and his ways of taking advantage of young girls. Trust me. It's okay, really. I'm not trying to harm you."

"I was fourteen."

"I was eight and close to eighteen during my last visit."

Lashawn whispers, "How'd you know I was a patient here? Did he tell you?"

"No, he never said a word. Let's just call it woman's intuition."

"Oh, okay."

"Can I ask you another question?"

"Go 'head and ask. I don't mind."

"Are there any other young, attractive female employees here?"

"Yes, ma'am. Renee's out of the office for the moment. She does the doctor's billing."

"Was Renee a patient here, too?"

"Yes, ma'am."

"One last question."

"Go right ahead."

"Did he ever put his hands on you or Renee?"

Before Lashawn can answer, Dr. Easley opens his office door and says, "Miss Goode, I thought you'd be long gone by now. I bet your family is starting to worry."

"Please refer to me as Mrs. Gaffney. I was just on my way out the front door."

"All right, then." He turns toward Lashawn and asks, "Are you okay?"

Lashawn tries to maintain her composure. "I'm fine. Everything's okay. I was just giving Mrs. Gaffney one of your business cards for a friend of hers."

"That's hard to believe. I don't think she'll be sending any referrals my way. Naomi, can I see you in my office for a brief moment?"

Against my better judgment, I reenter Dr. Easley's office. This time I don't have a seat.

"What do you think you're doing out there? Hope you're not conducting some sort of meaningless investigation."

"Sounds like you have something to hide."

"Nothing. I don't have anything to hide. I'm not about to get into another heated discussion with you. It's not in my nature to argue with a beautiful woman such as yourself. It hurts me to think that you don't believe me. Whatever happened to the sweet, innocent Naomi I grew to love and cherish? You were always my favorite. No one ever compared to you. I still love you. Don't you know that I love you?"

"No."

Dr. Easley steps in my direction, comes close to me. I'm really uncomfortable. He walks right pass me and picks up a cassette player off his desk. There's no way he's still using that old thing.

"C'mon, you remember how we used to be. I've got something for you. Listen to this."

Dr. Easley presses Play on his cassette player. A softer version of his voice says, "I love you, too, Naomi. But what makes you love me so much?"

A familiar voice emerges from the tiny speaker. "I don't know why. I just love you, that's all."

"C'mon, what did I tell you about answering questions like that? We need to keep the lines of communication open. I need more. If you can't communicate with me effectively, then I can't help you."

"Okay. Sorry. I love you because you're a wonderful person. You're kind to me and Serena. You're a good friend. A lot of times I see you as a father figure. I miss my daddy so much and miss my momma even more. I love them with all my heart. But you help me through the bad times. Thank you." There's a pause. "I wanna marry somebody just like you when I grow up."

"Is that right?"

There's a giggle in my voice. "Yeah! Somebody smart and handsome with a good job."

"You're so sweet."

Dr. Easley stops the tape.

I'm embarrassed. Never have I felt more exposed. My heart erupts with an indescribable pain and a barrage of uncontrollable emotions.

As tears pour from my eyes, I yell, "That's not fair! I was a child with problems and you're trying to make something else out of this. Oh God, I gotta get outta here!"

Dr. Easley jumps in front of me and shouts, "Wait! Please don't go!" He wraps his arms around me and says, "I'm sorry if I've done anything to hurt you or Serena. God knows I am. Can you please forgive me? I'll do whatever it takes. Please forgive me."

This is definitely another one of my weak moments. Hearing that old recorded session almost killed me.

"Let me go!" He holds me tighter. "Get the fuck off of me! I mean it!"

"All right! All right! I didn't mean to upset you with the tape. I was just trying to remind you of how close we used to be back then."

"Back then I thought the world of you, but I . . . you don't wanna know what I think right now . . . you cruddy bastard."

Dr. Easley puts both his hands up in the air and says, "I understand. I just wanted to hold you for a minute to help ease the pain."

I wipe my tears and say, "Thanks, but no thanks—I'm too strong to be broken by your weak-ass psychological games. You can't break me. I'm unbreakable and now I know why you never tried to have sex with me. I was too smart for your dumb ass. Am I right? Tell me I'm right!"

"I dunno."

"You know. Tell me I'm right!"

"You're right."

"You ought to be 'shamed of yourself."

Dr. Easley begins to cry. "I am ashamed. I'm not perfect, just a man. Can you ever forgive me?"

"No, I can't, but I'll pray for you. At least I got a partial confession out of you."

"I wouldn't call it that, but you can call it whatever you want."

"That's exactly what I hate about you. Your arrogance is off the meter. You'd think a man in your situation would display a little bit of humility."

"Humility, huh?" He gives me a fake smile. "Well, please, whatever you do don't ruin my good name. I'd rather give all this up before that happens."

"The only way to stop a person like you is to tell everybody about what you've done and what you're probably still doing. They need to know and they're gonna know. I can't wait to see you behind bars and to see your name on the North Carolina State Sex Offender's Registry. You're a threat to everyone and you need your license revoked. I'm gonna try me best to ruin you. That's all I have to say."

I make my way out of Dr. Easley's office. I storm pass Lashawn as she tries to calm the momma of the child with the one o'clock appointment. Hopefully they all overheard my encounter with Dr. Easley.

15

Naomi

When I get home Craig is sitting on the edge of our bed looking frustrated as hell with his head in one hand and a pen in the other. There's a major stack of bills on the bed next to him along with our Bank of America checkbook and a battery-powered calculator. I haven't seen Craig so flustered in a while. There's a six pack of Budweiser on the nightstand and four of the six cans have already been opened.

Craig drops his pen on the bed and reaches over to finish off one of his cans. He looks up and says. "Hey. Where you been all day?"

"I had a few stops to make. You're drunk, aren't you?"

Craig laughs. "I ain't drunk. I'm gonna be drunk, but I ain't drunk yet. Stop trying to change the subject. Where you been?"

"I said I had a few stops to make."

Craig shakes his head and says, "We need to talk."

"Where's everybody?"

"Oh, Momma and Daddy came by and picked up Morgan. Guess she's spending the weekend with them or something. Erika went to Reidsville with her friends and I don't have a clue where in the hell C.J. went. Oh, by the way, Darryl's outta jail. He came by here a while ago and picked up Serena and their evil seeds. Darryl acted like nothing happened. That sorry son of a bitch tried to sell me ten rolls of pennies. Serena wouldn't let him do it, said they belonged to the kids."

I roll my eyes and say, "Whatever. They're in serious need of money. I don't wanna talk about them right now. So, what else do we need to talk about?"

"Well, it finally happened. I got laid off today."

I sit down on the bed facing Craig. "Oh, no. Sweetie, I'm sorry. We knew it was coming, but not this soon."

"I know. I'm just sitting here looking at all these damn bills. We're all right for now, but I don't know how long our savings are gonna hold up, especially with us having to help out Darryl and Serena."

"Don't worry about them. I came up with another solution."

"Good, 'cause we've only got about eight thousand dollars to live off of till I can get something else going."

A look of concern covers my face. "What about your severance pay? Didn't they give you that at least?"

"Yeah. To be honest, it wasn't much, just a few thousand. I didn't wanna touch our savings at all, but now we don't have a choice."

"After eighteen years, all they gave you was a few thousand dollars? Shoot, I'm glad I did what I did."

I grab my purse, pull out Dr. Easley's check for two thousand dollars, and hand it to Craig.

He looks at it and says, "What's this supposed to be, a handout? We ain't exactly broke."

"He gave me that for Serena."

"Why? Was he in a generous mood or what was it?"

I take a few minutes and explain all that I went through today. Then I take a few more minutes explaining how Dr. Easley took advantage of Serena when she was a teenager.

After I'm done explaining, I'm shocked because Craig has the nerve to say, "Two wrongs don't make a right. Take it back! Better yet, I'll take it back."

"He ain't getting this back. I know that two wrongs don't make a right, but sometimes you have to do wrong and just pray for forgiveness."

"What? Okay, say your prayers, 'cause this one's on you. I guess we can use the extra money. God knows we can't afford to just give two thousand dollars away." Craig gives me this disgusted and disappointed look. "You're always doing something."

Like a child I say, "I know."

"I have to confess."

"Confess to what?"

"I . . . I overheard you and Serena talking last night in the laundry room."

My jaw drops. I'm completely speechless. All the things Serena and I talked about last night start to play back in my mind, especially the thing I said about not being sure if I was in love with Craig. I want to run and hide.

"You can close your mouth and try saying something. Say anything, don't just look at me like that."

"I don't know what to say. I'm not sure exactly what you heard because so much was said."

"Too much was said. I heard it all. I heard things I wish I hadn't and others I'm glad I did. I'm hurt, but what can I say? Life goes on."

"I'm sorry."

"So am I. It kills me to know that we've reached this point. Guess things have been bad for a while and neither of us wanted to admit it."

"Don't you even listen to me? I tried telling you that things were messed up between us last night, but you tried convincing me that we could get things back to how they used to be. Things haven't been right between us for a long time. Every time we discuss this relationship all we do is talk about how good things used to be."

"That's true. It's like we're living in the past." Craig frowns. "I don't wanna talk about this anymore. Everything's messed up now. My life is shit."

"How can you sit there and say something like that? I'm part of your life and so are the kids. Does that make your life shit?"

"That's not what I'm talkin' 'bout. My job is gone. There's nothing else here for me to do. What am I gonna do, work at Wal-Mart, Dollar General, or Dairy Queen? There ain't no more jobs here in Eden."

"I can always go back to work."

"Bullshit! You can forget that. You belong right here taking care of this house. We need you right here."

"For what, Craig? We don't have any babies. Look around. The kids are pretty much independent."

"We still need you here."

"No, *you* still need me here. Why? Why do you feel like I need to be here so bad?"

"I don't need this right now. I'm the man of this house and I don't have to explain everything I say. You ain't gonna work nowhere and that's final." He exhales loudly. "I went through hell at work today and then I'm forced to come home to this. I wish that white boy had pulled the trigger."

"What are you talking about? What white boy?"

"Nothing. You can read about it in the paper. All I'm saying is that a man should be able to find peace in his own house. Since I can't, I'm outta here."

He knocks the stack of bills on the floor, along with the checkbook and calculator. He grabs his keys off the dresser and rushes by me and right out the front door. I hear his noisy ole Ford Bronco start up. The muffler on that thing sounds as angry as Craig looked. The truck's tires screech as he takes off down the street. I don't even care because I have plans of my own.

Part II

ALL AT ONCE

16

Naomi

Kanye West's CD has me relaxed and in a zone. Although it's just an illusion, I have this intoxicating feeling of freedom. I love this feeling, even if it's only temporary. The kids are off doing their thing, Craig's off doing his thing and here I am.

I'm cruising along N.C. 87 on my way to Serena's house, just as happy as I want to be, as if I don't have a care in the world. It's pitch-black out here. My headlights cut through the darkness. Along this narrow, two-lane road there are wild skid mark patterns made by drunk drivers who lost control of their vehicles. My eyes are drawn toward the makeshift roadside memorials of crosses, flowers, and teddy bears which honor and mark the exact spots where accident victims lost their lives.

I gently accelerate, and just like that my mind shifts to something that makes me happy. Spike Lee's new movie was just released today and Serena and I are dying to see it. We always support black movies on their opening weekend.

The temperature is a crisp 61 degrees, a sharp drop from the humid daytime temperature of 93. My driver's side window is down. The cool night air blows forcefully on the left side of my face, in my ear and through my hair. I'm feeling adventurous, wind in one ear and Kanye West in the other.

All of a sudden I notice that my car begins to decelerate. I press down harder on the gas pedal, but it still won't accelerate and quickly becomes extremely hard to steer. The front tire begins to shake violently and I almost lose control. I'm forced to do something that I dread—pull over on this dark, deserted roadside. There aren't any streetlights or cars, just a bunch of trees and darkness. I'm all alone on a deserted country road without a cell phone and pretty much screwed. My husband was too cheap to even consider buying cell phones for the two of us even with a reduced family plan. Craig claimed that the reception in this area was too poor and the phone wouldn't serve any real purpose. Boy, was he wrong.

The movie starts at ten o'clock. According to the clock on my car stereo, it's 9:15 P.M. No way I'm going to make it there by ten. I take a deep breath and try to calm myself. The air is rich, smells like fresh tobacco leaves. My ears are buzzing. Sounds like I'm surrounded by thousands of crickets. The mosquitoes are relentless. They quickly sense my presence and try to feast on my flesh. This is unreal. I'm hungry, thirsty, and scared to death. I must look awfully crazy sitting here in the dark, swatting and scratching while chewing a piece of stale Wrigley's Doublemint gum.

The anger I felt for Craig just a minute ago has turned into fear and frustration. I need help. With each passing second I become more and more afraid. Before long the cool night air and insects force me to put up my window. I decide to crack it a bit to keep from feeling too claustrophobic.

Out of nowhere I notice the sound of an approaching vehicle and a set of extra-bright headlights in my rearview mirror. Something tells me to click on my hazard lights so this person can see me because this may be my best shot at getting out of here. The headlights get closer and closer, making me squint. Now they've got me completely blinded. As the vehicle pulls up behind me, I can't tell the make or model, but my guess is that it's a truck or van because of the height of the headlights. I'm not sure whether to get out or just sit here. Common sense tells me to sit my behind right here and let this person make the first move.

The driver of the vehicle behind me must be as hesitant as I am. For some reason this idiot clicks on his high beams for real. I'm sure this is some guy who knows I'm a helpless female who's scared half to death. A few minutes have passed, and the guy in the vehicle hasn't moved. This whole thing has become a weird waiting game. What a nightmare, and it's only getting worse, causing my body to tense up in a strange way. I can barely move. I'm petrified and I want to go home.

This weirdo knows that I'm scared to death and he's probably enjoying every minute of this. All kinds of bad thoughts begin to play out in the back of my mind. What if this guy isn't alone and has a pickup truck full of Ku Klux Klan members plotting to do something awful to me? They might be looking for a black person to lynch and I'm it. What if this is some type of crazed murderer or rapist? What if I end up like Momma? What if this is the person who abducted Carolyn Tinsley? What if I end up on the news just like her? I'm beginning to hyperventilate and shake all over. All I can do is close my eyes and pray.

Carolyn Tinsley's family was on the news this evening sending out pleas to her abductor for her safe return. My heart goes out to Carolyn and her family. They said that her search party has been unsuccessful in their attempts. Momma Pearl was even on the news tonight leading a candlelight vigil for Carolyn. After all this time I still hate my aunt with a passion. No matter what I just can't forgive or forget. She used a tragic event like this woman's disappearance to lead a candlelight vigil and announce the opening of her new church on East Stadium Drive. Evil witch. I wanted to call her something else, but I won't say it. God, please forgive me.

All of a sudden there's a loud pounding on my driver's side window that scares the life out of me. It quickly brings me back to reality.

Some hillbilly asks, "Ma'am, you okay in there?"

Blood rushes to my stomach, giving me a nauseous feeling. My arms and legs are numb and I can't stop shaking. My neck is tense. I'm actually too nervous to look in this man's direction.

"Ma'am, you okay in there?"

"No, I'm not okay. Could you please get me some help?"

"I can help you. Looks to me like you got yourself one hell of a flat. Your tire's all ate up. You got a spare?"

Beer breath and cigarette smoke flow through the tiny crack of my window. I slowly open my eyes and struggle to look to my left. As I look I can hardly make out the person in front of me. I've never laid eyes on this man in my life. He appears to be a scruffy-looking, middle-aged white guy with long, dirty-blond hair and a beard. He's smoking the shit out of his cigarette like it's the best thing he's ever had. His eyes are wild and intimidating like Charles Manson's or somebody out on a weekend pass from a mental institution. He definitely has this strange mountain man appearance going on, and there's no way in hell I'm getting out of this car. My momma didn't raise no fool.

He puts his cigarette up to his mouth and signals with the other hand for me to roll down my window a bit more. I completely ignore his gesture. My window is already low enough for me to hear whatever he has to say.

"You got a spare? 'Cause you're definitely gonna need one, no ifs, ands or buts about it."

"Please, sir, is there any way you can contact my husband or a tow truck?"

He appears to think for a few seconds. "The closest phone is probably three or four miles away. I can give you a lift down the road or put your spare on for you. Whichever suits you best." He smiles and nods. "I'll leave that up to you, little lady."

I just remembered that Craig isn't even home. He's probably out with his drinking buddies. My hands are over my face, trying to hide my fear and my tears. This man is up to no good and I'm trapped.

"Do you want my help or not?"

I look at his dirty hands and face and say, "No, I think I'll be okay."

"Alrighty then, but I don't think so. It's dangerous just sitting out here like this. Somebody could rear-end you or something. If you're afraid of me, you don't have to be. My name's Pat, short for Patrick. I'm just trying to help you—that's all, ma'am."

"Okay. I appreciate it, but I am afraid. Hope you're not offended or anything."

"Heck nah. Why would I be offended? I don't blame ya one bit, 'cause it's bad out here. Never know who you can trust."

"Uh-huh."

"But, looka here, ma'am, you can step out of your car and wait on the side of the road or have a seat in my van while I change your tire. How's that sound?"

"I dunno. My husband and his friends will probably be along here any minute looking for me."

"Okay, but I don't think so."

"Yeah, they will. My sister is expecting me at her house."

"Whatever you say. I just hate to leave you sitting here. Trust me, I'm harmless. Plus, I don't think there's gonna be anybody else by here for a while. God knows you gotta trust somebody sometime, even someone who looks like me. I gotta momma, a wife, two sisters, and two daughters, and I would hate for them to be in a situation like this. I swear I won't hurt you. You can trust me."

I take a deep breath. "I guess so. Normally I wouldn't do this, but I don't feel right getting out this car, sir. There's already one missing woman in this area."

Pat raises an eyebrow and says, "Well, guess I'ma hafta leave you alone then. But right 'bout now, you're stuck between a rock and a hard place and that's no lie."

"Please, sir, I don't mean to seem ungrateful or nothing. I really and truly appreciate your help, but I just wanna make it home to my family."

He laughs. "Shoot, ma'am, I won't hurt you. I wouldn't hurt a fly."

Out of nowhere, another set of headlights appear along with yellow flashing lights. It's a tow truck. I sigh and think, *Thank you, Jesus. My prayers have been answered.*

As the tow truck pulls up next to my car, I notice that Pat's facial expression changes dramatically. He looks angry and gets a twitch in his left eye.

The tow truck is parallel with my Camry. A very attractive young black guy rolls down the window of the tow truck and says, "Hey! How y'all doing? Is everything okay?"

The guy in the tow truck looks very trustworthy and has a nice, soft southern accent. I'm so glad he's here.

Right away, Pat says, "Yeah, everything is fine. I'ma help this lady right quick and get her back on the road. I got this, partner."

"All right." He looks at me just to be sure and asks, "Miss, are you okay with that or would you like my help instead?"

Pat gets offended and yells, "Hey, boy, I said I got this! You better get going!"

"Oh my goodness. Pat, please go about your business and let this man help me. I'd rather have him help me out. Looks like he gets paid to do this kind of work." I look at the attractive black guy in the tow truck and say, "Please don't leave me out here like this."

Pat turns toward me. "What? You fuckin' bitch. Wasting my goddamn time."

Pat takes a deep drag off his cigarette, then flicks it into the woods. He gives the tow truck driver a dirty look and shoots me the same. He blows out the smoke, then stomps away angrily, mumbling curse words all the way back to his van.

The tow truck driver pulls up and parks his truck directly in front of my Camry. He jumps out of his truck and makes his way toward me. From what I can see, this guy is gorgeous. I'm getting excited. As he walks toward me, I can see that he is extremely tall and well built. He has on a pair of faded blue jeans, a short-sleeved navy blue uniform shirt, and a pair of black leather work boots. I'm loving his athletic build. He makes me feel safe.

I lower my driver's side window completely because I want to get a good look at this guy and he needs to get a good look at me. On top of all that, I don't want to miss a thing he has to say. I just pray that this guy ain't some kind of handsome psycho killer.

"Hi, again. What did he just say to you?"

"I don't know and I don't care. I just wanted him to get away from me."

Pat peels off and zooms past us like a bat out of hell in an old white utility van. It looks like a torture chamber on wheels, the type of van a kidnapper or serial killer would use because it has no side windows, only two dark-tinted ones in the rear. I'm able to pick up a lot of quick details about the van, but unable to get a good look at the license plate.

"Well, he's gone now. Him and his crazy-lookin' self. Guess I scared him off."

"Thanks." I smile. "I feel so much better now. What's your name?"

He extends his big, strong hand and says, "I'm Brian . . . Brian Scales. What's your name?"

Brian knows how to treat a lady. I like the way he grips my hand. I wish he'd raise my hand up to his full lips and kiss it. Instead he keeps my little hand buried in his gentle but masculine grip. Brian has hands like an athlete. I can imagine him palming a basketball. His fingers are big and thick. I'm sitting here caught up in a quick fantasy of one of those big, thick fingers inside me. I clench my thighs tightly as I get a tingling sensation between my legs. I'm getting wet.

I play it off and say, "I'm Naomi Gaffney. Nice to meet you, Brian."

"It's nice to meet you too, Naomi. That's a pretty name."

"It's okay. Kinda old-timey if you ask me."

"I like it a lot. Bet your momma gave you that name."

"She sure did, God rest her soul. She named me after her best friend."

"Sorry to hear you lost your mom. I'm sure she was a wonderful person."

"She was wonderful."

"I can look at you and tell." There's an awkward moment where we just stare into each other's eyes.

"I know how you feel. I used go to school down at North Carolina A&T. I majored in biology 'til I had to come out when my daddy passed away last year."

"It's hard losing a parent. Sorry to hear about your daddy."

"Thanks, but I'm doing all right. I'm just trying to look out for my momma." He pauses. "Naomi."

Here we go staring at each other again.

"Well, let me do less talking and help you get back on the road. I'll talk you half to death."

I give Brian a big, pretty smile and say, "I don't mind. I don't mind one bit. As fine as you are, you can talk to me all night."

"Is that right. We just might have to make that happen. I'm gonna grab some flares from my truck real quick."

I feel safe with Brian, so I get out of my car and stand on the road-side as he lights a few flares. He seems very concerned about my safety.

"I was going to ask that you stay in the car because you don't know me from Adam. Then again it's not really a safe place for you to be when I jack the car up."

"You're right in both cases. I can tell you're a good person. Your parents did a good job raising you. There's something calming about you."

"I feel it too. There's something in your eyes that I like. Why do I feel like I've known you for a long time?"

"I dunno."

There goes that stare again. Brian squats down in front of my flat tire in a catcher's stance. He has good balance. Right away I notice the shape of his thighs through his pants. Within seconds I notice a bulge in his crotch. I look away because I don't want to be too obvious. His chest and biceps are awesome—even his forearms appear muscular. I just stand back watching in awe as he does his thing.

17

Craig

I'm standing here cutting up, acting a natural fool with my partners T-Boy, Brother, and Sonny at Knott's Landing. The place is packed and noisy from the music, balls crashing together on pool tables, laughter, and loud conversation. It seems like there's just a bunch of loud-mouthed men and women trying to outtalk each other. A few old-timers are on the dance floor looking stiff, while others shuffle their feet aimlessly or do a tired two-step as an old-fashioned jukebox blasts a song by Clarence Carter. The place has a real bluesy atmosphere. I'm surrounded by a bunch of chain smokers and I'm dying for a cigarette. It's hard to kick old habits. Been three years since my last drag, but I'm getting weak.

Every bar stool in here is occupied and there ain't an empty table in the house. This reminds me of how it used to be down here on a Friday night before everybody got all depressed and stressed out about the layoffs at the mill. Looks like the party is on again. This beats the hell out of folks sitting around with long faces, telling sob stories and getting pissy drunk at home. Things were getting mighty depressing around here, so I'm glad everybody decided to let their hair down and relax.

Knott's Landing is what folks in Eden refer to as a hot nightspot, old-school pool hall, or old-fashioned down-home dancehall. The holy rollers refer to this place as the devil's playground. To me this is my second home. People here know and respect me.

Two of my boys, Brother and T-Boy, have a low-stakes game of pool going. I won a few dollars earlier against my other homeboy, Sonny.

Don't ask me how T-Boy and Brother got their nicknames. They don't even know. All I know is that T-Boy and Brother are two of a kind. Brother is a single, fifty-two-year-old Samuel L. Jackson looka-like who thinks he's a revitalized playa, thanks to Viagra. He likes to talk a bunch of trash about the women he's supposedly sleeping with. T-Boy's a couple of years younger than Brother, married with three kids. His kids are all out of the house except for his youngest son. T sounds responsible, but he's not. His wife Zetta is the one who keeps their household going while he spends most of his time running behind everybody else's wife. If he isn't chasing some woman, then you can find him right here with a stiff drink in one hand and a cold beer in the other, or a couple of doors down at the barbershop running his mouth.

Sonny is actually old enough to be my granddaddy, but he refuses to let me or anybody else call him Mr. Sonny. He's a widower. For the most part he's a calm, cool, and collected kind of guy unless somebody does something against him. When somebody gets on his bad side, then he becomes a mean little son of a bitch just like me. I heard he was a stone-cold killer back in the day. Rumor is he shot a man in the head during a poker game for disrespecting him and trying to steal his money. That was nothing compared to the other rumor about him stabbing another man to death years ago for touching his wife's ass.

Brother, T-Boy, and I worked together at the mill. Sonny worked there, too, but during a whole different era. I was the last to get the ax, and this is like my going-out party. We're doing it up right with plenty of Jack Daniel's and Millers Genuine Draft.

Brother's always flapping his lips about whatever girl he's sleeping with and that's just what he's doing right now.

"I'ma 'bout to drop this stick like I did on that gal last night."

Brother leans over the pool table, sticking his ugly face under the Coors pool table light. He closes one eye and squints with the other as he lines the cue ball up with the eight ball.

"Eight ball corner pocket."

I say, "Always talking trash. Here's ten dollars. You make this and I'll pay you. You miss, you pay me."

Brother nods at me. "Get ready to pay up."

We all quiet down, watching Brother attempt to make his last shot. The eight ball drops.

"Game! Gimme my money, boy."

"Yeah, yeah, whatever. That ain't nothing but luck."

"What can I say, son? Call it whatcha want. I'm on a lucky streak."

"That ain't what I heard. Heard you got your ass whipped real good last week."

T-Boy laughs and says, "Ain't that the truth. Some dude whipped it real good."

Sonny says, "You always telling stories—tell us how that ass whippin' went down, Brother."

As I hand Brother a ten-dollar bill, he says, "See, what had happened . . ."

Sonny says, "Yeah, tell it. Tell it just like it happened."

I say, "That's right. Tell it, man. Don't hold back. We want the whole truth."

"All right. Y'all 'member that fine-ass high-yellow gal I was messing with over yonder?"

"Nah, but we might have heard about her a time or two in one of your nasty stories."

"Well, this is for real now. I had just popped one of them little blue pills a half an hour or so before leaving my house. Then I was over there fucking the shit out of that gal. Lawd, I was giving it to her good too, doggie-style. She ain't never had nothing that hard. Had that gal calling my name and begging for mercy, but I wasn't trying to hear that, though. I was relentless on that ass."

T-Boy adds, "Yeah! That's what I'm talkin' 'bout. Was she loving it?"

"Was she? Shit, is water wet? You best believe she was loving it."

Sonny cuts in, "You lying."

"I swear on my own grave—that's how serious I am. I ain't lying."

I ask, "What's her name then?"

"I can't put that gal's business out there like that."

"Why not?"

"If you shut the hell up, I'll get to that in a minute."

"Whatever you say stays between us. You know how the brother-hood rolls."

"Yeah, I believe that like I believed you when you said all of us would still have jobs at mill, Mr. Supervisor. Just let me finish telling my story."

My face drops as I try to hide my shame. "Gon' and tell it then."

"Like I said, I was doing it to her doggie-style when all of sudden a big-ass shadow came out of nowhere. I heard a deep voice say something about killing me, and then I felt this god-awful pain in the top of my head. Next thing I knew I was out cold. When I came to, the girl had me in her arms, crying. She thought her ole man had killed me and I thought he did, too, but the only thing was, I don't think he gave a damn. 'Cause when I looked across the room I saw this big, black, mean-lookin' nigga staring at me like he hated me with everything inside him. He looked like that big, greasy sucker from that movie the *Green Mile*."

We all laugh.

Brother points at his eye and continues. "This eye right here was swollen shut, my lips were as big as Jimmy Walker's back when he was on *Good Times*, and I could taste my own blood. I was so scared I damn near had a heart attack. Her ole man grabbed me by my neck, picked me up like a rag doll, and told me to get the hell out of their house. Before he let me go he said that if I ever told anybody about what had just happened, he'd kill me and my whole family. Keep in mind I could hardly stand, much less walk, but somehow I managed to get the hell outta there, and fast."

"Why you telling us this if the girl's ole man told you not to?"

"'Cause I ain't got no family and I'm half dead anyway."

"You's a damn fool, you know that?

I notice this girl named Pauline and her group of friends move from their table. As they head toward the front door my partners and I grab our drinks and head over to our new table.

These two ugly chicks get my attention as they walk through the front door.

I say, "Damn, y'all see what I see?"

"What's that?"

"Those two over there. Damn!" I look again. "Double damn! Either that's the ugliest woman I've ever seen or she's the prettiest monster I've ever seen. And that other one looks like she's wearing a wrinkled paper bag over her head with a wig sitting on top." I bust out laughing. "Oh no, that wrinkled bag is her damn face."

Nobody else is laughing. T-Boy looks mad.

"What? I know y'all found that funny. Look at 'em."

"Ain't nothing funny. That pretty monster is my sister and the wrinkled paper bag with the wig sitting on top is my wife."

I cringe in my seat. "That can't be Darcy and Zetta."

Sonny says, "Yeah, Mo, it is them."

I offer a lame excuse. "I'm drunk as hell. What do I know?"

T-Boy gives me a cold stare. "Just 'cause you're married to that pretty, half-white girl of yours, you think all the regular black women around here are ugly. You always act like you think you're better than us. You ain't!"

"Nah, you got me all wrong. Naomi is just as brown as you. Don't nobody love black women as much as me. That's all I know. In this day and time we shouldn't even be discussing simple issues like this anymore. And I don't think I'm better than anybody in here. I'm just proud of who I am. Some people mistake my pride as some sort of arrogance. I think somebody's got an inferiority complex, that's all. The way I see it, we're all in the same boat."

Now Brother feels the need to express his opinion. "Seems like you finally got your wake-up call. You just realized this morning that all of us were in the same boat when that white man handed you that paper and laid your black ass off like he did me and T a little while back. Bet that really showed you that you wasn't no better."

Sonny comes to my defense. "C'mon now! Y'all need to stop. Y'all know damn well Mo ain't like that. Let's be real, T-Boy—you know Zetta and Darcy ain't all that ugly or all that attractive, either."

"Man, fuck both of y'all. C'mon, Brother, let's gon' over here and talk to some real down-to-earth folks and leave these two phony niggas alone."

I say, "Hey look, a round of drinks for everybody, on me."

"Go to hell, Mo."

Sonny shakes his head. "That's all right, let 'em go."

When I look across the room I notice Darryl shooting pool with some other guys. He looks over in my direction and gives me a quick nod. I give him a quick nod back. I hope he stays his ass over there and leaves me alone. The last thing I need now is another trouble-maker getting on my nerves.

Ten minutes later T-Boy and Brother come back over to the table with me and Sonny.

T-Boy smiles and says, "Hey, Mo. What about those drinks?"

Brother goes, "Yeah, is that offer still on?"

Sonny looks at me, then at them. "Y'all gotta be kiddin'."

I ain't thinking about these two fools. "After the way y'all acted, somebody needs to be buying me a drink and apologizing."

Brother says. "All right, that'll work if you promise to forgive us. We didn't mean no harm."

T-Boy says, "We sure didn't."

I ask, "So what made y'all come back over here?"

"You was right about those two ugly jokers over there. I don't why I got so mad. Guess the truth hurts."

Sonny says, "Keep drinking and they'll get prettier and prettier with every sip, I promise."

We all laugh. The four of us make up real quick with hugs and handshakes. Their comments about me and Naomi hurt, even though they claimed they didn't mean anything by what they said. But now I know how at least two of the people I refer to as friends really see me. Sonny is the cool one, the one I trust most.

Within a few minutes everything is back to normal. One of our all-time favorites, Eden's own Cicero Jones and the Down Home Blues Band, take the stage. The lead singer is an old-timer who started singing the blues from the living room of his momma's house back in the late Fifties. Word got out about Cicero's talent and folks from all over town would pack his house to hear him sing. The ones who couldn't fit inside would sit on the front porch looking and listening through open windows. There was always a crowd around his house when he sang. He and the band got a record deal during the Jim Crow era. They started touring a few months later, going to juke joints all over the South.

As the band plays I notice my old girlfriend, Mia the home-wrecker, dancing by the bar. I'm sure she noticed me, too, but we act like total strangers. We give each other a look that says, *I've moved on and I ain't thinking about you.* I appreciate her ignoring me. Helps me stay focused. She continues doing her thing and I continue doing mine. It's better this way. I'm in no condition to talk to her right now anyway. This Jack Daniel's and Miller's Genuine Draft have me feeling all right. Lord knows if she started some of that sweet talk of hers, I don't know where we might end up. Just kidding. I've got something better at home.

Brother says, "Aw, shit, ain't that Mia?"

"Yeah, man. That's bad news right there. She's invisible to me and hopefully she can't see me, either. Only place I'm going tonight is home to my wife where it's safe."

"I heard that."

18

Naomi

I knew I was in trouble, real trouble, from the moment our eyes made contact. I'm probably more helpless right now than I was when Pat's van first pulled up behind me, but this is a different kind of trouble. With each passing second I feel myself falling deeper and deeper under Brian's seductive spell. I never realized it before, but there ain't nothing better than a fine-ass, young country boy. Something in his stare tells me that he wants to do a lot more than simply fix my flat and help me get back on the road. I bet Brian would like to finish our conversation later. I think we're both curious to see where this whole thing is gonna lead us. Being curious like that isn't exactly a bad thing. As a matter of fact, it's natural.

I need a friend like Brian. Oh, just listen to me, sounding like a little slut. I should have seen this coming. Serena warned me that I would meet a nice guy like this. Even Craig knew I'd eventually meet a guy like Brian. I was cursed from day one. Got Momma to thank for that. Infidelity must run in our family. But Brian is so fine that I just saw a vision of Momma's smile of approval and her giving me a big thumbs-up. Never got a vision like that from her when it came to Craig. This is the green light I was looking for and now I got both feet on the gas.

"If you ever get a flat in an area like this when you're alone, you should keep on driving till you get to a service station or a payphone 'cause it's not safe out here in the middle of nowhere. You had already driven on the tire when it was flat and you destroyed the sidewall. You're gonna need a brand new tire."

"I don't care. As long as I'm safe, that's what matters."

"Yeah, I'd hate to think of what might have happened to you out here with that weirdo."

"I know, but thank God you're here with me."

"God is good."

"All the time."

"And all the time . . . God is good."

"That's true. You got me smiling."

The smell of fresh tobacco leaves isn't the only thing in the air. A high dose of excitement is also present. I was too preoccupied to notice before, but I just realized that there's a full moon out tonight. Beautiful. It hangs high, illuminating the night sky along with the bright yellow flashing tow truck lights in front of me. The mosquitoes are gone and now the crickets are singing a much more pleasant song. The cool night air is just as refreshing and liberating as the breeze I felt through my bedroom window the other afternoon in the midst of the storm.

Brian's all finished putting on my spare tire. Neither one of us wants this to end. I think that's why he was taking his time changing my tire. We both lean against my car, staring at each other during a brief moment of silence.

I ask the first silly question that pops in my head. "How tall are you?"

"I'm six-six. Stand up straight and let me get a good look at you. How tall are you?"

"I'm five-nine."

"That's a good height."

"You play basketball?"

"Yeah. That's usually the first thing people ask me. Then most women ask my shoe size."

"That's so funny." I look down at his feet and think, *Damn!* "So what size do you wear anyway?"

"I wear a seventeen."

I lose my breath and feel myself get wet at the same time. "Dag, you got some big feet."

"I know—I get these big feet from my daddy. When he died my momma told me I had some big shoes to fill and she wasn't lying." He wiped his hands on his pants. "Well, sorry to say it, but I'm all done."

"That was fast, too fast."

"I know, but all you had was a flat tire. This little spare will do the trick for now. I'm gonna keep your wheel and you can stop by my garage over in Leaksville tomorrow to pick it up. I'll get you a brand new tire, have it mounted, and have your ride back to normal in no time. Here's my card."

"You're pretty slick. Is that your way of making sure you get to see me again?"

Brian smiles. "No, I'm a businessman. It's called professional courtesy. I just wanna finish what I started."

"Oh, is that right? I see, professional courtesy." I wink. "I thought that was what you were doing. Okay. Since this is business, how much do I owe you?"

"Don't even worry about it. My service is free to you. I enjoyed doing business with you. The new tire is the only thing you'll have to pay for. But I should be able to get you a nice deal on a new tire. I got a good connection. This guy gives me some sweet deals on all types of auto parts and tires."

"I feel bad 'cause I know this is how you make your living."

"That's true, but I ain't hurting too bad for cash. My daddy left me his garage with a reliable mechanic working for me. I make a pretty decent living."

"How can I repay you then?"

"Whatcha doing tonight?"

"Oh my goodness. I was supposed to pick up my sister at her house so we could go see that new Spike Lee movie tonight."

Brian looks at his watch. "Well, you done missed the last show. You might as well come by my place and have a late-night snack and a cup coffee with me. How's that sound?"

"Nice. I'd love to go, but I need to stop by my sister's house first to let her know I'm okay."

"I'll follow you over there, then we can head over to my place. I live alone in a nice, cozy little spot not too far from here."

"That'll work. Sounds real inviting. Thanks for everything, Brian. You're such a gentleman."

"Again, it was my pleasure."

This is sort of an awkward moment because I'm not sure what to do next. Brian is standing in front of me, looking down at me with a smirk on his face. Somehow we've been drawn closer together. The next thing I know I'm in his arms. He's bold. Brian feels so good that I'm about to melt.

I'm so wrong for hooking up with this man. No matter what, I just can't help myself. That ain't the only thing bothering me. I can't get up the nerve to tell Brian that I'm married with three kids, either. He doesn't need to know everything about me right now. I might scare the poor boy away.

19

Naomi

I just stopped by Serena's house to let her know that I was okay. I was in such a hurry that I didn't even go inside. We just stood in her doorway, talking. Right away Serena noticed Brian's tow truck, even though he parked halfway down the road from her house.

She asked, "What's that tow truck doing down the road?"

"I don't know. It's probably waiting for Darryl to come back so they can repo your Ford Escort."

"Please—that piece of shit is paid for, and anyway, don't nobody else want that damn thing but Darryl. Don't make fun us just 'cause you and your man are livin' large."

"Shut up! We're far from livin' large. Anyway, I told you I was gonna look out for you. We can go down to the bank in the morning and have a cashier's check made out to your mortgage company."

"Oh my God. Girl, are you serious?"

Serena hugged me and said, "Bless you! I knew you wouldn't let me down. You can skip the check if you wanna. You can always give me cash and I can get the check done up on my own to send off."

"Yeah, right! That won't happen. I can see you and Darryl now, spending all that money up in no time."

"No, we wouldn't 'cause we're gonna be a real responsible couple from now on." Serena was talking to me, but her eyes were focused down the road. "Tell your friend in the truck I said hi and not to be so obvious next time."

"What friend? I don't know what you're talkin' 'bout."

"Okay, but I bet you'll know what I'm talkin' 'bout when I stand here watching y'all pull off together. You following him or is he following you?"

"You're crazy."

"Whatever you say. You can't fool me. Been there, done that."

"What? You know him or something?"

"No, I don't know every swinging dick in Eden. I just know y'all are up to no good. Don't let me stop you. Do your thing, girl. You deserve to be treated special. Is he cute?"

"I don't know what your talkin' 'bout."

"All right, keep acting like that. I'll see you in the morning. You might have some extra time 'cause Darryl called and said he saw Craig down at Knott's Landing having a ball."

Brian and I arrive at his house. We pull into a gravel driveway barely large enough for two vehicles. The driveway is very similar to the one at the house where I grew up. I love to hear the grinding sound of tires moving over gravel. Brian lives about four or five miles from Serena in a small house with blue wooden siding. Looks like he has a real rehab project in the works here. I don't really think too much of the exterior. The most noticeable features on this house are the new windows and the new front door. Brian gets extra points for that because he sees the potential in this property.

Brian comes over to my car, smiling from ear to ear. "Welcome. This ain't much, but it's home. Hope you weren't expecting something real fancy."

"This is fine. No need to explain things to me. You're a young single black man with your own house. You get major props for that alone."

"Thanks."

"How long have you lived here?"

We head toward the front door.

"Four months. Momma found this place. She thought it'd be a good idea for me to start off with something small and inexpensive.

This is was actually a foreclosed property, but I'm hooking it up. I painted the siding, replaced the windows, roof, and doors. A lot of hard work for one man."

"I bet. Look at you, all proud and everything. You should be."

"I am. That's my motorcycle alongside the house."

I take a quick peek. "Ooh, a Ninja. I like that."

"I promise to take you for a ride on it one day."

"I'd like that. By the looks of that bike, I guess you're the adventurous type, huh?"

"I guess so. I like living on the edge sometimes. Gives my heart a good workout." Brian opens the front door. "C'mon inside."

Brian cuts on a lamp. He picks up the television remote and turns to the VH1 Soul channel. An Angie Stone video is playing.

I drop my purse on the end table and sit myself down on Brian's new sectional sofa.

"Can I get you a drink?"

"Sure. Anything cold. I know you said something about coffee, but I'm not in the mood for coffee." I quickly glance around the room and say, "I love your interior. This is really nice furniture. I always liked sectionals. The color scheme in here is warm, cozy and real friendly. Nice hardwood floors. I like a room with personality."

Brian returns to the living room with two ice-cold bottles of purple Gatorade. He acts like I'm one of his boys and we just got finished running a game of B-ball or something. I can't believe he brought out a bottle of Gatorade. I did say anything cold. But come on, Gatorade?

Brian sits down next to me and says, "Here's a Gatorade. Hope that's okay. It's the coldest thing I've got in the house."

I'm able to get a good look at Brian and I definitely like what I see. He's clean-shaven, has somewhat of a boyish face with dark, innocent eyes and a perfect smile. He's so fine that I'm not even going to complain about this Gatorade. I'm about to drink this stuff and be happy.

I take my first sip. "This is pretty good. I usually don't drink these, but it'll do."

"Are you sure?"

"It's fine. I did imagine you coming back with a chilled bottle of wine and two glasses."

He laughs. "I don't drink. I'm kind of a fitness fanatic. I've got a huge stock of Gatorade in the refrigerator and in the pantry."

"A little wine here and there doesn't hurt."

"Alcohol makes me urinate like crazy and kills my sex drive."

"Well, you definitely don't need any alcohol then. Trust me, this Gatorade is just fine. What did you have in mind for a late night snack?"

"I can have Domino's Pizza out here in thirty minutes."

"You don't have to do all that. What do you have in your refrigerator?"

"I've got part of a leftover rotisserie chicken, a chef salad with sliced, smoked turkey breast, and I got a ton of frozen dinners in the freezer."

"Earlier I felt like I was starving to death, but I think I'm good for now. Sounds like you've got a lot of food in there for a single guy."

"I mostly eat at Momma's. I can run in the kitchen and make you a plate if you want."

"No, I'm fine. I'm just sitting here looking around wondering who helped you decorate."

"For the most part, I did it myself."

"You know good and well your momma helped decorate this place."

Brian smiles. "Yeah, you're right. She did, but a younger woman's touch wouldn't hurt. As a matter of fact, when can I see your place? Do you live alone? Is it far from here?"

My facial expression changes and Brian sees it right away.

"Sorry to hit you with so many personal questions at once."

"It's okay. I'll let you see my place soon. And I don't live too far from here."

"But do you live alone? I bet you've got a boyfriend."

"No, I don't have a boyfriend. I definitely don't have one of those—not yet, anyway."

"Thank God. I never even asked if you were single. To be honest, I just instantly saw us as a couple. You're beautiful, Naomi. I love your eyes. Your entire face is perfect and your body is nice with plenty of sex appeal. Plus, you got a real sweet personality. I can't even look at you without smiling."

Brian moves in closer like he wants to kiss. I'm really feelin' him, but I'm not ready to kiss him yet. Somehow I'm so caught up in the newness and excitement of this friendship that I forgot about my family. Instead of kissing Brian, I try to cool off and take a quick sip of my Gatorade.

"Can I see the rest of your house?"

Brian gives me a puzzled look. "All right. You wanna start in the kitchen or the bedroom?"

Although I like the way Brian said *bedroom,* I say, "Kitchen. The kitchen is always a good place to start."

Brian shows me around his house. I think he can tell that I'm stalling. We go from the kitchen to the two bedrooms, the bathroom, and then back out the living room. He's got a cute little house.

"Looks like you've put a good amount of money into this house."

"I have." Brian gives me a curious look. "What is it, Naomi? Do I make you uncomfortable?"

"Actually, I'm very comfortable with you. You make me feel relaxed. Makes me forget who or where I am. There's just this strange feeling of déjà vu, like I've been here with you and done this before."

"I can relate. I keep feeling like this is a dream. So everything is okay between us, right?"

"Everything is fine."

"This feels so right to me. I'd just like to take this to the next level, that's all. I've been trying to find the right moment to kiss you, but you keep throwing me off."

"I'm sorry. My mind was somewhere else. I'm okay now."

Brian looks at me, I look at him. He licks his lips and I lick mine. We're so close right now that we're breathing each other's air. I like this. Our lips touch and it's nice. He caresses my face and moves my head in whichever direction he wants and I let him. My lips part. I feel his tongue as he begins to devour me with his kiss. I've never been kissed like this. His kiss takes me away. I'm lightheaded, energized, and extremely turned on at the same time.

I open my eyes and pull away slightly. "That was nice . . . really nice. I want this so bad. More than you probably realize. You make me feel like a teenager being kissed for the first time. I feel like I'm eighteen again."

"So why'd you stop? That's a good thing, right?"

"It is."

"Uh-oh. I see it written all over your face. You're setting me up for some bad news, right?"

"Sorry, but I am. You don't really know me."

Brian makes a silly facial expression. "I know damn well you're not gonna sit up here and tell me that you're a man. Are you?"

"No, crazy, I'm woman."

"I'm just kiddin'. I know good and well that you're a woman, one hundred percent. You looked so serious that I wanted to see a smile on your pretty face. Relax."

"You need to know certain things about me." I pause for a moment.

"What is it then? Trust me, we can work through whatever issues you might have."

"Okay, I should've just told you right away, but I couldn't. Guess I didn't wanna turn you off or scare you away. The last thing I wanted was to be rejected by you."

"Rejected? That won't happen. C'mon. What is it?"

"I have a daughter."

"Is that it? I love kids. When can I meet her?"

"That's not all." In an apologetic tone I say, "I have two stepkids and a husband."

"Whoa . . . that's not good! You're married?"

"Yeah. I'm dead wrong. I know this ain't good and I'm sorry for not telling you from the start. I've been married for eleven years," I swallow then speak again. "Can we still be friends at least?"

"We can be friends and that's it. I don't believe in messing around with a married woman. That goes against God and everything I believe in."

"I bet you believe in premarital sex, don't you?"

"I do. Having sex with a married woman is completely different than just regular ole premarital sex. That's another level of sin to me."

"Sin is sin. You sound real hypocritical to me."

Why did I have to open my big mouth? Now I've completely shifted everything in a different direction, the wrong direction. This is turning into an argument.

"Say what you want, but it's not the same to me. Sins are broken up into different categories and so are punishments."

"Well, I guess I should be going now."

"I'm not putting you out, but it is getting late. You should probably be heading home to your family, anyway. It's after eleven o'clock and they have to be wondering where you are."

Brian gives me a look that tells me that he wishes he never met me because I got him worked up for nothing. His look of excitement from a few minutes ago has completely faded.

I stand up, grab my purse, and say, "Good night, Brian. I wasn't trying to waste your time or play with your emotions."

He appears even more disappointed. "Good-bye, Naomi."

"I said good night and you said good-bye. You make it sound so final."

"Good night then. What else do you want me to say?"

"That look on your face says it all. Good luck with your house."

"You can still drop by my garage tomorrow morning and pick up your wheel. Look for a green Ford Explorer. That's what I usually drive."

"All right. Thanks."

Brian just sits on the sofa watching as I walk away. He doesn't even have the decency to walk me to the front door like a gentleman is supposed to. This is just what I deserve. But I depended on a male to be the voice of reason and surprisingly he was able to come through. It's rare to find a guy with such high moral standards.

Out of nowhere, Brian comes running toward me and puts his hand up against the front door, preventing me from opening it.

"I can't let you walk out that door. I don't want you to leave me like this."

I slide my hand off the doorknob. "Why not?"

"Because I was sitting over there thinking to myself, and an image of me forty years from now popped in my head. I was an old, miserable fool, lonely and full of regret for just sitting still and letting you . . . the most beautiful thing I've ever seen . . . walk out of my life. I don't wanna be full of regret. Now I see that no matter what, we should be friends." Brian takes me by the hand. "Don't go. Stay a little while longer. C'mon, please. I don't want the night to end like this."

Brian brings my hand up to his lips and kisses it.

I say, "Ooh. I don't even know what to say. All I know is that you give me goosebumps . . . butterflies . . . and you take my breath away."

"Does your husband make you feel like that?"

Without thinking, I say, "No."

"Does he treat you good? And are you happy with him?"

"He treats me okay. He used to treat me better. There ain't any romance in our relationship whatsoever. I'm not happy and I've told him on several occasions."

"He ever put his hands on you?"

"No. My husband isn't really physically abusive, but he is verbally abusive."

"He only does that because you allow him to do it. You need to do things that make you happy. It's okay to be selfish sometimes. I know it's easy for a wife and mother of three to forget about her own needs. When was the last time you did something for yourself?"

"I can't remember. Well, I guess being here with you like this is doing something for myself."

"Good. This can be your escape from all of the pressures, pains, and strains of everyday life. I wanna be here for you anytime you need someone to talk to or if you just need somebody to simply listen. I can be that shoulder to cry on or whatever you need, Naomi."

"Are we friends again?"

"I'll be your friend, lover, or whatever else you need. I wanna make love to you."

"Not tonight. I'm not that type of woman. We really don't know each other well enough to do that yet. I've only been with one man my whole life. I've never been into one-night stands."

"Neither have I. I can guarantee you that this will be more than a one-night stand. I'm telling you, I'm not a one-night stand kinda guy. I have a short list of girlfriends. I've only been with three women my whole life. One was a long-term teenage relationship with this girl named Shawana. And the other two, Natasha and Christina, were in college. See, I'm talking years, not just days or hours. Remember, whatever happens here stays here. You can trust me."

"I'd love to be with you like that, but not tonight."

"Just think. You can have me inside you or have me please you in any way you'd like. I'm not going to force myself on you. All you have to do is say you want me. All this can be yours."

Brian unbuttons his uniform shirt and reveals his sculpted chest and washboard abs. His body is unreal. It's becoming hard for me to resist him now.

"Brian." All of a sudden I feel myself getting weak and this situation is turning into a dreamlike state more than ever. My mind tells me to go home, but my body refuses to move because it's dying for Brian's attention. Out of nowhere I ask, "Can I touch you?"

"C'mere. Closer."

Brian pulls me in close to his bare chest. I run my hands all over his rock-hard chest and abs. He seems to like the feel of my fingertips and nails gliding over his skin. Like a crazy woman I begin to undo Brian's pants and back him against a wall.

He smiles. "I like this. Check you out being all rough."

"I wanna see something."

I'm curious to see if Brian is really packing or what. At first I'm not sure what he's working with, and then I feel the shape and texture of his big ole country dick. I'm impressed.

"It's okay you can pull it out all the way and take a good look at it."

I pull it out and wrap both hands around it. "Oh, this is nice and big."

"Keep touching it just like that and it's gonna get even bigger. You've got a nice grip. I like the way you stroke it."

"You've got the biggest thing I've ever seen. Look how hard you are. It's perfect, like I crafted it with my own hands."

"That feels good. I wanna make you feel good now."

The next thing I know Brian scoops me up and throws me over his right shoulder.

"Grab your Gatorade, 'cause you're gonna need it."

"For what? Are you about to help me work up a thirst or something?"

"You'll see. Stop asking so many questions. You'll be thanking me later."

20

Naomi

Brian spanks my butt all the way to his bedroom. I think he likes the way it jiggles. He tosses me on his bed and dives on top of me in a real aggressive manner. Reminds me of a wild animal attacking its prey. He begins to smother me with kisses, taking my breath away. Brian works his hands through my hair, massaging my scalp as his tongue works mine. I love how aggressive he is. My body is being stimulated in more ways than one. Craig could learn a thing or two from Brian. I never had a man lick my teeth and work his tongue around inside my mouth like this. He even throws in kisses to my face and ears.

Brian sucks my bottom lip, then asks, "You like the way I kiss?"

"I do."

He smiles, and just like that, he goes to work on my neck. My body begins to tingle all over.

"Oh, that turns me on so much. You found my sweet spot."

The kissing and licking is fine, but I'm quickly reminded that Brian sucking my neck is a big no-no.

"Wait . . . wait. You can kiss and lick all you want, but you can't suck on my neck. I can't go home looking like a high-school girl with nasty little passion marks all me. I think a certain crazy person that I live with might notice and get highly pissed off."

"Okay then—I'll just have to suck on you somewhere he won't notice."

Brian is so attentive. He drops his head and starts kissing my chest and unbuttoning my blouse at the same time. His mouth and hands are always busy. He has a hand on each of my breasts. My blouse is off and he's aiming to remove my bra. That's a problem.

"I hate to disappoint you, but I don't take off my bra for nobody, not even my husband."

"Why?"

"'Cause I don't."

Brian laughs. "'Cause *I don't* isn't a good reason. What's the real reason?"

I'm slightly embarrassed to say the real reason, but Brian's cool, and I have to keep it real with him. "'Cause I got small breasts and I don't like 'em."

"I mean, you do have small breasts and all, but so what? I like them. Men don't really care about breast size as long as you have firm ones with nice nipples. From what I can see, you've got really nice breasts."

"I'm glad you like 'em, but the fact that I don't like 'em overrules whatever you say."

"Is that right?"

"Yeah, that's right."

"I showed you my thing without hesitation, so the least you can do is show me your breasts."

"Oh, you're so cute. But sorry, sweetie, those little I'll-show-you-mine-if-you-show-me-yours games like that don't work anymore."

He laughs. "Man, I was hoping that would've done the trick. I used to use that on girls all the time when I was younger."

Brian tries another approach. He brings his mouth right up to my left ear and kisses it. He runs his wet lips and tongue around my earlobe. I get chills all over. This feels so good that it makes my eyes roll in the back of my head. All I can do is close my eyes and lie here enjoying being seduced. My issue with my breasts is starting to seem so silly.

I can feel Brian's warm breath as he whispers, "Wouldn't you love to feel my mouth on your cute little eraser-sized nipples?"

It takes everything inside me to say, "No." I'm lying.

Brian continues massaging my breasts and hard nipples with his hands. He moves his mouth away from my ear and starts kissing my breasts through my bra.

"If my titties were a little bit bigger, I'd whip them out and let you go to work on them. But—"

Brian cut me off. "But nothing. I can't believe a woman as beautiful as you would be ashamed to show her breasts. I'm not totally satisfied with my body, but I don't have a problem showing you whatever you wanna see."

"My breasts look way too small for my body. Your body is perfect and very well proportioned."

Brian gets serious. "I wanna see and love every inch of you. If you could see yourself through my eyes, then you'd be fully confident. I wanna see your breasts more than ever now that I know you don't even show them to your husband. It'd make me feel special. You can let down your guard and relax around me. You need an introduction to the three R's. Tonight is all about you and your *relaxation, rejuvenation,* and *rejoicing.*"

Oh my God, Brian sounds so good and convincing. I'm so focused on the three R's that I automatically say, "Okay."

Brian reaches around and slowly unfastens my bra, even though I never actually told him he could. I was more or less saying okay to tonight being all about me and the three R's. For once this is all about me. This is my time.

For some reason I trust, and feel extremely comfortable with, Brian. I'm trying my best to relax and picture myself with perfect breasts. I'm thinking along the lines of a D-cup. My mind tells me that Brian will close his eyes and won't even look at my little boobs.

My bra is unfastened, but out of respect for my comfort level, Brian keeps it in place, covering my breasts. He runs his hands underneath and touches them and gently pinches my nipples. He maintains eye contact, never taking his eyes off mine. I think his eyes and the way he stares at me are extremely sexy. We're both in a trance. He sends me a nonverbal message, telling me that everything is okay.

Brian stares deep into my eyes while giving my breasts the sweetest wet kisses. If anyone could see the way he's treating me right now, they would swear that this man was deeply in love with me. At least that's how he makes me feel. His mouth is incredible. He gives me the special attention that my body's been yearning for. I've been wanting to be treated like this for a long time.

Finally I'm comfortable enough to remove my bra and expose my breasts freely. This whole experience is so different. I'm different. Guess it took a new man to bring out my hidden qualities that my husband never cared about revealing.

Brian says, "Thank you. Look at them . . . look at you . . . beautiful. This means so much to me. You should never be ashamed of your breasts again because they're part of you and you're beautiful just the way God made you. Never forget that."

"Thanks. But still, I'll only expose them to you."

"That's fine with me. Means I'm special, right?"

"You are."

"Shhh. I'm not finished. Just relax and let me do my thing."

Brian kisses my abdomen. He makes tiny circles with his tongue down to my bellybutton and below. He moves down my legs and then to my toes. I nearly lose my mind when he puts my toes inside his mouth.

He reaches up under my skirt and slides my panties down. This is it. My panties are off. We've reached the point of no return. He's got me. My anticipation builds as Brian works his way back up, kissing my inner thighs. I'm dying to feel his mouth between my legs. Inch by inch he makes his way there. He touches me in the sweetest spot of all. His fingers part me and he applies a long slow steady stroke over my clitoris with his tongue. He begins to talk to me between licks.

"How's that feel?"

He licks me again the same way in the same spot.

I moan, "Gooood. I like it. No, I love it. I love it!"

"I'm glad. I want you to love it, 'cause I love doing this to you." He licks. "You're nice and tender. You taste so good . . . sweet."

He licks again and again. His tongue feels sensational against my clit. Stroke after stroke feels better and I get even wetter. Brian shortens his strokes and begins to flick his tongue from side to side and up and down, teasing me.

"You want it?"

"Yes!"

"Show me how you want it then. Grab the back of my head and guide it exactly where you want my mouth."

I grab his head and raise my hips at the same time, placing his mouth directly over my clit again. This time it feels even better because I'm controlling the force. He wraps his lips around my clitoris and gently sucks it. Feels so good that I get muscle spasms.

My hips continue to rise, and before I know it, his tongue is inside me. I grab Brian's head, forcing his tongue deeper inside me. Deep! Now I'm the aggressive one. He's fucking me with his tongue! Love the feeling. Brian probably can't breathe, but who cares? This is what he gets for going down on a woman who ain't used to getting her stuff eaten like this. I can't remember the last time I had this done. This is one time I won't forget.

This man does wonders with his mouth. Although the speed and motion of his tongue alternates, the pleasure remains constant. He can do no wrong. The pace slows and it's as if he is tongue-kissing me down there. He's completely loving it, loving me. He kisses me down there with so much passion and pure delight that I can hardly stand it.

I whine, "Oh . . . my . . . goodness. Oh! Oh! Uh! Uh! Feels good. Feels so good. So damn good, Brian. Oh, Brian, please don't stop. Don't stop!"

This is so intense. My heart is beating a mile a minute. It's like being on a roller coaster as it makes its way to the top, then rapidly descends, a complete rush. Pleasure beyond pleasure is all I know. Makes me wanna savor the moment, making it last forever.

Brian mumbles, "Talk to me."

"Ooh! You're gonna make me come."

"I'm gonna make you come a few times. Go 'head and let it go."

"Uh-huh! Uh-huh!" I start panting uncontrollably. "I'm coming! I'm coming!"

He keeps going. Before I know it, I roll right into another orgasm.

"Ah, yeah! Look at you . . . oh . . . so beautiful. We can't stop now."

Brian puts one of his big fingers inside me and maneuvers it around. He knows he's found the right spot because he can tell by my reaction.

He asks, "That's it, right?"

"Uh-huh. That's it . . . right there."

I reach down and feel his hard dick.

"You ready? Want it inside you?"

I just nod my head signaling. He reaches over on his nightstand for a condom.

"You don't need that. I want it raw."

"Are you sure?"

"Yeah. I wanna feel you."

Brian repositions himself between my legs. He spreads them a bit more, then bends my knees. The next thing I feel is a pleasurable pain. This is called being taken by surprise. A shocked expression is frozen on my face. He's so big and I'm so tight. Makes me feel like a virgin again. It hurts, stretches and then finally accommodates. Lord knows I'm wet enough. Brian penetrates deeper. I feel my insides mold to the shape of his dick.

"You okay?"

All I can say is, "Mmmm!"

"You okay?"

"Uh . . . huh." He thrusts.

He kisses me on the lips.

Brian is so fit. He moves like an automated sex machine. My personalized sex machine, who's been masterfully programmed to meet my every need. He lifts my legs over his broad shoulders and drives me deep into the bed. He holds me in one spot for a few seconds, and then the force is slowly released as he uses the mattress to counteract his thrust bouncing my body into his. He has no mercy. My head is banging against his headboard and now my neck is bent. No mercy from him and no complaints from me. I love it!

My thoughts shift to Craig and his sexual style versus Brian's style. There's no comparison. Brian's size, strength, skill, and overall sex appeal are overwhelming.

We shift through a variety of sexual positions. Sweat drips from Brian and I think I'm beginning to perspire, too. My breathing is labored like I'm running a race.

I know I'm dealing with a pro because he's even dominant when I'm on top. He has a nice way of working his hips from below.

I try to assume a more dominant role and he whispers, "Let me do all the work." He times his words with his thrusts when he says, "It's . . . all . . . a . . . bout . . . you!"

Brian moves me from left to right, top to bottom, to his dresser, against the wall, over to his weight bench. This is a workout. I'm standing, sitting, and then squatting. My legs go from being straight, to being bent, to being spread far apart, and then having them close together, making me feel tighter. I'm getting the workout of a life-time.

Another orgasm is moments away. I feel it building inside. Brian senses it, too, and works me even harder. Feels incredible, like my body is slowly changing, becoming electric all over. As I close my eyes, it's like I'm being transported into an exotic world of pleasure deep inside my own mind. I'm overflowing with sensual emotions.

"That's it. That's my girl. Feels good, huh?"

For a second I'm kind of ashamed to let Brian see me have such a powerful orgasm because I'd hate to let him know that he has such an overwhelming effect on me so soon, but he does. I'm starting to feel an emotional connection with him already.

The shame is gone. My facial expression must look weird, even ugly. This feels so good that I don't even care how I look.

"I like that. You're gonna make me come now."

I open my eyes because I want to see the expression on his face. The exact look that my pussy makes him feel. He goes from having a look of agony to a glazed look in his eyes.

Brian reaches down between my legs to pull out, but I stop him.

"I wanna feel you come inside me."

"Awwwwwww. Awwwwwww."

His erection becomes more intense. A warm blast occurs and sud-denly I'm filled with his juices.

He yells, "Oh shit!" and then collapses on top of me and holds me tight. I grab him by the back of his neck, give him tiny kisses on the left side his face.

Five minutes later Brian sips his Gatorade and hands me my bottle. I smile because I've never needed or appreciated a sports drink so much. That was one hell of a workout.

21

Naomi

Craig isn't home yet. He's still out there doing his thing and that's fine with me. I'm lying in bed all alone replaying vivid passion-filled images of what Brain and I did earlier. Seems like it happened a lifetime ago. Being here like this makes it feel like Brian and I are worlds apart and it seems unreal that we even crossed paths and connected on the level we did. Hard to believe I was just in his arms.

The fact that we had unprotected sex bothers me slightly. Part of me wanted to check his medicine cabinet before doing something like that. Then I looked at him and saw a picture of perfect health. His eyes and teeth were so white, skin was flawless, and his body was as fit as could be. Not to mention that his penis passed my initial inspection. I know all that doesn't mean a thing because there are healthy-looking people with full-blown AIDS. I doubt seriously if he has any STDs though. I pray to God that he doesn't.

A flashback comes to mind.

Brian stood up in front of me completely nude and said, "I'm gonna go take a shower. You're welcome to join me."

We had sex again in the shower before I left.

I showered at Brian's house and then again when I got home. I didn't feel dirty or anything, but I needed to wash away any traces of my new lover. Even after two showers, I can still feel him inside and out. Couldn't wash that away even if I wanted to. His smell is still with me. He had this faint but unmistakable scent of Johnson's Baby Lotion all night. After our shower we rubbed each other down with his lotion. On my way home I kept sniffing myself and thinking of him. I have a bottle of Johnson's Baby Lotion in the bathroom and I'm tempted to rub some on myself or just sniff it as I lie here thinking about him. All of a sudden I have a taste for Gatorade.

Brian was so attentive during foreplay. He was extremely physical and able to perform for a long time. His various techniques of pleasing me were a nice change. The workout bench sure came in handy—we did some creative positions on that thing. At some point I lost track of how many orgasms I had throughout the night.

He's too good to be true. It's rare to find a man who has the knowledge and ability to make a woman feel as good as he made me feel. I know he must have some flaws—I'm trying to convince myself that Brian can't be as perfect as he seems. If we were a real couple he probably wouldn't attempt to do half the things he did or make me feel half as good. It drives me crazy to think that he just might be that good, and it drives me even crazier to think that he isn't really mine. I have this wild urge to make him mine before another woman comes along and takes him away.

To me, most guys are full of games, and Brian is probably the same. In the beginning Craig made me feel special. He even made me feel good physically then he eventually slacked off and hit a rut. Somehow that rut slowed us down and threw us off course. It may be time for us to move on and go our separate ways. I can't settle for inferior sex or a lack of attention from the man in my life. From now on if Craig can't come correctly, then he might as well not come at all. If Brian wants to be the man in my life, then he has to be able to maintain the standard that he set tonight because I can't settle for half-stepping anymore.

I'm still having flashbacks.

I asked Brian, "Will you even know my name tomorrow?"

A serious expression came over his face. He held me close. "How could I ever forget you? I'm missing you already and you haven't even left yet. I'm gonna know your name for the rest of my life. You don't understand me. I want you to be with me on a regular basis. We shared some real intimate moments tonight and I just can't go around doing the things I did to you with any and everybody. I'm really feelin' you, Naomi."

That made me feel good. For a moment I did wonder how many women Brian had really been with and if he treated each one of them like he treated me.

I hear the familiar sound of Craig's truck making its way down the road. He pulls into our driveway. Instantly the vivid mental images of me and Brian together disappear quicker than my favorite television show, like when Craig picks up the TV remote and rudely turns the channel.

Within a couple of minutes Craig enters the bedroom and gets undressed. I lie still, pretending to be asleep. He climbs in bed, smelling like a brewery. His body seems to search for mine because I feel him slowly inching his way up next to me. He doesn't sense that I'm awake. Craig scoots up behind me and eases his arm around my waist. He kisses my spine with his moist lips and blows his warm breath over my upper back and shoulder blades. The fact that I'm not wearing panties must have him aroused. To him this is my way of saying that I'm ready, his for the taking. Actually, this is my way of saying that I'm too tired to put on underwear or nightclothes and I want to enjoy the freedom of nakedness. Well, lower body nakedness, anyway, because I'm still wearing a bra.

I feel Craig stroking himself with his free hand. I know what's next. Why do men think they can start arguments, roll out for hours, and then come home expecting sex without even apologizing?

I reach over to the nightstand and cut on the lamp on my side of the bed.

"What are you doing?"

He looks real stupid and says, "Nothing. I thought you were asleep."

"You thought wrong . . . I'm not. Were you about to have sex with me?"

"No."

"Lying ass. C'mon, I know you were. Guess you were about to have sex by yourself then."

"No. I was about to wake you. You still mad?"

"I'm still . . . kinda mad. I dunno. You still mad?"

"Not as much. Can we still have sex?"

"How do you figure we can still have sex? I can't believe you have the nerve to even put your lips together and spit out some foolishness like that."

"Even though we're mad at each other, that shouldn't interfere with the sexual side of our relationship. No matter what happens, a wife should never deprive her husband of sexual pleasures."

Craig's got a lot of nerve. His stupidity energizes me. I feel a burst of sexual energy come out of nowhere.

A devilish voice inside my head goes, *Pretend he's Brian and sex his little ass till he can't take it. Craig won't last but a minute, anyway. Ride him, girl . . . ride him!*

I spring into action, jumping on top of Craig and pinning his little ass to the bed.

"Whatcha doing?"

"Shut up!"

"What?"

"Shut up and let me do what I wanna."

He's irritated and it seems the more irritated he becomes, the harder his thing gets. I apply more weight and pressure, holding his shoulders down with both my hands.

"I'm in charge. You be the quiet one tonight and just lie there. I'm gonna have my way with you."

I take him inside me and begin to bounce up and down, riding him like a crazy woman. Seems I'm a bit too much for him already. Craig grabs my ass, trying to control my rhythm.

"Don't touch me and don't try to slow me down. Hands out to your side!"

Craig obeys me. He doesn't say a word. Only moans and groans. I change positions by coming to my feet and squatting on the bed for better leverage. Now I'm dropping my weight down on him harder and faster. The penetration is much deeper.

The bed is bouncing, rocking, and squealing. Never realized how loose this headboard was.

This is starting to get real good to Craig, and I can't lie 'cause it's starting to get good to me too. I like being like this, especially with Craig's overly dominant ass. The bedside lamp gets knocked off the nightstand. It's dark in here. Reality becomes fantasy. My mind tells me that I'm with Brian again. This is getting real good to me now.

"I'm about to come!"

Craig's voice just killed my fantasy.

"You . . . better . . . not! Not . . . yet! Me . . . first!" I pant.

"I . . . I . . . I!"

"Shut . . . up!"

That devilish voice inside my head has come back. *This is your second man tonight. Brian was just down there raw and he came inside you.*

I get so turned on that I reverse my position. Now I'm facing Craig's feet, holding his legs down. He reaches over and puts his hand near my clitoris. I push it away. He wants me to come so bad that he's willing to try anything. I begin to stimulate myself with my own hand. Within seconds that intense feeling comes. I'm getting warm all over. I slow down eventually stopping and then clenching my legs together real tight. I become tense, then completely relaxed.

Craig asks that same stupid question that most men ask, "Did you come yet?"

I don't even answer.

The devilish voice inside my head goes, *Don't let him climax. Lie down and go to sleep. Let him know how it feels to be sexually unfulfilled.*

Craig explodes before I can even move. It doesn't bother me too much because I got to do something different with my husband for a change. He seems to be very satisfied. I said I was different now and I am. Look at me, finally being wild and taking risks. Maybe hooking up with Brian wasn't such a bad thing after all.

22

Naomi

It's morning, 7:35. I feel Craig get out of bed. He seems to be in a pleasant mood. I described our relationship as a roller coaster ride and I was right. Never know what to expect from one day to the next.

I smile. "Good morning, Craig."

He smiles, leans over and gives me a kiss. "Good morning, baby."

"How you feeling? Did you sleep okay?"

"I slept good. I feel like a new man." He pauses and then gives me a peculiar look out of the corner of his eye. "What in the hell got into you last night?"

The devilish voice in my head goes, *Brian got into me last night.*

I ignore that stupid voice. "What's the matter, you didn't like it or something?"

"I loved it! I don't know what it was, but keep doing it."

He leans over and kisses me again.

"I think I'm in the mood for making omelets."

"I'd like that. It's been a while. What's the special occasion?"

"Oh, nothing. It's just a beautiful Saturday morning, that's all."

As Craig walks toward the bathroom, he looks out the bedroom window. Something automatically steals his attention because he runs over toward the window to get a closer look.

"Goddammit!" He drops to his knees and screams, "Oh, hell no! No! Noooooo!"

I jump out of bed to see what's going on. "What is it?"

He grabs me. "Don't look out the window. Please. I don't even want you to see what it is."

"Where are the kids?"

Craig holds me down so I can't see anything. "Morgan is still with Momma and Daddy. Erika and C.J. are in their bedrooms."

"Thank God! But, what is it? I need to know what's going on out there."

"It's okay. I need to go out there and do something. Go back to bed and promise me you won't look out back."

"If it's that bad, I won't look."

Craig slips on his pants and heads over to our closet. He pulls out his shotgun.

"Are those shells still in this drawer?"

"Yeah. You're scaring me. Should I call the police?"

"Not yet."

"I wanna see what's going on."

As Craig heads out of the bedroom, he says, "Give me a few minutes and I'll be right back."

I give him more like a few seconds to get out of my sight and when he does, I zoom over to the bedroom window.

Everything appears to be normal until I look up and slightly to my right. My stomach sinks and all I can do is scream. Chop-chop is dead. To make matters worse, she's hanging from a tree by her chain. Somebody intentionally hung our dog. Who could be so cruel? Even though I didn't like Chop-chop, the sight of her hanging disturbs me greatly. I look down in the yard and see Craig crying his heart out. He puts his shotgun down and tries to lower Chop-chop to the ground.

I grab my bathrobe and head out back.

When I get outside, Craig is on his knees holding Chop-chop. He looks like a grieving father who just lost one of his children.

"Who did this shit? I can't believe this. Why? Why my dog?"

"Craig, sweetie, calm down. Let her go. She's gone. Let's go back inside."

It's as if he didn't hear a word I said. "Whoever did this is sick as shit."

"I know, but you gotta let her go. Come on inside so I can fix those omelets we talked about earlier. We need to go inside anyway to call the police. We definitely have to report this."

Craig and I go in the house to prepare breakfast. We soon realize that neither C.J. nor Erika came home last night. Both of us were probably too preoccupied to notice. All we knew was their bedroom doors were closed, so we assumed they were inside sleeping.

We take a brief moment to cool down. Craig and I try our best not to think about what happened to our dog and try to function as close to normal as possible. Instead of getting himself even more agitated, Craig actually helps me prepare breakfast. He cuts up onions and peppers for the omelets while I whisk the eggs. I like to use green and red peppers along with shredded cheeses. The only other things I add is small hunks of butter and few pinches of salt.

It's strange having Craig around the kitchen like this. Chop-chop's tragedy has humbled him already. To be honest, neither one of us has much an appetite. Preparing these omelets is more or less a way of keeping our minds occupied.

After breakfast, Serena arrives for me to take her to the bank. When I open the door she appears to be really upset about something.

With tears streaming down her face, she says, "Good morning, Nay. Hey Craig."

Craig looks up and says, "Hey."

"What's wrong with you?"

"I got a lot of bad news this morning."

Craig goes, "So do we."

"Don't tell me you're having problems with Darryl again."

"No, it's not Darryl this time. Everything is fine at home." Serena holds up a newspaper. "Wait till you read this. There's two articles in here that are gonna bring tears to your eyes. Read this one first."

I read the title out loud so Craig can get the scoop at the same time: "*Local Girl Declared Missing.*"

My heart stops as I read the title because Erika isn't home. The same thought probably goes through Craig's mind as well. I haven't seen Erika since the other night, but I'm sure the article isn't about her. Craig saw her last night.

"The article is about the disappearance of seventeen-year-old Morehead High School senior Ginger Davis, whose parents reported her missing on Wednesday of this week." It hits me. "Oh my God, this is about C.J.'s ex-girlfriend."

Craig says, "Keep reading."

"The article goes on to say that authorities located Ginger's car along Harrington Highway late last night. Investigators suspect foul play and that this case may be related to Carolyn Tinsley's disappearance. Eden police are using all available resources in an attempt to solve both cases. Investigators are combing the wooded area along Harrington Highway, using bloodhounds and cadaver dogs. Crimestoppers has a one-thousand-dollar reward for anyone with information leading to an arrest. The services of the Rockingham County Sheriff's Department and the North Carolina State Bureau of Investigations have been added, due to the demanding nature of these cases. Investigators are calling the two disappearances suspicious and highly unusual since they occurred so close together in terms of time and proximity. Eden police would not elaborate any further."

Craig looks worried. No telling what he's thinking. "This is way too close to home now. The police better do something before someone else disappears. Man, I'm sitting here wondering where in the hell C.J. and Erika are."

"I don't even wanna think about that right now because I'm getting upset."

Serena asks, "What's going on?"

Craig says, "They didn't come home last night."

Serena says, "Hopefully those two are together somewhere. They probably stayed the night with friends or something."

I say, "I hate to say it, but I think something's wrong 'cause C.J. and Erika don't even hang out together. All we know is that they didn't call or come home last night. And to make matters worse, somebody done killed our damn dog."

"You lying. Craig, tell me she's lying."

"I wish she was, but she ain't. Somebody's gonna pay for that shit too."

"Did y'all call the police yet?"

Craig goes, "Nah, not yet."

Serena asks "Whatcha waiting for?"

"I'm gonna call in a minute, don't worry. I'm just trying to think this through."

"I'm sorry to hear about the dog. I think the kids are fine, though."
Serena pauses as if she isn't quite sure what to say next. "Well, y'all
haven't even read the big news yet. Take a look at the next article
down."

"I'm not interested in reading it. Just tell me what it's about."

"They found Dr. Easley dead in his office. Apparently he committed suicide."

I say, "That's crazy!"

Craig says, "You ain't talking about y'all's doctor, are you?"

"Yes, it's him. Our Dr. Easley. That's why I'm like this. Made me sick
to my stomach as soon as I saw it. Take a look."

I look down at the newspaper. One sentence jumps out at me,
which reads,

*Dr. Timothy Easley provided care for numerous children with psycho-
logical problems in the Piedmont Triad Area (Greensboro, High Point,
Winston-Salem, and surrounding counties) for over two decades.*

Too bad the article doesn't mention that the man was a child mo-
lester who probably caused his patients to have more psychological
problems than they had when they came to him.

Out of nowhere, Craig blurts, "That's a damn shame he did that.
Naomi just went to see him yesterday."

Serena's eyes widen and her head rises. "What do you mean, she
went to see him? Nay, what is he talking about?"

"Oh, girl, he don't know what he's saying."

Craig goes, "I don't know what I was saying. Naomi went to see another doctor. Her depression is coming back pretty strong again.
That's all I was trying to say. There's so much going on around here
lately that it's easy to get confused. Ain't that right, baby?"

I have this stupid expression on my face. I've never been a good
liar. "That's right. Told you he was confused."

"Don't give me that shit! I know you went to see him. Didn't you? I
bet you mentioned what you and I talked about, too. You stressed him
into killing himself. I know you caused him to do that."

"Don't say that. He did that on his own."

"I don't know what to say about you. See, that just goes to show that
you always need to be the center of attention. When shit ain't all

about you, you can't handle it and you go and ruin things for other people. That man had a family."

"Oh, is that right? You didn't think about his family when you were fucking him."

Serena's jaw drops. She looks embarrassed. "How do you know who or what I was thinking about when I was with him? And I don't appreciate you telling all my business in front of Craig, either."

"He took advantage of you and I don't know how many other young girls. The girl at his office, his damn receptionist, admitted to me that he fondled her and another young girl who works there. To make matters worse, he gave them jobs to keep them quiet. The man was sick. You weren't there yesterday to see and hear what I did. If you're trying to make me feel bad, it's not working because that's one less son of a bitch that society will have to worry about. The only thing I feel bad about is him not being around to face the embarrassment and consequences of a public trial. His suicide is a clear admission of guilt."

Craig says, "Think about it, Serena. The man killed himself so he wouldn't have to face the consequences. You have to admit Naomi's got a point there."

Serena wipes the tears from her eyes. "I guess you're right."

"I am. Have I ever tried to hurt you?"

"No. I'm so sorry. Sometimes I'm too stupid or stubborn to see what's really going on. You've always looked out for me. The reason I'm here now is 'cause y'all offered to help me. I ain't nothing but a fool."

"No, you're not."

Craig goes, "Yes, she is."

Serena and I both give Craig a funny look.

Our attention goes toward the front door as it opens and closes quickly. C.J. appears. He walks into the kitchen with muddy boots, trying his best to act like everything is normal and under control. As much as I try to help him, sometimes I have to agree with Erika. He is such a weirdo.

"Hey, how y'all doing this morning?"

Before I can even get my first word out, Craig puts his hand up and says, "Don't worry. I got this, babe. Where in the hell have you been all night, boy? And where is your sister?"

"I was at a party in Reidsville. I don't drive so I got home the quickest and best way I could. Sorry it took me so long. Erika was there, too. She should be here any minute."

I ask, "What was wrong with your finger? You couldn't dial a phone and tell us what was going on?"

"Babe, I said I got this. Why in the hell couldn't you pick up a phone and call us? Me and Naomi were worried sick."

"Sorry, I just wasn't thinking."

Serena shouts, "Don't you know that people are missing around here?"

"Serena, let me discipline my son, please. You got two little ones that need a whole lot more discipline than this one, so save it for them."

"Excuse me then, Craig. I didn't know you were the only person allowed to discipline your kids. That's what family's for."

"Thanks, but no thanks. Did you hear that something happened to Ginger?"

"Yeah, I heard she was missing."

"You don't even look upset or surprised."

"I'm not. To be honest, that girl did so much to me that I'm kinda numb right now. I don't have any real emotions about what happened to her. I don't know what to feel."

"Boy, don't say stuff like that. People might think your dumb ass did something to her. You didn't, did you?"

"Man, I know you must be crazy, asking me something like that."

Craig snaps and the next thing I know, C.J. is on the floor and Craig is on top of him.

"Craig, no! Don't do that!"

C.J. yells, "Get off me!"

"Back off, Naomi. This is my son and I'll raise him my way, and if that means knocking his ass out, so be it." His attention goes right back to C.J. The poor boy looks terrified. "I'll kill you in here if you ever disrespect me again. You better watch your tone with me . . . you hear me?" C.J. doesn't answer. "I said, do you hear me?"

"Yeah!"

"Yeah?" I said. "Do you hear me?"

"Yes, sir. I hear you."

"That's more like it. I was brought up saying, 'yes, sir,' and so were you. And don't you forget it. You hear me?"

"Yes, sir."

"If anybody asks you about Ginger, you better give them a good answer like, 'I'm sorry to hear about what her family is going through. I'm willing to help out in any way I possibly can.' I don't care what that girl did to you in the past. The past is the past. You just might mess around and give somebody a wrong answer about that girl and find your ass in jail. Don't forget, there are a lot of smart-mouthed, innocent black men in jail. Your mouth can get you in a lot of trouble, so you better watch what you say and how you say it. Now get up and go to your room. That's where you'll stay until I tell you otherwise. That means no phone calls, PlayStation 3, TV, or radio. Do you understand me?"

"Yes, sir."

Craig helps C.J. up, and then he heads to his bedroom as he was ordered to do.

"Before y'all open your big mouths, let me explain something first. It's not that I have a problem with y'all disciplining the kids, I only have a problem when it comes to C.J. See, 'cause it takes a man to raise a man. Women tend to be just a bit too lenient. At some point y'all become enablers."

I say, "I know just what you're saying. We should knock our boys to the floor every time we discipline them 'cause that really gets their attention and drives the message home."

Serena says, "Shoot, I guess I'm gonna have to start slamming Travis to the floor to get my point across."

"I ain't saying all that, but think what you want. That's how my daddy raised me and I didn't turn out half bad."

Serena says, "No comment."

I say, "You might be right about some of that. I'm always the one who caters to C.J. and I was in constant denial about him smoking weed. You were right about that all along."

"I'm glad you finally admitted to that. You give him more attention than you give the girls, braiding his hair sometimes twice a week. You gonna make a punk outta my son."

"Don't say that. It's called being a good momma. That boy has been through a lot and every now and then I like to show him some special attention."

"All right, enough of that for now. Check out this article right here."

Craig slides the newspaper over in front of me and Serena. There's an article in the paper about him saving his boss and himself from a gun-wielding, disgruntled employee.

"Is that what you meant when you said you wish that white boy had went on and pulled the trigger?"

"Yeah."

Serena looks at her watch. "Well, we need to leave now and get to the bank."

"Hold on a minute, Naomi. I need you to be here when the police arrive, just in case they have questions for you. And hopefully Erika will be here shortly and you can tear her ass apart 'cause I'm staying out of it."

Craig calls the police. Within fifteen minutes or so, Officer Hartwell, the same policeman from the other night, responds to take a full report. In the middle of the report, Officer Hartwell asks if anyone has some type of vendetta against us that we're aware of. A few names come to mind and I'm sure Craig has a few. I mention the guy Pat from last night. Hopefully this can give the police a concrete lead in their two disappearance cases. For a minute I think that maybe Dr. Easley hired someone to scare me. I refuse to mention anything about him because I might get arrested for blackmail.

Craig gets upset with me for not mentioning that I was stranded on the road last night. I quickly remind him that if I had a cell phone or if he hadn't been out at the bar all night with his buddies, that wouldn't have happened. All of a sudden he wants to apologize. Seems more like he's putting on an act for Officer Hartwell.

23

Naomi

Serena and I just returned from Bank of America. Our little trans-
action is history and so is Dr. Easley. Was that mean or what? As
much as I try, I don't feel bad. I'm just not sure if the punishment fit
the crime. Maybe it does in God's eyes. Who am I to judge?

Craig's truck isn't in the driveway and there's no telling where he is
or when he'll be back. I've been trying to ditch Serena, but she wants
to hang out with me today for some reason. My mind is on hooking
up with Brian so I can get rid of my little spare tire. Plus, I wouldn't
mind him giving me tune-up.

As Serena and I enter the kitchen, I can't help but notice that the
in-use light is lit up on the phone and the handset is missing. C.J. is in
his room, being punished. That can only mean one thing: Erika is
home. She uses the phone more than any of us.

"I think Little Miss Thing is finally home."

Serena gets all excited. "Ooh good, let's go question her about
where she was last night and who she was with. Lil' Nasty Girl. Erika
reminds me of myself when I was her age."

"Like that's a good thing." I think for a minute, doing a quick comparison. "You're so right, but I wouldn't brag about it."

"Shut up and get your butt down there to her room. And don't be
too hard on her. Erika can't help herself. She's young and pretty. I bet
all the boys find her irresistible, just like when I was her age."

"I'm gonna be sick if you don't stop."

We head down the hall. I knock on Erika's bedroom door.

"Who is it?"

"It's me. We need to talk."

Erika opens the door and says, "Hey, Ma. How you doing, Aunt Serena?"

"I'm fine, and you?"

"I'm a'ight."

"I need you to hang up the phone so we can talk."

"I'll call you right back."

Erika hangs up the phone. Serena and I have a seat on her bed. Erika starts giving us some lame story about where she was all night and how she thought we knew she was spending the night at her girl-friend's house after the party. Suddenly I'm not as mad because maybe she did mention to me or Craig that she was supposed to do a sleepover this weekend. Lord knows my mind has been on other things. Brian has me kind of distracted right now. Certain images pop back in my head. I miss him so much. Can't wait to see him and ex-periment some more. Damn, he's good.

Erika is in front of me, yapping about something. I swear I don't even hear her right now. She was trying so hard to convince me that she wasn't doing anything wrong. I was convinced like five minutes ago that she was just doing typical teenage stuff, just hanging out with friends, listening to music and eating pizza. Hanging out with a few boys here and there is part of growing up. I think we just had a break-down in communication somewhere along the way. Plus, how can I be mad at her? She even invited her annoying brother to hang out with her. That's definitely a sign of maturity. We're doing a great job rais-ing these kids.

Serena's voice disrupts my thought process. "Were there a lot of cute boys at the party last night? Tell me all about it."

"I don't know—I was only concentrating on one."

"No, don't do that, girl. I told you that you shouldn't settle for one guy. You need to explore more than one option. Enjoy your youth and freedom while you can. At your age the dating world is yours. You need to take advantage of as many of those little niggas as you can."

Erika goes, "Huh?"

I laugh. "You are so ignorant, Serena. Erika doesn't talk like that.

We're raising her to be a respectable young lady and you want her to mess around with every Tom, Dick, and Harry in Eden."

"Girl, please. Don't nobody be messing around with no Tom, Dick, or Harry. Those are white-boy names."

Erika and I bust out laughing.

Erika asks, "What's wrong with white guys?"

"Yuck, everything! Don't you know they used to force themselves on black women. I'm talking about raping us. They're perverts. Why do you think black people come in so many different shades nowadays? White men raped our women and got them pregnant."

"That was a long time ago during slavery days. White guys have a lot of respect for black women now. Sometimes more then the black ones do. There's nothing wrong with mixing races. Both of y'all are mixed and everybody around here talks about how pretty y'all are."

"That's different. Our daddy is black and our momma was white. Understand what I'm saying—black man . . . white woman."

"What's the difference?"

"When the man is black and the woman is white, that's called getting even."

"Serena! Stop it! Erika, don't listen to her. She learned foolishness like that from our daddy."

"So what. He was right."

Erika says, "All I know is that I wish I was mixed so I could have good hair and a complexion like y'all have. Morgan's got good hair like that and it's not fair. All the black guys at my school are drawn toward the light-skinned or white girls."

I say, "I find that hard to believe. No matter what, you're beautiful the way God made you. Was it that you felt like you couldn't compete and that's why you're dating whatcha-call-'em?"

"His name is Brad. And he's the best."

Serena puts her hand up to her forehead. "Oh no! Not a white boy, Erika. Forget Brad. You just need to give the black boys at school a minute to get to know you better that's all. I know they find you attractive. Don't get all caught up on hair and complexion. That's a bunch of bull."

"I'm tellin' y'all, they don't like dark-skinned girls with natural hair. They don't even notice me."

I'm getting upset. "I had no idea this was going on. Erika you're beautiful and you know it."

"I do know it, but the black guys can't see it 'cause they're too busy running behind the pale girls at school. I hate living here."

"Don't say that."

I never knew Erika felt this way. I give her a big hug because she needs it. She's so pitiful. My head turns to the side slightly when I hug her. I notice an unopened box of sanitary napkins next to her bed under the nightstand. My mind takes me back to the day about two months ago when I purchased them at Wal-Mart. I clearly remember Erika telling me that she was completely out of pads.

"Serena, can you excuse us for a second?"

"What's up?"

"Erika and I need a mother-daughter moment."

"Don't treat me like that. I'm her aunt."

"Serena, please. This is serious."

Serena senses the urgency in my voice and she leaves without saying another word. I get up and close the bedroom door behind her.

"I'm really upset with you right now. We talk about everything under the sun and now I feel like I'm looking at a stranger. What's really going on?"

"I'm sorry about all that stuff I said. Maybe the black guys at school aren't that bad. It's probably just me in general. I speak proper English and can be kind of bourgie at times. They probably can't relate to me."

"Cut it out! I don't have time for your little act. I figured you out. When were you going to tell me that you were pregnant?"

"Huh? I don't know what you're talking about. I'm not pregnant. Do I look pregnant? I might be putting on a little weight, but I'm definitely not pregnant."

"Stop lying to me. The door is shut and nobody else is here. You're different now. I can tell that you're hiding something. I told you a long time ago that you could always come to me and talk about anything."

Erika's eyes begin to tear. "I'm not pregnant . . . anymore. I had an abortion yesterday."

"Oh God!"

We embrace. Erika breaks down. She starts boohooing and crying like a baby. I've never seen this child like this before.

"Was Brad the one?"

"Yeah. He paid for everything."

"So there wasn't really a party in Reidsville, was there?"

"No, I made that up."

"Does that mean C.J. knew about this?"

"Yeah, one of my big-mouthed friends must have told him and I know he opened his big mouth and told you. I hate him because he promised not to tell you or Daddy. The last thing I ever wanted to do was to hurt the two if you. I'm so sorry. Now Daddy's gonna kill me for sure."

The tears flow from Erika's eyes harder than ever. Fear sets in as she thinks about Craig.

"Your daddy doesn't know about what happened and C.J. did keep his promise. I swear he didn't tell me anything. I figured it out on my own."

"How?"

"I'm not as old or as out of touch as you might think. Sometimes mommas have extra-special ways of figuring things out."

I pick up the unopened box of sanitary napkins and hold it right in front of her face.

"Good grief. I never thought about that."

"See, you told on yourself. C.J. kept your secret."

"Really. He did that for me?"

"Yeah, he came in here this morning, trying to act normal, looking all crazy." Things start to add up—C.J. wasn't at a party last night. "Oh my God, he had mud on his boots."

"Huh?"

"Did you even see C.J. last night?"

"I saw him early in the evening, but after that I was resting up at Brad's house for the rest of the night. Why'd you ask that? What's wrong with C.J.?"

"Nothing. Did you know that Ginger was missing?"

"Yeah."

"Please don't tell me that C.J. told you she was missing."

"Yeah, he told me yesterday. Why?"

"No reason."

"He's been trying to get back with Ginger for the past couple of weeks, but she was still seeing that other guy named Kevin or something like that."

I jump up and head out the door.

"What's wrong? Where are you going?"

"I need to ask your brother something."

I knock at C.J.'s bedroom door and there's no answer. I turn the knob. When the door opens, all I see is an empty bedroom. He's nowhere to be found.

24

Naomi

It's 11:45 in the morning and humid as ever outside. Feels like summer is here for real. I've got my car's AC blasting. This is one of those hot days where you can see the heat waves dancing in the middle of the road. Days like this makes everybody wanna stay inside and keep cool the best way they know how.

I'm on my way to Brian's garage. I keep asking myself what I'm doing, and why? The only answer I can come up with is simply having a good time because I deserve it. I'm having a good time and all, but in the meantime my life and everything in it is spiraling out of control. I'm dazed. I need to get a grip. Problem is, I don't know how to get a grip anymore. Feels like I'm eighteen again and this whole experience with Brian is overwhelming. For the first time in my life I'm starting to realize that I got married too young. And for the one-millionth time I'm reminded that I married the wrong man.

Erika and C.J.'s problems are taking a toll on me. And I still don't have a clue as to who killed our dog, or why. Nothing seems real except when I'm with Brian. He's the only thing I want to be real in life. That's nothing more than me trying to escape my problems. The kids aren't my problem right now. They're damn near grown and need to do their own problem-solving for a change. I just hope Morgan is okay.

When I pull up to Brian's garage I notice his green Ford Explorer and his tow truck parked outside. I begin to realize how many times I've driven past this place and never gave it an ounce of thought. Never thought about the building or the people who worked here. This garage had no meaning in my life whatsoever, and now I'm overjoyed to be here. At this moment it's a welcome sight—a place of refuge.

I feel like I'm being watched closely by someone as I approach the entrance. The fact that I'm excited about seeing Brian chases all my paranoid feelings away. I don't care who sees me. Being with Brian is the only thing that matters to me right now. My heart is beating fast and I even have butterflies in my stomach.

I must look so out of place among all these old broken-down cars and pickup trucks. The garage is dusty and smells like motor oil and old tires. I'm careful where I step because there are grease spots and puddles of antifreeze everywhere. If it weren't for sunlight streaming in through the windows and doorways, the inside of this place would be extremely dark. The only light I see is one of those hanging worklights up under the hood of a car. A noisy, large shop fan circulates hot stinky air all around.

A voice comes out of nowhere. "Can I help you, ma'am?"

"Oh, hi—you scared me. I didn't see you down there."

An older guy, some little grease monkey wearing a navy blue uniform shirt similar to the one Brian wore last night, slides out from under a car.

"Sorry, ma'am. Didn't mean to scare you. I was just down here doing some transmission work."

"I didn't mean to disturb you, but I'm here to see Brian. He's supposed to put my wheel back on for me today."

He laughs and wipes his hands with a rag. "I think he's gonna have me put that wheel back on for you. He doesn't do stuff like that around here. That's what he's got me for. I'm Otis."

Caution. A yellow warning flag goes up in my mind. Otis is being nosy. I know how people in Eden operate. If he thinks I'm about to tell him my name, he must be crazy. He'll be on the phone within minutes, asking everybody he knows about me. Hell no!

"How are you, Mr. Otis? Is Brian around?"

"Sure is. I'm doing fine, thanks for asking. Let me get him for you."

Mr. Otis stands up, turns around, and instead of going to get Brian, he yells out with everything he's got, "Hey, Brian! Brian! There's a lady out here to see ya!"

I laugh out loud and say, "Thank you."

"You're welcome, darling." He looks at me closely. "You any kin to Ms. Louise?"

"No, I don't think so. But around here, I mean, in a small town like this, it's hard to tell."

"Ain't that the truth? You look like some of her kinfolk."

I don't know what to say. "Oh, okay."

Brian yells, "What is it, Otis?" He peeks his head out of his office and sees me. His whole expression changes and so does mine. "Hey, Naomi!"

I wish he hadn't said my name, but it's too late to worry about that now. "Hey, Brian. What's up?"

"You can come on in."

"Thanks, Mr. Otis. I'll talk to you in a minute."

Mr. Otis continues wiping his dirty hands with his rag. "Uh-huh. Nice meetin' ya."

I feel his perverted eyes watching my ass all the way to Brian's office.

Brian closes his door as soon as I enter his office. He greets me with a hug and tongues me down.

"I'm so glad to see you."

"Me too. I haven't stopped thinking about you and that full-body workout you gave me last night."

"Was it good?"

"Yeah. It was extra good."

"I enjoyed you too. You felt too good to me. I was losing it. Had me all messed up. Can't wait to do you again."

"Neither can I."

"You don't have to wait. You're welcome to this anytime you want some."

"Umm. I like the sound of that. I've got a surprise for you."

"I'm ready."

I turn around and slide my jeans down, revealing my ass in this black silk Victoria's Secret thong.

"Damn, you're lookin' good. Aw man, look at you and your sexy-ass self."

Brian palms my ass with both hands, making it jiggle and bounce a bit. He kisses it. The next thing I know he has me bent over his desk and slides the little piece of material between my cheeks to the side. He starts doing that thing he does so well with his tongue again. It's inside. Feels so good that he has me gasping for air. Within a few minutes he reintroduces me to his big ole country dick.

For some reason, I feel like Mr. Otis might be outside the door getting his thrills. The noise from office's window air-conditioner drowns out most of my moans. All of sudden I don't care because I'm getting *my* thrills. Right now I don't care about anything—C.J.'s problems, Erika's problems, or the dead dog. I call this rejuvenation at its finest.

Brian turns me around and puts me on top of his desk. He gets between my legs, wraps them around him and goes to work. It starts getting real good to him because he picks me up in the air. This is like climbing a big, tall tree and riding one of its strongest branches.

About a half an hour later Brian and I are laid out, cuddling on an old black vinyl sofa that I usually wouldn't even consider sitting on, but since I'm with him that makes it okay.

Brian says, "I like this pace."

"So do I. You think we can keep on having sex every day just like this?"

"I dunno, but I sure hope so."

"We might have to slow up a bit 'cause we might get caught."

"I'm prepared for that. You know, I've already given it a bunch of thought and I figure it's worth it."

"Me too, but I'm still kinda scared. I think I have more to lose than you."

"True, but I'm here for you and willing to take the risk. You know I ain't lying. Remember, you didn't even think I'd know your name today, Miss Naomi."

"That's right. You proved me wrong. Do you think Mr. Otis suspects we're doing something in here?"

"Yeah, but don't worry. Otis would never run his mouth. He knows how to mind his own business."

"I don't trust him, but if you say so." I look up at Brian's dusty clock. "Ooh, look at the time. I need to run home and check in real quick."

"You think we can meet up later at my house?"

"I'll try my best."

"How does eight o'clock sound?"

"Sounds like a plan."

Brian and I get ourselves freshened up at his sink. Before we're done there's a knock at the office door. It scares the living shit out of me because both our pants are still off. I can't move or feel my heart-beat.

Brian scrambles around to get his pants. "Yeah, what is it?"

Otis says, "It's me. There's someone out here to see you or the lady who owns the Camry."

My life begins to flash before my eyes. I think of how I'm going to explain this to Craig because I know he's out there steaming mad and he has every right to be.

"Okay, we'll be right out."

Otis asks, "You want me to put that tire on for the lady right quick?"

"Yeah, go right ahead and do that." Brian looks over at me and asks, "You okay?"

"No, I'm not. I'm scared to death. I think my husband is out there."

"Really? Don't worry. He won't think nothing of this."

"You obviously don't know my husband. He's a nut. He'll know some-thing's up the moment he sees how attractive you are. He's knows the type of men I like."

"Well, you need to get your jeans on because one of us has to go out there first."

"You go first and then come back and tell me who it is."

"Since we're in this together, why don't we go out at the same time?"

"I love how brave you are. I'll just go out first, then you count to one hundred before you show your face."

"That'll work."

We kiss.

After getting dressed and checking myself very closely in the mir-ror, I decide to step out of Brian's office.

I'm not really scared anymore because I know Brian will protect me from Craig if he decides to get physical. As I walk out I see Serena smiling from ear to ear.

"So, now I see what you've been up to. Is this where he works?"

"Who are you talking about?"

"Your boyfriend. Can I meet him?"

"I don't know what you're talkin' 'bout? I'm here getting my wheel put back on."

"That's not the only thing you're gettin' on." Serena's eyes widen. "Oh my God, is that him?"

"Who? Where?"

When I turn around I see Brian walking toward me looking all buff, flexing his muscles in a brand new fresh white tank top.

"Hi, I'm Brian, the owner. Did someone ask to see me?"

"I did. How are you?"

"Fine."

"As hell . . . I'm Serena, Naomi's younger sister. You're the tow truck guy."

Brian gives Serena my special smile. "Yeah, I am the tow truck guy. Naomi's sister, huh? Nice to meet you. Is there something I can help you with?"

"I don't know yet."

I say a quick, "No!"

"Brian, how would you like to take me and Naomi out for lunch."

He looks at me. "I'd love to, but your sister looks like she isn't interested."

"Too bad. I know the three of us could have a ball together. Maybe another time."

"Yeah, maybe. You never know."

"Excuse us a for minute, Brian." I pull Serena aside. "What are you doing?"

Serena says, "Nothing. I noticed your car and decided to holla at you. Next time, don't park your car in such an obvious spot. It could have been Craig driving by."

"Next time, mind your own business and don't follow me around, especially when I'm not doing anything wrong. I knew somebody was watching me."

"Guilty."

"I said I was getting my car worked on. You see that man over there putting my wheel back on?"

"All I see is Brian. I like him . . . much . . . much better than Craig."

"What?" I mouth the words, *I hate you. Go home.*

Serena knows me too well. We're beginning to think and act alike—well, almost.

About ten minutes later, Mr. Otis and his slow-behind self has my wheel back on. Serena finally leaves. After a scare like that, Brian and I decide to say our good-byes and save some of our passion for later.

25

Naomi

Before I get into my Camry I look back over at Brian. He gives me his special smile that I'm starting to love and waves at me one last time. It's hard to say 'bye to him.

As I'm about to pull out onto the road, I stop for a passing vehicle, a white van. My stomach drops and my heart begins to pound. The white van from last night drives past me real fast. Glad it kept on going. The driver's face was a blur, but I could tell he looked in my direction. That was scary.

I might be overreacting, considering the fact that there must be a bunch of white vans like that one riding around in this area. By now the local news should have broadcasted a description of that stupid van. I'm sure the police are busy searching for Pat's van, and there's no way in the world he'd be driving around in broad daylight on a busy street like this, trying to abduct somebody. This van looked newer, unlike the older and dirtier-looking torture chamber on wheels from last night. After a few seconds I dismiss the whole thing and just go about my business.

I was at Brian's garage a lot longer than I'd originally planned, so that means I need to come up with a quick alibi.

I'm on my way to my in-laws' grocery store to pick up a few things. This way I can kill two birds with one stone. This counts as an alibi and a long overdue visit. I like shopping at their store, anyway. And at the same time I'm keeping the money in the family. No need to give Food Lion and Winn-Dixie all of my cash. My in-laws' grocery store is just a few miles from here.

When I pull up to the Draper Grocery Store I notice Craig's Bronco parked out front. The store is located right between Knott's Landing and the barbershop. The parking lot is a mess. It's made up of a mixture of dirt, gravel, potholes, and puddles. Right away I see this mildly retarded girl I've known all my life named Pee Wee standing under a green awning, sweeping around the outside of the store. I haven't seen this girl in a long time. Pee Wee is a big-boned girl who looks to be at least six feet tall and well over three hundred pounds now. She's still as knock-kneed and slow-footed as ever. Pee Wee's momma kind of gave up on her back when we were little and sent that poor girl away to special schools for years so she could learn to be independent and live on her own.

Pee Wee continues sweeping and never notices me walk up behind her. "Hey, Pee Wee. How you been? You remember me?"

"Huh?" Pee Wee sounds like she has sinus problems. She stops sweeping and turns around. She looks at me for a couple of seconds, drops the broom, and then puts her hands up to her mouth. With a surprised look she says, "Hey, Nay. I 'member you."

Pee Wee claps her hands a few times and jumps up and down. She charges toward me and wraps her arms around me real tight.

She asks, "How you doing?"

I smile and say, "Fine, and you?"

Pee Wee grabs me by the hand and leads me through the store's front door. "Look who's here, everybody!"

"Mommy!" Morgan is sitting on a brown metal folding chair next to her daddy, eating a Popsicle. She runs over and gives me a hug.

Craig goes, "Hey, baby."

I kiss Craig and then take in the smells of cardboard boxes, fresh fruit, and brand-new money.

I say a general, "Hey, everybody!"

A couple of customers greet me on their way out of the store.

Craig's daddy is at the register. He looks up and says, "Hey there, pretty lady. How you doing today?

"Hey, Mr. Maynard—I'm doing just fine. How you doing?"

He comes from around the counter and gives me a kiss on the cheek. "My back and my knees is killing me, but I'm making it. No use in complaining 'cause it don't do any good no-how."

"Well, just keep doing the best you can and everything will come together."

"See, that's what I like about you, Naomi. Always got something good to say, a real positive young lady. Craig is a lucky man."

Craig shakes his head and laughs. "I know, Daddy. You remind me each and every time you see Naomi."

Craig's momma comes out from the back office with an old-fashioned feather duster in one hand and a pricing gun in the other. She looks directly at me, twists her lips up, and says, "Well, look what the wind done blew in. We ain't seen you in a month of Sundays, girl. Maynard and Pee Wee is out here acting like we're being visited by royalty or something."

Pee Wee looks uncomfortable. "I'm going back outside to sweep."

"Hey, Miss Georgia."

She frowns, twisting her lips worse than before. "Naomi."

"Sorry I haven't been by here to visit."

She does that talk-to-the-hand thing. "Uh-huh. Whatever you say, chile."

"Momma, don't be mean to Naomi like that."

"You shut your mouth, boy, 'cause nobody was talking to you."

Mr. Maynard cuts in, "Georgia, you need to stop. I swear to goodness, our son is a lucky man. Just look at her. Naomi gets prettier and prettier every time I see her."

"Now don't go messing with that chile's head, telling her stuff like that. There ain't nothing worse than a conceited high-yellow woman."

I should be offended, but I'm not. "It's okay, Mr. Maynard. Miss Georgia is right, but I won't let nothing go to my head 'cause I don't consider myself high-yellow or conceited. I'm just a tad lighter than you, Miss Georgia."

"Momma, you're wrong for saying stuff like that to Naomi. Everybody's hating on my wife, even my momma."

"Gimme a break." She turns toward her husband. "Maynard, you don't get all excited 'bout me and tell me stuff like that no more."

"That ain't true. I said you were pretty this morning. Am I lying?"

"Yeah!"

Mr. Maynard laughs. "C'mere Gee-gee. Get over here with your pretty little brown self and give me some sugar."

Miss Georgia starts blushing as Mr. Maynard kisses her on her face and neck. She just eats it up. They eventually stop as a group of kids enter the store, looking to buy some of their favorite candies, chips, and pop.

Morgan says, "I hate when Grandma and Granddad act like that."

Craig says, "That's a good thing. Just means they still love each other."

I tap Craig on the shoulder. "I can't stand your momma. Why does she have to be like that toward me?"

"You know I don't like to be caught in the middle between you and her."

"She just hates when somebody says I'm pretty. Your momma burns me up, making fun of my complexion and calling me high-yellow. Why do we discriminate against ourselves like that?"

"Girl, you know good and well nothing's ever gonna change with black people. You read that Willie Lynch letter before. Whitey taught us to hate ourselves like that."

"Daddy, who's whitey?"

I say, "Don't worry about that, Morgan."

"That's right, Lil' Momma, you'll find out exactly what we're talking 'bout sooner or later."

"Enough of that kinda talk. Why is my friend out there sweeping? Hope y'all ain't taking advantage of her."

"Momma and Daddy are just giving Pee Wee something to do while she's here visiting for the next week or so. You know they'll pay her for helping out. Earlier they had her moving boxes and helping to stock the shelves. She's strong as an ox, but as awkward and clumsy as can be."

Craig and Morgan laugh.

"You should've seen her, Momma."

"Don't make fun of her. That ain't right."

"We know. Momma Pearl and Sister Clarissa are supposed to come by here any minute to pick her up. They're taking Pee Wee over to see the new church. They got it all decorated for their first service tomorrow morning."

"I hope I'm not here when my aunts arrive. I just stopped by to pick up a few things, then head back home."

"Just tell me what we need and I'll bring it home. I stopped by here to pick up Lil' Momma, then Momma and Daddy said they wanted to talk to me about something real quick."

"I'll stick around for a few minutes."

"Good." Craig looks toward his momma and daddy. "Y'all ready to talk to me?"

Mr. Maynard says, "Yeah. Give me a second to finish ringing these kids up."

Miss Georgia comes back over to us. "We need to talk to you and Naomi. I guess it's time I started treating her right."

"Oh, it's okay. I'm used to how you treat me. I mean, it's been like this for over eleven years. I wouldn't know how to take it if you changed now."

"Don't mess it up, girl. I'm trying."

"I was just playing. I know you love me."

The last group of customers leave the store. We all sit down on the brown metal folding chairs up front, except for Craig. He decides to sit on top of this big long white freezer filled with ice cream and frozen foods.

Mr. Maynard and Miss Georgia hit us with some shocking news. They've purchased a new home in a retirement community near Orlando, Florida, and plan to move there by the end of summer. Craig's facial expression changed as soon as they mentioned something about moving away from Eden. He becomes livid because they made him promise to raise his family here and always remain in Eden. Their news is like a big slap in the face.

Mr. Maynard says, "Calm down, Craig. I know exactly where you're coming from."

"No, you don't."

"Trust me, we do. Your momma and I promise not to leave you high and dry. We want you and Naomi to take over this store and keep the family business going."

"I can't believe this."

Miss Georgia says, "It's just that things are changing for the worse here and we're getting up in age. We need to get away while we still can. I'm afraid in this store. All I hear about night after night is how somebody's missing, somebody's house has been robbed, this one has gotten murdered and that one shot the other one, or somebody done overdosed on drugs. Somebody just got shot the other night in those apartments over there on Georgia Avenue. This ain't the same Eden we're used to. Can you understand where we're coming from now?"

"You can't let a few bad apples spoil the bunch or run you away," Craig insists.

Miss Georgia says, "I'm sorry, but we have to get away. You can make a lot of money here. This is pretty much all the people around here have, especially the ones who don't have a car."

Mr. Maynard says, "You can be your own boss."

Craig begins to soften a bit. "That's true. And I do need more income and all, but I never imagined y'all leaving here."

"We know. Sleep on it, son. Your momma and I don't expect an answer right now."

Miss Georgia asks, "What do you think, Naomi?"

"I think it sounds like a good thing for all of us. Then C.J. and Erika could even help out around here."

"Me, too."

"Hold up now. Lil' Momma, what I tell you 'bout being in grown folks' conversations? Grab another Popsicle and go in the back office and watch TV till we're done talking."

Craig slides his butt over so Morgan can open the freezer door. She grabs herself another Popsicle and heads to the back office.

I say, "I'm gonna miss y'all. Wish all of us were getting away from here and going to Florida together."

Miss Georgia says, "Y'all can come down and visit us any time you'd like."

"Everybody looks so sad now. I'm gonna head on home and do some laundry or something. Craig, I just need you to bring home a couple boxes of cereal, a gallon of milk, a loaf of bread, and a dozen eggs. I'll see you and Morgan at the house."

"All right, baby."

I give Miss Georgia and Mr. Maynard hugs and kisses as if they're leaving for Florida right now.

A blue church van with light blue lettering on both sides pulls up to the store as I head out the front door. The first person I notice is my Aunt Clarissa, and then I make eye contact with the woman on the passenger side. This is my first time in years coming face-to-face with Momma Pearl and Aunt Clarissa.

My anxiety rises to an all-time high. I wish I could turn around, but it's too late now.

26

Naomi

Feels like I wanna run and hide. Then I'm reminded that I'm a grown woman who knows how to defend herself. I can use the common sense God gave me and if that doesn't work, I can always use my hands. So, bring it on!

My aunts greet me with so many hugs and kisses that it's sickening. They're treating me so nice that it makes me confused. Momma Pearl smiles at me and so does Aunt Clarissa. I'm forced to stand back and take a good look at these two. Not much has changed. They're still dressed in white cloth gowns with head wraps made from the same material. All of sudden I notice that a lot *has* changed. I look at their faces and deep into their eyes, searching their souls. The evil appears to be gone. They're noticeably different to me and I'm sure others have noticed their changes as well. The weathered faces with hard lines and angry wrinkles have faded. Their faces are smooth and relaxed, frowns replaced by joyous smiles. Now they remind me of decent women. Momma Pearl looks like Whoopi Goldberg and Aunt Clarissa looks like Loretta Devine. They almost make me smile, but I don't. Instead, I see a reflection of myself in their glossy eyes and realize that they can see the look of confusion plastered all over my face.

Aunt Clarissa says, "God is good, ain't he, chile?"

"Yes, ma'am. He sure is good."

Aunt Clarissa says, "We went and visited our brother today and prayed with him."

"Daddy?"

Momma Pearl adds, "Yes, your daddy. He asked about you, but we didn't have anything to tell him 'cause we never see you anymore."

"How's he doing?" I ask.

"He's sad as usual, but, praise God, we were able to lift his spirits."

"I'm glad."

Aunt Clarissa asks, "Can you go visit your daddy to let him know he's not alone in this world? He's so pitiful."

"I'll try to go see him soon."

Momma Pearl says, "Don't wait too long 'cause tomorrow's not promised to any of us. It would do his heart good if at least one of his daughters cared enough to visit him."

"We do care about him, but it's hard to go there and sit all that time. You wouldn't understand. Plus, we refuse to take our kids into a prison."

"I understand what you mean, but he needs y'all. I'm gonna head over there and talk to Pee Wee right quick. I'll give you and Momma Pearl a minute or so to talk. I'm so happy and excited to see you Naomi. Praise God." Aunt Clarissa pulls us all together for a group hug. "Now all we need is Serena to make this reunion complete. How is she?"

"She's doing fine."

"Tell her that I asked about her and let her know that she's always in my prayers."

"I sure will," I say politely.

"Go 'head and talk to Momma Pearl. I'm sure she has a lot to discuss with you."

As cars drive by, people blow their horns and shout greetings to their beloved Momma Pearl. People on foot greet her with smiles, hugs, and well-wishes. Incredible. These people have a glow in their eyes when they look at her. Momma Pearl is a celebrity. They greet her with the kind of love and respect people have for a great religious leader like T.D. Jakes. I remember a time when people looked down on female preachers and now they love this one to death.

I don't know her, not this side of Momma Pearl. She has finally achieved the position in this community she's worked toward for so long. Holy woman. Inspirational spiritual leader. Matriarch of the family and black community of Eden. I wonder what happened.

Within seconds my mind is flooded by memories of her evil ways, all the name-calling and unjustified beatings she gave me and Serena. I can't forgive or forget. It's just too much.

Momma Pearl says, "Naomi. What is it? What's on your mind?"

"Nothing."

"Something is troubling you. I know you so well. Let the past go. I'm different now. You can see it. I know you can. You can see it with your eyes and feel it with your heart. I am different now."

"Don't tell me what I see and feel," I argue. "You don't know what I feel in my heart. You have no idea. You've never been in my position."

"But I *have* been. My momma took her frustrations out on me for years. I swore I'd never be the same way. That's probably why I never had kids of my own. Then you and Serena came into my life. I'm so sorry for how I treated y'all. Believe me when I tell you, I've paid for all my sins. I asked God to wash them away and now I'm as pure as this white gown. I've got a clean slate . . . praise God. I've been redeemed in the eyes of the Lord. I know that I've done wrong in the past. All I ask is that you let go of all of your bitterness and forgive me."

"I can't."

"Oh, I serve a merciful and forgiving God and if He can forgive me, why can't you?"

"Because I'm not God."

"But you are. He's in all of us, chile. I can teach you so much. Pray to God for forgiveness and you will forgive me. Do you think I'm worthy of your forgiveness?"

"No."

"God has filled me with a joy that's so fresh and new. This feeling doesn't fade and I want you to feel it, too."

"Thank you, but I have no interest in what you're doing. There's no way a person like you could change. You've got everybody else around here fooled, but not me and Serena. We know the real Momma Pearl."

"I'm not your enemy. I love you, Naomi . . . always have." Her eyes begin to tear. "There was a time when I couldn't cry, but now I can let go. I was your momma when you lost yours. God knows I meant well. I took you into my home and cared for you and your sister the best way I knew how. If you see me as your enemy, then love your enemy.

Love me. That's all I ask. We're all sinners, including you." She takes me by the hand. "Judge not and you shall not be judged . . . condemn not and you shall not be condemned . . . forgive and you shall be forgiven. Blessed are the merciful, for they shall obtain mercy. Blessed are the peacemakers, for they shall be called the children of God."

My eyes begin to tear now because I can feel something powerful move from her body throughout my entire body. But still I'm resistant to her message. "Don't preach to me, because I'm not one of your followers."

Momma Pearl smiles. "I'm done for now, but I won't give up on you, Naomi. I want you to be part of what I'm doing for this community. Will you come to our new temple sometime tomorrow? We have three services—eight, eleven, and three-thirty. Can I count on you to be there?"

"I doubt it. I doubt it very seriously."

"I hope you and your family can be there so you can see what I'm all about now. Naomi, you've just inspired me to do a new sermon tomorrow." She looks at me and I'm still unmoved. "Look at you, chile. You've got a good heart and God's spirit is in there somewhere. Do you remember when I helped you let Him in there when you were younger?"

"Yeah, I remember."

"The spirit is still there and where the spirit is, there is no room for hatred or bitterness. If your heart is broken, the spirit will help mend and make it whole again. Let me help Him help you. I love you, Naomi."

"I love you, too," I mumbled and left.

27

Naomi

I just walked in the house. Within seconds something tells me to check out C.J.'s bedroom to see if he made it back home. Hopefully he's in there and Craig won't even notice that he left. If Craig comes home and that boy ain't here, there'll be hell to pay.

C.J.'s bedroom is as empty as it was a few hours ago. I stand in his doorway for a couple of seconds, looking around his room. Then I'm reminded that I'm his stepmom and I have the right to search his room. I'm curious and want to take a closer look to see exactly what C.J. has really been up to. I can't stand how secretive he's become lately.

As soon as I step inside the bedroom a musty odor attacks my nose from every angle. I glance around quickly. C.J. has the nerve to have a bottle of Febreze Fabric Refresher and a bottle of Febreze Air Effects on his nightstand. Either he hasn't used any of the Febreze or the funk in here is just so powerful that it overcame both types of deodorizers. Guess you can only disguise funk for so long. I try teaching these kids that I can't do it all around here. I'm nobody's maid. Eventually they'll have to do something about cleaning up. They don't even make an effort to clean their damn bedrooms.

This room is a mess. Don't know why I didn't notice it earlier. The bed is unmade. Cups, bowls, and silverware are on the nightstand. An empty two-liter Coke bottle is sticking out from under his bed. I'm stepping over tennis shoes and Timberland boots. Clothes are on the floor, marking the exact spot where C.J. stood when he took them off. His hamper is empty because his dirty clothes are everywhere except where they belong. He's just plain sorry.

C.J. has a collection of *Jet* magazine's Beauty of the Week pictures on his wall. That's a hobby he got from his father. Craig admitted to doing the same silly thing when he was a teenager.

For some reason I'm nervous being in here, snooping around like this. I'm definitely violating C.J.'s privacy. Regardless, the search goes on. Among the tons of PlayStation 3 games I notice two African-American porno DVDs. I pick them up and study both covers for a few seconds. A freaky-deaky mess. I put them back, even though I am kind of tempted to confiscate at least one of them and view the evidence more closely.

I kneel down, lift his mattress, and find two *Playboy* magazines and a letter from Ginger. The envelope is already open. Looks like she mailed this to C.J. a little over four months ago. The letter reads:

Dear C.J.,

You know that we've been together for a while (four long years) and we've grown as individuals. But unfortunately we've failed to grow as a couple. I hope you understand how messed up that is. I've given this so much thought and I hate to break it to you like this in the form of a letter. I wanted to do this in person and I tried a bunch of times, but you always have a way of changing my words or totally misunderstanding or ignoring my point. This way there's no way you can misunderstand that I NEED TO BREAK UP WITH YOU. I need time to think. I need time for myself. I feel so trapped with you. You're cool and all, but most times I know we don't see eye to eye. I like to go to parties, shop, and meet new people, but all you want is for us to be alone and have sex all the time. For some reason you don't care or don't believe that there's more to life than having sex. You need time to discover new things. I know I was your first real girlfriend, but you will have others. It's not hard for me to let go, even though it will probably be hard for you. Just believe me when I say that IT'S OVER BETWEEN US. WE'RE TOO DIFFERENT.

At first I thought we just needed time apart, but now I know for a fact that it's best that we go our separate ways. And I know you're probably thinking that we can remain friends. NO, WE CAN'T. WE CAN'T BE

FRIENDS OR ANYTHING ELSE. AGAIN, IT'S OVER. Being friends will do more damage than good. I did have feelings for you a long time ago, but I know for a fact that I WAS NEVER IN LOVE WITH YOU. I'm not being mean, just being real with you. Sorry I can't go to the Senior Prom with you. Please respect my feelings and believe that this breakup has nothing to do with Kevin, I swear.

Thanks for finally giving me my school ring back. Have a good life.
—Ginger

P.S. You're not the weirdo everybody around here says you are.

There are tiny, circular impressions in the paper where I imagined C.J.'s tears must have fallen while reading Ginger's letter. No wonder he was so emotionless about her disappearance. She still doesn't deserve to be out there missing like that, and I pray to God that she's returned safely to her family.

In some ways I can relate to what Ginger was saying to C.J. about feeling trapped and about him ignoring or not understanding her point. I guess, like father, like son. It's sad, but that's how genetics work.

I open C.J.'s underwear drawer. Nothing interesting inside, except a bunch of assorted condoms. I fish around inside the drawer and come across a ring, Ginger's school ring. Uh-oh!

Out of nowhere a voice asks, "What are you doing?"

It's C.J., looking a little disturbed by the fact that I'm in his bedroom going through his personal things.

"Oh my God. Where'd you come from? You scared the life outta me."

"C'mon, Momma. Is this what you do when you think I'm not home? I was in the rec room. Why are you going through my stuff?"

"'Cause I'm your momma and I can. I should be asking why you have Ginger's school ring hidden in your drawer?"

"It wasn't hidden. She gave it to me the last time I saw her. Guess she wanted me to have something to remember her by."

"Do you know where Ginger is?"

"No."

"Have a seat on the bed 'cause we really need to talk."

C.J. takes a seat on the bed. "What's up?"

"Why are you acting so different? What happened to your eye?"

"I got into a fight with Ginger's boyfriend, Kevin. I had to step out of the house for a minute and go straighten him out."

"What was that about?"

"He was spreading rumors that I had something to do with Ginger's disappearance. But I didn't."

"So did you straighten him out? What I'm asking is, did you win the fight?"

"It was a tie."

"Looks and sounds like you lost."

"Nah, it was a tough one though. You should see his face."

"I need to know where you were last night and I don't want to hear that lie about a party in Reidsville again. I know there wasn't a party and I know all about Erika and Brad's situation. I hate to think about her getting pregnant and getting an abortion."

"Did she tell you that? 'Cause the first thing she probably thought was that I told on her. "

"She did think that, but I figured it out on my own. Enough about Erika—the focus is on you now. Where were you last night?"

"It really was a party in Reidsville. I couldn't go because the police picked me and Kevin up for questioning and held us all night. I know he told them all kinds of lies about me. I told the police that I was a minor and they needed to contact one of my parents. One of the policemen told me that they didn't have to do shit. They were going to run things the way they wanted and they did. That's why I was so mad when I came home this morning. Just hearing Daddy mention Ginger's name made me even madder."

"What about the mud on your boots?"

"I was walking down the road and had to step over in the mud every time a truck passed by. I hope you don't think I have anything to do with Ginger's disappearance. I love her and I'd never do anything to hurt her."

"I found that letter under your bed. And it's strange to me that you have her ring back."

"She told me that I could have it last week. That was the last time I saw her."

"All I'm saying is that you know what happened to my daddy," I explain. "I'm not trying to see someone else I know and love become a victim of southern justice."

"That won't happen to me."

"It can. All they need is someone believable to pin this on. Then they'll design a jury to put your butt away for a long time. You might be young, but you're not invincible."

He is silent for a moment. "I can't believe this. Since you first came into my life I've called you my momma because I felt close to you. You're the only person I can really talk to. I always felt like you believed in me more so than Daddy. He goes all crazy whenever I come to him with problems. Sometimes I feel like he's against me."

"He's not."

"I dunno. You've always been here for me. I've never lied to you except to protect Erika. All of a sudden Erika came to me in need of help and I couldn't let my little sister down, even though she gets on my nerves. All I'm saying is . . . please don't go against me now because of one lie. Believe me when I say that I didn't have nothing to do with Ginger's disappearance. I have no idea where she is. The police let me go because they knew that I was innocent. I *am* innocent."

"I never said you had anything to do with Ginger's disappearance. Things just look a little suspicious, that's all. I believe you. I don't know what else to say."

"I'm trying hard to make everybody proud of me for a change. I'm gonna walk across that stage Saturday morning. I'm proud of myself regardless of whether anybody else is. Everybody's against me. Sometimes I feel like I was meant to finish last in everything I do."

"That's not true. I'm really proud of you and I tell you almost every day. You have to learn to abide by your daddy's rules, that all. When he says stay in this room, he means it. When he says work hard so you can go to college, he means it. When he says he wants the best for you, he means it."

"He expects too much."

"No, he expects you to be better than he is. He doesn't want you going to work every day at the Mill, breaking your back like he did. Your dad wants you to be some type of professional. He always says he has to raise the bar for the next generation. He wants you to be the best."

"I'm trying. I just need to refocus my attention and stop letting Ginger distract me. I love her and I hope she's all right. I've been worried sick. I can't even cry anymore 'cause I'm all out of tears. It hurts when you love somebody so much and they don't even want to be around you. She probably gave me that ring back so I could get out of her face."

"Stop being so hard on yourself. Relax, and before you know it someone better will come into your life."

"Seriously, though, all I want is Ginger. We just seem to go together perfectly—she's the right fit for me."

"Stop it! Now I'm starting to see what she was talking about in that letter. Let it go. You need to just get her out of your system."

"It's even harder now because I'm seeing her name and face everywhere."

I sighed. "I think you might need professional help to get over her. You remind me of this girl I met when I was in therapy. She lost her mind over this guy who broke up with her. Is that how you wanna be?"

"No. I'm not that bad, am I?"

"I think so. You're like a time bomb waiting to explode. I love you and that's why I'm being honest with you."

"Thanks. I'm gonna work on it."

"And I'm gonna work on getting you off of punishment." I hear Craig and Morgan enter the house. "I'm gonna go work on it right now."

C.J. hugs me and says, "I don't know what I'd do without you."

28

Naomi

I take about ten minutes pleading C.J.'s case to Craig. I try my best to get him off the hook. At the same time I also try my best not to mention anything about Erika's situation. Before I started talking to Craig I went to Erika's bedroom to tell her that she would be punished until further notice. She was so out of it that all she said was a simple, "Okay."

Erika is an emotional wreck. Now I think the seriousness of what she did to herself is starting to sink in. I take a moment to console her the best way I know how. Then I'm back out to the family room to finish pleading C.J.'s case. Feels like I'm being pulled in every direction and trying to be everything to everybody at the same time.

After explaining to Craig that C.J. was at the police station all night being harassed, he decides to let him off punishment.

I take a moment to talk with Morgan until I'm interrupted by the telephone ringing. Craig ignores the phone and C.J. and Erika are too busy having miniature nervous breakdowns to even notice. This family is falling apart. It's my job to keep us together. I look at the clock and realize that I'm due at Brian's house in a couple of hours.

I pick up the phone. "Hello."

A white woman on the other line goes, "Is this Naomi Goode?"

"Yes, but my last name is Gaffney now. What can I do for you?"

"Sorry, Mrs. Gaffney. My name is Joanne Green and I'm Miss Magnolia Wilson's nurse. Do you remember Miss Wilson?"

"Yes, I remember Miss Maggie. She was my next-door neighbor from back when I was a little girl. Is she okay?"

"Not really. She's quite bad off and wanted to see you before she passed. I know this is short notice, but she's really in a bad way. Is it possible you could stop by here tonight?"

"Yes, ma'am. I'll be there as soon as I can."

"Thank you so much. I'll let Miss Wilson know she can expect to see you some time this evening."

It's going on six o'clock. I needed a way to get out of here so I could meet up with Brian. I promised to see him around eight. Looks like going to visit Miss Maggie is my way out.

I explain to Craig about what's going on with Miss Maggie and ask if he'd like to go with me to visit her. The only reason I even offered is because I knew he'd say no. Visiting a dying old woman doesn't sound inviting to me, either. The person I'm going to see afterward interests me the most.

My anxiety level is way up as I rush around the house, putting the final touches on everything before leaving. I order a pizza, breadsticks, and buffalo wings and make sure the kids are okay. I try to spend a few minutes with Craig because he's feeling depressed about his momma and daddy moving to Florida. He resents the fact that they made him stay in Eden and now he feels that he would have done more with his life if he had moved away like his older brothers and sister. I sit still and watch him down a couple cans of beer within five minutes or so.

I reassure him that everything will work itself out and that things happen for a reason. The whole thing could be a blessing in disguise.

He looks at me and says, "I hope you're right. Before you leave, could you put some more ice in my glass?"

"Where'd the glass come from?"

"Over here."

I look down on the floor next to the recliner and see less than half a bottle of Jack Daniel's.

"You don't have to hide it from me." I shake my head in disgust. "I see you and your old friend Jack Daniel's have been getting together on a regular basis lately."

"You know how old friends are. You might be seeing a whole lot more of J.D. around here from now on 'cause me and him are dealing with a lot of shit."

"You don't even know the half of it."

"Whatcha say?"

"Nothing. I'll be right back with your ice."

On my way out the front door I feel guilty and stop by Morgan's bedroom to check on her again. She's lying in bed reading a book.

"Morgan, I'm about to head out."

"Okay, Momma. I'll see you when you get back."

"Whatcha reading?"

"*The Bluest Eye* by Toni Morrison."

"Isn't that book a little too mature for you?"

"You're the one who made me wanna start reading books like this. Reading is a good thing, right?"

"I guess—all right, then. Do me a big favor and keep an eye on the family while I'm out."

"I will."

I give Morgan a hug and a kiss on her forehead. "Stay sweet. You're the best thing in my life right now. Promise Mommy that you'll never change."

Morgan smiles. "I won't."

29

Naomi

This is a strange Saturday evening. Beside the humidity, there's something in the air.

I get an eerie feeling every time I go back to my old neighborhood. Two years after Momma's murder, someone or something out of the ordinary burned our old house down to the ground. The whole incident with Momma and Daddy left a bad taste in people's mouths and a lot of bad memories.

The only thing that remains at the site of our old house is the foundation and ruins, shattered traces of my shattered past. Momma Pearl paid the taxes on this land for years and when I was old enough, I took over the payments. One day I might actually do something special with this land. All I know is that I'll never sell it because it means too much to me.

A small wooded area separates my momma and daddy's property from Miss Maggie's. I decide to pull into our old driveway first. I listen closely as the gravel churns under my tires. Still sounds the same after all these years. I'm surprised this gravel is even still around. Serena and I used to throw this same gravel in the woods for fun when we were little. Hard to believe we used to do something like that, because it seems so precious to me now. I reach down, pick up a handful of gravel, and place it inside a plastic bag. I set the bag inside my car for safekeeping.

One of my favorite things about the field behind our old house still stands as a constant reminder of my imaginative childhood, our weeping willow. That was our secret hideout. Sadly, there isn't a trace of our make-believe wishing well. I imagine that some bad kids probably came along and destroyed it with their grubby little hands.

I'm drawn back to the front of my house. I step over the remains of the brick facade and seem to be transported back in time. I'm reliving the day before Momma died. My memories lead me throughout my old house. In my mind everything appears just like I last remembered during the normal times. All the sights, sounds, and smells are here. This is the living room where I'm standing. I'm eight years old again, standing in front of our wood-burning stove. I can see my daddy slouched down on the sofa watching a baseball game with a beer in one hand and a cigarette in the other. He appears to be so content. He's completely absorbed by the game, too absorbed to even notice me standing here watching him. It's okay because he's relaxed and I love seeing him happy. His cigarette smoke irritates me, but I don't dare spoil his enjoyment.

I hear pots and pans moving around. Momma is in the kitchen trying her best to fry chicken extra crispy just like Daddy likes it. As I stand at the entrance of the kitchen, Momma doesn't notice me. She checks her cornbread in the oven and her pot of collard greens, then stirs her homemade mashed potatoes.

Serena is behind me in the hallway spread out on the floor with a coloring book. She colors really sloppy, all outside the lines. That girl could never color as good as me.

Everything appears in front of me just as plain as day. All of a sudden I'm struck by the urge to change the past. I rush up to my daddy and beg him to stay home with me, Serena, and Momma so we can remain a happy family. Because I know that if he stays home instead of going to work tomorrow that bad man won't come to take Momma away from us. She won't be murdered tomorrow night and Daddy won't go to jail for the rest of his life.

In the back of my mind I know this isn't real. Sound actually comes out of my mouth as I stand here like a crazy woman acting out what I would have said to Daddy that day.

"Daddy!" He ignores me. "Daddy, please listen to me! I need you to stay home with us tomorrow because Momma needs you. A man is gonna come here and murder her. Please don't leave us. We need you so we can stay a real family and me and Serena won't be forced to live with your hateful sisters. Momma's gonna die if you leave us. I don't want her to die and have you go to jail for a crime I know you didn't commit." I reach for him. "Do you hear me?"

Momma walks into the living room with a dinner plate and a cold beer for Daddy. She places it on the folding TV table in front of him.

"Thanks, Barb."

"You're welcome, sweetie."

Momma smiles at Daddy until he looks down at his plate and then her true feelings are briefly revealed. Her bright smile is quickly replaced with an unmistakable look of bitterness and disregard.

"Momma, please don't look at Daddy like that. And please don't let that man come here tomorrow night. That man is gonna kill you. Do you hear me? He's gonna kill you! I need you 'cause I'm nothing without you."

I'm so disturbed from being here that I'm having hallucinations. I can't keep from crying. I cry for my momma and daddy and the rest of my family. This is like visiting a cemetery. My fierce crying is a way of cleansing myself of certain emotions. It hurts like hell because no matter how hard I try, I can't undo what happened in the past.

After a few minutes I'm able to make my way up to Miss Maggie's front door.

30

Naomi

Miss Maggie's nurse answers the door. She's a big, dorky-looking white woman dressed in a pair of 6X-sized scrubs and a silly smock with a brown puppy dog pattern. If she were two inches taller and an inch wider, she'd be a perfect circle.

"Evening—you must be Naomi."

The house smells like liniment. The air in here opens my sinuses right up. Everything is still the same. Same old furniture and the same old smell.

"I am, and you must be Joanne."

"You're just as pretty as everybody said you were."

I smile. "Who said that?"

"Miss Magnolia and just about everybody who knows you. There were two colored ladies by here earlier, dressed all in white. Both of them knew you and talked about how pretty you are. They stopped in to pray with Miss Magnolia like they do all the time."

"Those were my aunts."

"Two very nice ladies and I'm not just saying that 'cause they're kin to you, either."

"I guess they're okay."

"Miss Magnolia is right this way."

Joanne directs me around the corner to the living room where Miss Maggie's hospital bed is.

"Miss Magnolia, look who's here."

"Sweet Jesus. Looka there. Is that you, Naomi?"

Miss Maggie hasn't changed a bit. She's still a pretty little brown-skinned woman with silver gray hair. Miss Maggie is just like the typical grandma, sweet and spiritual. Her heart has always been in the right place, but where her mind is, is another story.

"Yes, ma'am. It's me. How've you been, Miss Maggie?"

"Naomi, would you like some pop or some lemonade?" Joanne asks as she heads for the door.

"No, thank you. I'm fine."

"That'll be all for now, Joanne. Thank you."

"You're welcome, my dear."

Joanne exits the living room.

"She's nice."

Miss Maggie frowns and shakes her head. "She ain't nothing to write home about. What were you asking me before we were interrupted?"

"I was just asking how you've been."

"Blessed—and you?"

"Blessed as well."

"Come over here and give me a hug." We embrace. "Pull that chair up right here and have a seat next to my bed."

"I heard you've been bad off sick, but you look like you're doing well. I honestly expected to see somebody on her deathbed. Look how good you're doing."

Miss Maggie presses a button and raises the head of her motorized bed. "'Bout as well as can be expected for a dead woman."

"A dead woman? Whatcha talkin' 'bout, Miss Maggie? You look as healthy and alive as ever."

Miss Maggie looks like she's about to tell me a big secret. "You 'member Dr. King's speech where he says that he's been to the mountaintop?"

"Yes, ma'am."

"Well, I can relate to what he was saying. I've seen the promised land and I'm ready. There's a grave waiting for my body and God has made a home for my soul in heaven. That ole grim reaper come knockin' at my door last evening and the angel of death picked me up and carried me off to glory."

Miss Maggie gives me chills talking like that. I'm not sure what to say next.

"I guess the grim reaper is gonna come knockin' at everybody's door one day."

"You said a mouthful that time. When I heard the knock at my door I instantly began to praise God 'cause I knew where I was headed."

I'm not sure if Miss Maggie is really demented or what. She looks okay, but looks can be deceiving.

"How'd you get back here if you'd gone off to glory? I didn't know they let you come back."

"I don't know, exactly. I'm not a ghost or nothing. Guess my job wasn't done down here."

"Okay. How did it look up there?"

"Look at you. Sitting there thinking Miss Magnolia done lost her ever-loving mind. You don't believe me, do you?"

"I believe you. I'm just curious to know what you saw."

"I'll tell you, heaven is a much more desirable place than earth. An angel, a real nice black woman, took me soaring through the clouds—then we headed way up north into a bright light. It was blinding."

I play along and entertain her random remarks. "I heard that it was like that."

"Me, too, but what I wasn't expecting was to see that heaven was run by black folks . . . it's a whole bunch of us up there. The angel told me that heaven was a reward to blacks and oppressed people for their labor on earth and unwavering belief and faith in God. Throughout everything we've gone through, we never lost sight of God."

"That's true. So are there white people in heaven, too?"

"Yeah, but they don't have the same wealth or power they have here on earth."

"So, I still don't understand why you came back here or why you asked to see me before you died. I mean, I'm glad to see you and all, but I'm confused."

"I'm getting to that—give me a minute. Be patient with the old lady, okay?"

We laugh.

"I'm sorry."

"You know, Jesus is a black man who stands at the right hand of God."

This poor old lady is more delusional than I was earlier. Her comments are becoming more and more weird. I do believe that Jesus is a black man, but I don't believe Miss Magnolia went to heaven.

"I remember reading something like that in the Bible. Did you see Jesus?"

"I surely did. He is so wonderful. I didn't see God, but I know he was there somewhere. I did get the chance to speak to Jesus." She closes her eyes, looks to the ceiling and puts both hands in the air. "Thank you, Jesus. I just had to give him praise real quick for showing me something so beautiful. Everything was great up there—no terrors, sorrows, or grief. I didn't even mind being dead until I realized I had gone on to glory without telling you or somebody what I knew about your momma and daddy."

My eyes widen and I sit up straight in my seat. Miss Maggie has my undivided attention now.

"What do you know about them? Did you see Momma in heaven?"

"No."

"Oh!" I frown with disappointment as if Miss Maggie is actually speaking from experience.

"But that doesn't mean she wasn't there. I did see my momma and daddy. All of my brothers and sisters were there. My daughter Pattie and my grandbaby, who both died in that car accident a long time ago, were there. My husband, Lucious, and my first husband, James, were there too. Still don't know how James made it, but that's not for me to judge. I saw lots of people I knew. Old friends from way back. It was nice."

"So, can you tell me what you know about my momma and daddy?"

"I never told nobody 'bout this, but I know your daddy didn't kill your momma."

"How do you know that?"

"'Cause I was there that night."

"In my house?"

"No, in my yard when a man came busting out your back door. I was in my yard real late feeding my dog 'cause I couldn't sleep."

"Who was the man?"

"I don't know. I couldn't see his face, but I'm sure he was the same man who had been by there a bunch of times before that night. You see, I never been the nosy type or one to gossip, but I know your momma was having an affair with that man."

"I kinda figured that out on my own."

"I could never see his face on 'count of the woods being so thick. That night he saw me looking, and to this day his face is still a blur to me."

"What happened when he saw you?"

"He didn't see me till a car pulled up and somebody helped put your momma inside. Seems like it was against her will. When he saw me, I ran in the house and called your house to make sure what I was seeing actually happened."

"I remember the phone ringing and your dog howling."

"So you know I ain't lying, then. After that your daddy came home looking for your momma. I heard him calling for Barbara, but she was already gone off in the car with those people. I think it was two black men. In fact, I'm pretty sure the man who came out your back door was black."

"I still remember hearing that man and Momma laughing in our house. Why didn't you tell Daddy what happened when you heard him calling for Momma?"

"I don't know. I got scared and something told me to mind my own business. You know your daddy wasn't the easiest person to talk to. He was a mean son-of-a-something-or-another."

"He wasn't always mean."

"I used to hear how he beat on your momma."

"He did beat her, but he didn't kill her."

"I know he didn't and that's what I'm trying to tell you. I knew it for years and I almost took it to my grave. I don't guess I have much time to be here now that I've told somebody what I knew 'bout your momma and daddy all this time."

"I can't believe you kept important information like this to yourself for so long. You let Daddy go to jail for nothing. How could you? That was rotten of you, Miss Maggie."

"I know, but a little while after your daddy came home a man with a funny voice called my house. He called me by my first and last name. Said he knew what I saw and if I ever repeated a word of it he'd torture me like he was gonna do your momma. When I heard what he had done to your momma and where they found her, I almost died. That same man continued to call me almost every hour of the day—then it went to every day, then every week, then every month, then eventually a few times a year, just to remind me that he was still watching me. That man knew things about me that no one else did. That's how I knew he was really watching me. I've been a prisoner in this house for so many years that I can almost relate to what your daddy has gone through. I didn't exactly do anything wrong, but I was forced into seclusion. That has been my punishment for keeping my mouth shut."

"Did you ever think about having the phone calls traced?"

"I thought about that, until that man told me his calls couldn't be traced and if I mentioned anything about him to the phone company or the police, he'd know."

"I don't believe that."

"Well, when you're old as me and trapped in a house for so long, you begin to believe a lot of things no matter how ridiculous they might sound. Joanne is the only person who's been by here to do anything for me . . . her and your aunts. They know I don't go out, so they bring the church right here to my bedside."

"That's nice, but when was the last time that man called you?"

"Last month."

"Did he?"

"He sure did. He knew I was sick and close to dying and said I better take what I know to my grave. He said if I thought about telling somebody he'd help me meet my maker before I was ready to go. Fear ain't an option for me no more, so I told that coward that I was always ready to go because God had already prepared a home for me."

"What did he say then?"

"Nothing. What could he say? I haven't heard from him since. I just want you to be careful because now that you know the truth he might be after you. I'm sure he's out there watching right now. He knows you're here."

She's scaring me. "It's getting late. It's going on eight o'clock. I think I'm gonna get going."

"Why you rushing off so quick, leaving good company?"

"I have to go somewhere else before going home. It was good seeing you. I'll see you soon. I'm gonna stop by here tomorrow or Monday morning with a detective or somebody from the district attorney's office to speak to you about Daddy's case. I'm gonna get him out of jail 'cause he doesn't belong there."

"I won't be here."

"Yes, you will because I need you."

"I've done all I can do here and now it's time for me to go home . . . to move on to a better place."

"I'll see you soon."

"In heaven. 'Cause there's a place for you there, too. Jesus told me to tell you to slow down. He said you'd know exactly what that meant. He said don't be afraid to call his name when you need him most."

My eyes begin to water. Miss Maggie is really scaring me now, because she knows something. I don't know what it is, but she definitely knows something. Maybe she senses that I'm about to head over to Brian's house to do wrong.

"Thank you so much for giving me that information. I admire you, even though it took you a long time to tell somebody what you knew. Good night, Miss Maggie."

"Come give me one last hug. Good night, Naomi, and God bless you."

"God bless you too."

On my way out the front door I ask Joanne if she overheard what Miss Maggie and I had discussed in the living room.

"I did, and then again I didn't. I hear lots of things around here. Most times it goes in one ear and out the other."

"Could I get you to be a witness to what Miss Maggie said about my daddy?"

"I don't like to get involved in things like that. Take it from me, there are a lot of folks here in town that still haven't forgotten about your daddy . . . a lot of white folks . . . angry, Confederate-flag-waving white folks, if you know what I mean. Leave it be. Some things are better left alone."

"But not this. Thanks for nothing, Joanne."

"Good night, Naomi."

31

Naomi

Brian greets me in front of his house with a big ole smile and grill utensils in both hands. I can see big puffs of white smoke swirling around in his backyard. Something smells good.

"Hey, Naomi. Right on time."

"Hey—told you I'd be here on time."

"I know. You sure look pretty."

"Thanks, and you don't look half bad yourself."

"I'll take that as a compliment. It's hard to look good and work the grill at the same time."

"Don't give me that. You know you look good. Probably been getting compliments from women all day."

Brian laughs because he knows I'm telling the truth. He sets the grill utensils down on a lawn chair on top of a couple of paper towels and then gives me a passionate kiss. His touch is amazing. He touches me in a way that is so familiar and natural that I don't even complain about him kissing and holding me out here in plain sight. Seems like this is meant to be.

He picks up the grill utensils and puts his arm around me. "C'mon back here. I got a surprise for you."

"Smells goods out here. I bet you've got something good on the grill."

"You'll see."

Brian takes the top off the grill to reveal four big, juicy steaks. He's got a bunch of mixed vegetables wrapped up in aluminum foil grilling on the side.

"Whatcha think?"

"Makes my mouth water. Are those steaks for us?"

"Nah. They're just for show. I decided to go through the trouble of seasoning and marinating them all day, cutting up all these onions and peppers, and then grilling the steaks to perfection with a nice mesquite flavor so you could just stand here staring at them with your mouth watering."

I punch him in the arm. "Shut up. Stop being mean. I didn't know. Last night you didn't have any real food like this and acted like the only time you really ate was at your momma's house."

"I was just kiddin'. I eat real food here, too, not just salads and frozen dinners. I can cook a little sumthin' . . . every now and then, anyway. Have a seat right over there 'cause I'm about to make you a big plate of my best cookin'."

Brian has four citronella lights situated around the yard to repel mosquitoes. He lights two smaller ones on the picnic table. Dinner by candlelight.

"This is so nice. I ain't used to being served, especially by a man."

Brian stands behind me, massaging my neck and shoulders. "See, I figured that, so I want you to get used to having a man cook for you and serve you."

"My husband used to cook for me . . . in the beginning."

"Oh no! Can you not mention the husband? It kinda kills the mood."

We both laugh.

"Sorry."

"It's okay. It's just that when I look at you I don't see your husband or your kids. Hard for me to believe that they really exist. All I see is you and me being happy together."

I'm glad Brian can't see my facial expression right now. "No matter what, my family is part of who I am."

"I understand, but for now . . . let's eat!"

I think we just conveniently avoided our first argument. Somebody has a problem accepting me for who I really am. Well, I'll let it go for now 'cause here comes my food.

Brian is unbelievable. He sits this huge plate of food down in front of me. I'm looking down at a beautiful grilled steak topped with onions and peppers. On the side I have potato salad, grilled vegetables, and deviled eggs.

Brian holds his hand out over the food. "Well?"

"Thank you. Everything looks and smells delicious. I'ma try my best to eat as much of this as possible."

"Do the best you can 'cause it ain't like you can take it home with you. I can see you now, going home talkin' 'bout, '*Baby, look what I got. My boyfriend made me a steak dinner and it sure is good.*' "

"Oh, you're just full of jokes tonight."

"I'm in a good mood, that's all. Happy we could hook up again. And whatever you don't eat tonight, we can have tomorrow night for dinner."

"All right. Seems like you really like having me around."

"I love having you around." Brian pauses, blesses the table quickly, and then says, "Oh, look what else I have for us." Brian pulls three bottles of wine out of a small blue cooler. "I've got whatever you like— zinfandel, chardonnay, or merlot."

"Dag, you really went all out. I would have been happy with a plain ole bottle of Martini & Rossi Asti Spumante or something."

Brian sits down across from me. "You deserve better than that."

"I know, but you already did enough with dinner. This steak is the bomb."

"Thanks. Thought you'd like it."

"You went and paid for all that wine and you don't even drink."

"I do now."

"No—I'm being a bad influence."

He smiles. "No, you're not. It's okay for me to have a little taste every now and then, right?"

"I did tell you that, didn't I?"

"Uh-huh, you sure did. Look, you had a sample of my wild side and now I wanna bring it down a notch. You know, give you a sample of my romantic side."

Now I'm smiling. "This *is* romantic."

"I almost forgot the music." He turns on his CD player. "This is *The Best of Luther Vandross, The Best of Love.*"

"I love this CD. I wanna hear track four."

One of my all-time favorite songs comes on, "If This World Were Mine."

Brian says, "Dance with me."

"Let me finish eating first."

"Don't worry 'bout that. There's plenty more food left. I'm feelin' this song and we need to get up and do something."

"All right then."

I can't even remember the last time I danced like this. Brian is a smooth, passionate type of guy. He has his arms wrapped tightly around me. My head is pressed against him. We both sway from side to side, singing along with Luther and loving this moment. Brian grabs me by the chin. He leans down and kisses me.

I'm enjoying the moment and all, but I can't ignore the weird sensation of someone's eyes watching me from the wooded area behind Brian's house. Even with the music playing, I could have sworn I just heard something moving back there. I think someone has been following me all day.

"You hear that?"

"What?"

"That sound from the woods."

"Nah, it was nothing."

"But you did hear something, right?"

"It was probably some type of animal or something."

"Can we take this party inside?"

"All right. Whatever it takes to make you comfortable."

32

Naomi

Tonight is different. I told Brian that I was glad he decided to change the pace a bit. It kind of bothered me when Miss Maggie told me to slow down. Guess I'll have to heed her warning at some point. I feel that I'm really getting to know Brian better now. We're lying on a blanket on his living room floor in our underwear, talking and channel surfing.

I ask, "Where do you see yourself a year from now?"

"Hopefully I'll be back at A&T, finishing up my degree."

"I remember you saying that your major was biology. What do you hope to do with that?"

"My focus is mainly in medical research. Mostly because black people are at greater risk for HIV, high blood pressure, strokes, heart attacks, and diabetes. A lot of our people are developing Alzheimer's Disease too. I wanna do something to help prevent deaths related to the diseases I mentioned by finding better treatments and earlier interventions. See, my daddy died from a heart attack brought on by obesity, smoking, drinking alcohol, and lack of exercise. To him, going to work at the garage was exercise enough. He thought lifting heavy auto parts was a good workout. In reality it just put an extra strain on his heart. He worked day in and day out so I could go to college. During my freshman year at A&T he had a stroke and lost the use of his right arm and leg. His speech was slurred. Daddy became real bitter, said his body betrayed him. Then he had that heart attack. I had to leave school because of depression and on top of that, Momma needed me here. Now I wanna work to prevent other families from going through what mine went through."

"I keep saying that you're so different from other guys around here and it's true."

"I don't know about all that."

"Well, I do. It's so sexy to sit here talking to an intelligent and compassionate guy like you."

"Thanks. You ever think about going back to school?"

"Yeah, but I'd rather go into something that doesn't require a lot of schooling. I don't think I have the patience or dedication to go to college at my age. I was blessed with natural talents like cooking and being able to do hair. I hope you don't think I'm stupid or nothing for not going to college, 'cause I could have. I graduated from Morehead with honors."

"I can tell you have a good head on your shoulders. You don't need a college degree to validate your intelligence. Not only are you intelligent, but you're beautiful. It's such a pleasure being around you. I just love looking at you." He touches my face. "These little pouty lips, button nose, almond-shaped eyes, and high cheekbones are mesmerizing." He whispers in my ear. "You're gonna make me fall in love with you."

"Sure you wanna do that?"

"You just don't know. I really, really like you. I wish you were deeply in love with me. I want you to think about me when we're apart, even when you're with him."

"I do."

We kiss.

"I thought we weren't going to talk about Craig."

"I guess that's reality and it's time I face it. You're married . . . I hate saying that."

"I'm starting not to like the sound of it myself. You ever think about getting married?"

"No!"

"Man, that was a quick answer. So, what are you, one of those, why-buy-the-cow-when-you-can-get-the-milk-for-free kinda guys?"

"No, not at all. I don't want nothing for free. I think I work hard in

a relationship and pay for everything I get out of it. I pay close attention to detail, like when I knew you needed to have your toes sucked
or how I explored your body till I knew exactly what you liked and
how you liked it. And one of my favorite things—how I picked up on
the way you like to be kissed on the back of your neck like this."

Brian kisses me back there and I just melt.

"Oh . . . stop. We're supposed to be talking."

"Tell me you didn't like that, or when I touch you here."

Brian runs his fingertips up and down my bare inner thighs and
then rests his hand between my legs.

"Okay, I do like that. I still don't see your point."

"I might not treat my wife like that, but I'll damn sure treat my girlfriend like that. There's a big difference between the way a man fucks
or makes love to his girlfriend compared to how a husband has weak-
ass, two-minute sex with his wife."

"I'm starting to see your point and I don't like it because it's so
true."

"Tell me all the things you want from your husband, but he doesn't
give you."

"Let me see."

"I can tell you. More foreplay, more passion. Maybe he's not freaky
enough for you. Bet you'd love to have him go down on you every day
and night?"

"Every day and night? Shit, once a week would be nice."

We both laugh out loud.

"What are you afraid of when it comes to marriage? Do you think
you'd get bored or something?"

"I guess I could be married. Then I'd have *girlfriend sex* with my wife
all the time . . . have her butt-naked with both feet in the air every
night."

"Nasty. Are you afraid of commitment?"

"Not at all. I'm used to committed, long-term relationships. I think
that in some cases marriage spoils a relationship. That piece of paper
makes everything go sour. That's why so many married people cheat."

My whole facial expression changes, even though I know that wasn't
aimed directly at me.

"I'm sorry. Hope I didn't offend you."

"Nah, I'm fine. You're just stating your opinion."

"To a certain degree, married men who cheat seem to treat their mistresses better than they treat their wives."

"Why is that?"

"The wife has the husband's name, house, cars, money, benefits, and the majority of his time. So, the husband feels obligated to buy gifts and do extra-special things for his mistress. And to top all that off he lets the mistress know the real side of him, that side of him that's a big mystery to his wife."

"Do I really wanna be married now? After hearing all that, is it really worth it? I think about breaking up with Craig a lot. If it wasn't for the kids, I probably would have left his behind a long time ago. I wouldn't want to hurt them. That's the last thing I wanna do."

"But you don't mind hurting yourself. Would a breakup necessarily have a negative impact on the kids?"

"I dunno."

"I mean, don't think they don't sense the tension in your relationship."

"I'm sure they sense that neither one of us is happy." I pause for a second. "Can we talk about something else?"

"All right." A smile comes over Brian's face. "Tell me about the most embarrassing moment in your life. Don't hold back any details. I wanna hear it plain and simple, just like it happened."

"Let's see. When I was in elementary school a boy pulled down my tube top and everybody saw my little underdeveloped breasts. For about a month, boys came up to me offering Calamine Lotion for my mosquito bites. For a while I did't know what they were talking about. I looked at my arm and leg and didn't see any mosquito bites. Then it hit me—they were talkin' about the two little bumps I called breasts."

"That's terrible. Now I know why you're so insecure about your breast size. It came from that experience."

"Maybe it did start back then. I'm not sure. Now tell me about your most embarrassing moment."

"I've been tall all my life and kind of awkward in my early years. One Easter morning I was late for church and there was nowhere to sit on the first level. I had to go upstairs to the little cramped space in the balcony. You can probably see where this is headed. I noticed an empty spot on the far end of the pew. I forget that the ceiling was slanted up there. I kept moving further and further down the row until my head slammed into the ceiling and sent an echo throughout the entire church. Every head in the church turned in my direction. Kids laughed. Some adults frowned. The worst moment was when my pastor looked up at me with a disgusted expression for interrupting his sermon."

"That's so funny. I really enjoy being with you. I like talking about funny stuff like that instead of talking about marital problems. If I knew what I know now, I would never had gotten married. I've come to realize that my husband can't satisfy me sexually or any other way. Of course, when we first met I had just turned eighteen and had little-to-no knowledge about sex or relationships, so the smallest amount of attention impressed me. I was a virgin and a late bloomer. Plus, I needed a way out of a bad family situation. It didn't take much to hook me."

"I'd like to hear more about that bad family situation, but only when you're ready to talk about it."

"Okay. Just not tonight, because talking about that would definitely spoil the mood."

We both laugh.

"You've unlocked something special inside me," I confessed. "Look at tonight, for example. We had dinner, danced, talked, and laughed like crazy. And when it comes to sex, you make me see and feel things I've never experienced before."

"I'm glad you brought up the topic of sex. I've been dying to ask you about your opinion on oral sex."

"I love it!"

"Is that right? So you're pretty good at it?"

"Oh, hold up—you mean the other way around. I misunderstood."

"I'm talking about giving, not receiving. You see what I'm saying now."

"I see. There's an old saying that goes, it's better to give than to receive. When it comes to what you're talking about, I changed that all around to, it's better to receive than to give."

"That's not good. I haven't had anybody to do me right in that department in a long time."

"Well, tell me about it. Who was she? Don't leave out any details. I wanna hear it plain and simple, just like it happened."

"Stop trying to act like me."

"I can't help it. The more we hang out together, the worse it's gonna get."

"Okay. Let me give you the details. My first girlfriend, Shawna, used to do me right. She had a juicy mouth, a soft, friendly tongue, and a deep throat."

"Yuck."

"Whatever, girl. It felt good to me—she had skills. She could do it fast or slow. I still don't know which was my favorite. Both ways felt good, though. It didn't matter about sucking it 'cause there was hardly any suction involved. That's where a lot of women go wrong. That's why y'all jaws be hurting, from trying to suck too hard. The part about sucking is a myth. All y'all need to have is a juicy mouth. Shawna just knew how to position her tongue and teeth to make it perfect. She knew how to use her hands to add more excitement to it. She used to take my thing out of her mouth and kiss and rub it all around her lips and face like she loved it. She would slap it against her cheeks. Damn, that felt good. Then she'd play with my balls and lick 'em or put both of them in her mouth and massage them with her tongue."

"She must have been good. Look at you, getting all aroused."

"I can't help it. You asked for details. I was having a flashback."

"Wait a minute. You're not the only creative one. I got a sexy dessert game we can play. All I need is some chocolate syrup or whipped cream and a blindfold."

"Oh shit! Who's the freak now?"

Brian jumps up and runs to his bedroom, then to the kitchen in order to get everything we need for our little game. He comes back with a can of whipped cream and a blue-and-white bandana. I begin to explain the rules of the game to him.

"Here are the rules. I'll put the whipped cream somewhere on my body and you have to find it using your mouth only. You must be blindfolded, and remember—you can't use your hands."

"That's fine. One request."

"What?"

"Can I go first?"

"Sure."

Brian ties the blindfold around my eyes and I go to work searching for the whipped cream. Within seconds I find it on his top lip. Too easy.

When my turn comes, he finds the whipped cream just below my navel.

The next time around, things get a little more complicated. He puts the whipped cream in a very intimate spot. Let's just say I'm about to erase all his memories of Shawna and replace them with new, improved ones.

33

Naomi

Out of all the places I could have gone this morning, I decided to come to Momma Pearl's brand-new church, The Eden Temple of Light. I'm glad she decided to rename this church because the old name was too long and too unofficial-sounding. Eden Light Undenominational Church of Faith sounded more like a cult disguising itself as a regular church. Glad Momma Pearl left the old name behind along with that little old dilapidated white building. Now things are off to a better start. The old church wasn't air-conditioned. We were kept cool by two big, noisy floor fans that had to be unplugged every so often because they drowned out Momma Pearl's voice in the rear of the church. The other thing we used to keep cool was old, handheld church fans with Dr. Martin Luther King's face, praying hands, or an advertisement for the Perry-Spencer Funeral Home on the front.

This is a bright, beautiful temple. Craig and the kids refused to come here because all they wanted to do was stay at home watching television or doing something close to nothing. Craig said this was a lazy Sunday morning meant for getting plenty of rest.

I'm sitting here with my old church family, enjoying the choir as they sing "Blessed Assurance."

After the song, Momma Pearl comes out and the congregation erupts with applause and praise. After a few minutes of absorbing the congregation's love, she takes a seat behind the pulpit on what looks to be a huge throne. There are two seats next to her—Sister Clarissa is seated on Momma Pearl's left side and the seat on the right is empty.

Sister Clarissa makes some quick church announcements and then says a wonderful prayer. When she finishes, the choir begins another selection, "Amazing Grace."

I'm very familiar with the service because this is the same way it was at the old church. Only difference is now the congregation is a hundred times larger. Me and Serena were involved in almost every function in the church. We used to be part of the old church's junior usher board, the regular usher board, the junior choir, and the regular choir. I was named the assistant director of the children's ministry and Serena was my assistant. I can't forget to mention that we worked in the church kitchen with a bunch of old ladies every Sunday. Guess that's how I learned to cook so well. Don't know what happened to Serena's cooking skills.

As the song ends, Momma Pearl makes her way to the pulpit. The entire congregation rises to their feet. The choir finishes singing "Amazing Grace," but the music continues playing softly in the background.

"Praise God! Good morning, family. First off, I wanna thank each and every one of you who contributed to our building fund for all those years 'cause it finally paid off. I especially wanna thank the people who never questioned where all that money was going. Thanks so much for your faith. God is good . . . all the time. Praise His name! I see one of my favorite nieces made it here today, hallelujah! Thank you, sweet Jesus! I would ask her to stand, but her presence here is enough." The music continues in the background. The volume increases a bit. "*Amazing Grace, how sweet the sound . . . that saved a wretch like me. I once was lost . . . but now am found . . . was blind, and now, I see.* Thank you, Jesus! I love that song. Such beautiful words . . . there's strength in those words . . . healing in those words. 'Cause I too was blind, but now I see. Thank you, Jesus, for saving a wretch like me. Have mercy! Does anybody know what I'm talking 'bout? Can I get a witness?"

People start shouting and crying.

Momma Pearl continues, "Hallelujah! Thank you, Jesus! Thank you for allowing me to see. I wanna tell you a story this morning.

Once upon a time . . . a long time ago, the devil had his hands on me . . . had both of his hands over my eyes . . . so I couldn't see. I had slipped into darkness and I know somebody knows the place I'm talking 'bout . . . I know somebody's been there."

The spirit moves throughout the church, skipping all over me. Looks like I'm the only one standing still or with a dry eye.

"Through His grace I realized I was in a dark place that I didn't wanna be . . . I had no business there. I was lost . . . yes, I was. That's when Jesus pulled the devil's hands off my eyes and allowed me to see. The devil was gone and that's when I saw Jesus and I haven't looked away since. I knew I was lost, and then I was found. Amazing Grace, oh, how sweet the sound. Lord, I thank you for saving a wretch like me. I'm brand-new. Thank you, Jesus. Hallelujah! Praise God all around the church. Let the church say, Amen. God is so good."

The tempo of the music speeds up and changes over to some real shouting music. A lot of people are dancing in the aisles and clapping their hands. Bright rays of light shine down through the stained-glass windows. A feeling comes over me that I've never felt before. Sensations move throughout my entire body. Tears begin to flow for no apparent reason and there's nothing I can do to fight the feeling. To be honest, I don't want to fight the feeling. It's God.

Momma Pearl notices what's happening to me. She comes down out of the pulpit and wraps her arms around me and I wrap my arms around her.

I whisper in her right ear. "I forgive you. Sorry for judging you."

Part III

RIGHTEOUS WAYS

34

Naomi

I feel brand-new, like I have little or no interest in the things I used to. Momma Pearl prayed a powerful prayer for me after this morning's service, giving me a spiritual makeover. I'm not exactly ready to lead a one hundred percent decent Christian lifestyle yet, but I am going to make some significant changes in my life. The first major step I made was forgiving Momma Pearl. I just left the Rockingham County Jail. I stopped by there to see Daddy. His letters and collect calls stopped months ago and I hadn't seen him in almost a year. It was definitely time that I reached out to him.

It took a while for Daddy to come to the visitation room. He likes to look his best and I'm sure my unannounced visit caught him off guard. I imagined him trying to shave and do some other last-minute preparations to make himself look as presentable as possible.

As the guard led him through the doorway I noticed drastic changes in his appearance. Daddy always wore his hair close, but not this close. His head was bald. There were hard lines in his forehead and bags under his eyes. He wore gold, thin-wire-framed glasses. The amount of gray in his goatee had tripled. He'd gained at least twenty to thirty pounds. He looked old. His dark eyes expressed resentment for losing his freedom, frustration for everybody ignoring his impassioned cries of innocence, and a deep sadness that could only have been brought on by years of being misunderstood.

Tears welled up in our eyes at the same time. We held each for a good ninety seconds without saying a word.

Daddy said, "Hey, Boo-boo."

"Hey, Daddy."

"I thought you had forgotten all about me. Thought you'd given up on me, girl."

"No. I didn't forget about you. How could I? It's just that things at home started to take up more and more of my time, that's all."

"I understand. Only thing is I feared the day would come when my daughters would give in to the rumors and believe like everybody else that I had taken their momma's life. I feared the day when y'all would just give up on me completely."

"Never."

"I dunno. I thought it had happened."

"We think about you every day."

"How's everybody doing? How's that ole crazy husband of Serena's? My grandbabies doing okay?"

"Fine. Everybody's fine."

"Good, that's what I like to hear. One thing I never have to worry about is whether or not you're being taken care of 'cause I know Craig is a good provider and he knows how to take care of my baby."

"You're right. He's taking good care of me."

"I know. I'm surprised he didn't come here with you today. I remember the last time he was here and got mad 'cause all these inmates were staring at you. Shoot, Craig has to realize that he's married to very attractive woman and guys are gonna stare."

"Look who's talkin'. I remember you being the same way about Momma—overprotective."

"We're talkin' 'bout Craig, not me. Maybe I was like that a long time ago. I'm different now. I'm serious. Don't look at me like that. People change." He pauses. "Was Craig affected by the layoffs at the Mill?"

"Yes sir, but don't worry. He's got some other things in the works already."

"I ain't worried. You can't keep a good man down, that's for sure. Craig will be back to work in no time."

"He might be taking over his parents' grocery store. They're planning on moving to Florida within the next few months."

"That's good news . . . for them. Wish it was me. Then again, I probably wouldn't even know how to act if they was moving me outta here. Sometimes I feel like I've died a thousand times in here." He looks down. "Nothing to look forward to whatsoever. I look at some of these guys in here counting down their days, but I can't even do that. My only way out is death." He repeats. "Death. Can you believe that?"

"Stop talking like that."

"Can't help it. I ain't lying . . . just being honest with myself. I don't know what I did to deserve this life. I asked God a million times, but He won't tell me. One of these white supremacist guys in here told me that even if I didn't kill your momma, being in here was my punishment for marrying a white woman."

"That's not true."

"He said God was punishing me for race mixing."

"He's ignorant."

"I know, and I'd never believe foolishness like that. Believe it or not, there are some decent men in this place, both white and black. We sit down and exchange ideas on all kinds of topics. We learn from each other. During my time here I've come to realize that people have slight differences, but for the most part we're all the same regardless of color. If that wasn't the truth we wouldn't bleed the same blood or be able to make babies with each other."

"That's true. All right, you are different now because in the past stuff like that never came out of your mouth."

"See, everything in jail ain't exactly bad."

"I know. Guess who I saw yesterday."

"Who?"

"Miss Magnolia. You remember Miss Maggie, who used to live next door to us?"

"Yeah, I know who you're talkin' 'bout. Where'd you see her?"

"I stopped by her house yesterday."

"For what?"

"She told me some very important information about the night before Momma died."

Daddy's expression turned flat and he appeared withdrawn. "Don't believe that gossiping old woman. If she knew some important information, she wouldn't have waited all these years to talk about it."

"Don't you wanna hear what she had to say?"

"No, not at all. I'm not interested."

"It could help you get outta here."

"You don't know this, but there have been a few people to come forth over the past twenty years or so, claiming to have important information that was supposed to help get me outta here. But look where that got me . . . absolutely nowhere. I can't go through that again. Can't build my hopes up only to be let down and made to feel worse than when I started out. It's too exhausting. I'm just trying to find inner peace and this is the closest I've ever been to it since day one of my sentence. I'm getting old and set in my ways. I'd be lying if I said that being here hasn't taken a toll on me, but I'm learning to survive. As long as I live I'll never get used to it, though. I'm just surviving one day at a time." He laughed. "After all this time, what would I do out there anyway? Things have changed so much over the past twenty years that I wouldn't know mud from mess out there." Daddy's eyes began to tear. "You coming here today means a lot to me. All I ask is that you not mention anything anybody has to say about that night or my case because it's just a waste."

Out of respect for Daddy I changed the subject. No matter what, I'm going to do my best to get him out of that place, regardless of whether he's aware of what I'm doing or not.

I'm on my way to Serena's house for a dinner she promised me for giving her that check for her mortgage. My silly husband and kids knew I was going over there for dinner, but they still didn't want to join me. Craig said Serena was nasty, but not freaky nasty. This time he meant it in an unsanitary kind of way. The last time we had dinner at Serena and Darryl's house, Craig and I needed some hot sauce for our catfish. Nobody could find the hot sauce until Darryl went and found it somewhere in his bedroom. We weren't sure why the hot sauce was in the bedroom. I wanted to believe they had dinner in there the night before and forgot to return it to the kitchen. Most black people put hot sauce on everything. For some reason I think Craig and I imagined Darryl and Serena pouring that hot sauce on each other in the bed and licking it off. Whatever the case was, we didn't want to use any of that hot sauce on our food. I could have sworn I saw a piece of curly black hair stuck on the side of the bottle. Memories like that make me laugh and at the same time make me not want to eat there again. No matter what, that's still my sister.

When I pull up to Serena's house I notice Travis and Taylor unattended to in the front yard, playing. It's hard to believe their momma used to be a daycare provider. She can't even take care of these two. As soon as the kids notice me, they come running up to my car.

"Back up! Stand still till I pull into the driveway!"

One thing about these kids is that they obey me, if nobody else.

The kids come running up to me. "Y'all momma know y'all out here like this?"

Taylor smiles and mumbles something I can't understand.

Travis goes, "Yeah, Momma told us to come out here and play."

"What y'all playing?"

"Swimming!"

"How do you play swimming without water, baby?"

"Pretend. Hold our breath and move our arms like this."

Travis starts moving his arms in a circular motions and walks toward the house real fast.

He yells, "I'm swimming!"

Taylor looks at Travis out of the corner of her eye and imitates her brother. She yells out something incomprehensible that sounds kind of close to, "I'm swimming!"

"Poor babies—Aunt Nay is gonna have to buy y'all a swimming pool. Keep going. That's right. Swim y'all little butts right up those steps and in that house."

I'm standing in the living room and I can hear Serena in the bathroom with the water running.

"Travis, where's your daddy?"

"He with his friends."

I knock on the bathroom door.

Serena goes, "I'll be right out."

I've known my sister forever and I can tell when she's been crying.

"Serena, it's me. What's wrong?"

"I'll be right out."

I take the kids out into the living room so they can watch television. I need to find out what's going on with Serena.

Within a minute or so, Serena comes out of the bathroom with red, swollen eyes.

"What is it now?"

"C'mon in the kitchen. We need to talk."

"Travis and Taylor, y'all be good and sit right here till I come back."

When I get in the kitchen, Serena is sitting at the table with about four or five tissues in her hand, crying her eyes out. She's a mess. I don't see one trace of food, so I automatically assume that my appreciation dinner has been canceled. Serena looks like she has a good excuse for not making dinner.

"What's got you so upset?"

"I don't even know how to tell you. We've been trying to track you down all morning and half the afternoon, but nobody knew where you were. Craig said you went to church. I called there and one of the ladies there said you had left hours ago."

"I went to see Daddy."

As soon as I say that, Serena drops her head and starts crying even harder.

I put my arms around her and ask, "What? What is it?"

"You ain't gonna believe this shit."

"Try me."

"Somebody went to the cemetery . . . and . . . and . . . dug up Momma's grave, and her remains are missing."

My stomach turns inside out. "What! I don't think I understand what you said. Run that by me again."

"Just what I said. Some sick motherfuckers went there and stole her remains! They dug up the grave, broke into the casket somehow, and stole her remains. The police called Craig this morning while you were at church, then he called me. When I got to the cemetery the police were there. I saw the open grave and completely freaked out. The casket was still in the ground, busted open. I swear to God, I just fainted."

"I honestly don't know what to do or to say right now."

"You better do something. All I know is that early this morning the man at the cemetery noticed a big pile of dirt next to Momma's grave. He called the police as soon as he realized what happened. Whoever did it kicked over her headstone too. They won't even let our poor Momma rest in peace."

"Oh my God! What's next? Did they bother any other graves?"

"No, they only bothered Momma's grave."

"I can't believe this. Who's messing with us like this? That's just uncalled for and totally disrespectful. What could they want with her remains? It's not like she was buried with expensive jewelry or nothing."

"A policeman said that someone had robbed two old ladies and stolen their purses while they were visiting a gravesite two weeks ago."

"But that doesn't have anything to do with Momma."

"I know. He said people steal flowers and items placed at gravesites all the time, but he had never seen anything like this before. He was a real nice guy. He remembered Daddy. He said this could possibly be considered a hate crime."

"Why Momma? Why our momma? Why?"

"That's what I'd like to know. Why aren't you more upset? You haven't even shed a tear. I can't believe how calm you are."

"What am I supposed to do? I'm not used to this. This is unreal."

"This shit is unreal to me, too!"

"Shhh. Lower your voice. No need to get the kids upset, too, and try not to cuss," I say.

"What is wrong with you? Don't tell me how to act. My momma is missing."

"Please! Stop it! The reaction that you're having right now is what they want from you. They're not gonna get that from me. Momma isn't missing. That ain't her no more. She's an angel in heaven. All they have are her earthly remains."

"And that should be enough to piss you the fuck off! I'm ready to go out there and hurt somebody . . . right now!"

"Who are you gonna hurt? Huh?"

"I wanna hurt *you*! Stop acting so calm and get mad. That's our Momma we're talkin' 'bout," Serena declared.

"I keep telling you that ain't her. You need to pray."

"Oh my God—no, you didn't! You done went to church one time this year . . . oh . . . I forgot Easter . . . that makes twice this year, and now you're all righteous all of sudden. Don't give me that crap."

"This ain't crap. You don't understand. I felt God this morning and I'm trying to be a better person. This is just some kinda test . . . something temporary. The way I figure, whoever is behind this is gonna get sloppy sooner or later and the police will find them. Look at what they're doing . . . stealing remains . . . c'mon now! I think we're 'bout to find out all about Momma's murder. It's just a matter of time. I can feel it in my heart. You know I'm right."

"No, I hope you're right."

"You gotta believe. You just gotta believe what I'm telling you," I tell her.

I grab Serena's hand and say a quick prayer. Instead of her bowing her head and closing her eyes, she's standing there staring at me, all stupid with a look of disbelief.

35

Naomi

This is a real trying time for me. It's been a while since I've traveled this familiar path to Momma's gravesite. So many times I've carefully and respectfully stepped over graves to get to Momma's and today isn't any different. I'm superstitious. I heard it's bad luck to step on someone's grave. I can't see myself being disrespectful, even though somebody desecrated the one grave that means the most to me. I stop dead in my tracks because I don't feel the need to get any closer. From where I'm standing I can see the yellow police tape that surrounds Momma's gravesite like a typical crime scene. The police are still here. Guess they're over there trying to collect evidence.

This is a very disturbing site to me. For some reason I can't get my feet to take another step. My mind is bombarded by sad memories of Momma's burial. I remember placing a red rose on top of her casket. Moments later I watched from the family car as the groundskeepers lowered her casket into the ground and began to cover it with dirt. I never dreamed that one day somebody would unearth her remains. A big mound of brownish-orange dirt surrounds the top, bottom, and right-hand side of Momma's grave. Somebody put a lot of useless effort into digging up all that dirt. This dirt was never meant to see the light of day again. Grass had even grown over Momma's grave. Why disturb things after all these years?

An older black man, probably a groundskeeper, notices me looking at the gravesite from a distance. He makes his way in my direction.

"Excuse me young lady. Is there something I can help you with?"

"No. I'm fine. I just wanted to come out for a minute to see what happened out here, that's all."

"People been coming by here all day for a quick peek. Shame what they done did to that lady's grave. Ain't never seen nothing like it in all my years. I'll take you over there for a closer look if you'd like."

I look over toward the policemen. The man notices where I'm looking and tries to read my mind.

He says, "Don't worry 'bout them. We won't be in their way at all."

"I dunno. I think I've seen enough already."

"You look mighty curious to me. C'mon, follow me." The man starts walking ahead. He stops and turns back toward me. "By the way, my name is Floyd."

He extends his hand. I extend mine. The feel of Floyd's rough calloused hand is irritating. Makes me wish our hands had never touched.

"I'm Naomi."

Floyd smiles. "Uh-huh. Pretty name . . . pretty girl."

"Thank you. Can I have my hand back?"

Floyd's smile is slowly naturalized. "Sure thing. Sorry 'bout that. You kinda favor this one girl who came by here earlier and fainted."

"Really?"

"Ya sure do. I remember the white lady that was buried over there. Her husband killed her, and now this. I don't mean to sound racist or nothing, but I know it wasn't one of us who did this."

This man doesn't realize that the girl who fainted earlier was my sister and the white woman who was buried here is my momma.

"What do you mean, one of us?"

"You know what I mean, black folks. This is some of that weird stuff that white folks do. I've been working here for twenty-three years and I know for a fact that you won't find a nigger snoopin' 'round no graveyard at night. And I know whoever dug up that grave did it at night 'cause I was here all day yesterday. I take offense to this 'cause it's disrespectful to the dead and to me. I take a lot of pride in my job and this makes it look like I wasn't doing what I was 'posed to."

"Do you ever remember seeing any of this lady's family visit her grave?"

"No!"

"Did you actually know her husband?"

"I don't reckon so. Why you asking questions like that?"

"No reason." I say, backing down.

"For a minute I thought you might have been from the NCSBI."

"Who?"

"North Carolina State Bureau of Investigations. I just learnt 'bout that today myself. They were by here earlier. They're the same people who're investigating those disappearances. You know what I mean, the lady and the teenage girl."

"Oh really?"

"I know a lot, don't I?"

"Uh-huh, you sure do."

"See, I know how to act like I ain't listening when important people are talkin' 'bout important stuff. My momma taught me that. C'mon over here. I want you to get a good look at this gravesite. You'd have to see it to believe."

"All right, then."

Floyd and I get as close to the yellow tape as possible. We're standing on the opposite side of the big brownish-orange mound of dirt.

"Here, look down there. You can still see the casket. C'mon, gal, it ain't nothing to be scared of."

I feel myself trembling. Feels like I'm doing something wrong or forbidden. I shouldn't feel this way because this gravesite belongs to Momma. I get on my tiptoes and look over the edge of the hole, which looks like a dark, bottomless pit. The first thing I see is this old rusty, dirty, weathered casket that used to be a beautiful eggshell white. Then I see the inside. The satin and lace interior that was once a brilliant white are now a faded yellowish-brown. The sight of Momma's pillow is too much for me because I notice loose strands of her long black hair lying there, the last place I remember seeing her head rest. I become extremely light-headed. Tears pour from my eyes.

I scream, "No . . . no! Help me! Help meeee, God! I can't take this no more. Help me! I want my momma back."

I feel too weak to stand and I'm sick to my stomach. I drop to my knees. Now I understand exactly what happened to Serena when she was here earlier.

Floyd panics and asks, "Whatcha talkin' 'bout, girl? Calm down.

You're drawing too much attention. C'mon and calm down now. You hear me? It's okay. You're gonna be all right."

One of the policemen asks, "What's going on over there?"

Floyd answers, "I don't know. I didn't know this was her momma's grave. She'll be okay in a minute."

One of the policemen asks, "Ma'am, are you okay over there?"

I can hardly speak.

"C'mon and answer him. Gon' and say something."

Still crying, I say, "I'll be okay."

The policeman says, "A cold drink of water should make you feel better."

Now I really know how Serena felt. I feel like cussing this man out for making a stupid comment like that. How does he figure a cold drink of water will make me feel better? He has no idea how traumatized I really am. I'll refrain from cussing because I already made myself look ghetto enough by falling to the ground screaming and crying.

Floyd helps me to my car.

As I get inside my car, I say, "Earlier you said a few other people had been by here to take a quick peek. You got any idea who they were or how they looked?"

"Well, it was mostly some kids. Trust me, there ain't no way any kids could have done this. They just ain't strong enough. There was a white fella through here this morning just 'fore the police arrived."

"Did you tell them that?"

"Yes, ma'am, I sure did tell 'em. They lookin' for him right now."

"How'd he look?"

"He was a ole dirty-lookin' hillbilly with a beard."

"Was he walking or driving?"

"He was driving. Drove a white Ford van. He got away 'fore I could see his tag number."

I'm stunned. "You sure it was a white Ford van?"

"Just as sure as I'm standing here lookin' at you."

"And you're sure you told the police exactly what you saw?"

"Let me tell you something, Naomi—I think they was already looking for the same man 'cause all the police got excited, even the people from the NCSBI."

"North Carolina State Bureau of Investigations."

"You got it."

"Oh, Mr. Floyd, you have no idea what you've done."

"Did I do good, baby?"

"You sure did. I think I know who's responsible for all this craziness in my life now. Thank you so much for keeping your eyes open. God is good."

"All the time. You be careful driving home. Hopefully the police will catch that hillbilly before he does something else crazy."

"I pray they will. Thanks again."

I feel like my prayers have been answered. Sooner or later all criminals get careless. I knew it'd just be a matter of time.

As I turn on to Van Buren Road on my way back into town, I notice a tow truck speeding up behind me. It's Brian, blowing his horn and signaling for me to pull over. He pulls in front of me. I get out of my car and hop into his truck. As soon as I get in, he greets me with a kiss on my lips. At first I'm reluctant to kiss him, and then I remember that I said I'd make subtle changes.

He goes, "Ooh, Naomi, look at you. Ain't you lookin' pretty today."

"I looked even better earlier before I got myself dirty. Whatcha doing working today?"

"I'm really off, but I had to help somebody out down the road." Brian looks at me closely. "What you been doing? How'd you get your dress dirty like that? You look like you've got something in your eyes or like you've been crying."

"I'm better now. I had some family problems earlier."

"Was it the hubby?"

"Nah, it didn't have anything to do with him. I'll explain another time. Too much information and not enough time. I gotta get home."

"What's the rush? I missed you so much. God, I feel like I'm going crazy without you. Last night was out of this world. I'm falling in love with you for real. I know I love that mouth yours. You're something else."

I frown. "Shhh. Don't talk like that. I went to church this morning."

"So did I. The Lord don't mind me talkin' like that. He hears and sees everything we do. He knows what we're gonna do before we even do it. He's here . . . He's there . . . He's everywhere, and He was even there last night."

"You're right, but shut your mouth. I don't wanna hear or think about that right now."

"All right. Look, I need to tell you something. I need to confess to two things I did. Hope you won't be too disappointed in me."

"It's okay. I knew from the beginning that you weren't perfect, so I kinda prepared myself for at least one little slip-up from you. Whatcha gotta tell me?"

"Here's my first confession. That potato salad and deviled eggs from last night wasn't mine. Momma made 'em, but I figured it was no big deal because even if I had made 'em myself, I was gonna use her recipe anyway."

I bust out laughing. "You're so freakin' wholesome when you wanna be. It's hard to believe that there's a raging sexual beast buried in there somewhere."

"So, you ain't mad? 'Cause I felt like I kinda deceived you."

"Trust me, after the day I've had so far that wasn't even worth mentioning."

"Really?"

"*Really.*"

"Okay, here's the other thing. I told you a couple of days ago that whatever happened between us would stay between us."

My eyes widen. "Oh no! Who'd you tell?"

"My pastor. I told my pastor and nobody else."

"Oh my goodness. What am I gonna do with you? I don't mind that so much. I'm just glad you didn't tell somebody who actually knows me. That's confidential information, anyway. Don't worry, he won't tell anybody."

"My new pastor is a female. I went to the eight o'clock service at Eden Temple of Light this morning."

"Oh my God—Momma Pearl is my aunt. Boy, what did you do?"

"I dunno. She told me she was your aunt after I told her about us."

"No, you didn't use my name!"

"I did. She kept pressing and pressing, so I just came clean with everything."

"Why would you do that? You had no reason to tell her anything. Why?"

"That woman is something special. I trust her. The good thing is that she said she wouldn't judge either one of us. She just prayed with me, that's all."

I suck my teeth. "No wonder she was so surprised to see me this morning at the eleven o'clock service. I felt God for the first time in my life and I made a promise that I was gonna change my life and that means no more drinking, cussing, looking at worldly TV shows and movies, or listening to worldly music. And that means I'm eventually gonna have to give up on our relationship and give my husband more time and attention. If I do that right, then maybe he'll change for the better."

"I doubt it. How you just gonna give up on me so easily? If you leave him now, then we can do all the right things together. That's what I want more than anything in my life right now. I'll give you a ring and marry you if that's what it takes."

I don't even respond to Brian because my attention turns toward the road. I have this strange feeling that something bad is about to happen. Seems like I'm sitting here waiting for a sign. Out of nowhere I hear a loud vehicle coming up real quick from behind. That sound can only be one thing. All my luck-slash-blessings have just run out.

I look behind and yell, "Oh shit!"

"C'mon, Naomi, watch your mouth. Thought you were giving up on cussing."

"That's my husband's Bronco pulling up next to us."

Brian yells, "Oh shit!"

Craig pulls up right beside the tow truck and looks me and Brian dead in our faces. He looks pissed. After staring us down, Craig pulls up in front of the tow truck.

"I should have known we couldn't keep an affair like this a secret for too long in a small town like Eden. I hope my aunt didn't tell on us."

"Relax! I know exactly what to do. Listen, I just met you 'cause your car broke down and you needed roadside assistance. Hand me that clipboard real quick. I left my lights flashing—he won't know the difference."

"Yes, he will. He'll know. That's a brand-new Camry you're talking about."

"So what? Here he comes. Just act natural. Get out and tell him what happened to your car. Just make it believable."

"We are so dead."

Craig looks incredibly angry. He's been drinking and still has on the same clothes he wore yesterday. Hope he doesn't embarrass me too much. His cowboy boots are embarrassing enough.

"Naomi! What in the hell is goin' on? Where have you been all day?"

"My car was acting up and this guy spotted me and stopped to help."

"I must look like a damn fool to you, huh? Is that what I look like?"

"You're acting like one. I said I had car trouble."

"Give me your keys."

Craig snatches my keys out my hand. He goes over to my car, gets inside, and starts the car right up.

He gets out. "So what's the problem? Your damn car started without any trouble."

"I never said it wouldn't start. I had a problem with my wheel. It was wobbling like crazy."

Brian gets out of his truck and heads over toward me and Craig.

Craig looks up at Brian, who is about a foot taller, and asks, "What the fuck do you want?"

"I need the lady to sign this paperwork."

"Stop the lies and the games. I know what's going on."

"Craig, I can tell that you've been drinking. Please calm down and get back into your truck . . . I'm gonna get in my car and we can just go home."

Craig ignores me. "Look here, man, you better not open your damn mouth to me. You don't know me and I don't know you. But I swear if I see your big, tall, goofy-lookin' ass anywhere near my wife again . . . I'm gonna kill you! That's a promise and a threat."

Brian goes, "I don't know what you're talkin' 'bout. What am I supposed to say?"

Craig says, "Nothing. Don't say shit to me."

Brian puts both hands in the air. "I guess you got it then, big man."

"Yeah, I got you're a big man, you big, tall bitch! That's my wife you're messing with, not my girlfriend or my fiancée, but my wife. You know what that means?"

"Yeah, man, I know exactly what that means. Y'all take care." Brian turns around and walks toward his truck.

Craig grabs my arm. "Get your ass in that car and go straight home.

We'll talk about this later. I should go bust your boyfriend right in the back of his big-ass head."

Craig lets my arm go.

"Where are you going? Don't do nothing crazy."

"Take your ass home! Don't act like you're worried about me now."

Brian drives by with a disgusted look on his face and doesn't even look my way.

36

Craig

I think I handled myself real well in that situation with Brian. That boy could probably tell that I was a fighter and that I meant business. Fooling around with another man's wife can get a big goofy nigga like that killed in a hurry.

Now I'm about to pull over at this service station to use the pay phone and thank my informant for the reliable info she provided.

One day I might honestly consider putting some money into a cell phone. By the looks and smell of this receiver, that might not be a bad thing to do.

My so-called informant answers the phone. "Hello."

"Hey, it's me. Guess who I just ran into? You'll never believe it."

"Who?"

"Naomi and that guy, Brian, you told me about. You were right—I better keep a close eye on her."

She screams. "I told you! Told ya . . . told ya . . . told ya!"

"Calm down! Look how happy you are. You outta be ashamed."

"Not me. Your wife outta be ashamed. Did you follow behind them?"

"C'mon, Serena, you know me better than that. I'm crazy and all, but I ain't no stalker. I just rolled right up on them sitting on the side of the road in this nigga's tow truck in broad daylight for everybody to see. No shame in their game whatsoever."

"Did y'all get into a fight? Not you and Naomi, but you and Brian. 'Cause if y'all did, I know you passed the first lick."

"Nah, it didn't come down to that yet. I warned that big, tall bitch to stay away from my wife. Told him I'd kill him if he didn't, and I ain't lying. I mean it!"

"Don't go and do nothing crazy like that. I think you straightened them out. My sister knows better than to run around like that. She didn't learn that from me, that's for sure."

"Did you forget who you were talking to?"

"No, I do my share of running around, but don't nobody see me all out in the open like that. Maybe there's nothing really going on with the two of them or Naomi is completely out of her damn mind for being in his truck like that. Take it easy on her, all right?"

"We'll see."

"Did they admit to sleeping together?"

"I'm calling you from a service station pay phone not the county jail's pay phone."

"Oh, so I guess they didn't confess to anything then."

"No. You don't hear any sirens in the background. That's a good sign that they didn't open their mouths. As a matter of fact, I was the one who did most of the talkin'."

"Maybe you stepped in just before they reached that level, you know, sleeping together and all."

"Did Naomi tell you that they were sleeping together?"

"No. They just gave me vibes that they wanted to be with each other like that when I saw them together yesterday."

"What? They were together yesterday?"

"I told you 'bout that. That boy owns a garage over in Leaksville."

"I'm about to hurt somebody in a minute and his name is Brian. If he don't know that I'm a damn fool, then he better ask somebody."

"You ain't gonna hurt my sister, are you?"

"No. No way. I'd never hurt Naomi."

"You sound kinda funny how you said that. Now I'm starting to regret telling you about her and that boy. The last thing I need is for you to go off and do something bad to her. I don't want a repeat of Momma and Daddy 'cause I love my sister and need her more than you'll ever know."

"Forget all that. I'ma go home and chill."

"Oh, yeah? There's something else you need to hear."

"What's that?"

"Well, one night, a long while back, you and Darryl were over here drinking liquor. Darryl had passed out on the living room floor and you were just a step away from passing out your damn self."

"Girl, get to the point. Me and Darryl had quite a few nights like that."

"This night was different."

"Different how?"

"You came on to me kinda strong while Darryl was passed out. You and me was in the kitchen when you started touching my ass."

"Stop playing."

"I ain't playing. That's why I poked my butt out at you the other night after we had that argument. I called myself giving you a hint."

"You must be outta your damn mind."

"So you don't remember playing with my ass and telling me how phat it was?"

"No!"

"You played with my titties and told me how you wished Naomi's was as big as mine. You weren't trying to sleep with me . . . you just wanted to get some free feels in."

I'm thinking real hard and getting a damn headache trying to think that far back. It does seem kind of familiar. Feels like I need another drink right now to clear my head up.

Serena asks, "You still there?"

"I'm thinking. I might have had a nightmare like that, but I damn sure don't remember touching your body like that in real life."

"I'm not about to argue with you. Just know that it did happen. I swear it did. I never told anybody about it, especially not Naomi."

"Guess I owe you a big thank-you, then."

"It's the least your little smart ass could do. I just hope you realize that we all make mistakes, even you. I heard about your past, so take it easy on my sister."

"You ain't saying nothing. The past is the past. I never slept around on Naomi."

"I never said you did. Just do me one big favor and go on and forgive Naomi for this one. We'll never know. Maybe she did something with that boy and maybe she didn't. The only reason I said something to you about Brian is because I didn't want to see your happy home being broken up."

"Yeah, right! I'm sure our happiness means everything to you. Bet you wake up all the time in the middle of the night worrying about whether or not me and Naomi are happy. You're the one who encouraged her to go out there and find a man."

"Huh?"

"Oh, you didn't think I knew that, did you?"

"That was just girl talk. Nobody is stupid enough to really believe that kinda talk."

"Evidently somebody was. I think we should end this call right now. The only reason I'm being this nice is because I know you and Naomi are still dealing with issues related to your momma. Other than that, I'd really be going off on you."

"You don't even appreciate the fact that I called myself looking out for you."

"I do appreciate it . . . very much and thank you. One last thing—if I touched you the way that you said I did, then please accept my apology because I'm very, very sorry if I acted like that."

"It's okay. I have the same effect on ninety percent of the men in Eden. You already know the other ten percent are either blind, crippled, or crazy and that's the only reason why they're not sweatin' me."

I laugh. "Yeah, I know that's right. I'm gone. I'll be calling you soon to give you another update."

"All right . . . 'bye!"

I'm glad that's over with. It's hard to trust a woman who tells on her own sister. Serena is always saying that blood is thicker than water. That's a joke.

37

Naomi

I'm in the kitchen, minding my own business, when Craig comes home being all confrontational. He looks and smells bad. A mixture of sweat and alcohol is seeping out his pores. I don't know why people like to drink on hot days like this.

Craig yells, "Tell me what's been going on between you and your boyfriend. How long have y'all been seeing each other? Has he put his hands on you?" He shakes his head. "What in the hell do you see in him?"

"Craig, you really need to calm down. You look real crazy standing there like that. I bet you haven't bathed or shaved since Friday. You've been on a drinking binge. Now, please quiet down before the kids hear you. I'm begging you."

"You're gonna answer my questions and I don't give a damn who hears me. Stop trying to turn things around on me. You're the one who's been doing wrong. Everybody knows I've been drinking again . . . so what! And no, I haven't had a bath or shaved in a couple of days, but I washed up real good this morning and hit all the important spots. Is that good enough for you?"

"Leave me alone, Craig. You're drunk right now. Please go somewhere and sit your foolish self down. Let me finish frying this chicken and I'll have dinner on the table in less than a half-hour."

"Did you sleep with him?"

"Stop it, Craig!"

"You can't even deny it. Do you love him?"

"Please, go somewhere! I know the kids can hear you."

He yells even louder. "They need to hear me! I want the whole world to know what you went out there and did. I asked if you loved him."

"I don't love him. Are you happy now?"

"Hell no, I ain't happy. You don't love him and you don't love me, either. Who do you love and when did you stop loving me, anyway? Tell me that."

"I do love you . . . now go sit down somewhere." I say calmly.

"You're lying. Did you ever kiss him?"

"If I say that I kissed him, then will you go sit down?"

Craig steps right up in my face and says, "Stop playing with me! This ain't a game. What were you doing with him yesterday?"

"I knew somebody was watching me. You need to stop. I knew you were following me around."

"I don't have time to do dumb shit like that. Where did y'all go yesterday? Where'd he take you, to his house or to a motel?"

"Look, I'm going through a lot right now and you're not helping. Please stop stressing me out."

"Don't try to use your momma for an excuse. She's long gone and you're trying to kill me, but I ain't ready to die yet. I want answers and I want them now."

I ignore Craig and continue frying my chicken.

He snaps, "Fuck that chicken! Turn around and give me answers. You had sex with that man, didn't you? Be a woman and tell the truth. Was he better than me? Was his thing bigger than mine?"

I giggle a little. "You gotta be kidding me. Even if I did something wrong, I wouldn't tell you right now. You're a drunken mess and I'm getting tired of it."

"Damn you! You're doing it again. This ain't about me. You went out and fucked up, not me! You think you're going though a lot, then step into my shoes."

"I'm dealing with my own problems and a whole lot more. I got your problems, C.J's problems with police, Erika's abortion, and whatever else is after that. Now back up and get away from me . . . stinking!"

"Erika's abortion? What in the hell do you mean, abortion? When was she pregnant?"

"That's not an issue now. It's been taken care of."

"I'm tired of you! I asked you to stop doing things with that girl behind my back. Now look what you did." Craig lunges at me and grabs me by my neck. "You better respect me or I'm gonna choke the shit outta you!"

"Bullshit! Choke me then, Craig . . . choke me!"

I forgot how strong Craig is. He's got both hands wrapped around my throat. I'm trying my best to yell, "Get off me! Get the fuck off me!"

I can barely make a sound. I'm not crying, but tears are flowing from my eyes like a river from all the pressure on my throat.

Craig takes me down to the floor and gets on top of me. "I'll kill you in here, I swear I will! Don't make me do it, 'cause I will. Now I told you to stop playing with me. You're gonna take me serious! You hear me? I said, do you hear me?"

He begins to apply more pressure. Craig is so drunk that I'm not even sure if he's aware of how much he's hurting me. I'm not able to answer him because I can't get any air to pass through my windpipe. He continues to add pressure. Feels like my windpipe has been crushed. I totally underestimated Craig's strength and his sanity. He has completely lost his mind. I never imagined in my wildest dreams that my husband would ever put his hands on me like this. I never imagined dying like this, either. If the blood flow doesn't return to my brain or I don't take a breath within the next few seconds, then this is it for me. I'll never see my kids again.

A man yells, "Get your hands off of her or I'll cut your goddamn throat."

The pressure is slowly released. Air, pain, and more pain. I need more air. I can hardly breathe, but at least I'm still alive. When I open my eyes I see Brian standing in front of me with a butcher knife to Craig's throat. Craig is on his knees with his hands in the air. I blink my eyes and when I refocus I clearly see that it's C.J. with the knife to his daddy's throat. C.J. got the knife from the cutlery block on the kitchen counter.

I manage to mumble, "Stop, please don't. Don't hurt him."

My voice is extremely hoarse. C.J. ignores my pleas. He holds the butcher knife steady and directly over his daddy's throat.

Craig yells, "You better kill me, nigga, 'cause if you don't I'ma kill you first!"

"You ain't killing nobody!"

Erika yells, "Y'all need to stop! Let Daddy up and don't you hurt him."

Craig looks toward Erika. "You already hurt me more than this nigga ever could. I can't believe you or Naomi . . . doing all kinds of stuff behind my back. Went and got yourself pregnant. Thanks for being such a good role model for your little sister."

Erika goes, "I'm sorry, Daddy. This is all my fault."

"Nah, this right here is C.J.'s fault. My own son done turned against me. That ain't even your real momma, boy. If you're gonna kill me over that tramp, then I deserve to die. You don't even know what she went out there and done to me—to us, I should say."

"I don't care! You know you're wrong, Daddy, dead wrong for putting your hands on her."

Craig shouts, "I dunno! I dunno nothing no more!"

C.J. yells, "Shut up and get off your knees! Get up!"

Erika says, "Let him go, C.J."

"I'm trying to let him up."

I say, "Call the police. He's going to jail for putting his hands on me."

Morgan finally comes into the kitchen, looking terrified. "No, Momma. I don't want my daddy to go to jail. Please don't . . . don't call the police. Can't y'all just make up and eat dinner like we do every Sunday?"

It hurts me deeply to see Morgan like this. What she's really telling me is that she doesn't want to grow up like I did with a daddy in jail. Craig is at his lowest point ever and if he goes to jail now, he'll never recover.

Craig says, "We can't, Lil' Momma. Too much has happened now. Things are all messed up."

C.J. says, "I'ma let you up now, Daddy, but don't be a fool and try to hurt none of us."

As Craig gets up slowly, he says, "You don't have to worry 'bout that. I'm leaving. Y'all don't have to call the police. All y'all can have this house. I can't afford it no more, anyway."

Craig makes his way to the back door.

Morgan cries, "Daddy, don't go!"

I say, "Let him go. He tried to kill me. Get out."

"I gotta go. Erika, even though you broke my heart, I still love you and Morgan—I love y'all, God knows I do. But I wish that nigga right there was never born."

Erika cries out, "Don't say that, Daddy. He didn't mean that, C.J."

Craig looks directly at me with hate in his eyes. "And you—I don't care if I ever see you again in my life."

C.J. says, "Just get outta here before something bad happens to one of us. I would've killed you when I had this knife to your throat, but you ain't even worth it. You're killing yourself, anyway. You got the nerve to act like Erika's such a poor role model. I'm ashamed to call you my daddy. Get your drunk ass outta here."

"Shut the hell up, you . . . you pothead!"

Craig frowns and throws his hand at C.J. Craig starts out the door, then he turns around and reaches under the kitchen sink for his bottle of Jack Daniel's. I don't have anything to say to Craig.

C.J. says, "Look at you. That's pitiful."

"Go to hell."

Craig slams the kitchen door so hard that the mini blind falls to the floor. I hear him start up his Bronco and take off down the road.

I turn to Erika and say, "I'm so sorry, Erika. Really I am. Your daddy said so much to me that he made your secret slip right out of my mouth. I wasn't aware of what I was saying. Really I wasn't."

"It don't even matter now."

Erika gives me a mean look for betraying her. She eases away and goes off to her bedroom. C.J. and Morgan stand by my side and help me up off the kitchen floor.

C.J. says, "Momma, I love you and I won't let nobody put their hands on you, not even my stupid daddy."

"Thank you. Craig would have killed me if you hadn't stopped him."

"I know. You looked like you were unconscious when we got out here."

"I almost felt myself going away from here."

Morgan says, "I hate when you and Daddy fuss and fight. I don't want him to come back here. I wanna live in peace."

"I don't want him back here either. I'm gonna have to leave here for good if he comes back. I'm so glad I'm graduating. I can't wait till Saturday morning," says C.J.

"He'll be back as soon as he sobers up. Hopefully his senses will return. Things will be back to normal. I'm going to my bedroom to lie down," I say.

C.J. and Morgan support me on both sides like two human crutches as I walk to my bedroom. Meanwhile, Erika is in her bedroom, mad as hell at me for opening my mouth and telling her secret.

38

Naomi

The phone rings.
I'm lying in bed with Morgan next to me. She's dead asleep—I was knocked out myself until now. The phone rings again. It's the kind of loud, irritating ring that screams that something's wrong. I answer the phone quickly before it wakes up my baby.

Softly I say, "Hello."

"Naomi."

"Yes."

"It's Momma Pearl. Did I wake you, darling?"

"No, I was just lying here."

I don't know why I lied to Momma Pearl just now. That wasn't the decent Christian thing to do at all, especially lying over something as simple as whether I was asleep or not. Sometimes I try to act like I'm a superwoman, like I don't eat, sleep, or use the bathroom. I think I lied mainly because I didn't want to make her feel bad for waking me.

I look over at my alarm clock and it reads 11:45 P.M.

"Sorry to call you this time of night, but I wanted to let you know that Miss Magnolia just passed. She went peacefully . . . she fell asleep like a baby and gradually stopped breathing. Me and Sister Clarissa were right by her side, praying for her as she went on to glory."

"I'm so sorry to hear that she passed. I stopped by there to see her yesterday. She told me she wouldn't be here too much longer. Miss Maggie was a sweet woman."

"Yes, she was. She told me and Sis that you stopped by here to see her. Thanks for doing that. She was tickled pink about you coming by here yesterday."

"I'm glad I got the chance to see her before she passed."

"It was meant to happen like that I guess. You okay?"

I'm trying to keep my answers as short as possible because the fact that she knows about me and Brian makes me extremely uncomfortable.

"Yes ma'am. I'm all right."

"I was worried about you at first, but now I know you're in good hands. Just keep your faith in the Lord and you can't go wrong. You'll be all right. Thank you so much for coming by the church today. Did you enjoy yourself?"

"I did."

"I know you did. I saw the spirit moving through the church. It even moved you. I know you felt it."

"Yes, ma'am."

"Well, you know you're always welcome there. That's your home."

"I know."

"Good, so don't be a stranger. Kiss Craig and the kids for me."

"I will."

"God bless you, darling. You know you're always in my prayers."

"Thank you. Good night."

Morgan is still out like a light. I'm about to move her to her own bed because she sleeps wild. This girl likes to sleep in the middle of the bed and, at times, diagonally. Every now and then she turns into a little kickboxer, beating me up over half the night. I understand that she wants to be close to her momma, but I'm not in the mood for a stiff neck and an aching body in the morning. By the time morning rolls around, she won't know or care how she got in her own bed. As a matter of fact, Morgan probably won't even remember being in my bed at all.

When I return to my bed it hits me that my husband is gone. I'm not used to sleeping without him. All that drama earlier seems like something from one of my favorite soap operas. To be honest, my life has turned into a nonstop soap opera. Less than a week ago I was caught up in the fictional lives of soap stars wishing my life had a little drama in it and now I drowning in it. This is too much for me to handle on my own.

I decide to give Brian a call.

Brian says, "Hello."

"Hey."

"Hey, what's up? I was just lying here in bed thinking about you. Where are you?"

"Home in bed thinking about you."

"Where's the big man?"

"You mean, my little nuisance? Craig's gone. Sorry for the way he talked to you earlier."

"Don't even mention it. For real, though, I wanted to crush his little ass, but I couldn't because I deserved to be talked to like that. I'm the one who did wrong. I disrespected him in the worst way by messing around with his wife."

"I guess so. He said he was leaving and that me and the kids could have the house. He'll be back. I'm sure of it 'cause the only thing he packed was a bottle of Jack Daniel's, right under his arm."

"So, what does this mean, a separation?"

"I dunno. Who really knows what this means. I feel like we're through, especially after he tried to choke me to death."

"What?"

"He tried to kill me in here in front of our kids. My son had to put a butcher knife to Craig's throat to get his crazy behind off me."

Brian is silent.

I say, "Hello, you still there? Say something."

"I'm still here. I'm just at a loss for words. I feel bad because I'm to blame for what happened. Somebody could have been killed. I guess I didn't fully understand how getting in a relationship with you would affect so many innocent people. Your kids are being affected from this and that's not fair to them at all. If your son had killed his daddy or if big man had killed you, I wouldn't have been able to live with myself."

"By the grace of God, none of that happened, so relax. What am I hearing? Is this the part where you totally distance yourself from me because my life is filled with way too much drama for you to handle?"

"I never said all that. Your husband is gone and that's a major change in your life."

"Oh, I see what's going on. All of a sudden this is real to you now. I think you're starting to fear the total package. Now you can fully see that I have baggage . . . kids. Is that too heavy for you to handle?"

"I can handle anything, but two of them kids ain't really yours though. Are they gonna go wherever their daddy is?"

"No, they're really mine and they're gonna stay right here with me. How the hell am I supposed to turn my back on them after all these years? I'm their momma, regardless of who gave birth to them or whether their daddy is in this house or not."

"Honestly, things are moving way too fast. We never really settled into a groove. Now it seems like you're saying the ball's in my court and you're waiting for me to make the next move."

"Basically, I am saying that. What happened to all that stuff you said earlier—*I'll put a ring on your finger and marry you if that's what it takes?*"

"I mean, I still feel that way. We need to talk face-to-face. When are you available to talk?"

"I dunno."

"What about right now? C'mon over. I've got a space for you right here next to me. My pillow misses you."

"I can't come over there now."

"Why not? Your hubby ain't there to hold you back. We really need to talk because I think you have the wrong impression of me."

"Well, listen out for me. I'll be right over."

I took a few extra minutes to get fixed up real nice for Brian. I used a special body cleanser called Angel Wash when I showered and then afterward I rubbed myself down in Angel Touch Lotion. I'm wearing two of my favorite things from Victoria's Secret, my lilac lace bra and panty set and my Dream Angels Divine perfume spray. I feel so sexy and I look beautiful. My hair has incredible body, all bouncing and behaving. Brian has no idea what I've got in store for him. I'm in the mood for doing a lot more than talking.

The kids are all asleep. Morgan is off somewhere, deep in another world. C.J. and Erika fell asleep with their televisions on. I decided to just leave everything as is because they both have a tendency to wake up in an instant whenever I sneak in and turn off their televisions. I don't want the kids to know that I decided to step out for a minute. I'll be back before they notice a thing.

I tiptoe out the back door, then out to the carport. As soon as I get to my car door, a strange sensation comes over me. My mind quickly tells me that something's not quite right. I fumble with my keys and then look back toward the house. Suddenly it seems so far away. There's a rustling sound coming from the bushes behind me. Instantly I'm petrified, feeling like I'm backed in a corner with nowhere to run. My breath escapes me. I get this incredible urge to take off sprinting back to the house. All of a sudden I feel something heavy come crashing down on my head. I feel a warm liquid rush through part of my scalp and down the right side of my face. I'm bleeding. This isn't supposed to happen to me. Everything fades into darkness. The last thing I remember seeing was my house with the full moon in the background and smelling dirt and roses.

I must be semiconscious because I feel someone wrapping duct tape around my eyes, mouth, wrists, and ankles. They just continue taping me up in a very precise manner without saying a single word. Within seconds I'm tossed in the trunk of a car. My head rests on the side of a spare tire as we take off to God only knows where.

39

Craig

For some reason I keep forgetting how easy it is to lose track of the most important things in my life like my wife, my kids, and reality in general. That's exactly what alcohol does to a person like me. It's hard to admit, but I'm an alcoholic. This is a recurring issue that I've been dealing with for years. A problem like this became real hard to ignore, especially when I found myself drinking excessive amounts of alcohol and starting my day off by drinking earlier and earlier each day. I have a bad habit of using alcohol to escape my problems; instead, they only seem to get worse. The past week has been a total blur. Forgetfulness has become a common thing to me lately. Erika told me about how I tried to choke Naomi to death, but I can hardly remember a single thing that happened Sunday evening.

When I came home Monday morning, Naomi was gone and I haven't seen or heard from her since. The last thing I want is to have another woman leave me because of one of my stupid addictions. I lost Debbie because of my addiction to loose women and I refuse to lose Naomi to alcohol.

Today's Wednesday and I haven't been able to eat or sleep for the past three days. My stomach is pickled and whining like a baby. There's a jackhammer working overtime, pounding inside my head. I'm anxious as hell and it's time for me to get my mind right. Time to get my life back on track. I need to get my wife back, but I don't even know where to start or how to prioritize things anymore. Something tells me to start by calling Brian's house again. I've been calling him for the past couple of days, but since he knows it's me he won't answer the damn phone. He answered once yesterday, then hung up as soon as he heard me mention Naomi's name. Brian's number was still programmed into the phone in our bedroom when I pressed the Redial button. I kind of figured the whole phone thing out like detective. He was the last person Naomi called on Sunday. I imagine she called him and he came over here to pick her up. Bet they've been living it up since then. They've probably been having sex every day in all kinds of ways. I'm aiming to put an end to all that shit just as soon as I can put a plan together. My concentration is shot to hell.

Meanwhile, I'm just sitting here on the side of my bed, pressing the Redial button over and over again.

Finally Brian answers the phone.

"Who is this?"

"You know who this is. Where's Naomi?"

"Yo, man, what the hell is wrong with you? I told you . . . your wife ain't here. Stop calling my damn house. I ain't gonna tell you again."

"Where's my wife?"

"Look, you're about to see a different side of me."

I laugh. "What? Boy, you must be out of your damn mind. How you gonna act like that when I know for a fact that y'all talked to each other on Sunday right before she left here? Your fucking number was still programmed in my Redial."

Brian pauses for a few seconds. "Is that right? Well, that just goes to show you that your wife called me. I swear I haven't seen or talked to her since Sunday night and that's the God's honest truth."

"Stop lying to me! I know she's there! You don't have to cover for her. Don't play games with me, boy. That's my wife!"

The phone line clicks, goes dead for a second, and a dial tone comes through loud and clear. That nigga just hung up on me.

I begin to hit the Redial button over and over again.

I'm tired of playing games. Time for action. I'm gonna call Sonny and ask him to meet me at my house. We're about to find out where this boy lives and pay him a quick visit.

40

Naomi

I'm no longer a person, less than human. Flies are all around me, buzzing in my ears and crawling on my flesh. That's not even the worst of it. I've been in complete darkness, bound in duct tape. The tape is still wrapped tightly around my eyes, mouth, wrists and ankles. Dried blood has my hair matted to my scalp like some sort of tight-fitting leather cap. My body aches from head to toe from lying on my back in the same basic position. As a matter of fact, I don't have a clue as to what day it is. My clothes were cut off of me at some point during my first night. I've been lying here completely naked, gagged and bound on a funky mattress the entire time. As far as I know, I haven't been sexually assaulted, just forced to lie here naked while someone watches me suffer. This room is cold, emotionally and temperature-wise. The air is drafty and musty like an old cellar. Someone must have felt sorry for me last night and tossed me a blanket that smells just as bad as this pissy mattress I've been lying on. I can smell traces of kerosene in the air, but the foul smell from this mattress and my own body are the most dominant odors in the room.

This place is a huge basement that echoes all kinds of sounds. I heard a woman scream in horror last night for about five minutes and then there was complete silence. Her screams were gut-wrenching and suggested to me that she was being tortured. I cried for her and for myself. At this point I know that the same inevitable fate awaits me. I'm still trying to figure out whether I've been abducted by the same person who's responsible for Carolyn and Ginger's disappearances. Maybe that was one of them screaming. I keep asking myself why whoever is behind this hasn't killed me yet. If this is it for me, then all I can do is rest assured that I was able to reestablish my relationship with God. I believe that no matter what happens, I'm gonna be all right. God is with me.

Suddenly I hear doors opening and closing and footsteps overhead. Blood rushes to my stomach, causing it to knot up. I tremble. My heart pounds out of control and my breath escapes me. Every time I hear movement, I think someone is about to come and kill me.

At least two to three times a day somebody comes along and cuts off this tape around my mouth. Each time I scream like crazy. The person doesn't say a word, just slaps me in the face and begins to force-feed me an unusual course of bananas, saltine crackers, and water.

Out of nowhere, a door directly in front of me opens. I feel someone's presence. He kneels down and begins to stroke the right side of my face with his hand. I move my head from side to side, trying to make him stop. He finally stops, then covers me completely with this nasty blanket.

I'm tempted to try and roll away, but it won't do any good because I can't see where I'm going. Occasionally I hear mice running through here. That's another thing keeping me on this mattress.

I think at least two men are holding me captive. I'm guessing that by the sounds of their movement and their actions. This guy right here is the more compassionate of the two, if that makes any sense. This bastard won't say a word. All I hear is his breathing. He stands up, turns away, opens the door, and exits the room.

41

Craig

I'm mad as shit. I swear, I can't win for losing. Just before I left my house the mailman handed me a stack of bills and a notice from the Bank of America letting me know that a stop-payment was placed on that check Dr. Easley wrote. If it ain't one thing, it's another. That pervert got us in the end. That's just how my luck runs. Naomi and her men are driving me crazy.

I'm in my Bronco with Sonny. We found out where Brian lives and we're on our way to kick his ass. I'm more of a hands-on type of guy. I like to let my fists do the talking. Sonny on the other hand likes to pack heat and is quick to pull it out and pop off a couple of rounds if things get out of hand. That's the main reason I brought him.

We pull up to Brian's house. Sonny points to Brian's truck in the driveway.

"Looka there. Is that his truck?"

"I hope so."

"Yeah, I bet that sum-bitch is in there."

"Bet Naomi's in there, too." I look at Sonny and laugh. "That nigga is in trouble now."

"Betta believe that."

We hop out of the Bronco and head up to the front door, looking around for nosy neighbors at the same time. No one is in sight. Sonny stands to one side of the door and I stand to the other. I knock on

Brian's front door, real casual-like. Within a few seconds Brian answers the front door wearing a white terry cloth robe.

Brian looks surprised. He makes a motion with the door like he wants to close it, but then his own arrogance stops him.

I ask, "What's up, playboy? Bet you didn't expect to see me standing here. Next time you better ask who it is before opening your front door to two crazy motherfuckers like us."

Brian laughs. "Look, Craig, or whatever your name is, Naomi ain't here so I guess you and your granddaddy should just turn around and go 'bout your business."

Sonny yells, "Who the hell you calling granddaddy, you sum-bitch!"

"I got this, Sonny."

I push my way past Brian and step inside his house.

"Naomi! Naomi! Get your ass out here!"

Before I know it, Brian runs toward me and grabs me by my shoulder. He turns me around and bangs me right dead in my right eye. I fall backwards, landing on the floor. Nobody has ever hit me that hard. His fist felt like a big, heavy piece of steel slamming against my eye and forehead. For some reason I never really counted on Brian fighting back. He didn't seem like the type.

Sonny jumps inside the house, closes the front door, and pulls out his pistol.

"You take another step and I'll blow your goddamn head off, boy!"

I'm lying on the floor, feeling like I'm going in and out of consciousness. I feel sorry for myself. This boy beat me down and has me laid out on the floor, feeling like a complete failure. He beat my time with my wife and now he beat my ass.

Sonny asks, "Mo, you all right?"

Just as Sonny asks if I'm all right, I notice that Brian's robe is unfastened. It must have come undone when he hit me. When I look at him I see this big horse dick dangling between his legs. The damn thing is soft and is about twice the size of mine. All I see now is him putting that thing inside Naomi. I imagine the passion they must have shared and how much she loved being with him. I have no real proof, but as a man I just know and feel it in my heart that something sexual happened between this boy and my wife. Neither one of them did a good job of convincing me to think otherwise. Anger and a vicious flow of adrenaline take over me.

"Hell nah, I ain't all right."

I get up off the floor, lunge directly at Brian like a bolt of lightning, and manage to work my way around to his back before he can even make one move.

Brian yells, "I'm gonna crush your little ass!"

I jump on his back. He's still on his feet. Looks like he's giving me a piggyback ride.

"That's right, get his ass, Mo!"

I'm able to get Brian in a headlock. He starts spinning around and pounding me from every angle, but no matter what, I maintain a death grip around his neck because I know this modern-day Goliath will definitely kill me if I let go.

Sonny laughs. "That's right. You got him now. Don't let go."

Out of anger, I say, "See, boy, I've been fightin' all my life. You didn't know you was dealing with a damn fool. I'll fight anybody, especially a big, young punk-nigga messing with my wife."

After about a minute or so, Brian slows down. I feel the life slipping away from him. I'm taking it away from him, slowly but surely. Never knew I could kill a man until now, and the bad thing is, I don't care. He took the most precious thing in my life away from me. A vision from my wedding day of Naomi dressed up, looking beautiful in her white gown, plays in my head. That white meant something to me, meant everything. She was pure. Never been touched by another man. She was mine, all mine. Brian took that away from me. And now I'm taking his life for violating what was meant for me.

All of a sudden both of us come crashing down to the floor. I purposely force Brian to land face first.

Sonny laughs. "You did it, Mo! Look at that sum-bitch!"

I feel crazy and strong as shit at the same time. My hands are shaking. I'm so pumped that I can't keep still. Seeing Brian spread out facedown on the floor makes me feel redeemed.

"That's what he gets for fucking around with my wife."

Sonny says, "Hold on, Mo. Something ain't right. See if that boy is all right. I ain't seen him move yet."

I laugh. "I saw him move just a second ago. He twitched around like this." I do a quick imitation of what I saw Brian do. I kick him on his side a few times. "Get up, nigga." Brian doesn't budge. "Oh shit, I think he might be dead."

All that hate I felt just a minute ago quickly turns into fear and concern.

Sonny says, "I don't reckon you killed him. Turn him over right quick and see if that sum-bitch is breathing."

"I don't think he's breathing."

"Good enough. What's done is done. Let's get the hell outta here."

"Hold up! We can't leave him like this."

"Who can't? Let's go."

"I ain't no murderer."

Sonny kneels down to check Brian out. "He's not breathing and he ain't got a pulse, either. He's gone."

"Oh no. At least I can call him an ambulance and then we can get the hell outta here."

"Might be too late for an ambulance. Give him two quick breaths. Do it! You're wasting time."

I look down at Brian's bloodied mouth. This is too much for me. I'm being forced to put my lips on the man who's been having an affair with my wife. God help me. Only a real man would do this. I fill Brian's lungs with my breath.

Sonny took a CPR course at the YMCA a couple of years ago. Bet he never thought he'd actually have to use his skills in real life. He starts chest compressions, yells out instructions and coaches me on how to perform two-man CPR. Within a few minutes Brian has a faint pulse and is taking shallow breaths on his own. He's still unconscious.

Sonny says, "Call 911 and pretend you're this boy and tell them you can't hardly breathe . . . and to send you some help. C'mon, move!"

"All right."

I go to the kitchen and grab the cordless phone. The 911 operator answers. I put on a fake voice and make up a quick story. The fact that I'm being recorded bothers me, but I continue the lies anyway. While I'm on the phone I look around Brian's little-ass house. When I get to his bedroom, I imagine how he and Naomi must have looked in bed together. I look in the bathroom and imagine seeing them in the shower, embracing with soapsuds streaming down their bodies. Then I imagine another scenario of them bathing together by candlelight and Naomi positioned between Brian's legs. I blow it off and continue to move from room to room. The smaller bedroom is empty. I check under the bed and in the closet, but Naomi is nowhere to be found.

The operator tells me that an ambulance will be here within ten minutes.

When I return to the living room, Sonny looks at me and says, "You know what? I don't think Naomi is here. After all that ruckus, she would have come out here to see what was going on. You didn't see her anywhere, did you?"

"No. She ain't here. We gotta get moving. The ambulance is on its way."

Brian moans. He's starting to come around.

Sonny and I look in his direction. I move in for a closer look.

I yell, "Brian! Brian! You hear me?" He moans. "Good. We're even now. I gave you your life back. Next time you won't be so lucky. I need you to tell the police that you have no idea what happened. Tell them two strangers followed you home and did this to you. You hear me?"

He moans.

Sonny says, "He don't hear you. Don't worry 'bout him. Hard as his head hit that goddamn floor, he won't remember you, me, or a damn thing. Let's go!"

42

Naomi

Somebody just walked past me real slow. I didn't realize it, but he must have been standing there watching me all along. He goes over and slides open a door. I hear the door drag the ground, making a sweeping sound. As soon as it opens, I feel a draft accompanied by the unmistakable stench of death. This is the first time that door has been opened. The rancid odor overpowers any other odor I previously complained about by at least one hundred times.

It smells like a couple tons of old rotten meat topped with a thousand dead rats. My stomach turns. A sour taste seeps from under my tongue, then around my entire mouth. This is the worst case of nausea ever. My stomach begins to boil over from the stench of death and a combination of fear and anxiety. My eyes begin to water under this tape. My mouth is still gagged with a piece of duct tape that extends around my entire head. I fight like hell to keep from throwing up. Within seconds, I'm forced to vomit and the bad thing is that it has nowhere to go. I have to think fast. I'm forced to swallow it back down to keep from choking. The door is closed, but not as tight as before because the odor still lingers. The flies down here are having a field day.

A few hours have passed. I can't take this waiting. I'm lying here in a complete mess and nobody has the decency to try and clean me up. The adhesive has irritated my skin—it's raw. One of these sadistic bastards added a couple more layers of duct tape on top of the original layers over the past few days. I've been turning my head back and forth violently, trying to work this tape away from my eyes. Thanks to the oil in my hair and the moisture of my skin, I've been able to get some of the tape halfway loose, creating a little slit to peek through, but I still can't see well.

I'm trying to figure out what's real and what's part of my imagination because my eyes have been shut for so long. Everything appears shadowy, a dark shade of gray. There are two pull-string light fixtures with single bulbs. One hangs from this end and the other from the middle of the ceiling. It's extremely dirty and dusty—shovels, brooms, mops, and two buckets sit in one corner of the room. A fluorescent light flickers at the far end. A large wooden cross with two smaller wooden crosses on both sides hang on the wall under the flickering light, and right above the three crosses is the word INFERNO written in big, bold, bloody letters. That's the perfect word to describe this hellhole.

I'm able to make out something in the distance. My heart skips a beat, then starts pounding out of my chest. There's a man standing in the shadows near a stairway at the far end of the room. This is so weird. He's as motionless as a statue. I can't make out his face because of the shadows. I can only see his jeans and boots. He must be enjoying this. I'm not sure if he's noticed that I was able to work the tape halfway from around my eyes.

He walks away and disappears into the shadows.

I continue to look around the room. There are dusty shelves and a workstation set up with assorted knives, saws, and ice picks. A collection of necklaces, bracelets, wigs, and a long scarf hang from the wall of the workstation. Eyeglasses, belts, and shoes sit on the two shelves. I quickly realize that one of the wigs isn't a wig at all. It's actually human hair and I can see large skin tags still attached.

I wish I had kept this tape completely over my eyes because now I can clearly see that I'm in the lair of a serial killer.

I hear footsteps moving in my direction. That guy must have come back and he's going to hurt me for working this tape loose. My eyes are closed tightly and my entire body tenses. I begin to recite the Lord's Prayer in my head. This is it.

Someone says, "I'm here to save you."

When I open my eyes, Momma Pearl is standing over me, dressed in her typical white garb. This is like a moment of relief for me.

She looks directly in my eyes. "I said I'm here to save you, chile."

I'm unable to speak because of the duct tape. I thank her with my eyes. Momma Pearl unravels the tape from around my mouth. I take in some deep breaths because this is one of the few times I've been able to breathe fully through my mouth, other than my awful feeding times. She pulls the remaining tape from around my eyes to the best of her ability because some of the tape gets tangled in my hair.

While gasping for air, I say, "Thank God. I'm so glad to see you. Thank you . . . thank you so much. Where am I? How'd you find me?"

"Call it divine intervention. God led me right to you. Look at that old pew right there. You should know where you are now."

"This is the basement of the old church. It's way different from how I remembered it. Look at that weird stuff over there. C'mon, we have to hurry. There was a man here. All I could make out was his jeans and boots. Is he gone?"

"I didn't see anybody. How long have you been down here?"

"I dunno. At least a few days."

"Do you know what today is?"

"No. I'm kind of disoriented. What day is it?"

"Today's your birthday." Momma Pearl closes her eyes and bites her bottom lip. "I can't keep this up."

"What?"

In scornful tones she says, "Happy birthday, sinner. I tried to hate the sin and love the sinner, but sometimes hate overpowers love and this is one of those times."

"Huh? What are you talking about?"

Momma Pearl gives me a strange look that sends chills throughout my body. She places her right hand on my forehead, closes her eyes, and zones out. She starts speaking in tongues. She's saying some kind of prayer. She's scaring me half to death. I don't know what to do or to say. I want her to stop this right now.

I hold my hands up in front of me and cry out, "Stop it! Remove this tape from my wrists and ankles before that man gets back here. We gotta go. C'mon, we don't have time for this."

Suddenly she stops praying. Her eyes appear real intense. She gives me an evil stare that pierces me down to my soul.

"Today is your birthday and your death-day."

"You're insane. Stop it!"

"I'm doing you and everybody else a favor. The good thing is, you won't get any older. Thirty is a good age to die. Try to remember all your favorite people, favorite songs and movies."

"What are you talking about? I need your help. Whatever I did to piss you off, I'm sorry. You're my aunt." I start squirming around. "Now get me outta here before that man gets back. Help me, please!"

"I'm gonna help you. I'm here to help save you . . . here to save your soul and prepare you for judgment day just like I've done for so many others, including your sorry momma."

I'm crushed. Feels like a ton of bricks just landed on me. My world has been turned upside down and inside out. Momma Pearl just admitted to killing Momma. I scream.

"Go right ahead and scream all you want . . . nobody's gonna hear you."

I'm angry and stunned. "No! You killed Momma? Don't say that. No! You couldn't have."

"Yes, I did."

The pride in Momma Pearl's voice angers me even more and I still can't process what she's saying. Something just won't let it sink in.

"Why? Why would you kill her?"

"She was sleeping with my husband and I had to put an end to that. He's down here, too."

I get hysterical. "What do you mean, he's down here?"

Momma Pearl slaps me in the face. "Stop crying!"

"Don't hit me again."

"Whatcha gonna do?"

I try my best to calm down because my crying only seems to upset this maniac even more.

"Nothing. I can't do anything. Where's Uncle Henry?"

"He's in that room over there with the others. Are you ready to see them now?"

"No! No! I can't believe this. Why'd you kill Momma and let your brother suffer for all these years for nothing? I hate you! I hope you burn in hell!"

"That's right, let all that hate out. I love it." She laughs, "Your daddy is suffering for not controlling his wife. He disgraced our family from the start by marrying Barbara. I had to kill your momma. God told me to do it. He told me to put an end to your momma's life for trying to ruin a holy man . . . the most decent Christian man I've ever known. She was sleeping with my husband, the pastor of this church. We couldn't have that, so Sis and I had to do her in. Henry helped us, then we got rid of him and told everybody he moved up north to start a new church. He was the man you heard at your house the night I killed Barbara. Who did you think the man was that night?"

I can't even talk. I'm going crazy because there's no way for me to express how I feel. In my wildest dreams, I never would have imagined that something was going on between Momma and Uncle Henry. No wonder he was so fond of me and Serena. Now I understand exactly why Momma Pearl hated us so much and made our childhood a living hell.

Momma Pearl is so lucky that my hands and ankles are still bound. I would kill her old ass with my bear hands if I could.

"You're a sick, evil, twisted, psychopathic bitch. I hate you with everything inside me."

She slaps me in the face again. "Sorry for that. Sometimes it's hard for me to control my emotions. Watch your language—this is still a church. We have a small congregation that still worships down here."

"You've been part of a cult all this time, brainwashing people."

"We don't brainwash anybody. They just learn to embrace our beliefs. And I hate the word *cult*. That word is used to distort our mission and hinder our growth. People always try to label what they fear or can't understand, but we understand. I'm part of a growing organization called the New Fellowship for a Better Tomorrow. It's far from a cult. We're God's people. Chosen to do the work."

"What work, killing people?"

Momma Pearl laughs. "We work as catalysts in this wicked society to make sure things happen the righteous way, the way they were intended to, and if that means getting rid of certain people then so be it. Your momma got in the way. So did Carolyn Tinsley, Ginger Davis, and Magnolia Wilson."

"How could you kill that lady? You had just killed her when you called me?"

"I did, and I controlled Magnolia's mind until I got tired of her. There've been a few others who've gotten in our way. They were before your time, ones you probably never even heard of. One that you may have heard of was Debbie Gaffney. She was in the way of the destiny planned for you and Craig. I knew he was in love with you from the start. I knew from the way he used to look at you in church that he wanted to be with you, so I made that happen. Debbie's in there with the others, too."

"Oh my God! You need help. You belong to a doomsday cult. You need to be stopped. Y'all are no different from other cults like Heaven's Gate, the People's Temple, or the Branch Davidians."

"There's no stopping us, because we're better than them. We're determined to fulfill our religious manifesto and we won't allow you or anyone else to stop us."

"I don't care . . . just leave me alone. What did I ever do to you?"

"You judged me . . . for years you and Serena judged me. And you should never have gotten involved with Brian. We had other plans for him. He was a God-fearing man, but you ruined him. Now we've got to deal with him, too. The thing I detest most about you is that you're so much like your momma . . . you and that damn Serena. She's next on my list."

"You better leave her alone. Please, let me go! I wanna go home to my family. They need me and I need them."

Momma Pearl shakes her head. "You don't need them and they don't need you. Pretty soon they won't even remember how it was to have you around. If you needed them so bad, then why'd you mess up and start having an affair with Brian?"

"I made a mistake. It's over between us. I never wanna see him again."

"You won't . . . I promise. Look at you, you're just like your momma. I knew you'd find out the truth one day, just never knew it'd be under these circumstances."

"I don't understand. What happened to you? I started to believe in you. You were so convincing last Sunday. I'm glad I know how to separate the message from the messenger."

"What you witnessed during Sunday's service was real. I do what I have to do for our organization. The new church will help fund and attract new members to our alternative fellowship. Soon a whole lot more people will learn to embrace our beliefs."

"I still don't understand you."

"What is it that's so hard to understand? There are negative consequences for people who get in our way or speak against me or our church. Things have always been this way. Get in our way, and . . . you will disappear. People have been abducted for years. A lot of times it's the big religious organizations and small groups like ours that take sinners like you away before y'all destroy our entire society. People just never suspect religious people like me and my followers. You'll be part of a glorious ceremony tonight, just like Ginger was last night. I wanted to keep you around longer, but I'm tired of looking at you."

"I'm tired of looking at you too. Tell me, who was the man I saw here earlier?"

"That was Floyd from the cemetery. I've got my followers doing all kinds of odd jobs for me. Floyd was the one who brought you here. He brought your momma back to our collection after all these years. She ran away from us and I had to kill her out on the road that night. I wanted to bring her back here with the others, but I didn't have time."

"So you hid Momma's body in that storm drain."

"I sure did. By the time I got back to her, the police and everybody was there. I walked over to them and offered my spiritual guidance."

"Uh-huh, just like you did recently when they had you on TV, pretending to care about Carolyn and leading a candlelight vigil."

"Don't you hate when that happens? Always keep in mind that the main people involved in certain questionable situations are usually close at hand, keeping an eye on what's happening and throwing up smokescreens."

"Here I was thinking that a white man was behind all the disappearances."

"You and everybody else. We had the police confused. The stupid profilers said a white man in his mid-to-late-forties was the likely suspect. The man you met out on the road was just some honest hillbilly that you misjudged. I laughed when I heard about that. Just made it easier for us to do what we had to. I need to take you over to the baptism pool in the next room to pray for you and get you cleaned up for tonight. It's part of our ritual. I can do it, or I can get Floyd to do it when he gets back. If you cooperate, I promise not to hurt you."

Momma Pearl moves toward me.

"Don't touch me!"

Although I try my best to resist, Momma Pearl grabs hold of my arms and is able to drag my thin, naked body across this nasty basement floor all the way over to the baptism pool without much effort. I completely forgot this other room even existed. She props me up on the side of the pool, then bends down, takes me by my legs, and pushes me headfirst into three feet of cold water. She leans over the side of the pool and grabs a handful of my hair in order to bring me closer to her. Momma Pearl tries to punish me by purposely holding my head underwater. I'm trying to make this as difficult as possible for her. She leans over just a little too much, and in an instantaneous motion I shift to my side, causing Momma Pearl to lose her balance. She screams as she falls into the pool. I realize that she is just as vulnerable as I am now. We're both in grave danger because one of us isn't making it out of here alive.

The water makes me much more agile than before. I fight with everything inside me to get to Momma Pearl in hopes of getting my arms around her neck before she gets to her feet. Reality quickly sets in. Since my hands and ankles are still bound, it's almost impossible to get a hold of her. I make a sudden move toward Momma Pearl anyway, but I'm still unable to get my arms around her. An awful feeling of frustration and despair come over me because I missed my only real opportunity to get to her. Looks like the odds are really against me now. I probably won't make it out of here alive.

Momma Pearl appears visibly shaken when she feels me bump into her. She looks as handicapped as I do in this water, especially when she slips while trying to regain her footing. When she hits the water this time, I'm able to get my arms around her neck. She splashes water everywhere, trying to get away from me. Feels like I have the advantage over her and I'm determined as hell not to lose it. This is a crucial moment. I become a savage, going into survival mode. The only weapon I have is my mouth. My instincts tell me to bite down on Momma Pearl's neck. I bite into her like a pit bull until I'm able to inflict some major damage. Blood flows into the water, tainting it along with Momma Pearl's white gown. Her head wrap comes untied, releasing her long, thick, black snake-like dreadlocks. Momma Pearl fights violently to regain control. She lunges forward, and when she does, my body weight and her own momentum propel her headfirst underwater. I'm forced underwater right along with her. We're both submerged, on the edge of drowning in this shallow deathtrap. It's a battle to see who can hold her breath longer. This evil bitch is fighting to the end. Just when I think she has taken her last breath, she gets a quick surge of energy, which only makes her situation worse. She lifts me just enough so I can take a quick breath, but her head remains submerged and is now pinned against the wall of the pool. There's nowhere for her to go. Hell awaits her as big air bubbles are expelled from her mouth and nose. Momma Pearl has taken her last breath. I wait an extra minute to make sure she's dead. Finally, she's gone.

I scream for mercy because I just took a life. Tears of joy and sorrow pour from my eyes. Feels like I'm about to have a nervous breakdown.

"I did that for you, Momma."

I'm trying my best to get my hands free. I'm working my hands back and forth and the water helps somewhat, but not enough to get free. I'm starting to panic now, because I'm lying here trapped in a pool of bloody water with a dead body. I have no idea where Sister Clarissa is and I know Floyd is on his way back.

I close my eyes and ask God for help. After a minute or so, my right hand slides free. My ankles are bound way too tight. There's no way I can stand like this. I drag myself out of the water and manage to re-move the tape from around my ankles. When I stand, my legs don't feel like they belong to me. My mind is set on getting out of here as quickly as possible.

All of a sudden I hear something fall from behind the door where the bodies are. The door opens partially. I see a female torso lying against the door. Inside are stacks of big blue and gray plastic storage containers with black trash bags sticking halfway out of a few of them. That's more then enough gore for me.

I grab my stinking blanket and try to remember how to get the hell out of this basement. I rush over to a big metal trapdoor, but it won't budge. It's locked from the outside. It seems impossible to get out this way. I head over to the old wooden steps. As soon as my foot hits the first step, it lands right on top of a rusty nail that goes more than halfway through my foot. I scream out loud from the pain. I don't have much time to tend to my wound because I hear a car pull up to the back of the church. I ignore the excruciating pain in my foot and lift it quickly, removing the nail. I continue upstairs to the church's lit-tle kitchen area. When I look out the window I see Sister Clarissa and

Floyd, along with two crazy-looking female members of the church, Sister Brown and Sister Riley, heading toward the trapdoor. I take off in the opposite direction.

I bust through the front doors of the church and head up the street, running for my life, barefoot and bleeding, wearing nothing but a stinking, dirty blanket.

Soon I realize that I'm running along the same road where Momma's body was found. The sight of the ditch and storm drain along the roadside makes my skin crawl. Momma was naked just like this when she got away. I just pray that nobody catches up to me.

There's a house about a thousand feet down the road. I'm almost there. All of a sudden I notice a car pulling out from the church's driveway. They must have found Momma Pearl's body and realized I was gone.

I start screaming for help. Doesn't seem to be anybody around to hear me. Regardless, I still continue screaming. As I get closer I notice a lady named Miss Rebecca sitting on her front porch.

"Help me! Please, help me. They're gonna kill me! They're gonna kill me!"

Miss Rebecca jumps to her feet. "Naomi! Is that you?"

"It's me! Help—call the police!"

"Your husband reported you missing. It's been on the news and everything."

My foot hurts so bad that I can hardly make it. "Here I am! Help me! They're in that car right there. They're trying to kill me!"

The car is getting closer. I clearly see that it's Sister Clarissa and Floyd.

Miss Rebecca yells, "I'ma get my shotgun!"

I'm just a few feet from Miss Rebecca's house when the car pulls up next to me.

Sister Clarissa yells, "What have you done? Do you have any idea what you've done?"

"Get away from me!"

A shotgun blast goes off in the air and seems to echo for miles. The car's tires screech loudly as it pulls off down the road. Miss Rebecca saved my life.

43

Naomi

Miss Rebecca helps me inside her house and gives me a night-gown. I lie down on her sofa. She calls 911 and explains to them what happened.

Paramedics and policemen arrive at the same time. Flashing lights are everywhere. Neighbors from the immediate area form a small crowd outside of Miss Rebecca's house as a result of all the commotion. I guess most people had given up and completely written me off for dead. As the minutes pass, the crowd grows larger with people from all over Eden. They seem to have popped up out of nowhere to get a glimpse of the woman who cheated death by escaping from a crazed serial killer and her followers. These people around here must sit around listening to police scanners or something. Where were all of them when I needed help? Where's my family?

Both national and local media arrive. This experience has *déjà vu* written all over it, but this time it's a different ending. I can't stop thanking God for allowing me to get away.

A lot of people shout questions and comments at me as the paramedics take me out of Miss Rebecca's house. The crowd is watching—I feel their eyes. All of a sudden I'm stricken with a feeling of paranoia because I know at least one person who's watching me right now has some sort of bad intentions. I think about what Momma Pearl told me about the people involved in certain questionable activities being close at hand, keeping an eye on what's happening. Any one of these people could be a follower of Momma Pearl, looking to get revenge. In the back of my mind I imagine somebody from the crowd lunging toward me with a knife, or maybe one of these policemen finishing me off with a gunshot.

I'm delirious, exhausted, and slowly going into shock. I'm placed safely and securely in the back of the ambulance.

The nursing and medical staff at Morehead Memorial Hospital are outstanding. They didn't allow any investigators or reporters to come anywhere near me until I had received an initial medical and psych evaluation. I ended up getting an IV and a ton of blood work. They cleaned up the wound on my foot, bandaged it, and gave me a tetanus shot. For the most part, I'm fine. I'm just lying here having flashbacks and thinking about what could have been. I'd just lived out a scene from a real-life horror movie.

The police took my official statement detailing all the events of my ordeal, from my abduction to my escape. I refused to speak to the media because the police had already put me through enough questioning for one night. I didn't feel like fooling with the media tonight anyway, because I'm tired and on top of that, I look a mess. They're supposed to set up a time for me to meet with the press tomorrow morning in the hospital's conference room.

A nurse steps from behind my privacy curtain and asks, "Mrs. Gaffney, I just got word that your husband and children should be arriving shortly."

"Thank you."

"Would it be okay if your sister comes back to see you now?"

"Sure. Where is she?"

Serena steps from behind the privacy curtain. "Here I am."

"C'mere, girl. I'm so happy to see you."

As we embrace I think about Momma Pearl saying that Serena was next on her list. She has no idea how close she came to being abducted. We are both in tears.

"Nay, I thought we had lost you, but you're a survivor. I don't think I would have made it outta there alive."

"Good thing we don't have to worry about that." I pause. "She killed Momma."

"I know. I'm not even surprised. I'm just glad you took care of her."

"I did that for all of us, especially for Momma and Daddy."

"I've been telling you for years that Momma Pearl was one crazy and deranged bitch, but you wanted to give her a second chance and start going back to her weird alternative church with all those assholes that allowed her to use mind-control techniques on them."

"I don't even wanna think about it. Where's my husband and my kids?"

"He said he was on his way. They all should be out there by now."

The same nurse who escorted Serena brings Craig to my bedside.

"Excuse me, ma'am. Mr. Gaffney is here to see you."

When I look at Craig, the first thing I notice is his eye. It's black and blue and swollen all to hell.

Craig greets me with a hug and a kiss. "I'm so glad you made it outta there, baby. We had no idea what happened to you. You all right? Did they hurt you?"

"I'm all right, besides a wounded foot and being a little messed up in the head. I'll be fine in no time. But what about you? What happened to your eye?"

Serena says, "I'm gonna leave y'all alone for a minute. Looks like y'all need some private time. I'll be right out in the waiting area. Craig, are the kids out there?"

"Yeah, I wanted to get a preview before I brought them in. Looks like things aren't as bad as I imagined, so you can send them back here in a couple of minutes."

Craig squints and makes an ugly face. "All right, what happened was, I got into a fight with your friend Brian. Don't judge by my eye, 'cause I actually got the best of him. He won't ever bother you again." He makes a pitiful facial expression. "Is that okay with you?"

"Yeah, but what did you do to him?"

"Me and Sonny went to his house and scared him. I roughed him up a little, but he was okay when we left."

"You took Sonny?"

"Yeah."

"That murderer. You were probably hoping Sonny would kill Brian, huh?"

"Nah. I took Sonny just in case things got out of control. I was under the impression that you ran off with Brian or something. I never suspected your aunt had her people from the church abduct you." He laughs. "That's some crazy shit for real. And to think we were all members of her church at one time. I'm glad I left when I did and never looked her way again. On a real serious note, I need to ask you a couple of questions."

"Go ahead. Ask whatever's on your mind."

"Is it over between you and Brian?"

"Yeah. I promise. Can you ever forgive me for betraying you like I did?"

"Only if you forgive me for putting my hands on you. I'll never do that again. I don't know where my head was."

"Don't worry. I forgive you."

"I don't wanna talk about Brian anymore. As far as I'm concerned, it didn't happen. So, where do we go from here?"

"I dunno. Where do broken hearts go?"

"I think they get back together and begin a healing process. This time we'll do it right. That means me taking the time to learn how to appreciate the simple things in life."

I smile. "Like sunrises, trees, grass, and gentle breezes?"

"You're really pushing it now."

"C'mon. Don't be like that."

"All right, I'll learn to appreciate stuff like that, too. I can do that for you. We're gonna take it one day at a time growing stronger every day."

"No more Jack Daniel's when times get rough."

"No more J.D. for me, even when times are good much less when times get rough."

"I promise to be right by your side through the ups and the downs. We can make this work. I'm sure we both realize that nobody's perfect."

"That's right. Even as great as I am, I have a few personal faults."

"That's cute."

"I'm just kidding. But seriously, though, we can't give up on each other so easily."

"We definitely deserve another chance. I heard things are better the second time around."

"I always say that I love you more than you'll ever know, but I can honestly say that I love you more than any man could possibly love a woman, and that's unconditionally. You and those kids are my everything."

"You may not believe me, but I love you with all my heart, and as time goes on I'm sure I'll fall deeper and deeper in love with you."

We kiss.

I hear the kids on the other side of the curtain. Morgan and Erika's snickering and laughing give them away.

C.J. says, "Be quiet, y'all. They're being serious and y'all are acting silly."

"Sounds like you've got some more visitors out there."

Morgan asks, "Is it okay if we come back?"

"C'mon in."

The kids bombard me with hugs and kisses. Surprisingly, Erika seems to have forgiven me. I'm overwhelmed with emotion because I've got my family back. Only problem now is that Craig and C.J. still have some issues to iron out. I'm so thankful that I've been given another chance to be a better wife to Craig and a better momma to my kids. After what I've experienced, I'll never complain about being bored or having to do housework again. Predictability isn't exactly a bad thing. Now I know that uncertainty brought a lot of misfortune and heartache into my life, more than I could ever have imagined.

I'm happy with who I am—Naomi Gaffney, wife, momma, and homemaker.

Epilogue

It's been six months since my ordeal and I'm still haunted by disturbing images. I've never been so frightened in my life. I'll never forget what happened—the pain, the stench, or my cries that went unanswered. How could anybody forget a living nightmare? Unfortunately, nothing can erase the horror I experienced.

I'm back in therapy because of multiple bouts of depression. I'm seeing Dr. Dandridge down in Greensboro. He disclosed some shocking information to me about Dr. Easley, who called Dr. Dandridge moments before putting a gun to his head, asking him to look after his wife and kids. In a desperate attempt to deal with his demons, Dr. Easley admitted to making some costly mistakes that affected the well-being of some of his female patients. Dr. Dandridge said Dr. Easley never mentioned anything about sexual abuse, but he knew exactly what he was insinuating. The phone line went dead. When Dr. Dandridge called back, no one answered the office phone. Within a half hour or so, a member of the housekeeping staff found Dr. Easley slumped over his desk in a pool of blood and brain matter from a self-inflicted gunshot wound to his right temple.

Dr. Dandridge wanted me to have a better understanding of Momma Pearl and her motives. We've spent hours and hours discussing her. He gave her a clinical diagnosis, saying that judging from her actions she was a paranoid-schizophrenic caught up in delusions, hallucinations, and amoral behavior. That bit of information wasn't a shocking revelation to me at all. It was just Dr. Dandridge's way of making sure that I wouldn't become overwhelmed by feelings of guilt for taking my aunt's life. That was the least of my concerns. I knew she was crazy, even without an official clinical diagnosis. She got what she deserved for ruining so many lives. Authorities removed the remains of twenty-seven bodies from the basement of the old church.

Eden Temple of Light is still going strong and the membership seems to keep growing. A new pastor has taken over, but a lot of the same old faces remain. I get an eerie feeling every time I drive by there. Those people know who I am and what I did. They don't say one word to me. They just stare at me in a strange way because they know that I know the truth.

Sister Clarissa and Floyd haven't been located yet. I guess they're still out there somewhere, doing what they call God's work. So far no one within the church's organization has been arrested or charged with any crimes.

Things are so different now. Craig and I don't really talk about the past. With the help of Alcoholics Anonymous, he's been sober for the past six months. We strictly live in the present, planning a bright future together. We're running the Draper Grocery Store—I'm kind of living out my dream of being a cook at a restaurant. I do a fish fry every Friday night and serve barbequed chicken and ribs every Saturday night at Knott's Landing. They call me the Queen of Soul Food around here now.

The kids are doing great. C.J. is going to school full-time at Rockingham County Community College, taking general studies with his new girlfriend, Dayna. Erika is focused on completing her senior year and going away to college. She hasn't been on a date in months and plans to be single for a long time.

Morgan is still Morgan and I love her for that. I pray that my baby will never change. She's still the top student in her class. Lately her thing is giving me and Craig financial advice on how to invest our money wisely and plan for an early retirement so we can move to Florida with her grandma and granddad. We're planning our first family trip to Orlando next summer.

Serena and Darryl separated. Serena says it's just a trial separation and they'll be back together soon. I doubt it. The two of them seem to be enjoying their freedom just a bit too much to ever hook up again. Overall, Serena and the kids have been doing better without Darryl. He's still drinking and carrying on like a fool. He's supposed to be staying with some friends of his down in Fayetteville. I heard he shacked up with a young girl and her four kids. He might get enough of that nonsense sooner or later and bring his butt back to Serena.

Daddy was released from prison four months ago. He received an apology from the prosecutor for falsely accusing him of Momma's murder. The state refused to compensate him for wrongful imprisonment for over twenty-one years. I expected Daddy to be bitter, considering the fact that he lost everything while in prison, except the land his house once stood on. He was fine with the decision. Daddy is just trying to enjoy his life and family, especially his grandkids. He's having a new house built on the site of our old one. Daddy's story gained national attention—Home Depot donated building supplies and two local contractors volunteered to rebuild his house.

Two teenage relatives of Russ Peterson, the disgruntled employee from Craig's old job, were arrested for killing Chop-chop. They called themselves getting even with Craig for getting their cousin arrested. The two boys would have gotten away with the crime if they hadn't started bragging to all of their friends. We still haven't gotten another family pet because Craig said Chop-chop was irreplaceable.

My sweet Brian isn't anywhere to be found. I haven't heard from him since that Sunday night we last talked. A new family has moved into his house. My heart was crushed when I realized that he had given up his dream of fixing up his house. Some strange men have taken over his garage. I ran into that guy, Otis, who worked at the garage with Brian, and he acted like he didn't have a clue where Brian or his momma had run off to.

I learned so much from Brian. Things I never even knew about myself. The saddest thing is that I never got the chance to tell him that I loved him or hear him say that he loved me. My heart misses him since he's been gone. I understand that everything happens for a reason. I'm just thankful to God that I had the chance to be with him, but I'm even more thankful that I have my old life back.

I'm on Wal-Mart's parking lot, loading bags in the trunk of my car.

I picked up a bunch of household goods, mostly cleaning supplies. A motorcycle rides up behind me. I expect it to keep moving, but it stops directly behind me. When I look up, Brian is smiling at me. He turns the motorcycle off.

I'm excited to see Brian, but I refuse to let it show much.

"What's up, Naomi?"

"What's up? After all this time, is that the best greeting you can come up with?"

Brian gets off his motorcycle. "How've you been? Still beautiful, I see."

"Thanks. Things are going well. How 'bout you?"

"I'm fine. Glad you're okay." He gives me a friendly hug. "I couldn't believe when I heard what happened to you."

This is an awkward moment for me because I'm so afraid that Craig might appear out of nowhere. Things are different between me and Brian now, but Craig still wouldn't understand. Something inside of me tells me that Brian has probably found a new love. The thought of him being with someone else shouldn't hurt, but it does.

"I'm just gonna get right to the point. Where the hell have you been?"

"My mother passed away and I needed to get away from here."

Brian pulls his momma's obituary from his inside jacket pocket and hands it to me.

"I'm so sorry to hear about your momma. And I'm sorry I never got the chance to meet her."

Brian smiles. "I know she would have liked you."

"You never said where you ran off to."

"My cousins came here for Momma's funeral and they asked me to go back to Chicago with them. I was out there for the summer."

"What about your house and garage?"

"Oh, I decided to rent my house to a family and rent Momma's house to my uncle. I leased the garage to some guys I know."

"Wow, that's a lot of changes in a short time. Did you forget about me?"

"No. How could I forget about you? I'm always thinking about my girl. That's why I'm back in Eden. I need you, Naomi."

"Is that right?"

"That's right. I need you right now."

There's so much passion in his voice that I'm not sure what to say next.

"Where are you staying?"

"I'm back at A&T. Been there since the fall semester. Told you I'd be back in school."

"That's good to hear. I like to see people stick to their goals."

"You ready for that ride I promised you?"

"I dunno."

"C'mon and go away with me. I know you're in the mood for some relaxation, rejuvenation, and rejoicing."

I smile. "Oh yeah, the three R's."

"Don't tell me you forgot about those."

"I didn't, but I've been trying to."

Brian's happy expression breaks down. "Huh?"

"I'm not the same Naomi you remember. I went through an experience you wouldn't believe."

"I heard about it. Eden was in the news quite a bit a few months back. I'm still in shock about Momma Pearl and the church. That's crazy. They had all of us fooled."

"I know. I thought for a minute that the weirdos from the church had done something awful to you."

Brian laughs. "Nobody from the church has done or said anything to me since the last Sunday I was there."

"Good. Well, I don't wanna talk about that foolishness anymore."

"I understand. I was excited to hear about your daddy coming home."

"He's making out pretty good. This community is finally doing something to help him."

"That's good. Now back to you. Trust me, I understand that you went through a life-altering experience that really put everything into perspective. I can relate. When I lost Momma, nothing in my life mattered except you. No matter what, my thoughts seemed to come back to you." Brian pauses, then looks deep into my eyes. "I love you, Naomi, and I think you love me, too."

My eyes begin to water. "I do love you. I love you so much that it hurts, but I'm determined to make my marriage work. I'll never betray Craig again."

"Craig? That's another story. He should have killed me like he said, 'cause now I'm here to get you back and I'm not gonna give up on you. C'mon and go with me."

"Where? Where are you trying to go?"

"Anywhere, everywhere, or nowhere at all. It doesn't matter as long as we can be together."

Brian goes over and starts up his motorcycle. He revs it up. "C'mon. Hop on." He revs the motorcycle again. "C'mon and run away with me."

Part of me is tempted to hop on the motorcycle and go off wherever Brian wants to go and make love like we used to. I start crying like a baby. The other part of me wants to hop in my car and speed away in the opposite direction.

A vision of my family sitting around the dinner table with smiling faces plays in my head. I take a step closer to Brian. I'm reminded of how it felt to be gagged and bound on that mattress. The stench of death and a vision of the word INFERNO written in big, bold, bloody letters go through my mind.

Brian revs the motorcycle up again.

"C'mon."

"I can't. Please, Brian, just go on without me. It's meant for me to be with Craig and my kids. Thank you."

"For what?"

"Thanks for teaching me how to smile and to love again. I love my husband too much to leave him. He's a good man. All the time I thought that I was missing out on something, but I wasn't. I've got everything I need at home. And if I can't get it at home, then God just didn't intend for me to have it."

"Is that how you really feel?"

"Yeah. Good-bye, Brian. If and when you come back this way again . . . do me a favor and don't look for me. Please, just let me be. And know that I'm happy with the life I've chosen."

"You're gonna miss me, girl. You'll come around in a minute. I need to give you time, that's all. You just go 'head and take care of home for now. I'll be here whenever you're ready."

"You better get going."

We embrace. Brian and I stare at each other one last time. He gives me a cute but confident smile, winks his eye at me, and takes off without saying another word.

I think of my favorite saying, *You live, you love, you learn.*

Now my new favorite saying is, *You live, you love, you learn, and then live another day to love again.*